Dedication

I would like to thank the following people for help material and meta-physical with this book.

My Husband Robert Duncan, Rebecca da Silva, Jenn Myers, Hazel Johnson, The Incomparable Deeble, Simone Wu, R.E.C. Thompson, and Grace Fry-Dolloff. All of you have encouraged me, you should be ashamed of yourselves.

About The Author

Weyodi Squid doesn't like to brag but she once knocked Ernest Hemingway unconscious in a bare knuckle fist fight. She has also been banned from the state of Indiana. Over the years she has developed a finely honed ability to trigger a burglar alarm with a fast food taco thrown at high speed from a moving vehicle.

Monster Bride

by Weyodi Squid

Table of Contents

Chapter 1 : A Spanner in the Works

t was a dark and stormy night, or rather a gloomy wet morning somewhere in the vicinity of 10 a.m.; pissing down rain, and fairly fateful in that it set into motion a chain of events that would not only bugger up one curmudgeonly professor's life but over turn a fair few number of apple carts in the process. Truth be told, said apple carts would be more than upset, they'd be burnt to the bloody ground.

That morning the Director's daughter came in and immediately set to poking about in Stephen Magesteri's half-finished projects. As sodding usual. Tracking in mud to boot. Typical.

"What is this?" Polly, short for Polycorpus Singularia Plumber, asked, looking at a pile of broken metal.

"It is the way of science to make its way to discovery through a process of trial and error," Stephen said glaring down his nose at her. She made it easy by being shorter than him, not everyone did.

"Well whatever it is, your gears wouldn't be so worn if you used a jeweled movement," Polly said extending a half-melted gear whose rounded teeth supported her argument. She leaned in and began carefully sorting the salvageable bits from those that would have to be melted down and recast.

Magesteri raised a solitary brow at her in consideration but he wasn't sure if Polly noticed him at all in her excitement at the wreckage. Pity. That look made

1

the apprentices nearly soil themselves.

"What is it?" she asked raising a globule of glass at him. "These are lenses, or were at any rate. What are you doing? Is this meant to be a weapon?"

"Then it would be fall under the aegis of the department of munitions, would it not?"

He trusted Polly to take his meaning; surely she wouldn't want her idea ripped out from under her either.

"What's it meant to do?" Polly asked squatting down to examine the melted wreck in a most unladylike posture. As ladies went she wasn't much to write home about, funny, that, since the Director's work was usually irreproachable. Still what did one expect of a girl cobbled together of random parts?

"Emit an intense beam of light," Stephen said, hoping for, yet dreading, an idea from the girl, but all he got was a grunt as she picked her way through the debris twisting a spring back into shape.

The next day was even more fateful though Stephen would have openly mocked the notion at the time. What's more the bleeding atmospheric conditions were worse; with the sort of violent storm foreigners always seemed to think was common in Londinium. Stephen did not take the weather into account despite the fact that this was no common every day drizzle, this particular day was nothing but pouring rain and black skies punctuated by blue lightning and not common at all and Stephen was thrown off kilter when Polycorpus failed to arrive in the lab to irritate him.

Off-kilter graduated to on-edge when he couldn't find his best spanner, the one so perfectly weighted it would have made Hephaestus weep, and had to make do with a clumsy clot of an instrument more suited to one of the spastic children of the aristocracy Henry Plumber usually saddled him with than a master engineer such as himself.

He could only stand so much.

Every man had his limits and Stephen Propertius Drusus Magesteri's limit was a second rate spanner.

He knew that girl nicked it. She was always pulling some sort of shenanigan in order to vex him, when she was thinking of him at all.

More often than not Polly couldn't bother to apply her focus to anything that didn't hum when you tripped the right lever. He wished his apprentices were that singled minded.

All the same he wanted his spanner and he wanted it right sodding now.

Where was that dreadful girl?

When Eleven o'clock tea came and Polly had still failed to materialize he poked his nose out to the work station Canavan and Ouellette shared across from the one-man-disaster-Edney. She was not there. She had not been there. Had she spent any time in the area their work would not be half so pitiful.

Unsure of what other options were open to him, Stephen distractedly wandered down to Henry Plumber's office, awkward shit of a spanner still in hand, and his shirt sleeves rolled to the elbow.

There Plumber was sipping tea across from Mrs. Brolly.

"Plumber…Aunt Augusta," he said, feeling foolish and wishing he could discover Polly's whereabouts without asking.

Henry Plumber sucked on his cigar, a look of vague surprise confined itself to his brow but Stephen knew how to read Plumber's signs.

Stephen frowned and Aunt Augusta shifted subtly in her seat and turned her head toward the rain lashing the window behind Plumber's chair.

Plumber's brow smoothed itself and a smile broke round his cigar. "You'd be looking for Polycorpus, then." It was not a question.

Stephen folded his arms across his chest.

"Weather like this she'll be on the roof, boy," Plumber muttered around his cigar.

Stephen didn't see why he should break precedent and explain himself now, so in lieu of parting words he saluted the two with his spanner and turned on his heel.

"You're welcome, Professor," Plumber said merrily.

"Don't forget your mackintosh, Stephen," Aunt Augusta called after him.

"Take one of mine from my cloak room if you like," Henry Plumber added.

Of course Stephen did no such thing. What sort of fool's errand had brought Polly up to on the roof in such weather? He pictured her wet and ill, sneezing and coughing all over his laboratory. Her nose would likely drip and that would be disgusting. It was highly inconsiderate on her part.

He was nearly to the roof when he nearly tripped over Dr. Noor, sitting on the 5th step from the top, smoking the small pipe he carried in his vest pocket.

"Ohhh," he said puffing superciliously "Have you come after Miss Polly?"

Stephen glared but said nothing.

"You'll find she always comes up when the weather is like this." Noor puffed on his pipe. "Personally, I wouldn't go out right now for love or money."

Stephen said nothing, merely stepped round him and opened the door to the roof.

There, beyond where the airships were moored, stood Polycorpus in the pouring rain, her wild hair streaming and her arms raised to the sky. He was near enough to see her maniac grin but not close enough to do anything but watch as a bolt of lightning branched down from the clouds and Polly, looking nothing like Plumber's funny little spinster daughter, fairly strained to greet it.

More than greet, she embraced the blue white light. Wet as she was, her breasts strained against the fabric of her dress and in the earth shattering crack her corset popped, ripping off her belly as her dress burnt away in a flash. Stephen did not know what to make of it. She seemed unharmed but what clothes had not been burnt off in an instant hung tattered. Indeed, more than unharmed Polly seemed …stimulated.

Were she a whore Stephen would say her thighs were thick and her breasts, while abundant, sagged a bit. But this was not a whore. This was Polly, the director's girl. Polly, who of all the female creatures in Londinium, he despised the least, sometimes even tolerated. It was Polly. And foul as it was of him to admit he could fairly taste the juice of her cunt in the air.

As she embraced the raw electricity the blue radiance enveloped and surrounded her. Singularia. The name made sense on an entirely new level in light of the storm. Not only was she a singular creation she was also singularly mad.

"Yes!" she cried to the gathering black sky.

And Stephen found that he felt something akin to jealousy. He envied a force of nature but he was not certain whether that force was the lightning or the girl. His skin prickled with it and his prick strained in his trousers. It was horrid and exhilarating.

She stood panting as the electricity receded even as the storm raged on. Her arms were spread wide and tiny snakes of blue electricity leapt from finger tip to finger tip and crackled at the ends of her unbound hair that spread like a cloud round her face and shoulders. Great sizzling multi-colored arcs chased from one shining bolt in her neck to the other, ringing her head like a crown.

Stephen took four steps toward her and …damn the rain slicked landing strip, lost his footing and tumbled to his knees.

In his scramble to right himself he caught Polly's attention and a wide smile split her face. Her laugh echoed in his ears above the storm's din and for the first time he was aware of Stephen Magesteri was afraid of someone other than himself.

Slipping backwards on the wet tar he gave up and sat, unsure of what this creature before him was. Singularia. Singularia rang in the back of his mind.

Seemingly without taking a step she advanced on him. Still his traitorous cock leapt.

Before that instant Magesteri had never put any store by the old truism that Lust and Terror were sisters who slept in the same bed, making it difficult to awake one without rousing the other. For the first time in his life Stephen felt as though his very being, his entire mind, soul, not to mention body, was aroused by a single girl, Plumber's girl. His own personal pain in the backside. He could not help but shiver as she rapped the knuckles of her left hand twice against an airship in passing to dispel the electrical charge.

Knock. Knock. She rapped on the next she passed as well and it was ominous. And it was exciting.

He did not know if he had any say in the matter when she climbed astride him. He shouldn't have been able to feel her erect nipples through his wet shirt, but he did. Her cunt was searing hot. Her eyes were mad and unthinking, as if she wasn't quite herself.

This was not proper.

More than that it was dangerous.

The result of this course would be unforgivable.

None of that seemed to concern her much.

Or at all, really.

Rocking back and forth like a mad thing she certainly seemed to know what she was doing.

Better than he did, frankly. It was as if his desire called to her even as his fear held him immobile. He did not know how her touch could be as hot as it was. Inside her was hotter still. The pleasure of it seared his brain. Yet as she slid up and down the length of him every inch of him that was bereft of her burning embrace screamed for the pleasure/pain to return. The only thing that could be more unbearable than this sexual execution was the notion of his torment coming to an end. Every bit of his skin burned hot then cold, the hairs on his arms and legs stood on end, his breath came only in gasps. She towered over him a queen. His body was wracked by jarring waves of ecstasy. She had to stop before it was too late. He prayed to all the gods and goddesses she would not make it stop. But he couldn't bring himself to say a word to her. Behind his shuttering eyes minute pin pricks of light expanded until a sun burned white hot inside his brain.

How was either of them still alive?

Then he was complete and knew no more.

Had either Stephen or Polycorpus been paying attention they would have noted that the door appeared to open and close quite on its own almost as if some unseen person was excusing themselves from the scene.

When Professor Magesteri came round to consciousness he was in the camp bed he kept toward the rear of his office. He had a hot water bottle clutched to his belly and was acutely aware of the sensation of being in love with his director's daughter. He could not deny that it seemed shamefully simple of him but there it was. The creature's capacity for danger had worked some alchemy and grudging tolerance had given way to respect, which in turn had been transformed to passion by the revelation of her true self. He hugged the water bottle close, shamming sleep as he lifted his eyelids just enough to see the flicker of her presence. Chills ran through him.

What fool could doubt the uncommonness of such a creature? Now his was the added burden of not making an utter arse of himself over her.

He'd known from the beginning that Plumber had made Polly specifically for him, specifically to suit what was delicately referred to as his "uncommon nature" back in the days when she was just so many fat little limbs floating in different jars, but while Stephen had tried to imagine some scenario in which his heart quickened at the sight of her he never thought it would be terror that thrilled him.

For her part Polly was mostly relieved that her only consequence was that once Magesteri chided her vaguely, while keeping his gaze trained on his work, for her carelessness at "being familiar with him" as he called it. She imagined he meant atop the roof where they were vulnerable to interception from all and sundry. But he didn't tell her papa, or worse, Mrs. Brolly. Sometimes she went a bit mad under the influence of a good storm.

When no more censure came she did her best to think no more on the topic, simply watched the sky for the next gathering clouds.

Polly continued to badger the head of Inventions. She had the most intriguing idea for a ruby and intermittent power source for the super-focused light emitting beam they had been mucking with the day before the storm.

Stephen Magesteri had known Henry Plumber since he was all of eight years old and the aforementioned Plumber had nothing in his lunch pail but a moldy crust of bread. Having been so long and well acquainted with the Museum director he was not in the habit of making appointments with his secretary or even, if the truth were known, announcing himself.

He would go speak to Plumber and perhaps, just perhaps, if the mood was right and he was able to keep his temper even he might broach the subject of Polly with the director. It was a thorny dilemma but surely Henry could help him sort it out. Certainly, Stephen hated admitting he was wrong, but surely he could bring himself to tell Henry, yes, he was right, he wanted the girl, Polycorpus, afterall.

He usually entered Henry's office through the service entrance that connected with the director's coat room. So there was nothing to blame but habit and familiarity when he stood among Henry Plumber's spare umbrellas, best and second best coats, assorted hats and a half dozen mufflers and distinctly heard Titus Albinus's drawl.

"You lied to me, Plumber," the tone had only the lightest edge of anger to it.

"About what?" Plumber asked sounding only vaguely interested.

"That blasted girl of yours," Albinus said.

"Did I?" Plumber said as disingenuous as ever.

"You led me to believe the female was common as cabbage," Albinus sounded distinctly put out.

"What did I tell you?" Plumber asked, playing the bumbling fool. It was Stephen's experience that most noblemen were all too ready to trust appearances and let Henry play the part. More fool them.

"You told me she was constructed entirely from the corpses of common infants, thus common in the extreme, which is most certainly untrue," Albinus said.

"Why do you say that?" Plumber said. Stephen could hear him lighting a fresh cigar.

"I observed your so-called daughter on the roof Wednesday last," Albinus said. "What I saw was anything but ordinary."

Stephen's experience with Plumber taught him to envision a disinterested shrug on the old man's part.

"When I asked your assistance in finding a suitable wife, I had the clear understanding that the girl was beneath my interest," Albinus was beginning to lose his temper.

At this Henry laughed. "So you want Polycorpus."

"Let's just say my curiosity has been piqued," Albinus said, coolly.

Stephen's guts tied themselves into a pretty knot as he realized precisely what Titus Albinus was saying; what Albinus had seen. Albinus who, for his part, said nothing to deny Plumber's accusation.

"Too bad for you, old chap, Polly is rather smitten with our Professor Magesteri," Plumber chuckled.

"I wouldn't consider that a terribly vital bit of information," was all Albinus had by way of response. "Girls are notoriously changeable."

"Point taken," Henry said easily. "And if I were to suggest the feeling might be reciprocated?"

"Pfff," Albinus said. "It's not as though he's willing to marry the girl himself. You know Stephen, beneath his volatile surface beats a heart of molten blancmange. If he was going to marry the girl he would have done it by now. Most likely before plucking the fruit and believe me he has taken quite a bite."

Plumber had the temerity to chuckle. "Has he now? That's most intriguing." Where was his fatherly concern? Shouldn't he be the least bit outraged? Stephen was somewhat outraged and he had been the transgressor.

"I witnessed a scene between the two of them with my own eyes on the roof of this very building, Wednesday, last, and has my cousin made a proposal? No, he has not," Albinus said answering his own question. It was an annoying habit of his. Titus was a smug self-satisfied twit.

Stephen fought the urge to burst in and demand an explanation from Plumber and Albinus knowing full well it would be utterly fruitless.

Stephen braced himself against the wall his heart pounding, the sound of blood rushing in his ears drowning out any more eavesdropping, inadvertent or otherwise.

What did it mean? He was well aware Henry had no scruples and would not so much as bat an eyelash before lying in service of a goal he considered worthy. And Albinus? By the Scaly Prick of Apophis, Titus Albinus made it a rule never to let a little thing like deceit stand in his way when it came to achieving a goal. Standing there in the dark the only question Stephen could ask himself was why in the name of the Nile Delta fate had chosen the two of them to be his closest confidants.

He needed to clear his head. He needed to get some sodding air. He was suffering the effects of too much wet wool. Between the coats and the umbrellas, it was like being buggered by a herd of hound's-tooth sheep. Of course, on the way out who should he nearly run straight into in the corridor but Guy Bleeding Ouellette.

"Tell my, tell, tell," Stephen paused unsure of what should come next. "Tell Miss Plumber to get the fuck out of my laboratory and put my tools back in their proper place once she's finished playing with them."

Ouellette gaped like cod.

Once he had left behind the pristine marble halls of the Museum for the filth and clamor of the Londinium streets he was able to think.

He bought a bun from a girl on the corner because her funny little broad upturned nose reminded him of Polly.

His first realization was that everything he had just learned was completely irrelevant; at its core the situation between Polly and himself had not changed one iota. He had not changed. He had never been a truly suitable choice for Polly.

And then there was Polycorpus herself. She had been as misled as he, and arguably received the worse end of the arrangement regardless of which man she chose. He considered revealing all but stopped short, what exactly would he say?

No, a difference that made no difference was no difference. He would not speak of it to her. He would not speak of it to anyone.

Halfway through picking out a selection of rubies large and perfect enough to suit Polly's scheme for the focused light device, his nerve endings began that peculiar ache that came from his dubious distinction of having survived, mentally intact no less, the tender mercies of the Cyrillic curse unlike every other member of the old battalion, besides Titus Albinus, of course. Titus had been out on a lark and missed the entire attack. Stephen swore if Titus Albinus lost his footing on a pile of shit he'd land in a field of diamonds.

He had recently acquired the habit of combating the hazy pain with dark chocolates as well as hashish; only a half step away from bitter. So he made a stop at a chocolate shop. While he was there, the sour cherries caught his attention as well. Aside from a tendency to buzz slightly when first placed on the tongue, they were pleasantly free of gimmickry, simply tart and delicious.

As he returned to his laboratory, half a sack of tangy sweets in his hand, he was greeted by the quick smile of Polly Plumber. He should have known Ouellette didn't have the bottle to tell her to get out of the lab.

She looked different, adult. Her normally intrusive bramble of hair had been braided, although it was already beginning to escape the confines of her plait. She was obviously making an effort not to look like either a school girl or a confirmed frump. When he realized she had removed her shoes, he couldn't decide whether she succeeded in her illusion or not.

Despite her attempt, she was still more than half wild barefoot girl.

He felt faintly ridiculous to be caught like a school boy with a sack full of sweets.

He held out the bag in his hand. "Would you like some candy, little girl?" He frowned.

Her grin split itself into the wide smile of pleasure. To be honest, it took him aback.

"Thank you, that's very sweet," she said, taking the shocking liberty of kissing him on the cheek, in his laboratory where any apprentice could have wandered by and seen.

"No," he said, correcting her stiffly, "they're actually fairly sour."

"I meant you," she said. "That was quite sweet of you."

He stood dumbstruck for several seconds before he had the presence of mind to recall that he wanted nothing to do with Polly Plumber. "Didn't you get my message, or did Ouellette bollocks that up as well? You're to get the fuck out of my laboratory."

Polly wrinkled her nose at him and turned away, sweet still in her mouth.

"And stay out," he called to her back.

As soon as she was gone he settled into his office with his sweets and his hashish pipe.

A week later Titus Albinus came and asked him to make the proposal on his behalf to Plumber. How could he sodding refuse?

Chapter 2 : A Confounded Spinster

y her own estimation Polly Plumber was a middling sort of a girl. She was not tall, by any definition of the word, but neither was she freakishly short; she was not hideous to look on, but she was hardly a ravishing beauty either. She was neither light skinned nor dark skinned but rather a patchwork of both with neat stitching between. Her hair was neither straight nor exactly curly but rather tended toward the texture and temperament of an Airedale Terrier.

She was quite good at some subjects, like maths and blueprint reading, and beastly bad at others; dancing and embroidery, for instance. At twenty-two she had successfully dodged marriageable age but was still young for a spinster. She herself had little money or property beyond her monthly allowance but her father had quite a bit more than other Common people she had been exposed to. While she was observably not Common, neither had she been born to the aristocracy, having been built by her father from parts he had gathered together in the back rooms at The Imperial Museum.

Oh, there had been others made the way she had, from common parts; but they were all male, and stupid. She didn't mean it badly, but the others like her, the reason they were called reccs - short for "reclamations" - was that they were wrecks. From Common casualties of war, the army doctors took the most functional bits, sewed those bits together, reanimated them and gave them back to the generals. The results were aware enough to follow orders but couldn't speak and had less initiative than the average spaniel. Of course they were usually just a week or two reanimated before they were put back on the front lines. They never lasted long.

It had been an idea of her father's that a recc made of common infants might learn and grow as other children did. And she did, although she wasn't quite ordinary, being stronger than common girls and a bit less coordinated. Her duties were to be examined, take tests, and be measured every fortnight, although she hadn't grown in years.

Other than that she had had the run of the Museum until she started bleeding, when Mrs. Brolly began to oversee her education, which was far from educational if you asked Polly, not that anyone did.

Still, it was a comfortably agreeable grey area she inhabited, replete with exemptions and privileges. The very fact that her life had such clear lack of definition rendered it subject to interpretation and therefore malleable. She could and did shape her niche to suit herself. She would be the last to complain. Polly liked falling through the cracks of social expectation. She could do as she pleased, provided she observed the niceties and kept her dress clean. What's more life was full of puzzles to be solved.

Polly's Papa, for instance, was an interesting subject. She often wondered exactly how her father ought to be classified. He had been born to a Common mother and a Common father and begun life as an errand boy. Yet now he moved among those born Men of Note as a matter of course. He counted the great monsters of the age among his closest confidants. True, sometimes it did happen that Common women bore monsters. But Henry Plumber did not grow hirsute under any phase of the moon, be it full, crescent, or gibbous. He had neither scales nor feathers. He did not possess gill, nor horn, nor tail. He could not fly unaided or walk through walls or speak to the dead. He wasn't even hump backed. And yet…and yet… her father, for all his Common birth, and Common parentage, and Common appearance, had a mind as quick and ponderous as a winged elephant and nearly as likely.

It was her father's mind that made him indispensable to Her Majesty and her father's mind that enabled him to rise to such a position of power and prestige as director of the Londinium branch of The Imperial Museum, where scholars and scientists unraveled the secrets of the universe on a daily basis and inventors from the breadth of the empire and beyond produced wonders of every water with delightful regularity. Perhaps that was it; it was her Papa's brain that made a monster of him.

Polly was knocked out of her reverie by a delicate clearing of the throat and looked expectantly at her companion, though more likely it was she who should be referred to as Mrs. Brolly's companion. In any event, the jolt left Polly as confounded as if she had been awaken from a sound sleep. Still Mrs. Brolly cleared her throat in reproach.

There was no question as to what sort of person Mrs. Brolly was. Mrs. Brolly was so decidedly unCommon anyone who gazed upon her naked face was turned to stone. An aristocrat of the first order, Mrs. Brolly, like most of her father's intimates, made his acquaintance during the Afghan campaign. Perhaps it was not quite the done thing to refer to a widow of Mrs. Brolly's class as her Papa's intimate and Mrs. Brolly was correct as a rule. It was her defining characteristic. But, correct or not, it was true that Mrs. Brolly came to dine every Saturday, and tea twice a week. She instructed Polly in those subjects she considered unfit for a paid tutor. It was also true that of all his associates only Mrs. Brolly's opinion was solicited, much less deferred to, on the topic of Polly.

Polly stared hard trying to glean some clue as to her crime from Mrs. Brolly's perfect composure, perfect grooming, perfect attire, and perfectly opaque veil.

"Polycorpus Plumber, your posture is an insult to both your father and your upbringing. Have you no respect whatsoever for the labor that went into your construction? Sit up straight, child," Mrs. Brolly lit into her as though slouching were a deadly transgression. She feared Mrs. Brolly would still be upbraiding her and referring to her as "child" when she was fifty; it was disheartening.

Polly righted herself and flipped open the necessaries box. Without thinking, she retrieved the mirror to make certain her hat was at the proper angle. In doing so, she snagged her glove on a bent corner of the carriage clock, ripping the kidskin loudly and knocking said clock directly into Mrs. Brolly's lap. The visiting cards, pencils, social registry, and scheduling book spilled willy-nilly on the coach floor.

Polly fully expected to be upbraided by Mrs. Brolly and braced herself accordingly. She was more than slightly taken aback when all she got was a sorrowful, "Oh, Polly!" instead. Frankly the tone of it unnerved her. It wasn't what she was accustomed to hearing from anyone, let alone Mrs. Brolly. It sounded vaguely like...pity.

She couldn't imagine why her snagging her glove on the carriage clock today was any more pathetic than last week when she had laughed so hard at Mr. Cottingham's impersonation of her Papa she had accidentally snapped the handle off her cup of tea and ruined her blue taffeta dress. There had been no "Oh, Polly!" then. Not even a little one. No, she had been sent up to her room to change and was lectured on decorum and carelessness for a good three quarters of an hour.

So obviously there was some difference between today and last Thursday. She wondered what it could possibly be. Perhaps it wasn't her at all but rather Mrs. Brolly who was not the same as last week. She had never known Mrs. Brolly to be changeable but perhaps she had suffered some disappointment Polly wasn't privy to. It had to be a dreadfully lonely life with perfect poise, perfect behavior, and perfect seclusion behind three layers of heavy veils. Polly's Papa had told her more than once, in the Afghan campaign, when Mrs. Brolly met the enemy and turned them to stone, the expression set on their marble faces was that of pure ecstasy.

Polly moved her conjecture to the back of her mind as she saw the horses draw near The Imperial Museum.

"For goodness sake, Polly, if you could but this once exit the coach in the manner of a well brought up young lady rather than a stevedore we would all be eternally grateful," Mrs. Brolly sighed.

Taking her anticipation in hand Polly waited patiently, more or less, for the footman to help Mrs. Brolly from the carriage first and even suffered to be "helped" as well. She took the marble steps one at a time. She didn't swing her reticule from side to side or hike her skirt scandalously high in order to make her way more quickly.

She did draw the line at not stopping to chat with everyone she saw on her way to visit her Papa. She could never be one for Mrs. Brolly's cool bob of the head. She simply wasn't that subtle or refined. She was patently overenthusiastic. It was one of her defining characteristics. She waved vigorously at Mr. Virgil, the head of all the Museum cleaners, who scowled in response to her grin, as was his habit.

Polly couldn't help herself. The Museum was quite possibly the best place on earth. Down every corridor was a fresh wonder to be studied and for some reason today Mrs. Brolly seemed intent on steering her past every one of them. She gripped Polly's arm with not only her gloved hands, but a will of iron, preventing her from taking the narrow stairwell that led to the roof where Polly could easily spend all day with Dr. Noor improving the performance of his various flying machines. Mrs. Brolly's grip only tightened as they passed the doorway leading to the Department of Munitions with its delightful explosions. Likewise she was dragged past The Arboretum, where plants of all sorts were grown and researched, and the Menagerie, where a thousand beasts were housed.

How unfair, not to mention unusual. After a standard admonishment not to make a nuisance of herself, Polly should have been set free to roam where she pleased. It was what she did. Why the change? Why the secrecy?

When she was practically frog marched past the Department of Inventions she could bear it no longer, she snorted. Professor Magesteri, who headed the most exciting department of them all, might be gruff and he might have intimidated her when she was younger, and he might still take great exception to her interrupting any of his multitudes of underlings with questions, but he always allowed her access to his works in progress. Always. She was allowed to put her hand to any disappointments or failures, and chances were she would have them running before the day was out. Sometimes it took him that long to recall that he found her annoying and shout her out of his laboratories. And that was before. Well. Before. Perhaps this had something to do with that.

Polly wondered.

Professor Magesteri hadn't betrayed her, had he? He couldn't do that without betraying himself as well, and surely, surely her papa would be more than a bit put out with him as well.

Wouldn't he? Maybe?

Oh Mighty Isis!

Polly was in trouble.

When they arrived at her Papa's office it became quite clear it was not possible to join Professor Magesteri in his laboratory because he was currently in full gale force bellow at her Papa. The heavy door might as well have been a beaded screen.

Polly did her best not to give anything away in front of Mrs. Brolly.

The argument was already quite advanced; she heard them as she and Mrs. Brolly took their seats in the ante chamber. That they were quarreling at all was out of the ordinary to say the least. Of all her Papa's associates only Professor Magesteri was as close to him as Mrs. Brolly. She did not know how long her father and Professor Magesteri had been friends but she did know their acquaintance predated even the Afghan war. While it could not rightly be said Professor Magesteri's manners with her father were good, it would not be a misrepresentation to say the head of the department of invention tended to be better behaved with her father than he was with the rest of the world.

Really mostly what she heard were rude words. Oh, no.

"I can't bear to listen to those two going on, do you mind?" Mrs. Brolly said, setting down her valise.

Polly blinked and would have obliged if she had any idea what was expected of her.

"What would you have me do?" she asked.

"Anything to drown them out so we aren't forced to listen to Mr. Magesteri's self-indulgent thunderings. Do your recitations," Mrs. Brolly decreed.

"Which ones? Square roots or prime numbers or…" Polly asked.

"For the sake of all the gods, girl, no, something comprehensible, do the Ad Imperium Condita," Mrs. Brolly said in clear exasperation, despite her veils.

She supposed Mrs. Brolly was aiming to distract her. But Polly kept an ear to the other room, performing her task with less than her full concentration; precisely the sort of thing she was always being upbraided for.

"In the beginning was the city, and most of the monsters slept, while others lived in shadows and in the deep hidden seas…"

"This is idiocy!" bellowed a loud voice she knew full well belonged to Professor Magesteri.

"It is, nonetheless, the situation in which we find ourselves," came the calmer one, clearly her Papa. Unflappability was one of her father's chief characteristics. That and a love of cigars.

Mrs. Brolly cleared her throat from behind her veil. "Continue."

"Until the full moon before the battle of Actium, Cleopatra, wisest of the race of the Ptolemies, using both magic and science called forth to the corners of the Earth, enlisting all the great monsters of the age to aid her and Marc Anthony as they waged war against the villain Octavian," Polly said trying to continue reciting while still keeping an ear to the shouting in her father's office. "Umm…and…umm so it was that after the glorious victory of Anthony and Cleopatra honors and titles were heaped upon the Uncommon Regiments and their brethren…." Without meaning to, Polly trailed off.

"So you are simply going to sit there, Plumber, and go along with this?" said Magesteri.

"That is no way to address the director of The Museum," a female voice she could almost place took him to task.

"It seems to me, the best possible choice is to accept the offer, even if it seems somewhat unexpected," Papa said gently and was for some time answered only by the sound of restless footsteps.

Professor Magesteri was pacing.

"Somewhat unexpected? It's bleeding absurd, is what it is! It's like he drew a name out of a bloody hat," Magesteri screamed.

"If you've a better proposal, I am perfectly willing to hear it, Stephen." There was the sound of clinking dishes. "Cigar?" Polly's Papa offered. Polly had never even considered that the Professor might possess a first name.

"Henry, please," came Mr. Magesteri's voice in what was perilously close to a whine. She had rarely heard him call her papa, or anyone else for that matter, by their first name before. Perhaps he had an aversion.

Polly's eavesdropping was interrupted by Charlie Edney, Mr. Magestri's least favorite clerk in the entire Invention Department, arriving with a bound folder full of half-finished schematics.

"May I join you, Mrs. Brolly?" Big as Charlie was he cowered as he said it. "I'm desperate for a bit of help."

"Very well, Charles." Mrs. Brolly nodded.

"Oh Polly, I'm so glad to see you," Charlie whispered. "I was up all night burning incense before Imhotep but I can't seem to get these right."

"Let me, Charlie," Polly said, taking the papers in her hands.

Charlie had been Polly's especial friend since he came to the Museum as roly-poly thirteen year old apprentice with horns and a tail. Over the years he had grown both taller and more muscular, until all that was left of his former appearance was a face like a cupid on a chocolate box. Charlie silently took a seat beside her, his tail switching. With less than half her full attention, she distracted herself by looking over the papers in his hands, making notes to keep Magesteri from hurling whatever heavy object was close by at poor Charlie's head.

Of all the departments Charlie's granny had insisted he work with Professor Magesteri -on account of the prestige Polly supposed - but Charlie was constitutionally unsuited to any sort of engineering. Charlie looked uncomfortable and scratched his left horn. Thus occupied it was some time before she was able to continue her "overhearing." It took a bit to set Charlie's schematics to rights but, at least it gave her something to do.

"As you know, Mr. Edney has petitioned for her hand despite the fact that he's still apprenticed and his master refuses his consent. How did you think Edney stacked up beside Albinus, again?" her Papa asked in the lightest, most inane voice Polly had ever heard.

Polly gave Charlie a hard look, but all he did was turn his head and scratch his horn again.

"Pfft," came Magesteri's reply. "And yes, being as I am the cretin in question's master I am well aware that his request to marry was denied."

"And a wise decision it was, Stephen," said Papa. He sounded as though he had something in his mouth, likely a cigar. "So you propose what? We let the girl go on as she has and simply wait for a scandal to erupt? As you're aware she can be a bit impulsive. Dare I say…passionate as well? Noor is of the opinion with a few extra thousand pounds in his budget he could send the child to the moon providing…of course, speculation about the moral laxity of the moon men is correct. We can only hope that she might find moon men marginally less enticing than Museum employees. Are you absolutely certain you wouldn't care for a cigar?"

"It would hardly be more ridiculous than what you propose," Magesteri said sharply. "Not that you could be expected to bring the girl to heel."

"I do have a Museum to run. May I remind you, Stephen, of the part you've played in forcing my hand; besides, I'm not the one doing any proposing," her papa sounded almost amused.

What had Mr. Magesteri suggested? That this girl, who ever she was, actually marry Mr. Albinus? Mr. Albinus, Duke of Londinium Austri, was horrid. Not horrid looking, no, when he wasn't invisible he was said to be rather handsome in a pinch-yourself-to-see-if-he's-real sort of way. The horror of Mr. Albinus was his four, count them, four, wives dead in childbearing. Whatever it was he put in them with his seed, it was deadly. Polly was surprised that Charlie had proposed to anyone, especially in competition with Mr. Albinus and against the wishes of his master, Professor Magesteri. She counted Charlie a good friend of hers and she hadn't heard anything about any girls from him, not anything noteworthy at least.

"It most certainly was not my proposal. That was a joke, and not a very good one at that," Professor Magesteri hissed adamantly. "A girl of her …temperament is hardly suitable for someone such as Himself…more importantly he is not suited to her, Henry, even you must realize the sheer bloody bleeding fuckwitted wrongheadedness…"

"I suppose you believe we should disregard the political advantages of such a match," her Papa said.

"Hang the political advantage!" Professor Magesteri said "The girl is wholly unsuited…"

"Who is she suited for then, Stephen?" her papa asked.

"I was under the impression…" Magesteri started before lowering his voice so Polly couldn't quite pick out what he was saying.

Whatever it was it made Polly's Papa snort with laughter. "Where did you come up with that idea?"

"You let me pick out her hair!" came the shouted reply.

"I've consulted you about my choice of overcoat as well, doesn't necessarily follow I mean for you to wear it, does it, my boy?" Polly's Papa said. "So why did you come to me on Albinus's behalf?"

There was more low muttering from Mr. Magesteri.

Logically it sounded as though they were discussing Polly, but that couldn't be. There was no world in which she would ever be in danger of marrying The Duke of Londinium Austri.

The female voice piped up again. "Even so …She's past ripe for marriageable age. When the fruit is already off the tree, you don't leave it to the crows if you can help it, especially not if a Duke is hungry for it."

Henry Plumber cut her off, "What I realize, Stephen, is that for the girl to refuse would be a mistake of Olympian proportions. She's 22 years old."

At that point, the Head of the Department of Invention let loose a string of profanity the likes of which Polycorpus Plumber had never heard before. He was still swearing, making suggestions to Polly's Papa regarding both his grand-mother and mother that were certainly illegal and likely physically damaging, if not impossible as well, when Mrs. Brolly led her through the door clearing her throat dramatically.

"Sit down, Polly dear," Polly's papa said pleasantly. "Let me reassure you that since I have become your father I have had nothing but the tenderest of pater-nal hopes for you; that you might grow and learn as other girls, and you have not disappointed me. In fact, you have grown and learned so much like other girls that now I find myself facing the same conundrum as all the other papas in the world. In fact, Mr. Magesteri and I have devoted the majority of the day to attempting to come to an understanding. In case you have any doubts about our decision, both Mr. and Mrs. Canavan and Mrs. Edney are in agreement with our conclusion, as is Mrs. Brolly."

Mrs. Brolly sighed. "I am at that."

Polly wondered what part the Canavans played in this.

Magesteri turned and gave Mrs. Brolly a betrayed look. "I thought, you, of all people, Augusta, would take my side."

"And which side is that? Because you appear to be arguing both for and against," Mrs. Brolly said.

Magesteri answered with an obscenity so raw it made Mrs. Brolly "hhhmph" at him.

"Stephen, the boy is my nephew," Mrs. Brolly.

"As am I," Professor Magesteri said, his mouth in a twist.

Henry Plumber sighed looking over the tops of his glasses and tapping the ash off his cigar. "I believe Mr. Magesteri has something to say to you, Polly. Don't you, Stephen?"

Professor Magesteri moved to stand before Polly and, lifting his chin so he might look down his nose, he all but snarled, "In the name of Titus Post-humous Albinus Duke of Londinium Austri I would like to request you do him the honor of becoming his wife, Miss Plumber, or die an old maid and a burden to your father."

"I beg your pardon?" She couldn't help blinking.

"Surely you can do better than that, Stephen," Henry Plumber said, still smiling. Or perhaps not smiling exactly, but rather holding his mouth in an approximation of a smile.

"Very well," Magesteri hissed. "Please, Miss Plumber, marry the wealthy and respected Mr. Albinus because it is preferable to the alternative of dying a spinster or worse yet bringing shame on your father which is clearly the way you are headed."

It was true. A mistake on her part could ruin her Papa, as well as herself. Polly wasn't stupid, she knew that, and she knew how to avoid an accident. She'd learned from Mable, the girl who lit the morning fires ay the Museum, how the female commoners went about it; wild aoesfoetida extract. Polly was nothing but bits of commoners sewn together and reanimated, so it worked for her and there wasn't anything wrong or illegal about it. It was only criminal sorcery to inhibit the conception of monsters, plain old common babies were twelve for a tuppence on the open market.

Polly could find no reply other than to go slightly green at the notion of marriage to Albinus just the same. Pulling herself together she looked about the room. The mysterious female she had heard was none other than the senior apprentice, Will Canavan's, mother. The Canavan family were most accurately described as the polar opposite of Polly's Papa, very noble, very financially embarrassed, and very nearly common, or at least terribly prolific as far as the nobility went; there were Canavans everywhere.

"If you want me to cooperate, Papa, you must tell me what all this is about," she straightened her skirts and pulled off her torn glove.

"A bit blunt but sensible," said Mrs. Brolly with what sounded like approval.

"This very morning Mr. Titus Albinus asked me for your hand in marriage," her Papa said, looking at his cigar rather than her face. "Or rather sent our Professor Magesteri as his go between to ask for your hand, as well as the rest of you."

"Couldn't he just take the hand, instead?" Polly offered. "I can always get another."

"That's right, make joke of it, the way you do with every sodding thing," Magesteri said sourly. "Perhaps you are suited to Titus after all."

"Stephen!" Mrs. Brolly reprimanded him.

"What on earth does he want to marry me for?" she asked, incredulous. It was a reasonable question. What could a stylish, wealthy, powerful, man possibly want with a wife her age, a wife of no birth, no breeding, and only passable looks?

Her father did not answer; instead he looked abashedly at his cigar again.

"An heir, obviously. Having tried his luck with his own class I imagine this is as close as Albinus can come to stooping to consort with the hoi polloi. You have, have you not, noticed your rather unseemly physical strength?" Professor Magesteri said scowling at her. "Perhaps you're under the impression all the girls accidentally snap the banister on the way down the stairs."

"That seems a bit much, even for Mr. Albinus…I mean I'm common as dirt," she started rolling her eyes but Magesteri butted in rudely.

"It seems the much vaunted brain your father endowed you with has fallen short. It also would appear you haven't been paying much attention to your lessons on society or history or any dog-buggering thing that lacks gears and springs and doesn't spark up under the proper circumstances. For thousands of years the Aristocracy has largely kept to itself …as far as breeding goes, at least. Thus, many of us find it increasingly difficult to produce viable offspring. There are, of course, common females, but there is a rather high morbidity rate for both mother and child as a result of these unions. As you, and everyone else on these accursed islands knows, the Duke has killed four separate wives trying to get an heir. Four Noble ladies have gone straight from their childbed to their graves. Albinus believes this problem could be solved with a female made of rather sturdier stuff," Magesteri went on but it seemed too terrible to believe so Polly felt compelled to stop him.

"It sounds to me like there is an awful lot of conjecture involved in what you're saying," Polly said, deciding to take off her other glove rather than wear

the torn mate. "He's no idea if I'm any different than those other females…
where it matters."

"It's a chance he's willing to take," Magesteri said blankly.

To that Polly had no reply. It wasn't much of a risk, on his part, she supposed. If she succeeded in giving birth Albinus would have what he wanted and
if she didn't he would still have her dowry and could try again with someone
else.

That was a cheery thought.

"Well?" Magesteri snapped at her.

She straightened in her chair. "Am I correct in assuming this would not be a
real marriage, simply a formality for breeding purposes, Professor?" she asked,
attempting to clear her head. "If I prove infertile, if I don't get, you know,
familial, we can undo the whole business?"

Magesteri stood over her, continuing to glare. "Your ignorance as well as your
indelicacy is astounding, Miss Plumber," Magesteri said coldly.

It seemed to Polly that everyone in the room inhaled at once.

Neither Mrs. Canavan nor her own Papa seemed willing to look her in the
eye.

"The Conferratio Ritual is unbreakable and it is also de rigeur at our level of
society, child. Without it the marriage would have no more legal weight than
a fancy dress play," the Mrs. Brolly said, laying a hand on her shoulder. "The
offspring of such a union wouldn't be recognized as a legitimate heir without
a legal adoption by their own father. Unfortunately, the Conferratio cannot be
broken except by death."

Magesteri sneered at no one in particular. "The girl would no doubt prefer
her father's social degradation, nevermind the consequences. It's all about
Polly's little whims."

"Calm down, Stephen, the child said no such thing," Mrs. Brolly clucked.

"May I speak to the Professor alone, please?" Polly asked. She was hardly a
child by any definition; sometimes Mrs. Brolly was exceedingly tiresome.

"Of course, not," said Mrs. Brolly. "For you are impetuous and he is impossible and…"

"My entire life I've come and gone in the Museum as I pleased. Yesterday. I spent half the day in the department of Inventions without your supervision. I don't see why Albinus's proposal should suddenly mean I can't be trusted on my own. I should like to speak to Professor Magesteri, please, about the man I'm being asked to marry, without all of you butting in." She was trying to hold onto a sense of decorum, even though all her self control seemed to be failing at the moment.

Her Papa sighed sadly, Mrs. Brolly seemed to hesitate, Mrs. Canavan shook her head in horror but Professor Magesteri threw himself down in the chair opposite her as though there were several hundred other places he would rather be.

"After you, Augusta," Her Papa held the door for Mrs. Brolly and Mrs. Canavan although he addressed only Mrs. Brolly.

"Certainly, Mr. Plumber," Mrs Brolly said graciously.

"And Polly, while you are perfectly free to deny Professor Magesteri's offer, I do wish you would make me proud," her papa said quietly, merely a nose and cigar peering round the edge of the door. "It really is a great honor."

Polly forced herself to smile and wave as he left, even as her heart sank. No matter her natural obstinacy she'd never gone counter to her papa's direct wishes.

"Well," Professor Magesteri said, eyeing Polly suspiciously.

"Well," she repeated, "I would like to know why you are going along with this."

"Miss Plumber," Professor Magesteri said running his hands through his hair as dark and heavy as mechanical grease. When he next spoke it was under his breath. He was, of course, just as aware as she was that someone had their ear pressed to the other side of the keyhole he whispered, "Believe me when I assure you I would offer you an acceptable alternative but I cannot. I am not an acceptable alternative."

"Of course I understand perfectly. I never imagined it otherwise, but are

you afraid of him? Like my papa and Mrs. Brolly? I would like to know …"
she asked, trying not to sigh, only partly lying. Why couldn't she marry Mr.
Magesteri? Why did everyone seem to think Mr. Albinus was ideal? Why? Polly
wanted to understand. She knew her papa only had her best interests at heart
but how was marrying a man who had been the death of four women already
in Polly's best interest?

Professor Magesteri leaned back in his chair and he did sigh; he sighed so
heavily that melodrama was the only word Polly could find to describe it.
He sighed melodramatically; perhaps the sigh came with swirling tails of the
smudged red frock coat he was wearing in lieu of the leather apron and shirt
sleeves he reserved for the laboratory.

"You think me such a fawning lackey to the Duke I would sacrifice my
own…benefit at his whim?" he asked.

"I'll admit that didn't seem likely either," she said. "So, why?"

Professor Magesteri scowled while looking pointedly away from her. "You
know, I imagine, were you not hopelessly female and were you not joined at
the hip with the least imaginative clerks in my employ, I might find you barely
tolerable."

Polly found this last accusation patently unfair, Will Canavan was not in the
least bit dull and Guy Ouellette was actively clever. Even Charlie Edney was
only slow when it came to engineering. Although she had been told a hundred
times not to she folded her arms across her chest.

She also knew the words were dangerously close to a declaration of affection
on his part.

"Likewise, when you forget you are supposed to be an ill mannered wretch I
rather enjoy your company," Polly said obstinately, returning kind for kind. If
Mrs. Brolly heard her she would be dragging her home by the ear any minute
now. She knew she ought to feel ashamed of herself, but she didn't.

"You should be given to understand the full impact of the decision you are
about to make, Miss Plumber," Magesteri said speaking quickly and quietly
"Miss Plumber, the truth is, I am an unsuitable husband, far less suitable than

Albinus as you would no doubt learn in time. Certainly no less dangerous. This is no insult on Albinus's part; The Conferreatio he offers is, as you know, the most sacred ritual of our society, open only to the Uncommon," he said, watching her reaction closely.

"Which rules me out, I might have been made in a laboratory but all the pieces are common. Why do I keep having to remind everyone of that?" she said and immediately felt asinine when she saw Magesteri's disdainful look. "Why can't I marry you instead?"

"Because I am not an acceptable husband for you, or any woman," Magesteri said.

"And Albinus is? More importantly how am I an acceptable wife for him?" Polly said.

"Pfft," he snorted. "And they say you are a bright girl! Where was your head when you were supposed to be studying the history of the empire?" He cocked his head.

"I have other concerns, as well, professor," Polly said folding her hands in her lap, afraid to elaborate.

"What are they?" he asked archly.

"You do realize my current state?" Polly said circuitously giving him a hard look; he knew the issue as well as she did.

She watched as a light seemed to dawn on Professor Magesteri's face. "You think Titus Albinus gives a fig that you've disposed of your maidenhead? Well, so did most of his other wives before he married them, it's nothing to him. You might be surprised to learn those who live and die by the hymen tend, for the most part, to be overly zealous nursemaids, spinsters, and elderly widows," Magesteri said tersely. "Besides no one expects a female of your class to be intact past 15, 16 on the outside."

"Mr. Magesteri!" that was too much for Polly, lumping her in with the girls who sold violets on the street corner and would probably do it for a potato.

"Don't you 'Mr. Magesteri' me," he said folding his arms across his chest and looking pleased with himself. "I'm only telling the truth and you're sounding more like my Aunt Augusta every day."

"You are so exceptionally charming... I ought to thump you for that," Polly said contemplating making a fist; it wasn't the least bit proper.

"See what I get for trying to set your mind at ease, Miss Plumber," Magesteri said rolling his eyes.

"At least I treat you with a minimum of respect," Polly said, seething.

"So much respect you have, over the years, been an enormous pain in my back side. Stealing my best spanner…" he glowered. "In and out of my laboratory without so much as a by your leave…taking untold liberties."

Polly gave a hard look first to the keyhole, then to Magesteri.

"You're a fine one…" she whispered.

Magesteri returned a look that was both sheepish and annoyed.

She would have continued glaring and bickering but there, before her hovering in mid-air a silver cane came into view, like dissolving in reverse, growing more solidly visible by the moment.

The cane was followed by a pair of gloves in pale lavender. What Polly was seeing didn't actually take foothold in her brain until she saw the amethyst links in the French cuffs. And if she had a spoonful of the delicacy expected of her Polly would have either swooned or lost control of her bladder because there, towering over the two of them in their chairs was the terrifying Mr. Albinus, with a lavender waistcoat to match his gloves. His velvet frock coat was dove grey. As he solidified the effect was strangely like a shimmering shower of gold. He was quite tall and quite slender and looked surprisingly…gormless. Maybe his reputation among the ladies was enhanced by his finances.

He bowed ostentatiously. She was quite surprised to find he was a ginger. How peculiar. No one had ever mentioned that little detail.

"A fine one for what, Captain Magesteri? Liberties, was it? Hasn't Stephen brought you up to speed, Miss Plumber? No one has any secrets from the Duke of Londinium Austri, least of all you. Best to disabuse yourself of the notion here and now," Mr. Albinus said pleasantly. "Now, what have you to say to Miss Plumber, Captain Magesteri?"

Magesteri exhaled loudly and his shoulders sagged.

"Polly, would you please consent to marry Titus Postumus Albinus, Duke of Londinium Austri, Colonel in Her Imperial Majesty's Service, Order of Apophis 1st class?" Magesteri said with his lip curled. "It does appear to be the best course of action under the circumstances."

Everything in her balked but Polly knew she was expected to accede to the wishes of her elders and betters. She wondered what would happen if she crossed her arms and simply refused? How would she face her papa and Mrs. Brolly if she turned up her nose at arguably one of the most eligible bachelors in all of Londinium?

"I suppose it does," she looked down at her hands, one brown and one milk colored with freckles.

Professor Magesteri looked like he might almost smile for a moment before his face returned to its blank state. "We are agreed, then?"

Polly nodded.

"Technically, you should say 'Nubo' to indicate your acceptance; it means..." he started.

"It means "I veil myself" ... Nubo, then," she said resignedly.

Albinus nudged Magesteri. She never seen anyone do that before, nudge Professor Magesteri.

"And I should do this," Mr. Magesteri said, standing to unceremoniously dump a handful of gold and a delicate golden ring from his pocket into her lap. "Miss... Polly," he said, uncomfortably shifting from one foot to the other as he stood over her. "I... Um... We are not friends, but we are somewhat acquainted with one another. You understand I am not a particularly nice person myself but I wish to give you my word."

"Yes?" She answered him with similar lack of ease. She was supposed to marry Albinus? The whole situation seemed bizarre and dreamlike.

"Albinus will be a good husband to you, better than I would have been in his place, I swear it," Magesteri stumbled then gave Albinus a hard look.

Albinus clapped him on the back and laughed "You're a good man, Stephen.

I couldn't wish for a better go between."

"That's all very nice," Polly said in what she hoped was a business like tone; she felt like retching.

"I'm glad you think so," he answered blankly before continuing, his voice suddenly brisk. "Mrs. Canavan will be accompanying you to their ancestral home aboard Dr. Noor's airship, there should be time to complete the adoption in time for the invitations to be issued..."

"What adoption?" she interrupted him.

"The Confereatio may not be entered into by any parties whose parents were not joined in Conferreatio themselves. Under the present circumstances, Arthur and Livia Canavan have agreed to have you join their... brood in return for compensation. I understand Henry and Arthur have everything they need set up in advance," Albinus announced beaming.

She looked at him puzzled.

"We marry in a month," Albinus grinned as he said it. "The First day of April."

"Isn't that rather sudden?" she asked her head starting to swim.

"It is sudden, but today is the ninth of the month as well as perilously close to the full moon and no part of the Conferreatio may take place on the ides or the nodes or the waning of the moon or any number of holidays for a host of arcane reasons. That will be our last opportunity for nearly a year," Albinus said. "The oracles have been consulted."

The awkward pause that would have surely followed was interrupted by Mr. and Mrs. Canavan sticking their noses through the cracked door.

Chapter 3 : the Wedding March

Polly wished she could account for the short weeks between her proposal and her wedding in some sensible sort of way. She could say, if forced, that she was adopted by Artorius Canavan, although she didn't move house. What would be the point, when she would have to pack up her things and take them to Mr. Albinus's house almost immediately thereafter?

She must have passed the time some sort of way, doing something, because the time did pass. Quickly in fact. It seemed no time at all before a barouche was sent to fetch Polly to have tea with Mr. Albinus's mother and grandmother.

Polly walked up into the room, turned left at the portrait of the imposing man with great green wings, consciously working at keeping her right and left feet stepping in a pleasant rhythm as opposed to their usual lurch. She didn't know if she succeeded. She was also rifling through her catalogue of collective nouns. Mrs. Brolly insisted on proper speech and "Scads of dowagers", first inclination though it might be, was not correct.

If she was to have tea with Mr. Albinus's mother, great grandmother, and auntie, Mrs Brolly, and every one of them a Dowager Lady, that was an awful lot of dowagers for one afternoon. Scads.

Frost... that was it. A frost of lady dowagers. Or was it Dowager Ladies? Ladies Dowager? Either way, that's what they were. Polly would do her best not to catch cold at the sight of them.

Bracing herself she raised her fist to the door reminding herself to knock lightly, she absolutely did not want to bang a hole in the door, or knock it off its hinges, or well, any of the things she was apt to do unintentionally if she was over-nervous.

Polly's fist was a hair away from making contact when the heavy wooden doors swung wide to reveal a pair of maids who bowed at her like she was a lady and ushered her onto a deceptively plush looking settee directly across from what appeared to be a desiccated ape in black mourning garb.

"Leave us," the ape croaked in a heavy foreign accent. Alexandrian, like fancy ladies with pretensions tried to mimic, but this was not for show, this was as real as the Empress herself and it made Polly sit straighter than she had before.

"Polycorpus Singularia, I presume," the ape, who after a moment of staring Polly decided was probably just a very, very old woman, said.

"Yes, ma'am, I'm her," Polly said. the instant the words were out of her mouth wondering if her grammar was correct. "Would you be Mister Albinus's grandmother? I was to have tea with his mother and grandmother and and and also his Aunt Augusta."

There was metallic scraping sound it took Polly a moment to recognize as laughter.

"My name is Nefrit Magesteri. I am Titus Posthumus Albinus's Great Great Great Grandmother and Stephen Propertius Drusus Magesteri's as well, come to that. I believe he says grandmother out of laziness. I told the boy as I told his mother and her sister, I wished to speak to you alone before tea was served and I had to struggle to make my self heard over all the small talk and the clinking china," the old woman said forcing her heavy drooping lids wide enough that Polly could see the glowing red eyes.

Polly had never been more horrified in her life.

An oracle. She'd never met an oracle before, not in person. There were only said to be two in the whole of the Isles.

Albinus said he'd consulted the oracle about marrying her. He'd just neglected to mention the seer in question was his own elderly relative.

Every school child knew they lived practically forever. Or hundreds of years at any rate.

Every primer told the story of the Sybil at Cumae, who was told by Apollo to scoop all the sand she could hold in her hands. Like the countless grains of sand so would be her days. Only when the arrogant cow refused the god her bed did he neglect to grant youth and beauty to go along with the long life. So the oracle grew so old and dried up the priests had to hang her in a sack on the wall because they could no longer bear to look at her. Every time she was moved it caused such excruciating pain, until one day she simply collapsed into so much dust.

Albinus's great-great-great grandmother was only half-way there by the look of her.

"Are you paying attention?" Mr. Albinus's great-great-great grandmother said, whopping Polly up side the head with her ibis-headed cane. "There's precious little time before we're interrupted."

"Yes, ma'am," Polly said. Honestly she had no idea what else she could say. But it was a lie, her mind had been wandering.

"You're lying, but never mind, as long as you are paying attention now," the oracle, Nefrit, said, and Polly caught a glimpse of teeth as worn as stones. "You may have wondered why my…my descendent chose you for his bride. He chose you because that is the choice I led him to."

"What in Set's name for?" Polly blurted before she could help herself. One day her mouth was going to get her into trouble and today might possibly be that day.

"Because I am the oracle of Apollo. The only possible continuation of my line I have seen is through you," the ancient woman said.

"Why tell me if you already know it's going to happen?" Polly said. She had put her foot in it already, why try to practice restraint now?

"The future is not a mosaic that has been set in mortar on the floor. Rather, events flow one after the other a like a river, so it is always possible to divert the stream with a well placed branch. It is worth a great deal to me to see that this child be born," the old woman said. "I have seen the mother but the father remains unclear, either the dark brooding one or the dapper young duke. Both will share your bed. As both are my descendents it makes no difference to me who does the deed so long as it's done."

A shiver ran down Polly's spine "Are you, are you suggesting, I, I, I?"

"I am not suggesting anything. I am almost two hundred years old. Don't be foolish enough to believe you are capable of shocking or offending me. Let us understand each other. The Nobility, the male half at least, consider any impediment to conception Dark Arts. And for hundreds of years it has been the law; it is forbidden to interfere with the conception of monsters. It has been named the blackest of sorceries. They think a woman is a thing to be bought. Well, they are correct; a woman may be bought, not merely a whore but any woman, provided her father likes the price. But what money and power can buy a thousand times over only bonds of affection may make secure. Not many men grasp the subtlety of marriage. Titus has convinced himself you are bought and paid for and will remain convinced of that until he learns otherwise. The boy suffers a deficit of imagination. But you are a modern middle-class English woman, you were raised a commoner or something like a commoner, and I imagine you have no such foolish inhibitions. I, on the other hand, am a woman of the world, 187 years old. In Alexandria, everything is permitted, despite the law. We both know women the world over do their best to control their fertility every day and there is nothing unseemly about it. They give their favor to the man who pleases them most, sometimes they do it wisely, sometimes they do it foolishly and out of desperation. They are often less than successful, either in stopping a birth or in causing one to occur," Nefrit said evenly. "I would have you exercise your best judgement. That is all."

Polly was absolutely gobsmacked. She had no idea what she was supposed to say so she told the truth. "You don't think you're giving too much credit? I mean the ones with any pretense of respectability ape the nobility every way they can and the poor ones are too busy trying to stay alive to exercise much choice in anything."

The glowing red eyes closed and scraping laughter set Polly's teeth on edge.

"I can see why the gods meant you for me, it took 100 years for me to lose my tact but you seem to have been built without it from the beginning," Nefrit said between gasps of laughter.

Polly would have told Nefrit she didn't believe in any gods except that the doors flew open and there stood Titus Albinus, arms linked with Mrs. Brolly on one side and a woman she could only assume was his mother on the other.

"Polycorpus Darling," Albinus said bowing low and kissing her hand "Mother, may I present my fiancé, Polycorpus Singularia Canavan. Polycorpus, my mother, the Lady Aurora Albinus."

"Pleased to meet you, Mrs. Albinus," Polly said as the woman took her hands.

"Delightful to meet you, my dear," the woman said leaning close. "Polycorpus? I thought Hathor's little sister was called Sekmet." Her voice sounded exactly like Mrs. Brolly's.

"No, Mother dear, Polycorpus is the late Mrs. Albinus's other sister," Mr. Albinus said gently and technically it was true.

She had known vaguely that one of the four wives had been Will and Sekmet's sister, but since Polly hadn't known Hathor Canavan it hadn't registered.

Titus Albinus's mother patted her hand. "I'm sorry, darling, there are so many children in your family I have trouble keeping track. Imagine that, too many children! It's like having too much money," she laughed gaily.

Polly had heard Mrs. Albinus was not only Mrs. Brolly's sister but her twin. She had been a bit baffled as to how that worked seeing as no one could look on Mrs. Brolly's face without turning to stone but now she understood; Mrs. Albinus was blind. More than blind Mrs. Albinus had no eyes. Not even pits where eyes should go. Her face was perfectly smooth from forehead to nose. Not only were there no eyes there were no lashes and no brows either. Her hair was red like her son's. Polly wondered if Mrs. Brolly's hair was ginger too, underneath her veil, and hoped she never found out.

Polly had only seen Mr. Albinus the one time before, and it occurred to her he was not quite as common looking as he seemed in her papa's office. His eyes were both too big and too narrow, angled strangely in his face over cheekbones so prominent they were the widest part of his narrow face. As if he had both his mother's eyes and his own. His mouth was a woman's mouth, as well, too full for his thin face, or for any man really. It was nearly identical to Mrs. Albinus's. He was tall and weedy but despite his elegantly cut clothes, he had the look of not being quite full grown. His hands were too big for the rest of him and looking down so were his feet.

Polly looked back up at him, just in time to get a narrow-eyed scowl. He'd caught her looking at him. She was allowed to look at him, wasn't she? There were to be married, after all.

Or perhaps he had been looking at her as well.

"I have made a decision," Mr. Albinus's great great great grandmother announced as if it were a royal decree. "I am passing you the Lares Familiaris, the shrine to my husband's first ancestors. From now on, you will sacrifice wine to them on the feast days and incense each morning." She gestured to a triangular shaped piece of furniture wrapped in cloth opposite the parlor from them.

Mr. Albinus stared at Polly even harder. "She never gave anything to any of the others," he squinted.

"That's because they weren't going to be the mother of your child," Nefrit smiled and looked more apelike than ever.

Chapter 4 : Proceeding A Pace

A fter that, events became a blur. Polly, whose mind had always more or less glazed over when that sort of thing came up before, because-honestly-why-on-earth-would-she-ever-need-to-know-this-rubbish, it-wasn't-as-though-she-expected-to-get-married, learned her part in the wedding, which did, agreeing with Mrs. Brolly's description, seem very much like a play.

Perhaps it all happened too quickly for her to do anything but go along.

It began with, of all unlikely things, ritual hairdressing.

Mrs Canavan sat her down in a mostly empty room, dressed Polly in a simple tunica recta of linen, tied her belt with the most complicated knot she'd seen in her life, and plaited her hair into six sections, marking each part with the tip of an ancient rusted spear point. Having eight arms was helpful in this case.

Will's sister, Sekmet Canavan, said a gladiator had been killed with it once. The spear not the hairdo, though Polly thought it might go either way.

"SEPTENTRIONES, MERIDIES, ORIENS, OCCIDENS, CAELUM, INFERI," Mrs Canavan said intently, sectioning Polly's wild mane, then paused before intoning triumphantly, "META."

Polly's hair was not her best feature. Originally her head had come with some sort of stick straight black hair but when her papa had switched out the brains he also saw fit to exchange the black for golden curls, leaving a row of telltale stitches below her hairline. The biggest problem was as she aged the golden curls had turned to indeterminate light brown with a tendency to stick up from the scalp at perfect right angles.

Polly watched in the mirror as her hair was arranged by the many-armed Mrs. Canavan into six overlapping wreathes atop her head.

"You look like a table decoration," said Sekmet, wrinkling her nose.

"She looks like a bride," said Mrs. Canavan haughtily. "Flameum - Lutei Socci," she said with her next breath and opened a box Polly hadn't even noticed before. Inside was a veil and slippers, or at least they appeared to be a veil and slippers, wrought of flame.

With help from two maids Polly's feet and head were draped with a cold fire. It was surprisingly ticklish.

Polly was surprised when they placed the wreath on her head and it didn't burn.

In retrospect there were certain things she remembered better than others.

Mr. Canavan burning her clothes on the altar at the Canavan family home was not liable to be forgotten any time soon.

But the airship ride to Mr. Albinus's country house literally flew by, pardon her pun.

She was startled by her first sight of Mr. Albinus. He was such a dandy it was easy to forget he was a colonel in Her Majesty's Service, but his brass buttons shone and his uniform was a brilliant blue. The wreath on his head looked romantic and festive and all those things it was supposed to be. When Polly had looked in the mirror that morning she felt nothing but foolish.

Then when Colonel Albinus strode up and wrenched her out of Livia Canavan's arms in the village square, there were tears in her eyes and it stopped feeling like a play altogether, even though she knew the moment was coming. Had been expecting it all day, in fact. Weeks actually.

He seemed to pause the shortest split second that could still count as a hesitation before he spoke his part. "Ubi tu Gaia, Ego Gaius," he said, pressing a bough of whitethorn into her hands.

If she thought there had been a crowd in village square, it was nothing compared to the sight of every Museum employee, commoner, and monster she could name as well as quite a few others lining each step she took along the main road. She kept hearing snatches of the fescinni the revelers sang. The dirty nuptial songs had always been Polly's favorite part of any wedding procession she'd seen, probably because they weren't her wedding.

Now they seemed a bit rude, perhaps even intrusive.

Mr. and Mrs. Canavan took her hands again. They were flanked by Aidan Wallace and Drusilla Everidge. Will, Guy, and Sekmet came a half step behind. She hadn't had a chance to speak to them, but they seemed perfectly calm. Perhaps she was the only one who was verging on hysteria.

Before her, a perfectly ordered line of boys, the youngest apprentices marched. She wondered exactly what Professor Magesteri had threatened them with to make them so incredibly well behaved. One carried a vase with the Jumeau doll she'd never played with that she'd been instructed to bring from home; another carried a heavy grained cake; yet another, a torch lit from the altar in the Museum tower. Each bore something. Two particularly handsome boys, twins conjoined at the side, toted dolls in the likeness of her and Mr. Albinus on ornate pillows.

Up ahead strode Titus Albinus, at his side were Professor Magesteri, Mrs. Brolly, and of all people, Mr Virgil the cleaning man.

Albinus led them on and on, would the procession never stop? The parade continued on to the crest of hill and when Polly reached the top she saw... a dark squarish stone castle, modest for a castle but huge for a house, above all it was hardly welcoming. Finally, at the... what Polly would call the front door, over the drawbridge and past the moat, of course, Albinus paused and dug in his pocket for a set of iron keys.

Every mouth stopped, over a thousand people held their breath, waiting as Mr. Albinus held out the keys to his ancestral home.

"The doors are locked, Lady," he called. "Unlock the doors."

The procession parted to make way for her.

She did it. She unlocked the doors to Mr. Albinus's house. Albinus faltered twice lifting her up, as if he'd expected her to be lighter. She wondered that no one had warned him. She affixed her whitethorn above the lintel and Mr. Albinus finally gave up and tossed her over his shoulder as though she was sack of rocks and carried her that way through the entry way, up the stairs and into the great cold stone hall with all of the wedding party trailing and guests and all the great rush and throng of every Uncommon Gentleman and Lady of the Isles behind them.

"Well done," he whispered into her ear as he set her down.

In all the mad mad day, it seemed like a hysterical joke. How exactly had she done well? By not running away screaming? She fought to keep a straight face.

The wedding continued.

Would it never end?

After gifts of fire and water, she burned her childhood toys on an altar dedicated to Albinus's Primogenitors, whoever they were. She gave the Albinus a symbolic coin for her keep and threw another into the fire; the last, she presented to Arthur Canavan.

The Duke of Londinium Austri pledged her his life and made solemn vows to various gods, ancestors and, it seemed to Polly, every member of the wedding party.

There was a pause and the assembled crowd quieted as Livia Canavan again stepped forward.

Under her eye, the boys placed the dolls side by side in a tiny ornate bed set up prominently in the centre of the room.

The motherly many-armed and gilled woman took Polly's hand and placed it in Mr. Albinus's, speaking with only the slightest gurgle.

"By the ancestors Immortal, I join you, Polycorpus Singularia and Titus Posthumus both in matrimony. Ever after shall you be intermingled like the abundant clouds and by this either be in shame or in glory."

"Foedus lecti," called Arthur Canavan loudly as he placed his hand over theirs.

The Pledge of Fidelity. As it had been explained to her, it meant Mr. Canavan was personally vouching for her faithfulness as a wife. It wouldn't be binding until Mr. Albinus did his part and consummated the marriage.

Polly watched Mr. Albinus's cheeks color a bit as Mrs. Canavan led her away.

He had blushed. Him a Colonel in the Imperial Service. She couldn't help being taken aback by the terrible wonder of it all.

The bedroom, Mrs. Canavan was taking her to The Duke, Colonel Albinus's bedroom. She was probably blushing herself.

She couldn't bring herself to say a word as Mrs. Canavan led her to the bed strewn with saffron and violets. A bed that perfectly matched the tiny bed where the dolls lay. Under different circumstances, she would probably have found it very romantic.

"Polly," Mrs. Canavan said, taking down her ridiculous braids. "You know … my Hathor... Well, it wasn't meant to be, but this way Titus has given a new daughter to Arthur and I." She cleared her throat as though trying not to weep again. "Now when he comes in, it's expected you'll resist him; say 'no', once. When he calls you 'wife,' you can go along, it's the way it's done."

"I think I can manage that," Polly said, trying not to sound cheeky.

"I had better be getting along now," Mrs. Canavan touched her cheek. "Don't be afraid, love, Titus is a good man, you're a very lucky girl."

Without another word, Livia Canavan let herself out of the room, leaving Polly to feel ill in peace for a few minutes.

The next person who entered the room was the Bridegroom, tall, graceful, strange. She couldn't decide if he was rather ugly or quite handsome. Polly wondered what he thought of her.

"It's traditional that the bridegroom untie the bridal knot," Colonel Albinus said, Polly did know that, she'd just forgot for a moment.

She stepped toward him and looked down at the knot, this was going to take forever.

"Hold still," Albinus squinted at her in that way she was coming to dislike. Oh, that was it, he was too tall or she was too short or some combination of the two, he was hardly in a position to untie the knot at her waist the way he was supposed to. Albinus dropped to one knee and forced a smile. He had it untied in twenty-eight seconds.

"That was quick," Polly said and immediately felt stupid as he let the belt fall to the floor.

"I am not unfamiliar with the procedure," he smirked at her. "Raise your arms," he said as he stood and lifted her dress up over her head.

Polly had no idea why tiny bumps were raising themselves on her arms and shoulders and...oh yes, breasts. On sheer reflex she folded her arms in front of her and sat down on the center of the bed.

"Miss... Polly, you do understand what is to come is required," Albinus said and it wasn't a question, he had his eyes on her face and it made it very difficult for Polly to keep her eyes on the floor his deep voice as smooth as silk, "but there is no reason it should be unpleasant."

"No, I mean, yes, I mean, I don't know what I mean; this is all a bit sudden, you know? I don't know you," she said hating the whinging sound of her own voice.

"We will no doubt become more familiar with one another in time," he shrugged, then seemed to consider for a moment. "I could accomplish the con-summation while invisible should you like, if the sight of a naked male makes you uneasy."

"What a horrid suggestion!" Polly said. "That would be positively uncanny."

"I beg your pardon," Albinus said "My other wives liked it."

"Well, I find it distasteful," Polly told him. "I want to see you, while, while I'm doing it."

Colonel Albinus blinked. "I believe doing is my purview," he said bending to bring his face close to hers.

"Well, that's dull," Polly said, forgetting in her indignation to keep her arms over her breasts.

Colonel Titus Albinus's brows shot up toward his hairline.

He opened and closed his mouth without making a sound. "Very well, now you refuse." He reached out and touched her fingers with his hands that dwarfed hers.

"No," she said half-heartedly, pulling away from him.

"Wife," he said passionlessly, as though it was word entirely new to his tongue.

"Yes," she said, as though she agreed with him then paused pursing her lips. "But why?"

"Because this is the way it's done. This is the way it has always been done since time immemorial. The way it will continue to be done in the future. Now if I may resume the ceremony?" he said irritably.

"I'm simply saying the ritual isn't very logical," Polly

Albinus looked as though he would like to toss her out of the bedroom. "I dare say logic and ritual are mutually exclusive spheres," he said gesturing toward the bed. "Do you mind?"

He stepped away from the bed and began to slowly unbutton the row of brass buttons running down the left side of his uniform.

"Must you stare?" Albinus said pausing.

Polly looked down at her own naked body for a moment.

"Hmmpphh," was the only answer she gave him.

Now oblivious to her own undress, she crawled toward the edge of the bed on all fours.

It took him forever to get his clothes off.

Over his heart was a soldier's tattoo. A regimental insignia Polly had never seen before, the wadjet eye between the rampant Roman she-wolf, teats dripping and Apophis as a crocodile . Polly leaned closer to read the motto.

MALUM AD QUI MALUM COGITARE
EVIL TO HIM WHO EVIL THINKS

He was far bigger naked than he looked with his clothes on. She was dazzled a little by the sculpted look of his chest, the tight woven muscles of his abdomen.

She would never see him the same way again, partly because his body was like the statue of a god in a temple, and partly because he seemed to be unable to look her in the eye. Instead, he stared fixedly at a point on the wall. In that moment, she slowly began to like him a little. He was concerned about what she thought. It was strange. Polly felt aroused at the sight of him and a bit embarrassed by the fact. He still had an odd face. With his eyes cast down and apprehension clouding his features, he seemed rather dear all of a sudden.

It was only then that she thought to look between his legs.

Oh.

Her first thought was that both Charlie's and Mr. Magesteri's had been much more purple.

Colonel's Albinus's penis was the same bright red colour his face turned when Mrs. Canavan took her away to the bedroom. It appeared to be longer, if not thicker, than Professor Magesteri's but neither so long nor so thick as Charlie Edney's. Charlie Edney's penis. She hoped it never came up in conversation.

She also hoped he wouldn't hurt her. He didn't seem to be much concerned about her feelings, and she'd heard girls were sometimes hurt on their wedding night. She wondered idly if he'd hurt Hathor Canavan. Polly had rarely been hurt before but perhaps this would be different.

"Do you do it the same way you do the, umm, the invisible thing?"

"What are you talking about?" Colonel Albinus said, wrinkling his nose.

"Looking physically perfect, it's an illusion, like when you appear invisible? Am I wrong? How do you do it? Control what people perceive?" Polly said forgetting everything else.

Colonel Albinus straightened his back and took a step straight back "I rise every morning before dawn and spend four hours at the gymnasium," he said looking down his nose at her. "As for my Uncommon ability I, I, I simply do it. I find that quite sufficient."

Polly thought about it. Charlie and Mr. Magesteri were engineers. They had engineers bodies; soft guts and hard arms and shoulders. What muscles they had had come incidentally, from work, not from specific calculated effort, like making one's own body into a building project. Mr. Albinus's body was the sort only a man of leisure could afford to have.

"You don't know how you do it?" Polly asked, puzzled. "Aren't you the least bit curious?"

"Of all the impertinent…we are not all born scientists," he snorted.

"If I could keep people from seeing what's right in front of their noses I'd certainly like to know exactly how it worked. Perhaps there are some simple experiments…" Polly said thinking aloud.

"I am not a subject to be poked and prodded!" Albinus said his eyes wide.

"I wasn't planning to do anything invasive," Polly defended herself.

"Never the less, your husband is hardly an appropriate victim for your… research. Yes, um," Albinus said looking as though he'd like to adjust his uniform except for the unfortunate fact that he was naked. "Polycorpus Albinus, Duchess of Londinium Austri, now that you've seen to it that I am taken down a notch, perhaps we should proceed."

"Are you certain all the doing should fall to you? I'm a pretty fair doer myself when it comes down to it," Polly found when she didn't have Mrs. Brolly standing beside her she was apt to say whatever was on her mind. It was exhilarating.

"It seems a bit excessive for a wedding night, don't you think," he said, still facing the wall. "We can't go on like this indefinitely, distracting as this… banter is, we must complete the ritual."

"I realize that," she said inanely, expecting some snide retort to follow; none did.

Instead, he cleared his throat. "I shall give you two options. I can either make this as brief as possible or as pleasant as possible. I cannot manage both; the choice is yours."

"I would prefer pleasant, thank you, besides whatever happens tonight sets a precedent, don't you think?" she said, trying to force herself to be blithe.

"Indeed I do," said the figure, still standing at the foot of the bed.

Slowly, he advanced on her. Slowly, he looked her body up and down.

"Well?" she asked. She may not have been extremely experienced, there had only ever been Charlie and the one time with Professor Magesteri, but she knew enough to recognize desire when she saw it.

"You were put together poorly, like a machine made of spare parts, though, admittedly not quite so bad as the others of your species," he said, but there was no weight behind the words. His voice sounded far away as he slowly drew his right hand up the stitching that ran the length of her calf. "No doubt it will be akin to congress with a tinker's bicycle."

"Velocipede or penny-farthing?" she shot back.

He answered her with a snort then inhaled deeply "I expected you to have the odor of the charnel house about you," he said tilting his head. "And yet… you do not."

"What do I smell like?" Polly asked, sitting up. It was a question she had never asked herself, much less anyone else.

"A woman," Colonel Albinus said simply, and left it at that.

What followed was nothing like what she expected.

At first all he did was brush the very tips of his fingers against the most innocuous parts of her body, her face, her arms, the soft skin directly below her navel carefully tracing the stitching. He seemed to pay special attention to the seams that joined the freckled skin with the dun color. His forefinger traced the bolts at the base of her neck sending a shiver racing up and down her body.

She shuddered, anticipating each slow caress.

He continued as her body went from wire taut to languorous under his hands.

He held her eyes as his fingers trailed over her hips with feathery delicacy. The softest of touches glanced over the inside of her thighs without coming near her sex.

She all but convulsed and he groaned in response. She felt fierce satisfaction that she had moved him and she opened her legs in reply.

He deliberately chose to give her far less than she wanted, drawing one long finger over the cleft where her labia met, barely touching.

She arched her back against her will. Writhing. Willing him to touch her where it would do the most good.

Again, his fingers willfully avoided the plea of her body. The cruel man was teasing her. He stroked her softly without making direct contact with her clitoris, the fiend. Every terrible thing anyone ever said about him was true. He was a beastly, beastly man to taunt her so. She absolutely hated him. He was horrid.

Hesitantly, almost tenderly, he dipped one finger between her legs; there was an audibly wet sound as he removed it.

"I believe," his deep, smooth voice came out choked and ragged for once. "I believe you ought to be ready now."

"I want you," she stuttered. "I want you... to... do... it already."

"If you want me, ask me. You know my name, girl, say it. Say my name," he commanded.

She thought she could manage that, barely. "T,t,t, Titus come to me, please. Titus."

"Your wish is my command, Wife," he said. If there was any sarcasm in his tone, it was lost on her.

Then in an instant, he was on top of her. She'd made a mistake; he was not comparable to Charlie in any way, but a great looming force, a grown monster. There was far more to be afraid of in him than she thought. It was as if suddenly it was the first time she had been allowed in Mr. Magesteri's laboratory unaccompanied and there he stood looking for all the world like Caesar himself asking her tiredly to, "Cease your infernal chatter, Miss Plumber, you are giving me a splitting headache."

She felt arousal and terror in equal parts and she understood for the first time the intrinsic vulnerability of her situation. She might be clever. She might be brave, but she did not know everything and he seemed to be well aware of the fact. She smelled the faintest lingering trace of liquor on his breath.

"I am genuinely sorry, Miss Plumber," he whispered as he thrust into her. "Now say the words, woman, complete the ritual."

"Ubi... tu ... Gaius," she stuttered, amazed that she could even manage to breathe. She wasn't sure how but it felt much sharper somehow than being penetrated by Charlie Edney. As if she was losing her virginity all over again.

"You can do better than that," he chided her, grunting as he continued to thrust.

"Ubi tu," she started again.

"On top," he said roughly, managing to stay inside of her even as he switched their positions.

Now that might as well be conjury, she thought.

"Sit up," he instructed through clenched teeth.

Her head began to clear a little, enough, at least, that she could focus her mind and say the words, "Ubi tu Gaius, Ego Gaia."

She began to move instinctively. "Ubi tu Gaius, Ego Gaia," she repeated.

She didn't have to ask him if he felt it. He moaned, his lips reddened, face flushed, hips rose, and the flush spread across his chest. She felt a strange tug and the oddest flood of emotion that was not emotion, closer to a state of being, swept into her, over her, a state that was darker and more seductive than she would have been able to imagine, like a brain full of eels.

Was it the sex or some bit of wedding conjury no one had bothered to tell her about?

"Fine," he muttered, or something like it, his head tipped back and breathing shallow as he slipped his hand between them to stroke her clitoris. She wanted to ask him to repeat himself but it kept slipping her mind. In her defense it had been a very long day. The rubbing of his hand may have done something to curb her tongue as well.

Her body began to tense of its own accord and another feeling entirely washed over her, not unlike being run over by a coach and four. He was better, far better at this in fact, than Professor Magesteri, far better than Charlie Edney.

Without warning, he was above her again, pounding, his breathing harsh. She felt him spend himself in a gush of heat and fluid.

He collapsed beside her, panting like a winded greyhound.

She lay her head against his chest to feel his pounding heart, heedless of the wary look he gave her. She couldn't help it, she'd been laid low.

"I should like to ask about future," she couldn't think of an appropriate term "... unions."

"Nightly should suffice, Madam, until you manage to conceive," he said rubbing his face with both hands. "Or in the mornings should you prefer."

Polly wondered if when she died he would have same conversation with her replacement. She thought it but she didn't say it. Perhaps Mrs. Brolly had rubbed off a bit. "I'm not at my best mornings."

"Evenings it is, then," he said, attempting to ease out from under her.

"Where are you going? I was just getting comfy," Polly said, not meaning to whinge as much as she did.

Mr. Albinus's eyes crinkled as he spoke, as if he was a bit amused. "Pleasant though it may be to lounge about one's marriage bed, tradition demands we make an appearance to our guests."

"Oh," she said dumbly. "I forgot about them."

And then Colonel Titus Albinus, Duke of Londinium Austri, who had buried four wives before marrying his fifth, fell back on his bank of pillows and he laughed.

In the cold castle an already slightly intoxicated Professor Stephen Magesteri watched Charlie Edney and Guy Ouellette attempt to calm a rather outraged Will Canavan.

"Look, Will, I know it seems terrible but I don't think she'll end up the same as…you know…your sister," Guy said, winced, as if not quite believing it himself.

Will Canavan and Charlie Edney sat morosely, flanking Guy Ouellette, openly watching the two dolls on the tiny bed across the crowded room.

The ginger-headed doll vibrated visibly on the saffron sheets as the smaller doll slid down its length. Charlie licked his lips anxiously. Will clenched his teeth and suppressed the groan that rose in his throat no doubt in a combination of despair and imagining his sister Hathor in Polly's place.

The rhythm of the figures was undeniable. Will's knee bounced uncontrollably even as Guy kept careful hold of the back of his neck. He glanced over at Charlie, who looked like he was about to weep again.

Stephen officially hated all his employees.

He watched as the doll with hair carved of… what was it, cedar? It had to be cedar, seemed to overtake Polly's doll and started labouring hard against it. He could have sworn he saw sparks. That bastard.

"Let it go chaps," Guy said quietly. "It can't be undone now. There's always the next life."

When he could take no more Stephen stepped in front of them, obscuring the gutless cowards' view of the small bed.

"Canavan, Edney, you two young cretins look to be in need of more cake," Stephen said. "Trust me when I say our Miss Plumber has made the wisest choice under the circumstances."

"But, Sir," Charlie began.

"I'd like to know why nobody believes Polly can fend for herself," Will said sullenly. "She could hold off the Czar's forces with a cocktail fork."

Stephen peered over his tinted glasses at the slightly greenish young man. "Polly is a girl, like every other girl in the world, she must marry eventually, Canavan. Mr. Albinus is a powerful man, he has it in him to give her anything she desires. I hazard to guess more than you or I are aware of, and while Polly is extraordinary, her future at The Museum is rather limited. Is it worth so much to have her for your own?"

"For myself? I don't even like girls," Will blinked. "You ever think I just want her to be free? For her not to wind up like…like… Hathor? "

"If I were you idiots, I'd have more cake, as your master will likely be hung over and handing out extra assignments when you return to work," Stephen ordered frowning at his own largesse in warning them. "You too, Ouellette. Eat up. Some things can't be helped," he added.

Leaning into Albinus's side, in a gown of brilliant green that didn't quite suit her, Polly was presented to the packed room.

"May I introduce the Duchess of Londinium Austri, Polycorpus Singularia Albinus," the Colonel said loudly, his face void of expression for the split second before he remembered to put up a dazzling smile.

There were in all likelihood a thousand things she didn't know about Mr. Albinus. Her husband, a thousand things she didn't know about her husband. She wondered if she'd live long enough to uncover half of them. There was something utterly unreadable about his eyes as he scanned the crowd.

Whatever it meant it gave no warning of Colonel Albinus's next move to take Polly in his arms, bend her backwards, and kiss her full on the mouth.

The cheered response was surreal.

She wasn't sure why Mr. Virgil the cleaning man was among those to come before her and kiss her hand followed by a throng of well connected monsters.

Across the packed room she could see Professor Magesteri leaning against the far wall, his eyes on her, or perhaps it was Mr. Albinus he was looking at.

Her stomach went inexplicably queasy.

She had known Professor Magesteri as far back as she could recall and had never taken a proper look at him before that minute, it seemed. Had she been asked the day before to describe Professor Magesteri she would have noted the air of ill-grace that seemed to surround him like a cloud, if pressed further she could have said he had ill-kempt generally unwashed black hair and perpetual sneer that revealed teeth so decisively viciously crooked they were his most distinguishing feature and after that the well would have been empty. Now it occurred to her that she could stare at him all day long and never cease to be surprised with his fascinatingly ugly face. He had a wide mouth like his cousin Mr. Albinus. And eyes the same swamp colored blue-green-grey only several shades darker. Nostrils that seemed to like to flare. He was shortish, with a broad, almost barrel-shaped chest and arms a bit long for his body. His colouring in general was nobler, on the fairer side of Egyptian but nowhere near the milk-and-water bumpkin shade of his cousin, Titus.

Mr. Albinus put his arm round Polly's waist and looked dead at Mr. Magesteri.

Professor Magesteri in turn tipped his glass in their direction, but he didn't come close.

Chapter 5: Coming to Terms

The first full day of their marriage was somewhat hellish.

Titus would have preferred to have a routine to adhere to. Unfortunately, he was in the most boring place in the British Isles; his own country house. He would have left his chambers and gone for a walk round the grounds but the probability of running into some sort of house guest was high and it wouldn't do to be seen without his new wife so soon after the wedding. Of course taking a walk didn't require he allow himself to be seen, but that would still mean leaving the newly minted Mrs. Albinus on her own and he hadn't quite acquired the knack of predicting her behavior yet. In short, he didn't quite trust her.

Uncertain of how to entertain himself without leaving his rooms Titus read the first novel he came to in his new wife's luggage, sandwiched between a handheld telescope and a tatty corset. His new wife, however, slept. Apparently, she was not an early riser.

He glanced over her periodically with microscopic carelessness as he found himself caught up in a gun battle between the hero and an airship full of barbarians. Whatever else could be said of her literary preferences they were not dull. He supposed he could count himself fortunate he had not been compelled to read a romance with heaving bosoms and swooning heroines.

Titus's eyes wandered back to the bed and quite against his will he tried to discern the female shape under the wildly rumpled sheets. She was sleeping a very long time.

And when she finally did wake she laid abed for some time feigning sleep.

"Stop pretending," he said tired of waiting for her to arise, "your sham has convinced no one."

"What sham?" she asked groggily opening one eye.

"Your false representation of unconsciousness," he said pleasantly. "You won't get out of playing the hostess that easily. Tea is in two hours and I am not greeting my guests without the mistress of the house."

"It's only nine?" she seemed incredulous and then, inexplicably covered her face with the pillow.

Titus went back to his novel only to be interrupted by an indignant cry. "You've taken my book."

"Such as it is," he answered her.

Mostly, he spent those morning hours reading, pausing occasionally to ask an uncomfortable question or two, and surreptitiously observing Polycorpus Singularia Plumber; newly Canavan, and even more newly Albinus as she lounged.

Titus Albinus had always been given to understand the female toilet to be a lengthy and involved affair, requiring armies of servants and the blessings of various gods to be successful, which was why he was taken aback that Polycorpus would even think to attempt such an undertaking on her own.

That she emerged from his dressing room in nothing but a thin chemise and a half undone corset did not surprise him.

"Would you mind helping...?"she said.

"I am hardly a lady's maid," he said, raising the book to form a barrier between him and the sight of her in her under things. It seemed to him much more shameful than seeing her

naked.

"Surely you're capable of pulling a lace," she said.

"Again I would point out that it is neither my occupation, nor is it a pastime of mine, to dress ladies," he shifted in his chair and trained all his focus on the words before him.

"Colonel Albinus…perhaps Mrs. Canavan is capable but my arms are neither long enough nor correctly angled to allow me to corset myself. Please… ," she said.

"I will fetch you Mrs. Hepworth from the kitchen," he tried to offer as gallantly as he was able but the impossible girl ignored him, fairly shoving her backside into his face.

"Isn't the kitchen is on the other side of the castle? It will only take a moment," she said brusquely. "Besides who's Mrs. Hepworth? The serving woman, she's a hundred if she's a day."

"Has anyone ever told you that you were utterly insufferable?" he said, giving up and taking the laces in hand.

"Mrs. Brolly tells me that at least thrice a fortnight," she squeaked out, grasping the bed post as he pulled the laces for all he was worth.

"Even a broken clock manages to be right twice a day, dearest," he said, in spite of his generally even temper.

"Tighter," she hissed and he complied grunting and feeling somewhat embarrassed as he did so, straining for purchase he braced his body against hers and pulled. He could feel the heat of her, the firm muscle and feminine silken layer of her. Just beyond her flimsy shift was the vast expanse of her skin. He was at a loss as to how to respond.

He hadn't thought her especially appealing before their mutual wedding night; useful, clearly, but hardly desirable in and of herself. Now, having spent more time in the female's presence she seemed less bearable and more interesting simultaneously. He was at a loss to explain it.

"Now tie them," the girl ordered and he surprised himself by obeying.

To his surprise Madam Albinus managed to turn herself out passably well in time to reach the eleven o'clock table. Her sky blue dress was far more complimentary than the green the night prior. She was no gracious household goddess like Hathor had been, no charming domestic nymph like Chandi, or Lobelia or even Drusilla, for that matter, though she managed to play the hostess without incident.

He did his best to disregard the proceedings at the unimportant end of the table until young Edney opened his mouth.

"We; Will Canavan, Septimus Prosser, Guy Ouellette… and some others ….we thought we would escort the young ladies into the village to visit the sweet shop. Mrs. Brolly has graciously agreed to chaperon, of course," the young cod said.

Out of the corner of his eye Albinus noted that Edney kept glancing first at Henry Plumber then at Madam Albinus then in his own direction.

Plumber had the decency to cover any smirk with his napkin try to mask his amusement with a cough but young Polly spoke first.

"That sounds lovely," Polly said gaily.

"Then you will join us?" Edney asked.

That was an interesting question; would she join the throng of young people, Titus wondered, and embarrass him?

"No, Mr. Edney, I'm far too occupied," she laughed. The girl laughed far too loudly for Titus's comfort. Still he felt relieved that propriety had been maintained. At least the girl had some feeling but she could stop being so immoderate.

"Precisely," said Plumber with a chicken sandwich still mostly in his mouth. "She should accompany me to collect her things from Londinium."

Titus looked down the table at the generous repast. He wondered whether he or Plumber had paid for it.

"Surely I can get my things when Mr. Albinus and I return to Londinium next week," the girl said, she had the most peculiar way of gripping her tea cup.

If what she'd packed for the wedding was any indication her wardrobe was hardly worth collecting.

Toward midnight, Stephen Magesteri lit a fire in the hearth, because it was his habit to turn on the heat to his rooms in The Museum evenings and he wasn't going to freeze to death simply because he was at his cousin's country estates. He imagined with the spring storms there was no way to heat the old heap effectively without extensive renovations. Titus no doubt felt he didn't spend enough time at the place to warrant the expense. Stingy Bastard.

He put another log on the fire and singed his sleeve. For a moment it was literally a smoking jacket.

"Fuck me," he muttered patting out the smoldering silk.

"Frankly, even if I were so inclined I'm entirely too spent to entertain the offer," Titus said from the doorway. "Not that you're not appealing…in your own way…to someone…somewhere…without a dress sense. Good start on the lounge wear, by the way. It's hopelessly out of fashion."

"I got the bloody thing from you last year," Stephen said examining his sleeve.

Titus squinted coming close. "That is a bald faced lie, Stephen, that jacket was perfectly stylish when I gave it you to three years ago. I'm hardly to blame if you keep your clothes past their spoilage date."

That was too bleeding absurd of a statement for Stephen to make the effort necessary to respond. Instead he inhaled, only to have his nostrils assaulted by the smell of the marriage bed; Titus fairly reeked of Polly Plumber. He'd done it on purpose, clearly. Titus Albinus never took so much as an uncalculated shit.

Stephen asked himself, not for the first time, why he'd encouraged Polly to marry him, although the answer was obvious; while Titus might be overly subtle he was also wealthy and well positioned and as husbandly a specimen as Stephen had ever known.

There was a twinge of something in Stephen's gut, either he had broken his own heart or it was the result of over indulgence at Titus's table. Regardless Titus Albinus was to blame.

Stephen inhaled again, relishing the smell of congress even as it sickened him.

Titus lifted his chin and peered at him through slitted eyes before drawing back two steps.

"How do you find your new wife?" Stephen asked crossing his legs and poking Titus a bit with the toe of his boot.

A shadow crossed passed Titus's face so quickly Stephen reckoned anyone else would have missed it.

"A bit indelicate round the edges but enthusiastic, all in all a girl like any other I suppose," Titus said, his back ramrod straight, chin high. "Aunt Augusta assures me she's a bright little thing and will no doubt take to her duties like a duck to water as soon she understands what's expected of her."

The statement was so absurd Stephen didn't bother to stifle his laughter.

"I fail to see what you find so amusing," Titus said hands in his dressing gown pockets.

"I'm trying to imagine Polly," Stephen managed to choke out amidst the laughter, "Our Polly, terror of the British Museum, playing the dutiful little wife. Has she told you to piss off yet? If anyone can bring Tight-Arse Albinus down a notch or two it's our Polly."

"I do wish you wouldn't call her that, it makes it sound as though I'd a married a laundress," Titus said.

"What would you have me call her?" Stephen asked wiping his eyes.

"I am rather partial to Singularia," Titus said, toying with the hem of his ornate golden silk dressing gown. Stephen had no doubt it was the height of sodding fashion.

"You can be partial to whatever you like, Titus, she won't answer to anything but Polly," Stephen said.

Titus stood for a moment, rubbing his forefinger across his lip.

"She is proving slightly less tractable than I imagined a confirmed spinster would be," Titus admitted.

"Intoxicating, isn't it?" Stephen said, honestly.

"Hardly," Titus answer with a scowl.

Titus was a shit.

It was on her third night as a wife that Polly saw her husband's naked back.

After they had dinner, and Polly found some interesting talk at the table with Mr. Magesteri and Agamemnon Boyle about the difficulties of maintaining magnet trains across the Empire as opposed to the Museum workshop drawing board. Mr. Boyle called them "real world" problems. Mr. Magesteri, though she was supposed to call him "Stephen" now she was married to his cousin and kept having to remind herself, snorted and said the only difference between the Museum and the "real world" was that there were fewer idiots at the Museum. And at the Museum they were able to identify them early and put them where they could cause the least amount of trouble, theoretically, at least.

It was great fun. Really. The logistics of maintaining sufficient tanks full of electric eels to power the rails was intriguing. They talked animatedly until Polly had to go into exile in the drawing room with all the other ladies. She supposed it was the done thing that Mrs. Albinus sat on the settee with Mrs. Brolly across from Polly's chair, a piece of furniture that looked lovely and felt awful, while the two regaled her with tales of Mr. Albinus's accomplishments. Of course they called him "Titus" and Polly managed to follow suit, as if he were someone she knew.

She smiled and nodded and pretended to care but for the most part she was looking round the room despairing of finding a single conversation worth joining or even eavesdropping, in the entire parlor.

Still she managed to keep her eyes open and the smile plastered on her face until the gentlemen returned, smelling of whisky and cigars.

Her papa came and kissed her forehead, looking strangely sad. Well, he deserved it. If he felt sad he had no one to blame but himself so letting this ridiculous marriage business take place.

Then Mr. Magesteri and Mr. Boyle came and kissed her hand. Mr. Magesteri looked like he'd been up to no good. Good for him.

Lastly Mr. Albinus swept in with all his long legged, long armed, grace. Just because she didn't have it, didn't mean she couldn't recognize it.

"My darling, is it possible you have grown even more fascinating in my brief absence?" he said leaning down to kiss her cheek.

"You do know how to set the bar low, don't you?" Polly murmured in his ear.

When he pulled away, drawing himself back to his full height, Mr. Albinus looked as though he didn't know whether to be annoyed or amused. Polly had got a great deal of that from him over the past three days.

At least, that night when they went to their bed chamber he didn't balk at untying her corset. He was getting better.

"I'll have my valet engage a lady's maid once we're back in civilization. I must admit it never occurred to me you wouldn't bring a girl with you for this sort of thing," Polly's husband said as he pushed his hips against hers, likely for purchase. "Who did this for you when you were at Plumber's house?"

Polly wondered at the idea that there were anything uncivilized about three dozen house guests and more courses per meal than even she could finish.

"Mable, the girl who brings the morning tea, usually does it…did it," Polly said grateful to be able to breathe deeply. Mable had also made certain Polly had two months supply of wild asafetida extract before Polly left home and Polly had seen to it Mable had a new position at the Museum so Polly could get more whenever she needed it. Thank all the gods and goddesses for Mable.

"I don't see why your former father never engaged a lady's maid on your behalf," Mr. Albinus said, behind her.

"Perhaps because I wasn't a lady," Polly said turning round to see Mr. Albinus slip his shirt off his shoulders.

She had never seen him shirtless from behind before.

The perfectly articulated muscles of his back, like an artist's rendering of what a male back was supposed to be, with complementary freckles thrown in at no extra charge, were marred by what Polly could only reckon were the marks of a lash. Polly was horrified on a purely aesthetic level, it was like carving your name in the middle of the dining room table. It was a crime to ruin nice things. Or it ought to be.

"What happen to your back?" Polly asked.

"Precisely how is that any of your look out, my dear?" Albinus said still facing away from her.

She paused only an instant before answering him. "I should think I have some right to concern over the condition of your person. I at least ought to rank the privilege of knowing what sort of vandal marked it…and why?"

"It's hardly a topic fit for the weaker sex," he said.

"I'm warning you, I can be relentless. I will be relentless," Polly said, "if you don't tell me."

"Military discipline," Mr. Albinus said, his shoulders tensing visibly.

"That must have been before you were a duke," Polly said, automatically.

"I've always been duke," he said turning to face her. "I didn't become fully titled until I'd been confirmed Uncommon and officially named at two months of age, but I was Londinium Austri three months before my own birth."

"How? The sounds physically impossible." Polly tried to imagine a fetus doing ducal things. It made her bolts itch.

"That's when my father died," Albinus said, his face oddly relaxed, not leering, or sneering, or looking down his nose at her.

"Oh," Polly said. She didn't know if it was the fact that she had asked Albinus a question and he'd managed to answer her without being stroppy, or if it was the fact that he was shirtless, but she felt rather pleasantly inclined toward her husband at that moment. She tended to like him better the less dressed he was.

No matter what her new calling card said, Polly would never be a lady in her heart.

Having seen him so unarmed Polly wanted Titus Albinus, and for the first time she touched him on her own initiative, reaching up and cupping his chiseled cheek in her hand.

Her husband's eyes went wide and his lips parted.

Polly was undecided about the whole business of having a husband, any husband at all not just Albinus specifically. She had been perfectly content as a spinster. It was easy and she could see no good reason to change, but everyone had been so adamant that she take Albinus up on his offer she imagined there was some good solid reason that was eluding her. Now she wasn't so certain, but here she was married to him all the same.

Polly took a step forward and Albinus took a step back. So Polly stepped forward again and The Duke of Londinium Austri fell backwards onto the bed.

"Couldn't have worked that better if I'd planned it," she said dropping her shift to the floor.

He was nice looking, she'd grant him that, very appealing when he wasn't disapproving of the way she…oh breathed.

The Duke was blinking rapidly as if he wasn't quite certain what she was doing or what it meant. He seemed for an instant as if he was beginning to shimmer.

"Don't be afraid, I'm not going to hurt you," Polly said using her most careful voice and laying her hands on his half undone trouser buttons.

"Don't be ridiculous," he said licking his lower lip, it made Polly want to lick his lip herself. "Why… Would… I… Be… Afraid… Of… You? As if a soldier of the Empire…could be…afraid…of a girl."

The Duke was breathing rapidly and Polly watched, enchanted, as he swallowed hard and his throat bobbed.

To hear people talk, she was the one who had reason to be frightened. Still Mr. Magesteri had assured her, and the oracle had assured her, whatever it was in Titus Albinus that had killed his other four wives, was no threat to her. She had no idea why she believed them. Neither had shown her any empirical evidence. On the other hand, she didn't have any proof the other wives hadn't met with anything beyond ordinary death in childbirth. On average one in four Uncommon females met her end trying to bring life into the world. Perhaps Mr. Albinus was simply awfully unlucky. A cursory study of probability showed that these things did happen. Even for commoners the odds were not good.

Polly hoped that was it. The alternative being some sort of pathological condition, which didn't precisely hearten her, since sexual congress was the one thing about being married, and being married to Titus Albinus in particular, that Polly didn't have any misgivings about. In either event, she had her asafetida.

"Really, I'm harmless, I've never killed a living thing on accident," Polly said, nodding reassuringly as she climbed astride his still partially clothed body.

"That's good…good to know," the Duke said, clearing his throat as if it meant something.

"I think we should stop talking now; it's distracting," Polly told him, because really, it was for the best.

The Duke nodded pressing his lips together.

Polly could feel him, very stiff on the other side of his perfectly tailored trousers. She leaned forward and ran her fingers through his short ginger hair, wishing it was longer.

Her breasts pressed against his scratchy chest hair, also gingery.

She had held in. She had been as good as she could be for as long as she could be, and now she was going to enjoy herself.

Polly slid forward to kiss him and was delighted to realize the difference in their heights was mostly attributable to leg. She was perfectly capable of rubbing against the front of his trousers while she kissed him. The scrape of late evening stubble on his cheeks was especially delightful.

Her arms steadied her on the bed so she could press press press against him. Oh, he was lifting his hips and hitting the perfect spot without any coaxing and with his trousers still on, Charlie never could have managed that.

His lips were soft and his tongue was beautifully pliant when he opened his mouth to her. She might not particularly like him when he was standing up and dressed and everything but Polly reckoned the Duke was more or less acceptable when he was like this.

She broke the kiss to catch her breath.

"Please," he whispered raggedly. "Please, let me."

His hands grasped, flailing a bit, trying to, she wasn't sure what…switch their places or take his trousers off or something.

"I told you, I'm doing the doing tonight, no more talking," she said crawling down the length of his body to reach down and fumble with his buttons. She wound up simply ripping the stupid things off, they were so fiddley.

His member sprang forth from his newly torn trousers like the cuckoo from a clock. It should have made a noise. He seemed a bit taken aback when she laughed.

Then she recalled how well he liked his clothes, and she had spoken sternly to him in addition to having uncharitable thoughts about him, poor man buttoned up since before he was born having to be The Duke, so she felt a bit bad. She ran her tongue down his length as a sort of apology, and also frankly, to aid penetration. The wetter the better.

In response, he made the most surprising sound in the back of his throat, like a strangled sob. He trembled a bit when she lowered herself onto him.

She was so excited to not be pretending to be "ladylike" any longer, it took less than a minute for Polly to reach her first climax. It was glorious, made even better by the fact that she knew there were plenty more where that came from.

When Polly finally fell back on the feather bed exhausted Titus Albinus gawked at her as though he was seeing her for the first time.

She in turn took a good hard look at her husband, Colonel Titus Posthumous Albinus, Duke of Londinium Austri, Order of Apophis First Class. She had no idea what to make of him. He seemed to be a study in opposites. He was a decorated soldier and a dandy. He could turn invisible but loved to be looked at. He was easily as proper as Mrs. Brolly but put absolutely none of the fear in her his Aunt Augusta did.

He was still staring at her with hooded eyes.

"Are you yourself?" Polly asked. "I know I can be a brute at times. I haven't injured you, have I?"

"Don't be insulting," Albinus said, not seeming the least bit uncomfortable about his trousers bunched up at his ankles and the fact that he was still wearing his shoes. Still, he seemed to be studying her. Polly didn't much like it. She studied things, not the other way round. "Did Plumber do it intentionally?"

"Do what?" she asked, folding her hands behind her head.

"Did Plumber intentionally build you to be so…" Albinus licked his lips nervously, "so brazen?"

What a funny question but it was the first bit of scientific curiosity she'd heard from him, so she supposed it was a start.

"A bit of copper, but iron for the most part, no brass at all that I can think of," she told him.

Albinus seemed surprised by that, though she had no idea why. He blinked like he was a surprised, at any rate.

She wished she had some one to discuss it all with. Someone besides the marble bust of Ctesebius in the corner.

Chapter 6 : Settling In

itus Posthumous Albinus spent the entire ride back to Londinium without speaking a word, though his wife didn't seem to notice. She was busy reading another novel. By the cover it was more or less the same as the others in her luggage. A great deal of intrigue, a great deal of shooting, stabbing, and getting one's clothes muddied. If espionage were anything like that in real life, Titus Albinus couldn't have been forced at cannon point into taking it up as a line of work. Luckily, it wasn't anything like that. Not for him at least.

Really, spying usually only got dramatic if one was inept enough to get caught. Titus Albinus was not inept.

He looked across the train car at the newly minted Duchess, unsure whether it was a matter of him not speaking to his wife, or his wife not speaking to him.

He decided to test it out.

If only he knew how to address her. Polly sounded so common, and while he quite liked Singularia he'd never heard anyone actually call her that.

"Singularia?" he tried experimentally but that got no reply, she didn't so much as start at the sound of the name.

He could not, would not, call her Polly. He refused.

"Darling?" he said pleasantly.

"Hmm? Yes?" she said eyeing him over the top of her book.

So they were speaking, that was good.

"I believe I see my man awaiting us on the platform," he told her. "Please allow him to help you to the carriage."

"If I must," she said, still reading.

"Propriety would insist," he said forcing himself to continue smiling.

"Gods forefend we strain propriety," Polycorpus Singularia Albinus said, turning the page.

"Any more and I fear it may snap," Titus said.

"Not unlike Londinium Austri himself," his wife answered him.

Titus would have had a witty rejoinder but any answer would have been drowned out by the sound of the train pulling into the station.

For what it was worth, Mrs. Albinus was as good as her word, although his driver, Moots, stumbled under her unexpected weight.

Unfortunately, she was as distracted in the coach as she was in train compartment. Titus was uncomfortable being ignored, particularly by women, most of all, his wife.

Titus found himself tensing as Moots drove the horses ever closer to home. He found he wanted very badly, to impress Polycorpus. His other wives had been impressed without any real effort on his part, but Polycorpus seemed to be stifling a yawn half the time.

What was wrong with her? She ought to have been grateful, the most grateful of them all in fact, seeing how he'd rescued her from a life wasted in spinsterhood. But she wasn't.

Again, what was wrong with her that she was blind to his charms?

Females in general adored him. Old women loved his lively conversation and his impeccable manners. Little girls loved his whimsy and ability to amuse. And women in their prime? Well, that was obvious, wasn't it?

It seemed he had married the only female in the Empire who was immune. Oh, that would never do.

That wouldn't do at all. He would simply have to woo her, then. Seduce her with his intelligence and presence, his charm and good looks. She would fall in love with him. She would be impressed. Whether she wanted to be or not.

It settled his nerves a bit to feel the coach round the corner and see the familiar sights.

His was one of the seven finest houses in the city. She couldn't help but like that.

He smiled to himself in anticipation of his wife's wide-eyed admiration. He would wait until the coach had come to a full stop before dazzling her with a glimpse of what she had gained in him.

"Home at last, my darling," he said once the horses stopped.

Polycorpus set down her book, and, holding her place with one finger, looked out the window.

"That your house?" she asked, her expression blank.

"And yours as well, dearest, now that you're my wife," he informed her, all largesse, all generosity.

And then her nose wrinkled. "And I thought my Papa's house was too big for two people."

"Oh, my love, you shall simply have to endeavor to fill it with children, then," Titus said warmly, pleased at his own gentle, loving answer.

Polycorpus only curled her lip at him. He didn't find it an appealing expression.

It was at that precise moment that it occurred to Polly Albinus nee Plumber (technically Canavan but that was more or less immaterial as far as she was concerned) that not only had she married a Duke, she was now a Duchess. She would live in a duchess's house and no doubt be expected to do the things a duchess did, whatever that meant. She suddenly wanted to lock the carriage door and demand to be taken back to the train station.

Not certain what else she could do she allowed Albinus's driver, Moots, to help her to the ground, careful not to let him get hurt while he did it.

"Allow me," Albinus said as she headed for the front door and he scooped her up. He'd clearly been planning ahead because he didn't stumble a bit this time.

Moots darted ahead to open the door.

Polly could feel the tension in his arms and ramrod stiff back as Albinus strained to carry her through the foyer, but he kept smiling and he appeared outwardly unfazed even as he set her down gently in what appeared to be the drawing room in front of a line of …servants.

Oh Mighty Isis, a line of servants; and a ridiculous house, and he expected her to look at them, and say something.

It was bewildering. He took her to room after room.

He took her up stairs.

He took her down stairs.

He took her down corridor after corridor. Yes, it was pretty but exactly how much pretty was she supposed to feign interest in? It seemed Albinus could stare at pretty things indefinitely but it bored Polly to tears. She was barely pay attention at all by the time he dragged her back to the ground floor and stood grinning coquettishly at her before the door to the peristylium.

"Behold the piece de resistance," Albinus gestured grandly, opening the door wide for her.

Well, that was interesting.

What had once upon a time been the expected peristylium, the sort of inside-out room all but the meanest houses had, enclosed by the walls of the house on four sides and open to the sky above, had clearly been improved extensively. The ceiling had been glassed in for starters. There were electric pumps, which Polly could hear but not see, powered by eel tanks, as well as tanks of some sort of small shellfish. The pumps, on close inspection, were powering three separate and distinct artificial streams. There were trees and ferns and …what was it all for?

"What's all this then?" she asked.

Something genuinely merry glittered like a bit of polished metal in Albinus's eye.

"I'll show you," he said the corners of his mouth curling and he made a funny little trilling noise with his tongue. "Oh bendeeeeeeees," he called.

And there from holes and streams and seemingly burrowing from out of the mud dark wet muddy shapes bigger than Polly's arm. As the shapes slithered closer Polly could see they were great mottled brown salamanders with rather dorso-ventrally flattened bodies, strange thick folds running down their sides, tiny arms and legs and broad flat heads.

Polly watched as Albinus crouched down and scratched the largest on the top of its noggin with his gloved hand. The others crowded round Albinus's feet, she would say fawningly but who could tell what fawning looked like from a salamander.

"Are those Hellbenders?" she asked. Polly had seen pictures in books, but she'd never seen the animal live, and considering the amount of time she'd spent at the Museum Menagerie that was notable.

"The only breeding colony outside their native continent," Albinus said proudly. "I've had old Cronos here thirty years. He was a gift from my uncle when I was a boy."

"Mr. Magesteri's father gave him to you?" Polly asked. She'd never heard anyone mention either of Mr. Magesteri's parents but they were somehow related to Mr. Albinus through his mother. She knew that much.

"Hardly," Mr. Albinus said as if he smelled boiled cabbage. "He and Rhea were seventh birthday presents from Prince Brolly, Aunt Augusta's late husband. Who's a good pressie?" he asked the giant salamander. "You are!" he answered, still stroking its apparently adoring head.

"You knew Prince Brolly?" Polly asked, amazed, of all the people in the world she had a burning curiosity about Mrs. Brolly's late husband was very high on the list.

"Quite well, actually, my own father was dead, and he had no child of his own, we were quite close. I was even assigned to the same regiment in Afghanistan. Of all the dead in Jalalabad massacre only Prince Brolly was completely excoriated," Mr. Albinus stood abruptly. "Though that's a story for another day."

Then Albinus whistled again and the hellbenders wiggled away back to where they'd come from.

"You've got a great deal of environmental equipment; may I take a look at the controls?" Polly asked, itching inside to get at them.

"If you wish," Albinus said, as though he wasn't quite sure why she cared.

Frustrated though he was at his new wife's lack of response to anything in her new home, save the pump room, Titus Albinus was relieved to be back in Londinium and back to his daily routine. The sooner his darling wife was worked into that schedule and stopped being a general nuisance and his days resumed their accustomed sameness, the better.

Titus lay in his bed feeling rather uncomfortable. His mind and body had snapped awake the way they always did at this time, and he was ready, more than ready, to face the day's requirements, but he had the strangest feeling that Polycorpus was dragging him into a sort of quagmire, with which he was utterly unfamiliar. He didn't like it. He was inclined to say he didn't like his wife, but that would have been unseemly and not entirely accurate.

What he disliked were the feelings of confusion she inspired in him. She was rather stimulating - too stimulating in fact - there was nothing demure and wifely about the woman. He had the oddest suspicion the two of them would be great chums if she were male. If she were male? What a bizarre notion.

He would have to see to it Polycorpus was settled into her new role before he went mad with distraction.

Titus reminded himself it was the gallant thing to rise without waking his young wife. Part of him smirked, internally of course, at the terminology. In truth, at 22, Polycorpus Singularia was his most elderly wife to date.

He slipped from the bed carefully and drew on his dressing gown in the dark. The trouble was that she needed to be won over. If she loved him she would submit to him, she would automatically become docile. It was the way with women.

He would begin with a love note.

Polly woke up with a piece of paper stuck to her face. Why there was a piece of paper in the bed she did not know, but it tasted of perfume. She nearly retched.

She blinked twice and struggled to read the large looping florid script replete with curlicues. It was smeared in spots. From her drool she imagined.

My Most Dear and Precious Singularia,

I use the name Singularia because you are such a rare and decidedly Uncommon creation, my heart quickens at the thought of you. Last night the joy I found in your arms was exquisite. I know it is an immoderate thing to say to a lady, but, to quote Cicero, "A letter does not blush" and I mean you to know the depth of my appreciation.

Unfortunately we must part as daily matters at the gymnasium and public baths demand my attention but I swear to return faithfully to your side in time for elevenses, today and always.

It is my honor to adore you,
Colonel Titus Posthumous Albinus, Duke Londinium Austri
Order of Apophis, 1st class

And a full queue of x's and o's at the bottom.

"Well that was unnecessarily florid," Polly murmured to no one in particular. "Could have just said said, 'Gone to the gymn, see you at tea, last night was fun.'"

Polly wasn't sure how she felt about Albinus's foolish letter. Was he trying to impress her? Make her believe he loved her when they both knew he didn't? What did he take her for?

Polly certainly didn't love Mr. Albinus.

She didn't even know if she liked him. Still she was willing to make the best of the whole marriage business. Not that she had any intention of doing anything mad, like giving up her asafetida extract any time in the near future, but she could be pleasant and live up to her responsibilities. She simply didn't feel compelled to risk her life for the sake of his family name. That was hardly a reasonable expectation on his part in any event. Not that he would likely agree with her, but Polly didn't feel it was necessary to mention that she was taking measures to impede conception. It would do nothing but cause problems to let him know. He wasn't risking bleeding to death or breaking his pelvis or what have you, so he didn't deserve a say, as far as she was concerned.

In return she would try to be a good sport about becoming a duchess.

"What was that, Ma'am?" squeaked a voice on the other side of the room. There was a maid on her knees starting a fire in the fireplace.

"Is there something wrong with the hypocaust?" Polly asked. "Why is this floor so cold?"

Titus came home, perfectly on time, as ever, his cousin Stephen in tow, secure in the knowledge that whilst he had been hard at work in Her Majesty's service, his love note had been at work as well, softening Mrs. Albinus up, making her more pliable.

Cook had been at work, as well. Titus looked forward to his favorites. He looked forward to a pleasant tea with his wife and his closest, it might be argued only close, friend and relative. The other relationships he had were too tainted with questions of power and persuasion and perhaps the faintest whiff of blackmail, to compare. He had nothing to gain from Stephen; Stephen had nothing to gain from him.

Except perhaps for some fashion advice.

Not that he ever took it.

Not that anything he bought would hang properly in his current condition.

"Stephen," Titus said walking through the foyer. "Why don't you ever accept my offer to join me at the gymnasium? It would do no end of good to the fit of your suit."

"Need I remind you, Titus, that there are those unfortunate souls with occupations beside the figure they cut in the dressing mirror? Besides, I fear, were I to wander down to your gymnasium I might be in mortal peril of breaking into a sweat," Stephen said, hands in his pockets. "Never mind that I'm responsible for an entire department full of idiots, armed with everything from forges to bandsaws to blow torches to etcetera etcetera, idiots, I would remind you, who lie in wait for the opportunity to kill and maim themselves and one another the minute I so much as blink. Bloody morons."

"A threadbare excuse if ever I heard one," Titus said throwing open the door to the parlor. It was empty. "Where's the Duchess?" he asked the maid with a tray full of dainties in her arms.

"Her ladyship is occupied," she said her eyes downcast.

Stephen quirked his eyebrows.

"The dear little thing is no doubt taking extra pains with her appearance on the first full day in her new domain. She's so eager to impress," Titus soothed himself, remembering his rather charming note he'd left on her pillow.

"Polly?" Stephen said loading his plate with biscuits, taking care to get all the chocolate ones. "Polly Plumber?"

"Polycorpus Singularia Albinus, if it's all the same to you," Titus reminded him. "And do wait for your hostess before you shove that in your mouth."

Stephen, being an insufferable clod, leaned back in his chair with his plate balanced on his knee, looking singularly pleased with himself.

Titus watched the clock and said nothing. Any comment on his part would be met by a calculatedly infuriating rejoinder from his cousin, and he was not in the mood for it. Minutes dripped by. Still Titus watched the clock wondering where the bloody hell his wife had got to.

Then 15 minutes in to his discomfort Titus wondered no more, because there she stood in the parlor, a disheveled mess. She was in her bloody dressing gown, only the hem was now ragged, sodden and the piping torn, the neckline of her nightgown was half-ripped, her nails were caked with mud and there was a smear of dirt beside her chin. It was astounding.

"Have you seen the state of your hypocaust? Your heating system is a shambles," she said a massive spanner in her pocket, causing her dressing gown to gape open, exposing her rather scandalously for such mixed company. Anyone who cared to look could see the dark shape of her pubic region through the thin fabric of her night gown. She reeked of sweat. How dare she.

"Would you mind if we discussed this in the corridor, my precious flower?" Titus said.

"Fine," Titus's embarrassment of a wife bit out at him.

In the corridor Polycorpus stood, hands on her hips, like a fishwife.

"I assume you realize what an embarrassment…" Titus started only to be cut short.

"Good, you ought to be ashamed, have you done any maintenance on this wreck…ever? Besides cosmetics, I mean. If you spent half what you spend on imported wallpaper on keeping the bloody place from collapsing in on itself perhaps I wouldn't have nearly frozen my feet off when I got up this morning."

"What?" Titus asked taken aback by her barrage.

"Your heating system is an inadequate antique and you're a ninny for not taking an interest…not taking responsibility, for your own house. This house is just so much pretty paint and paper over a poorly kept, badly managed, machine. The only part maintained with any sort of pride is the conservatory. You ought to be ashamed! It should be a crime to let nice things fall to ruin by sheer lazy ignorance," she said angrily.

Titus felt a cold burn of rage mix with a hot rush of confusion. Him? She took him to task? Over the care of his house? What in Hades led her to get so worked up over that?

"On the contrary, my dear, you are the embarrassment here," Titus said.

"Me?" Polycorpus asked, wide eyed.

"You marched into your own parlor, reeking of perspiration, clothes dirty and torn, shouting at the top of your lungs about the bloody plumbing…"Titus said his voice getting louder at each word, he was unable to stop himself.

"Heating, not plumbing," Polycorpus interrupted him.

"Who bleeding cares? Not I, that's for certain," Titus roared.

"And it shows in the state of your house," Polly shouted back. She could be nothing but Polly, this uncouth creature.

"My house is certainly in a better state than your..." Titus flicked his eyes up and down her wrecked appearance, "person, though I use the term loosely."

Polly rolled her eyes.

"You appeared before a guest in a manner that would be inappropriate... in front of the servants. Even if you've no pride of your own, you could at least consider that your husband might have some dignity. You've done nothing productive all morning, have you?" Titus said "The soiree for the Earl of Caledonia is this evening and you've nothing to wear. All stupid little Polly can do is muck about with the hypocaust..."

"Stupid?" Polly asked her grubby little hands balling into fists "You call me stupid?"

"Yes," Titus said grinning to have evoked some sort of response from her. "Yes, I do."

"That's rich," Polly said, narrowing her eyes.

"Is it?" Titus asked grinning back at her.

"Very, coming from a great ninny like yourself," Polly said head cocked to one side.

"Ninny?" Titus repeated. He'd been called many things, over the years, most of them behind his back, but he'd never in his life been referred to as a ninny.

"Precisely, You're like some great overgrown girl, concerned with nothing but clothes and parties and..." Polly said.

Titus could listen to no more, he interrupted and began advancing on her until he stood towering over her, stooping to confront her nose to nose. "And you, Madam, are an oaffish, unsubtle, brute."

"And you're both utter shit as hosts. My tea's gone cold while you were rowing," Stephen said from the doorway. "First rule of married life, don't bother to take your domestic squabbles into the corridor if you're going to shout so loud everyone on the ground floor can bloody hear you."

Titus wasn't quite sure how to reply to that.

"Near as I can tell, you're both right. It's a draw and I'm too hungry to listen to the two of you point out the sodding obvious any longer," Stephen said.

Polly sighed and tromped after Stephen into the parlor.

"Could you at least close your dressing gown?" Titus said.

Polly looked down and laughed, actually laughed, before tying her gown.

"Shove over," Polly, horrid unsubtle Polly, said to Stephen, plopping down beside Titus's cousin on the settee.

Titus watched aghast as the Duchess Londinium Austri proceeded to take a biscuit from Stephen's plate. At the very least she could have washed her hands.

"What now?" she asked.

Stephen appeared to be fighting back a smirk. "Sorry, Titus, she's been doing it since she could toddle. You've married a biscuit thief."

"Not my fault you take all the best ones for yourself, greedy guts," Polly said wrinkling her nose.

Stephen smiled a tiny smile that seemed almost...warm. "Not my fault you're slow."

Titus felt every hair on his arms stand at attention. He felt...no, he couldn't possibly. There was no way under Nut's starry sky he was jealous of the filthy uncouth little sow on his settee.

"May I?" Titus gestured to the narrow space on the other side of his wife, and Polly grudgingly made room for him, though it was a tight squeeze for the three of them. Stephen needed to lose weight. It was no joke.

Polly opened her mouth to speak, but appeared to think another biscuit from Stephen's plate was a better option.

"May I offer you something from my plate...dearest?" Titus said taking up a forkful of stargazy pie as soon as Polly swallowed her biscuit.

The normally excessively intrepid girl looked a bit taken aback. Perhaps she was unfamiliar with the dish. Never mind, it was one of Titus's personal favorites, and it would be hers as well.

Polly opened her mouth and Titus fed her delicately. He'd never fed anyone before and he wanted to do it with aplomb.

Polly chewed and swallowed fairly politely. At least she kept her mouth closed.

"So?" Titus asked.

"Not really to my taste," Polly said.

Titus carefully took a portion of his kidney pie on his fork and put it in her mouth.

Polly chewed slowly, a look of anxiety on her face.

"And?" Titus asked.

Polly slowly shook her head. "Sorry."

Titus's hand hovered over the tray, his own plate exhausted. Personally, he preferred meats, fish, sausages, and bread. Sometimes mushrooms.

Titus scooped up a toast point with a perfectly sautéed mushroom in the center and popped it into Polly's mouth before she could protest.

She chewed with a look of concentration that was nearly vulgar. Well, at least she kept her mouth closed.

"I suppose you despise mushrooms as well?" Titus said feeling irritable.

"The way Florence makes them at my Papa's house, yes, but that's quite good, I rather like that," Polly said reaching for another.

Titus stopped her; her hands were positively unhygienic. "Allow me," he said gently feeding her another.

The tip of his finger touched her lower lip this time and he felt a strange warmth in his chest and fluttery feeling in his gut. It was absurd, ridiculous and wrong that he should be so moved by this clownish little person's approval.

"None of my other wives were this difficult to please," Titus observed as Polly enjoyed her mushroom on toast.

Polly licked the corner of her mouth. "And they're all dead, aren't they?"

Stephen broke in chuckling. "Technically speaking you're dead as well, aren't you?"

Polly laughed an oddly metallic little laugh. "I suppose I am. Poor Titus, I'm dead and I'm still a pain in his arse."

Titus would have agreed except that he was too busy being horrified by his wife's language.

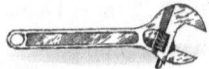

Polly stared at the ornate ceiling trying to puzzle it all out. Things between she and her husband were strange that night, which was to say Mr. Albinus was strange.

Albinus picked out her clothes and her jewelry, even her shoes. He chose a perfume after the ladies maid his valet had chosen had painted her face. They went to the stupid party for the stupid Earl of Caledonia.

The food had been good. Though Polly wished she'd brought a book because it was otherwise dry as dust. Colonel Albinus seemed to be everywhere at once though at the same time elusive. She saw him here and there, seemingly every place she turned at the party, but could never quite pin him down because every time she actually sought him out he was gone.

She was on the brink of being quite put out because she'd like to know when it would finally be permissible to go home. She was bored with the company and bored with herself and her corset wouldn't allow her to cram any more shrimps or toasts or delightful little cakes down her throat.

Or tiny potatoes.

Polly loved the tiny potatoes.

On consideration what Polly was truly bored with was Titus Albinus.

Mister Everywhere-and-Nowhere, weaving among the gossips…

Polly stopped mid-thought, tripped by the realization. What better occupation for an invisible man than that of spy? And what better camouflage than an overly-fussy tailor's dummy?

It was an interesting idea. At least it kept her thoroughly distracted until it was time to leave.

Polly found it difficult, but she managed to keep her idea to herself until the carriage door was shut and the two of them were alone.

"The potatoes weren't quite as good as they had a month ago at Bertie's, same shipment but an inferior grade, I believe. Tsk, tsk, not winning any points with Caledonia cutting corners at a party in his honor," he said, though Polly had no idea who Bertie might be. "I think Diana has stolen Clytemenstra's dressmaker, I imagine that's what got up poor Clytie's nose. Did the soprano sound sharp to you? I believe the soprano at the entertainment was a trifle sharp."

"I imagine your memory for that sort of thing is quite good, all the little details," Polly broke in to Albinus's prattling.

Albinus stopped, turning his head slowly to look Polly in the eye. "Why do you say that?"

"It seems to me a spy would necessarily have to possess excellent powers of memorization," Polly said, pleased with herself for working it out. That explained the gymnasium and the baths every morning as well. It wasn't his vanity. Well, it wasn't only his vanity. He was gathering information.

Albinus didn't say a word, only looked at her appraisingly, his fingertips covering his mouth.

"I'm not wrong am I? It's the logical conclusion, after all. How long did it take the other wives to work it out? Am I the quickest? I'd like to be the quickest," Polly said, starting to feel a bit uncomfortable. Perhaps you weren't supposed to tell people when you worked out they were spies. Perhaps it made them feel too obvious.

Albinus shook his head very very slowly. "They didn't."

"Not ever?" Polly asked, taken aback "Were they thick or something?"

"No, they weren't thick, they were girls. I am not longer entirely certain what you are, Madam," Albinus said, his eyes slitted.

"Oh, come on, they have to have known," Polly insisted in spite of herself.

Perhaps they simply had enough sense not to let on they knew. Polly felt rather stupid for telling Albinus she'd worked it out.

"No one knows," Albinus said in a different tone of voice than she'd heard from him before. "Tell me, how did you come to know the truth?"

"Because," Polly said, "you were everywhere at once. It was as if you wanted to be seen and that made me wonder why it was so important that you constantly make yourself conspicuous…and it just followed, logically. When you say no one knows, what do you mean by no one?"

"Only Stephen, and of course, Her Majesty," Albinus said. "Are you certain my cousin didn't play a hand in this? He didn't clue you in?"

"Professor Magesteri knew about you and he didn't warn me? That…that.. that…shit," Polly said the words tumbling out before she could stop them.

"He took a blood oath not the reveal my secret to anyone," Albinus said. "There's no exemption clause for paramours."

"He is not my paramour; he's never been my paramour," Polly said feeling annoyed with Albinus all over again. It was true, what passed between them was very nearly an accident, like tripping on an unexpected stair.

Albinus mirrored the expression she knew was on her own face, "Whatever you say, dearest. Still, for Stephen to have taken you into his confidence would have been high treason."

But Polly's thoughts had moved on.

"When you say 'Her Majesty' you mean…" Polly could hardly bring herself to say it, it was so, unbelievable and exciting at the same time.

"The Empress," he answered.

"The one in Alexandria?" Polly asked, so loudly Mr. Albinus winced.

"Unless we've some other Empress I've never heard of," he said peevishly. "Look, Polycorpus, it is of paramount importance you not breathe of a word of this to a single soul," Mr. Albinus said earnestly.

"Who exactly do you imagine I have to tell, Mr. Albinus? Now that I'm a bloody duchess no one speaks to me except for you and Mr. Magesteri, and you both already know," Polly said.

"My name is Titus, you know, you ought to call me Titus," he said. "You are my wife."

"I am, aren't I?" Polly said, feeling uneasy.

"Either that or I spent an inordinate sum of money merely to get an uncoordinated little spanner wielding snoop into my bed," he said. "Either way, money well spent, I'd say."

"You're awful," Polly said slapping him lightly on the shoulder, like she would have done Charlie Edney once upon a time.

Only Mr. Albinus…no, Titus seemed to be knocked backwards by the tap.

"Don't use slang, dear, it's dreadfully unbecoming," Titus smiling just a bit.

Chapter 7: Curses and Collusion

That night in bed Titus felt an inexplicable embarrassment before her. One that seemed to confound Polly as much as it did him. The intercourse itself was uninspiring and uncomfortable, which was stranger still.

Titus could not help feeling he had been exposed in some way he had never expected. What was this creature he had married? For all her supposedly common origins she seemed far more Uncommon than any woman had ever known, for both good and ill.

He lay awake in bed half the night composing, discarding, and composing anew the message he would leave her when he arose.

Oh Wife of Mine,
I had no idea when I married you that I could come to so dread a woman in less than a fortnight...no.

He turned on his back and tried again.

My Darling Polly,
I find myself questioning if I ever was in love before last night...no

The woman in question, snored loudly, flinging her arm into his face. He rolled on his left side to get away from her and found himself teetering on the edge of the bed. And considered again.

Dear Polycorpus,
I am aware that the Conferratio is considered insoluble before the law but perhaps there is
some way to circumvent...no

Titus clung doggedly to the cliff face of the bed and wracked his brain for the right words.

My Dear Polycorpus,
I feel I must reiterate my statement from yesterday's note; you truly are an extraordinary
female. Be that as it may I would appreciate an attempt on your part to be dressed and pre-
sentable by tea time, as I fully expect the Viscount Londium Oriens to join us.

Your Ever Vigilant Husband,
Colonel Titus Posthumus Albinus
Duke Londinium Austri
Order of Apophis 1st class

Polly woke up, bleary-eyed as usual, and remembering her promise to the oracle lit the incense before the gods of her husband's family. Nearly burning her fingers she reminded herself this was to become part of her daily morning regime.

It wasn't until later, poking about the house, that she noticed her husband's personal shrine in his locked study when she was looking for something to read. She hesitated a moment, but the key had been so easy to locate; he couldn't have meant it to stay locked.

Polly had never seen such a well used shrine. The gods were nearly worn smooth with touching. The smell of incense permeated the altar cloth. The dish for food and wine was stained dark purple. The holder for candles and incense black with carbon.

The gods.

Apollo Alexikakos. The Averter of Ills.

Apophis. The God of Soldiers.

No.

Officers.

The God of Officers.

There was a difference.

Mr. Albinus worshipped them both and he meant it.

Like many men Professor Stephen Drusus Nero Magesteri, Viscount Londinium Oriens, had a code of conduct; personal rules of behaviour that he never
violated no matter the circumstance. The first and foremost of these was to
never, ever, pass up a chance at a free meal.

Titus had extended a standing invitation to tea now that he had taken Polly
away from Stephen and the British Museum, even if it was for the best. So at
10:45 a.m. Stephen was honor bound to give his apprentices a stern warning
not to do anything too horrendously stupid and walk the half mile to Titus's for
tea. His cousin's cook was without parallel. He was absolutely not going to see
Polly. He was in it for the food and that was the end of it.

So it was that Stephen was surprised to see Titus waiting for him as soon as
he set foot outside the Museum, looking like the cat who meant to swallow the
canary but got a mouth full of crow instead.

"You do know I was on my way? I'm not late," Stephen said slightly taken
aback.

"Perfectly aware of that, cousin," Titus said fairly pulling Stephen down the
street alongside him. "I want to…talk."

"This is about Polly, I assume," Stephen said feeling as though his waistcoast
was a bit tight. He would need to take it to his seamstress but he couldn't recall
if he'd paid last months bill and she'd given him a stern lecture about credit last

time he was in.

"She knows, Stephen," Titus said faking a smile but apparently unable to unclench his jaw "she knows."

Stephen hesitated a moment and very nearly asked Titus what he was on about. Oh. That. No wonder Titus had his silk knickers in a twist but it had been inevitable, Polly being Polly and all.

"I told you she was clever," Stephen said falling into step with him.

"I thought you meant, I don't know, she knew more embroidery stitches or played the lyre better than the other girls," Titus said walking briskly.

Stephen willed himself not to show too much exertion trying to keep up with Titus's long sodding legs.

"I'm still not sure how she worked it out. The damnable woman said I tipped her off by being too 'conspicuously present' at the do for Caledonia last night," Titus said.

"Do you realize what you're doing? You're shitting your pants because you realize Polly's cleverer than you," Stephen said thrusting his hands into his suit pockets because what else was he to do with them?

The glare Titus gave him warmed the cockles of Stephen's heart. It was nice to know he could still get a rise out of old Tight-Arse after all these years. Best of all he'd simply told the truth.

"If that's the case," Titus said, taking his handkerchief from his pocket and cleaning the face of his watch as they walked. "Then she's easily cleverer than you as well."

"Oh you think so, do you?" Stephen answered, unsure how he felt about Titus's hypothesis.

Titus stopped when they turned the corner to stand before his great honking display of a house, if Titus was a peacock, and he was, this bloody house was his tail.

"Yes, I do think so and it concerns me," Titus said striding up the walk to the front door.

"Any reason? Beyond your vanity, I mean?" Stephen asked following him.

"Of course; the obvious question. How does she intend to use the information?" Titus asked stopping just short of the step. "Which was why I wanted to speak to you. You're familiar with her, understand her motivations…"

"She hasn't any," Stephen said.

"Don't be obtuse, everyone has motivations," Titus said. "Even you."

Stephen didn't like the sound behind that, he looked up at Titus. "Yes, cake, I'm motivated by cake."

"Oh, is that a pet name or something?" Titus said lightly.

"And why did you issue the invitation in the first place, what were your motivations? Tantalus always was a favorite story of yours when we were in the nursery," Stephen said, something he didn't want to identify welling up in his chest.

"Nonsense, Stephen, you're free to grow as fat as you like at my table, but I believe the question was my wife, Polycorpus Singularia," Titus said.

"Fine," Stephen said, suddenly beginning to itch indefinably under his skin. "Polly Plumber has the motivation of a Retriever; she likes food, praise, and to have her belly rubbed. Clever as she is her interest in subterfuge is non-existent."

The belly rubbing remark must have struck something in Titus because, knowing full well the danger he rounded on Stephen and lifted him up by his arms holding him against the wall of the house so the two of them were nose to nose.

"Her name is Albinus, Stephen," Titus warned. "You had your chance and failed to take it."

"Sorry, must've slipped my mind," Stephen grinned a wide wide grin at him. Let him know exactly how intimidated he was, meaning not one whit.

"The, the, um retriever business, you're not saying that to humor me?" Titus asked and Stephen could feel his breath on his face.

"Believe me, Titus, humouring you is the last thing on my mind," Stephen warned.

Titus exhaled loudly and dropped Stephen to the ground, throwing his arm over the shorter man's shoulders in the same move.

"Come along, we don't want to keep The Duchess waiting," Titus said suddenly his jocular self again, Stephen wasn't half sure he liked it.

Stephen didn't know how to respond to what he found when he stepped into his cousin's parlor. It was, needless to say, Polly, but Polly in the same sense, that an ingot and the coil in the new motor he was working on back at the laboratory were both essentially copper.

Her normally somewhat dowdy and haphazard dress was... well, she was dressed attractively. She looked good. Stephan hadn't Titus' obsession with couture but he didn't need it to know the dress suited her, in color and cut. Polly's hair had been thoroughly tamed into some elaborate style that made sort of crown on top of her head and spilled like a braided stream down past her shoulders.

Stephen was shit at describing women's hairstyles. But it was flattering. But her face.

Her face was...completely different and exactly the same. Her squinty black eyes had not been made any less squinty, but somehow they looked frightfully exotic now. Her lips had been painted in a way that made him think kissing her would have been like brushing his lips against a rose in full bloom.

Stephen began at that moment to contemplate the true price of a free meal.

"Where's the Viscount?" Polly said. "The note said a viscount was coming to tea."

"Londinium Oriens, at your service," Stephen said, doffing his cap with all the sarcasm he could muster.

"You're him? He's him? Why didn't you say so, Mr. Albinus? Isn't it mad, Professor Magesteri?" Polly laughed spinning in a circle, presumably to give him the 360 degree view. "Mr. Albinus did it."

Titus shrugged and smiled ever so slightly. "Ladies maid, actually. What have I told you, dearest? Titus...Stephen, we can't have you addressing your own family as though you're reading from our calling cards."

Stephen didn't trust himself to offer an opinion so he sat down and took a plate full of biscuits.

Polly was telling Mr…she was telling Stephen and Titus about being make-upped and hair dressed.

Stephen was trying to see how many cakes he could eat while nodding like a toy in a shop window but Titus seemed interested, or at least amused.

"You almost sounded like a girl for a moment there…right up to the point where you started dissecting the chemical properties of lip rouge," her husband said, his eyes twinkling and a smile splitting his narrow face.

Polly stuck her tongue out at him, exactly the same way she would if Guy Oullette or Will Canavan had said it to her, it was like something one of them would have said.

"Not in front of guests, Mrs. Albinus," Titus leered. Charlie Edney would never have said or done anything like that. Her husband really was filthy, in his heart. It was one thing Polly liked about him.

"Stephen's not a guest, are you Mr…Stephen?" Polly said leaning forward on her chair.

Mr. Magest…Stephen was wincing as he swallowed his…whatever was in his mouth. He'd been shoveling it in so efficiently Polly hadn't kept good track. My, but he looked pale. There seemed to be spots coming up on the cuff of his left sleeve, red spots that were quickly bleeding into solid marks.

Quick as a wink Titus was out of his own chair and on his knees in front of Stephen pulling off his velvet frock coat and satin waistcoat. Stephen's white shirt was stained with rapidly spreading words written in blood.

"Opium!" Titus called out. "Bring me the opium, Now!" he shouted to no one in particular, but Polly could hear the sound of running servants. She found herself attempting to read what was written on Stephen's shirt but it looked to be written in Cyrillic. She felt strangely detached, as though she was floating above the room. It was all so unreal.

"What are you gawking at, woman, have you never seen blood?" Titus said between murmuring low to Stephen.

"No," Polly answered. "Not like that. What is it? Is he going to die?"

Polly knew about death. She'd seen the dissections of plenty of dead commoners in Dr. Ng's laboratory. The thought of Mr. Magesteri dead made her want to run, fast and far and never never stop.

"Don't be silly, of course he's not going to die, he's merely going to wish he was dead," Titus said then turned round to look at her, surprised. "You mean you don't know?"

"Sir?" came a throaty male voice and there was Lewellyn, Titus' valet, with a very small oil lamp in one hand and long pipe in the other. Behind him one of the maids had a great blanket that appeared to be satin.

"Not a moment too soon," Titus snapped. "I've your opium, Stephen. All that's left for you is to do your part and inhale. Polly, I need you to wrap the blanket round his shoulders as soon as I've peeled his shirt off."

Polly did her best not to hurt Stephen as she wrapped the satin blanket round him, fascinated to see the bloody letters drip rapidly covering his chest. It looked like Cyrillic. She was fascinated and at the same time ashamed of her fascination. She didn't know where to look.

She watched as Titus moved Stephen to half lie on the settee. She'd offer to help but she was afraid she'd hurt him.

She was also quite fascinated to see how expertly her husband prepared the opium pipe and heated it over the tiny oil lamp Llewellyn had brought, holding it gingerly to Mr. Magesteri's lips.

Polly watched in captivated horror as Magesteri bled and trembled and sucked the pipe then trembled all the more before bleeding from his wounds anew and once again sucking at the pipe, over and over through the same actions in endless combination until finally Stephen Magesteri, Professor of Invention, Viscount of Londium Oriens, the poor bleeding lump, lost consciousness, his satin coverlet soaked through with red rusting to brown.

Polly looked at Titus. He'd been wearing his blue gloves. They were no longer blue. Neither was his waistcoast. His trousers no longer entirely yellow. There were foreign words, in a strange alphabet, backwards, Polly imagined, on the chair Stephen had been sitting in when it started.

"What does it say?" Polly asked. "Can you read it?"

"It's not appropriate language for a lady," Titus looking away.

"Now you're being absurd," Polly told him. "I've spent my life up until now in the Museum, have you heard how the apprentices speak? Have you spoken to your cousin? You think that's fit language for a lady?"

"Fine, this word, here, is abomination. This is evil spirit. This is mother. Sucks. Leperous. Phalluses. Fornicator. With. Dead. Dogs," Titus said pointing to each word, his voice clipped.

"What is this? Who did this to him?" Polly asked. "Why did they do it?"

Titus tilted his head and gave her a sideways look then slowly walked to sit down on a clean chair. His back ramrod straight, Titus removed his gloves, and placed his hands on his thighs as if posing for a photograph.

"It was 24 years ago, during the war. The regiment, our regiment, the 87th Superlatives, were encamped outside Jalalabad. We were impervious to attack by traditional means. Someone on the other side - you do know we fought the Russians in the war?"

"I'm not stupid," Polly said.

Titus nodded "Someone on the other side, a Cyrillic curse doctor...." - here he inhaled deeply - "found a covert method of attack using, quite literally, a poison pen letter. A missive, slipped in with the mail that arrived from home, that when opened attacked the regiment, one man after another, the very ink itself ensorcelled, carving words into their skins, leaving them to bleed to death."

"How horrid. How bloody cowardly!" Polly said, feeling very angry all of a sudden. War had always seemed so distant before.

"It wasn't cowardly, it was clever," Titus said coldly.

There was something in the whole business Polly didn't understand.

"Why weren't you affected?" she asked.

Titus looked at her very matter-of-factly and answered "I wasn't injured because I wasn't there. Because I had deserted."

"I see," Polly said trying not to seem too shocked, but she was. She was shocked and angry and, and, soldiers were supposed to be brave and honorable, and she didn't know what Mr. Albinus was.

"When I returned, having reconsidered my course of actions, I was surrounded by my dead and dying comrades. I was young and far from full grown myself, even the horses had been attacked, I could save only one man, and one man small enough for me to conceivably carry back to a medical unit. Rations had been thin for some time," Titus said, "and Stevie was small for 14."

"How old were you?" Polly asked, trying to picture it.

"I was born three months before my cousin," Titus said.

"Were you small for your age as well?" she asked.

"Average, I'd say, but weedy," he answered, looking her in the eye.

Mr. Albinus was not being charming, or arrogant, or foppish or any of those things that frequently got up Polly's nose. He was telling her the most horrible story she had ever heard with all the emotion of an automaton. Not a made up novel that was sort of fun in its terrible-ness because it was only make-believe, but a true horror that had happened to real people, real people she knew.

If it had been a book, she would have said Colonel Albinus was a coward and deserved to be caught out for his dereliction of duty and horse-whipped as an example. But now she knew that his desertion had wound up saving Stephen's life it was hard to label it as an irredeemably bad act, and Titus as nothing more than a bad actor. The youngest apprentices were 13 and 14 and they were little more than babies, really, and liked to skive off to play ball or chase when they were supposed to be working. Polly tried to imagine Charlie Edney at 14 fighting the Russians at the Khyber Pass; it was both comedic and pathetic. The more Polly experienced life outside of books and theory the more it appeared that there was no simple mathematics of morality, no simple formula for right and wrong.

Was she somehow deceitful to marry Titus when she loved Stephen? Even though Stephen urged her to do it and Titus was fully aware of the fact?

Was it perverse to grow fonder of Titus and Stephen at the same time picturing them as weak and frightened boys?

If so, then why did she like him better when she heard unflattering things about him?

"Then what happened?" she asked.

"Stephen was shipped home and returned to the museum an apprentice as soon as he'd convalesced. I remained and was assigned to a new regiment. I served out the duration of the war and opted to continue serving my Empress in the capacity for which I am most suited," Titus said, looking ahead, hands still on his thighs. "Stephen suffers almost daily pain from the curse, though the bleeding and the scars come and go with no warning. Sometimes weeks go by without incident. I live in hope some day my cousin forgives me."

"Forgives you?" Polly repeated, surely Titus didn't think a 14 year old boy could have possibly prevented an attack that killed an entire regiment of monsters.

"For saving his life, Polly," Titus said for the first time looking her in the face.

Stephen Magesteri woke up in one of his cousin Titus's dozen or so spare bedrooms, the sheets smeared with blood despite, he was quite sure, having been changed while he was unconscious. He kept his eyes closed and laid quite still.

Primarily he remained still because he could barely move with the amount of opium that tit, Titus, had forced on him but also, secondarily because Polly was sitting at his bedside, keeping fucking vigil. His eyes were closed but he could hear her. The girl had all the stealth of a bull elephant. Girl? Stephen nearly laughed at the preposterous use of the word. A married woman of twenty-two was not, by any definition, a girl, though her marriage was mostly his own handiwork. He wondered, vaguely, if he might have been able to find a way to marry her himself, had he worked at it. Bah, that was, without a doubt, nothing but an opium dream. Even if he weren't ugly, ill-tempered, and badly in debt, he was hardly husband material.

"Stop shamming," Polly said, "Ow!" accidentally stubbing her toe on the side of the bed when she crossed her legs. She'd taken off her shoes, which meant she'd likely been there some time. Stephen wondered how long. He threw his pillow over his face, hoping to avoid conversation.

"G'way, Polly," he groaned into the pillow.

"Do stop being… that way," Polly said. "Titus told me everything."

Even on a good day, Stephen Magesteri thought his cousin Titus was a pompous twat, however this was far from a good day. Stephen pulled the pillow down just enough to peer at Polly.

"Define 'Everything'," Stephen said.

"About how he deserted your, your regiment and the…the poison pen…how you were wounded and the only survivor," Polly said. "All that. Everything."

So, almost nothing then. Stephen covered his face again and considered what Polly must think based on Titus's version, a version that no doubt contained more hole than story.

"Don't be angry with him; he was only a boy," Polly said.

"Did my cousin tell you why he ran away from our camp?" Stephen asked, sure he knew the answer.

"He was afraid, wasn't he? It's only natural, he's just not as naturally brave as you are, I mean…" Polly said as though she were granting Stephen a rare glimpse of Titus's internal processes. What a laugh.

Stephen laughed at the bloody absurdity of the statement, and it hurt. "Fuck," he coughed out between chuckles. "No, he's a good deal braver. The reason, Polly, that my cousin left camp and missed the Russian's successful attack, was because our commander, Commander Khufu, was using Titus as a whipping boy. And he hadn't yet had enough military stupidity drilled into his head at that point to accept another minute of it."

"Whipping boy?" Polly repeated, leaning forward.

Stephen nodded "I reckon you've seen his back by now. Didn't you wonder how it got that way? I was a bit insolent in my youth, not exactly the picture of gentlemanly decorum you hold before you. Our Commander found it …effective to mete out my punishment to Titus whenever I broke discipline."

"But it was you he saved, out of the whole regiment, he chose to save your life," Polly said in something like wonder and something like bewilderment.

Stephen nodded, he'd often asked himself the same exact same question.

"Why didn't they whip you?" Polly asked.

So Titus hadn't told her that part. He'd left it to Stephen. One thing he was sure of, he'd be fucked if he was going to be the one to turn all the family dirty linen inside out for her inspection.

He gave Polly his best hard stare, the one that was famous for making junior apprentices bawl like babies.

"Because they were afraid," Stephen said slowly.

"Why would anyone be afraid of you?" Polly asked, her forehead wrinkled.

The impertinent excuse for a duchess.

"G'away, Polly, and leave me in peace," Stephen said throwing himself backwards on the bed and covering his face once more with Titus's goose down pillow.

Polly marched straight to Titus's study, forgetting to knock on her way in.

He was, as could be expected, writing a report to send to Alexandria and began shimmering out of view when he heard someone at the door.

"Only me," Polly said. "Nothing to be afraid of."

"I'm not afraid," Titus glared. "Merely startled. You could knock first."

"Sorry," Polly said dutifully. "Why was your commander afraid to whip Stephen? He was only a boy. Is he umm a werewolf? I know he's Uncommon but I've no idea how. He seems rather ordinary but then again he doesn't seem at all ordinary. What is he? Why were they afraid? And why did you save him?"

Titus looked up at her, his eyes wide, his mouth open, for the briefest of seconds, then went back to his writing. "I volunteered to take the lash for him."

Polly now understood even less than she had a moment earlier, if such a thing were possible. "Why? What in Osiris's name for?"

"Because discipline must be maintained, speaking of which, this report must be filed by dusk, if you would be so kind as to keep yourself occupied," Titus said staring at the page.

"In other words 'g'way, Polly, leave me in peace'," she said turning to leave.

She swore later she could hear her husband sighing heavily as she shut the door behind her.

It occurred to Polly as she walked down the corridor that Stephen and Titus probably meant "afraid" in a completely different sense than she'd first took it: as in afraid a real whipping might be too much for a 14 year old boy who was small for his age. Titus was protecting Stephen, that made sense all the way round. As hypothesis went it wasn't bad. At least it fit the facts as she knew them. Too bad neither of those puddingheads were more forthcoming.

She was walking aimlessly and trying to think, trying to find a way to test her theory, when she narrowly missed running into Malcolm barreling out of Titus's conservatory. By Mr. Albinus's own admission the little man occupied an unusual position among the servants, he had one job, and one job alone, along with the authority to conscript other servants if he felt it was warranted, to tend the Hellbenders and their environs. And also by Titus's own admission Malcolm was something of a favorite.

"Could you tell me something, Malcolm?" Polly asked, smiling cheerfully at him. Malcolm wasn't bad to look at, although truth be known, Polly found something appealing about most men, but Malcolm, despite being decidedly short and bandy-legged, with close cropped hair and otherwise unremarkable features, had the most amazingly long lashed eyes.

"As best I'm able, Ma'am," Malcolm said, looking down at his perpetually muddy boots. In actuality, Malcolm was muddy everywhere, it came with the job.

"When the Duke was lashed on his cousin's account, did he volunteer in order to spare Mr. Magesteri from harm? Is that what happened?" She asked.

Malcolm never once looked up at her but he did answer. "I'm sure I don't know, Ma'am."

Oh, that got right up Polly's nose. "On the contrary, I'm sure you do know," she said.

"If you say so, Ma'am," Malcolm still wouldn't look at her. "But if his lordship were to take a punishment that wasn't his own, I would say he'd have a good reason."

"What sort of reason?" Polly asked.

"His lordship puts a high value on duty," Malcolm said.

"You mean, duty to his family? Like Professor Magesteri? Protecting Mr. Magesteri? Or his military duty? His duty to the Empire?" Polly asked.

"Yes, Ma'am, all of those, Ma'am," Malcolm said "I've got to check the pumps, now, Ma'am. If the waters stop movin' the bendies stop breathin'."

Polly couldn't tell if that was a confirmation or not.

Chapter 8 : The Tedium

itus sent Llewellyn with his apologies at supper. Mrs. Albinus would have to dine without him. In fact he stayed locked up in either his study or the spare bedroom with Stephen until he imagined Polycorpus would be in bed.

Only she wasn't. Of course she wasn't. The woman could never make anything easy. She was wide awake, naked, on the divan, reading a book on planetary motion, like some bluestocking Odalisque.

"What are you doing up?" Titus asked.

"We agreed on nightly conjugal relations, didn't we? I'm ready to conjugate," Polly grinned at him.

"Aren't you cold?" he asked.

"Only my feet get cold, ordinarily, and I'm wearing slippers," Polly said wiggling her left foot at him.

"Oh," he said but he hadn't been looking at her feet.

He made a point of telling himself he was not in truth hesitating; rather he was exercising prudence in approaching a person who had managed to glean nearly all the pertinent facts of his life in a few short weeks, about whom he knew precious little. He had assumed initially this was because there was nothing to know. What exactly could a girl get up to with no viable social life available to her?

In reality, he realized he didn't even know where she'd come from, even if she was made of common pieces, which he was no longer sure he entirely believed, where had the pieces originated? They were different colors so were her pieces English? French? Roman? Egyptian? Afghani? Persian? Titus took her hand and examined it.

"What are you, Mrs. Albinus?" Titus asked.

"Several jars full of bits, pieced together with a clockwork spine, and reanimated by lightning, but you knew that," Polycorpus said holding her place with her index finger until he took the book from her.

"Where did Henry Plumber get the pieces?" Titus asked taking her left hand and comparing it to the right. In his own her hands were tiny, his fingers stretching more than a full joint beyond hers. He compared them further. The smallest finger on his hand was longer than her index finger. She was terribly small, for all her strength.

"According to Mr. Mage...according to Stephen he brought most of them back with him from the war. My hair is English though." she said looking from one hand to the other "They don't half match, do they?"

"So you've no idea at all?" Titus asked. It was a strange idea. He knew commoners bred like rats, but he could not imagine being unaware of his own provenance. His history was inextricably linked to who he was. He couldn't imagine having a self without having ancestors, it seemed impossible.

"Some parts are very light, so perhaps some camp follower's baby, I suppose? And some are dark, but there quite a few different peoples in the area, so ..." Polly looked at her arm. "Pashto perhaps? I'm sort of squarish and there are a few Nepalis there abouts...I've no idea, to be perfectly earnest."

"I wonder what color our children will be," he said idly bringing both her hands to his mouth and gazing from one to the other.

"If we have children, you mean; none of my kind has ever reproduced before," Polycorpus said pensively.

In a way it reassured Titus to know she worried over the same things as other women.

He bent low to tuck a kiss inside her freckled elbow, then closed her arm carefully, locking away the kiss for safe keeping.

"Don't worry, little Polly," he said unfastening his trousers as he reassured her. "It was foretold by the oracle, I heard it from her lips, myself, you will be the one who gives me a child."

Polly tried to get used to having tea with her Mother-In-Law and her twin sister.

Mrs.Brolly and Mrs.Albinus, although Polly supposed she was Mrs. Albinus now too, sat, as usual, side-by-side on a long velveteen divan under their own portraits in what Titus informed her was the second best parlor. But no matter how usual it was, Polly still felt uncomfortable.

Literally, over each woman's head, hung her likeness, posed with a man. It was funny how evident it was that the portrait over Mrs. Brolly was herself, despite the fact that it was in truth a painting of clothes and hat and veils beside a well dressed brown skinned man with huge vivid green wings. Polly would recognize that ramrod stiff posture anywhere. And the man must be Prince Brolly.

The man in Mrs. Albinus's portrait had to be their grandfather. He was white headed with a long bony face and arms and legs twice as long as a Commoners would be, and bent the entirely wrong way, spiderlike. Mrs. Albinus looked impossibly young, but her belly was high and round.

"Titus certainly favors his great grandfather," Polly said cheerfully.

"Oh, no," Mrs. Albinus laughed her high tinkling laugh. "That's his father, Arachnus. I was his second wife. He was married to his first wife for 60 years and no children. Imagine."

Titus gave her as close as he could come to a nasty look.

"86 and 17, before you ask," he said under his breath.

Polly swallowed hard and buttoned her lip.

It was a bit funny. Polly had convinced Charlie Edney to have intercourse with her because she'd been concerned that if she didn't talk someone into it she would die a virgin, which was all very well for people who were concerned about propriety and virtue but from the point of view of a naturally curious girl it was rather distressing.

Only she needn't have worried.

From the beginning Mr. Albinus had been…impressive, yet distant, at first, almost as though he were giving a performance. And then after Polly grew to know him better, he became slightly awkward, as if he wasn't accustomed to being intimate with women who knew his secrets. By the end of May they were fairly jocular with one another, although she still thought he was a bit precious, and Titus made it perfectly clear he found her somewhat coarse.

Unfortunately sex only occupied an hour or two of the day, at best.

And then the hour or so they spent in the conservatory, in the evenings, playing with the Bendies, as Titus called them. That was pleasant, too.

Still, for the first month Polly had to endure almost daily sessions with the dressmaker to bring her wardrobe up to standard, with ever present hovering from Titus, keeping a running commentary on cut and color as well as the relative quality of the fabric on offer that day. And pipings and buttons. Bloody buttons. Polly had never known anyone to care so deeply about bloody bleeding dog-buggering buttons. More than once she thanked Stephen for giving her the vocabulary to describe the tedium of spending time trapped between two people who knew the names for thirty distinct styles of button.

Titus blamed it on his social calendar, which was, she supposed, the reason for the dresses, though Polly strongly suspected even if he weren't a spy and didn't have to go to an average of four parties a week, even if there were no parties to attend, Titus Albinus would still delight in having dresses made for her. Not that Polly had anything to do but read the book Mr. Albinus held open for her while she was fitted. Still it was dull.

And there were the parties themselves, which amused Polly in as much as she knew that Titus was laughing and telling stories and charming the knickers off everyone while covertly uncovering all their secrets. The beginning and end of Polly's responsibility was to follow every rule Mrs. Brolly had taught her about society. That was all. Even though it nearly killed her and she couldn't wait to break into a foaming diatribe and throw off her shoes when they got into the carriage. More often than not Titus either rolled his eyes or laughed or both.

And then there was tea. That quickly became a routine as well.

Stephen came and ate all the chocolate biscuits every day with the exception of the first day of every week, when Mrs. Albinus and Mrs. Brolly gave Polly what would easily be the most nerve wracking 90 minutes of her week. Tea with her mother-in-law, was the sort of thing she imagined was designed to make you clench muscles you didn't know you had. It was so trite, so clichéd, and yet that didn't fail to make it true. Why couldn't she have a relaxing tea with her mother-in-law and Mrs. Brolly? Although she wondered a bit if anyone had ever had a relaxing tea with Mrs. Brolly. Was it possible to accomplish or more like an unreachable goal you could learn by striving towards, like building an immaculate machine?

Not that Colonel Titus Albinus would lower himself to have tea with Polly's Papa, ohhh no, he managed to change the topic, or distract her in some way or another every time she brought the topic up so that Polly finally resolved herself that if she wanted to see the Museum and her papa, and more importantly, Mable with her asafetida, she would simply have to go there herself while Titus was at the gymnasium.

Polly's asafetida was running low, and while she might be getting to like Titus, a bit, she was nowhere near interested in risking her life every time he took off his trousers.

Without her asafetida she'd be too anxious to have any fun with him anyway. If he had any sense at all he'd be grateful, not that she was about to tell him.

All in all Polly's life was strange and new and utterly bizarre in a mundane sort of way. There were no explosions, no fires, all the machines were at least somewhat out-moded. All the transportation focused on getting from point A to point B and sometimes point C as well. The only animals were the Bendies, though she liked them.

For twenty-two years Polly's life had been one way, without even a suggestion that it might change, and now in a few dazed months it had changed dramatically.

There were so many new demands and it all seemed a great stupid muddle to Polly. Polly wasn't used to muddles. She was a creature of the Museum. She understood disagreements, differing agendas and points of view. What struck Polly most was the realization that the world her husband lived in, society, politics, all that bother, seemed to be the equivalent of a cobbled together machine that no one noticed until it stopped working. This made her consider even more questions, things about her own position, about women, commoners, the dirty air. It seemed the questions were endless. If it had been a machine she would have drawn a schematic.

Instead she sat down beneath Titus's cherry tree in the Salamanderium with a pen and paper and began to puzzle it out, scruffing Titus's oldest bendie, Cronus on the head as she worked.

Polly was a bit disappointed when the salamander salamandered off to dig in the bank of the artificial stream the pumps kept running. He was intent too. Looking about Polly noticed some other Bendies doing the same thing.

She would have asked Titus, or Malcolm, who tended the Bendies, if they were available. Instead she wrote in her book.

From where does authority derive?

A husband's authority?

A father's authority?

Governmental authority?

The authority of the gods?

Titus noticed that while Polly was no more tractable than she'd initially been upon the commencement of their nuptials, neither was she more combative, he supposed that could be counted a victory.

By the end of the month she realized she was writing a treatise on moral philosophy, the first ever that took women and commoners into account, as far as she could find.

It was something to do at least.

She worked on it the in Salamanderium whenever her husband wasn't demanding she do something stupid or tedious . Mostly when he was at the baths or writing his reports to the Empress.

She sat on her favorite stone and opened her book.

What constitutes nobility? she wrote then stopped and pondered.

The Bendies were at it again, a good many of them digging madly in the muddy banks.

"Malcolm," Polly called to the little man in the pump room. "Malcolm, what are they up to, digging like that?"

"Building nests, Your Ladyship," he said, sticking his head out the pump room door, scrambling to take his hat off his head when addressing his betters.

As if Polly cared.

She was familiar with the habits of many exotic creatures from her days at the Museum.

"Is that how the Bendies attract a mate? Building a nice clean nest for them to lay their eggs in?" Polly asked. She knew quite a few species of bird mated on the basis of house building skills.

"Not exactly, Your Ladyship," Malcolm said his head disappearing back inside the pump room.

"How do they do it, exactly?" Polly called over a sudden spate of banging and clanking at the pump controls.

Malcolm appeared in the doorway very quickly, maybe on account of her shouting.

"You see, Your Ladyship, The Papa Bendy builds a nest and then he does what he can to trap a Mummy Bendy in his nest. And he keeps her there until she does her duty and lays her eggs, then the Papa Bendy fertilizes them with his seed. Do you know that word? Fertilize?" Malcolm said carefully.

Polly rolled her eyes "I know lots of words, Malcolm. I was raised in the British Museum and I had the run of its departments before I married the Duke."

"My apologies, Ladyship, breeding of rare animals isn't in the education of most young ladies. None of the others troubled themselves to come in here much," Malcolm said then looked as though he wished he could take the words back.

Polly did her best to smile reassuringly.

"I'm likely not as well brought up as the others were," Polly said feeling equal parts proud of herself and awkward.

"Please don't say that, Your Ladyship," Malcolm said sounding pained.

"What do they do after the female lays her eggs, the males, after they're fertilized? Raise all the little bendies until they can fend for themselves?" Polly asked.

"Them they don't eat," Malcolm said nodding.

Polly couldn't help grimacing as she went back to her writing.

Titus Posthumous Albinus was well acquainted with the workings of matrimony. He ought to; he'd been married four times. Five, if you counted Polycorpus. Not that she didn't count, but she was somewhat unorthodox.

He had thought, before they were married, it would be like marrying a workman's daughter, an exceptional girl born in unexceptional circumstances, who would be grateful to be amongst her own kind and soon fit into the society she should have been born to.

As much as he was loathe to admit it Titus had been much mistaken.

For instance, none of his other wives were so inquisitive. He was beginning to think no one alive was as inquisitive as Polycorpus.

Or as quarrelsome. The woman took issue with even the most innocuous of actions.

He'd learned that when he took pains to neatly fill out the new engagement book he'd picked up for her on his way home from the baths.

At tea that day he'd kissed her cheek and placed the eel skin book in the folds of her dress.

"What's this?" Polycorpus had asked, before, in her peculiar little way of hers, kissing his cheek in return.

"An appointment book, Kitten," he'd been trying on pet names since they'd returned home from the honeymoon, but thus far none of them suited her.

Polly gave him a skeptical look.

"It's been written in," his wife said looking puzzled.

"By me; I saved you the trouble of copying out my schedule," he said and awaited her thanks.

Polly didn't say a word.

"In my own hand," Titus pointed out, it was the sort of thing he usually delegated to Llewellyn, but he hadn't. She should appreciate that.

"What of my schedule?" Polycorpus asked.

Did Polycorpus have a schedule?

"My schedule is your schedule, is it not?" Titus asked.

Polly shook her head but didn't answer, she was too busy flipping through the book.

"What's this?" she said pointing out the solidly booked days from the 7th to the 15th of February.

"Our Lupercalia ball is generally considered the high point of the social season," he said earnestly trying to impart both the pride and the responsibility of the event to her.

"Our?" Polly repeated.

"Yes, we've been THE event for the last dozen years," Titus said, suddenly aware he was worrying the cuticle of his thumb with his teeth. How did she reduce him to this?

"What we? I've never thrown a party in my life. I've never even been to this party of yours. Or do you simply mean you and your wife of the moment when you say we?" Polly was squinting at him.

"Of course not, dearest," Titus doing his best to appear unfazed while below the surface he was grasping like mad for a way to save face. "It's simply that in these brief weeks, I've grown so attached I forget you haven't been with me, always. Cook will need you to begin discussing the menu before December."

"Do you call me 'dearest' to keep from confusing me with one of the other ones?" she asked. "I know you've other things on your mind, deceiving everyone you know and keeping up with all the latest fashions but I'm a living being, not an automaton. You're not the only one in this house with a personal name; mine is Polly. And yes, I have a schedule, you may not realize this, but I don't fall into a heap in the corner the minute I'm out of your sight."

"Yes, Dearest Polly," Titus said emphasizing her blasted name.

It didn't occur to him until later to wonder what she did when he wasn't about. What had the others done? For the briefest of instances it occurred to him he might easily practice a touch of domestic espionage, then he was shamed by the very notion. That was granting the girl entirely too much import. He hardly cared enough to find out what she did when he wasn't watching. Did he? Gods above and below he prayed he didn't. Caring was the purview of wives.

Stephen Magesteri, on the other hand, was genuinely confounded. Every day at tea, not early but soon enough, the newly minted Mrs. Albinus, instead of bursting into his private laboratory, a place where even his senior apprentices were forbidden, and diving headfirst into whatever caught her fancy, picked over his brain for the latest doing at the department of inventions in her absence. Granted he had rarely seen her equal. He'd seen articled engineers who were rank amateurs in comparison. Not that he would ever tell her such a thing but she certainly put his dimwitted employees to shame. The department of invention seemed slow and stupid in her absence.

Still he could have done with a bit more reserve. All his life he had cultivated a certain zone of regulated terror between himself and the rest of the world. Apparently no one had told Polly Plumber she was supposed to fear him ... or death for that matter. Perhaps it was because she had already been dead and seemed none the worse for wear.

In any event Stephen Magesteri had been under the impression that successfully ensconcing Polly Plumber in marital life would sever his connection to her. He was wrong and perhaps it was his own doing. Still, Titus renewed his standing invitation. And the food was as excellent as ever. Polly was as much Polly as she'd ever been. Marriage to Titus had not transformed her into a sober and dull Grand Dame in training. Stephen found the whole business disquieting, if not precisely unpleasant then not wholly pleasant either.

Chapter 9 : A Great House Revealed

And then one day she came to Titus. Polycorpus, his wife came to him, when he had hardly seen her for days on end because she'd been shut away with her menses, and not in a humor to speak to anyone, but after six days she came to him. She'd made it clear that for the duration of her monthly sorrow she didn't want to so much as look at another living being.

Initially, he had been grateful for the quiet and lack of questions, but he'd soon felt uneasy and irritable. If he had used his powers to check in on her without her knowledge, as her husband it was his prerogative. He hadn't stayed long at any rate, she was either sleeping or reading each time he looked in on her, and without her crude badinage Polly was not terribly engaging.

But now she had come to him.

"Polycorpus," Titus said unsure whether he should give her a smile or not. Polly gave him a wave of her hand from the doorway.

"Are you finished, then, with your... inconvenience?" he asked.

"Not quite, another day or so, but the worst is over," she said stepping over the threshold to his study.

Titus was not stupid, he understood that Polycorpus was up to something. He wondered if it would make a difference to ask her. She was so lacking in artifice there was likely little point. She would no doubt be unable to keep it from him regardless.

Then she dropped to her knees before his chair.

An apology?

Was Polycorpus Singularia going to make a humble heart-felt beseeching apology for the most frustrating two months of marriage Titus Albinus had ever endured?

Titus exhaled silently, he had won. All his patience and kindness had triumphed. She recognized his right and from here on out the road would be smooth.

He expected his wife to speak but instead she scooted forward just enough to rest her cheek on his thigh.

Titus couldn't work out if it was Polly's version of supplication or something else entirely. He nearly swallowed but saved face at the last minute, forcing a benevolent smile.

Then his wife did the most extraordinary thing, she put her little hands on his trousers. He quite nearly jumped out of his skin. Needless to say he tried to stand, to disappear, to…

"I believe I am beginning to grow a little fond of you, Titus," Polly said, holding tight to his hips though he had gone quite invisible. "Let me show you, Please?"

Titus found he did not have it in him to make a single utterance in response. It was not possible. Polly might be a trumped up workman's daughter, she might be impossibly bold but she could not possibly be threatening to do what he imagined she was threatening.

Clearly he was mistaken.

Even as she smiled up at him, feeling her way to his buttons, although she could not see them. Feeling his trousers all the way off, despite not being able to see a thing. It had to have been accidental on her part the way she brushed her face against him. She couldn't see him after all, there was no way she could know what part of him her cheek had touched.

That kiss had been meant affectionately and had not been intended for the tip of his member. He wasn't certain why he didn't struggle, it was merely that he felt as though he literally could not.

Then, slowly, feeling her way, Polly, his wife who felt at times like his arch-nemesis and at others like a dear comrade, ran deft little fingers across his front until she found his sex and held it, gently, in her fist, and though she could not see it, slipped his member into her mouth.

Without ever taking him out of her lips, she guided him back to a sitting position. This was vile, and wrong, and the sort of thing only a whore would do, and even then for a good sum of money and she was counting the moments until it was over, but Polly, terrible little Polly, seemed to be luxuriating in the experience, stretching it out, going slowly. Her mouth was wet and her tongue was agile and by all the gods it was the most sublime experience of his life. He found himself whimpering, though that was not possible. Titus Posthumous Albinus did not whimper, was incapable of making such a noise despite the fact that it issued from his own throat.

He opened his eyes to see he had gone quite visible and Polly was watching as she slowly took more and more into her mouth until there was no more to swallow. Titus was going to die.

Had her mouth been so obscenely pleasant inside before? This must be what it was to be a god; her tongue moving in waves back and forth across his shaft. It was taking increasing effort not to spend in her mouth.

Then.

With a single thought he was devastated.

Stephen had lied to him. What Titus had witnessed on the roof of the Museum was no singular occurrence, skill like this took years to perfect. Clearly his cousin had spent time and effort corrupting poor little Polly as an insult to him.

Titus looked at Polly, the corners of her mouth curved upwards. She was smiling at him with his cock in her mouth. Depraved and degraded.

Clearly the dear was not to be faulted any more than a hammer is to blame for the work of the carpenter. She was indisputably Stephen's tool.

He had no idea that his cousin could hate him so much.

He felt his end coming, unstoppable, and tried to wrench himself free, but no, Polly was too strong and held him fast by the hips, she would not be satisfied until their mutual debasing was complete. By the virgin Artemis, she even milked the very last of his seed with her hand, catching the drops on the tip of her tongue, appearing to savor the taste, not relenting until he was utterly spent.

Polly felt quite pleased with herself. She'd done Titus a good turn and had fun while she was at it. It was a nice feeling. She laughed as she licked a stray blob of semen that leaked out of his organ after she'd already let it out of her mouth. She'd thought she got it all.

Titus was giving her an odd look, though.

"Bet you didn't know I could do that," Polly teased him.

"Indeed, I never imagined you capable of such a thing," Titus said in a very careful voice.

"Pleasant surprise, no?" Polly said wiping her mouth on the back of her hand.

"A surprise, at least," he said pressing his lips into a thin line. "Where did you learn that?"

"Books, mostly," Polly supplied, because it was true "You didn't like it?"

She was suddenly worried for Charlie Edney. It hadn't occurred to her before that Titus might be jealous, but she'd read that some men were, sometimes, in novels. She didn't think Titus would actually hurt Charlie but he certainly could make a career difficult, and Charlie could hardly manage as it was.

"Knowing you, my dear, there was no doubt a good deal of book work involved, but on whom did you do your practicum?" he said standing to loom over her and pausing a moment to button his trousers. "And don't cloud the issue."

Polly closed her mouth tight. She didn't want to get Charlie into trouble.

"What do you know of my cousin? How much do you truly know?" Titus said leaning down and taking Polly by the hand and pulling her to her feet. He must have used all his strength to manage it.

Polly wanted to tell him Stephen had nothing to do with it, but then he would press for a name and she might accidentally get Charlie into trouble. Stephen could take care of himself. Charlie, she knew, could not.

"I've known him since I was made," Polly said, then closed her mouth, biting her lip to make certain they stayed. Titus still hadn't let go of her hand.

"You know he is Uncommon, but the details remain obscure is that not what you said? Speak up, do you know what he is? What he can do?" Titus bit out.

Polly shook her head. It had often confounded her. She knew Professor Magesteri was noble, and others sometimes alluded vaguely to his gifts, but she was always sternly quieted if she asked for clarification. The Canavan family's gills and tentacles were apparent and there was no missing Charlie Edney's horns but she knew some signs of nobility were more subtle. She was quite curious but so much had happened lately she hadn't had the opportunity to throw decorum to the wind and ask him now that she was in a position to do so.

"He is Osiris personified," Titus said with finality.

"Death Personified? What's that supposed to mean?" Polly asked.

Colonel Albinus tilted his head to look at down at her, his eyes suddenly gleaming with thought. "It means, my dear Polly, he has the power to kill with the touch of his hand as well as the power to banish death as long as that touch remains."

"A necromancer?" she asked, fascinated, having been cobbled together out of dead people herself. "A true necromancer?" It was the sort of thing one heard about but never saw first hand. She didn't even know there was a living necromancer in the Empire, the gift was so rare.

One huge hand wrapped itself round her right wrist.

"That dear man," she said. Perhaps she shouldn't have said that, it seemed to incense Titus.

"Don't wax too sympathetic, Little Polly," he said lightly, his eyes gleaming down at her.

"He had killed more than a hundred men in the Eastern Wars by the time he was old enough to have been taken on as an apprentice, as well as nearly another dozen quite by accident." His eyes focused on another place and time. "Stephen was a model soldier; he lived and breathed to please our superiors. The first girl he ever fucked he fucked at our captain's command." Mr. Albinus clasped her other wrist with his other huge hand and held her fast. He never used that kind of language. Polly didn't know whether she was more shocked by what he was saying or by how he was saying it.

Polly kept herself still as the grave waiting for him to go on. There seemed to be much more but the silence stretched itself like tungsten wire.

"She was quite dead before my cousin laid hands on her, quite beautiful but quite dead all the same…until he violated her. I believe he was initially under the impression she was responding admirably, until he saw the arrow in her back. She was a vizier's daughter, I believe our commander meant the act as a punishment to her father's support of the Russians," Titus snarled, his eyes blazing. "A week later Khufu took us to a brothel and we learned he had the opposite effect on living females. You are the first female to have ever survived intimacy with Stephen Magesteri. I believe it has something to do with your construction. And yes, of course I know about the two of you, I knew before we married. You may consider yourself forgiven."

"He was just a boy," Polly said unsure of what she should say and blinking a bit at being pardoned for something she never imagined apologizing for. "It was a long time ago. He's not like that now, he would never, of his own accord…it shouldn't color his future."

"I assure you all will most certainly not be well, nothing has ever been well nor will it go well for my cousin, Stephen, in the future," Tightening his grip on her wrists he yanked Polly away from him and held her at arms length his eyes glassy with rage. "It is time you understand what sort of abomination I have saved you from."

He fairly dragged her down the corridor in her dressing gown.

"Where are we going?"

"Going? For some illustration. I've a chart, I should think you'd like that," he bit out.

"What sort of chart is that? Surely, it can wait until... haven't we had enough drama for one night?" she said, stifling a yawn. Yes, of course, she was curious but she was also rather sleepy and a strange sense of dread was growing like a lump in her throat.

"No, it cannot wait until the morning or next weekend or the summer holiday or whenever you were going to suggest, it has waited too long already. Stephen should have told you before you agreed to be my wife. I should have insisted you know what your other option truly was, what dreck you were pining after," he said with a harsh tone in his voice. "The crime, you see, is Stephen, his existence, and if I wait any longer, I fear I shall lack sufficient... motivation to tell you."

She looked up at him bewildered. "What on Earth are you trying to say?"

"If you could stop your mouth and do as I say, we would no doubt be half-way to an explanation by now," he said, exasperated.

She snorted.

"Now, the stairs," he said.

She nearly tripped following after him, he was pulling her so close behind him and going so quickly, her pupils contracted painfully to suddenly find herself beside Colonel Albinus in a brightly lit basement room.

"And now, my dear, if you could curb your tongue for long enough to allow me to explain," he bowed, ushering her towards the end of the long room, "I believe most, if not all, of your questions will be answered."

He stopped at the long end and she realized what had appeared from a distance to be a mass of cracks in the white plaster was, in fact, a wild snarl of lines dotted with names written almost too small for her to make out. She leaned in close.

"My family tree, Polly. Here," he said, pulling her to the far end, "am I. Your name has been added as my wife."

She looked, forgetting for a moment that Mr. and Mrs. Canavan had, for purposes of the wedding, adopted her. Her name glistened in tiny black letters:

Polycorpus Singularia Canavan.

He seemed to be waiting for her to speak, so she said, "Oh."

His eyes glittered as though he could not decide whether to be angry or amused.

"Here you see the name Sidhe," He pulled her somewhere roughly three-fourths of the way along. "She was the last...Common-born to marry into my line. It was said her ability to disappear and reappear at will so terrified her common parents the ignorant pair left the child to die of exposure in the middle of winter. Sidhe's husband, Clodius Albinus, built this house a mere twelve years after Marcus Antonius defeated Octavian at the battle of Actium and founded the Cleopatrick Empire. Look at it, my dear, look at the whole and tell me what you see. Look at the family line."

She walked back and forth, scrutinising the names and branches folding in on themselves. His parents were second cousins, his grandmothers were sisters, the same dozen surnames repeated endlessly. She saw nearly every member of the nobility she knew on the wall. Augusta nee Brolly was Stephen Magesteri's Aunt. His father Aurora's and Augusta's Elder brother, Aurelius. Titus Albinus was his first cousin as well as his second cousin. The Canavans were intermingled with the Martins and the Edneys. Who would imagine?

"He's dangerously inbred and so are you," she said, fighting not to fidget or wince. "Not just you either, I see all the rest of society here. There hasn't been fresh blood in a long time."

"Congratulations for noticing the obvious," he said flatly, "and the primary reason we find ourselves in this marriage and, also... the reason Stephen is such as he is."

She was dying to make him talk faster, shake him, or… something. Then she realized how profoundly uncomfortable he looked.

"I have never told this tale before, it has not been necessary," he glowered, "every one in the British Isles over the age of forty knows it from reading the papers, the rest from rumors. Look at the wall," he instructed.

"What am I supposed to be seeing? Or am I not allowed to speak yet?" she said crossly.

"Stephen's parents," he said, "Aurelius and Euphemia Magesteri, how many times have their lines crossed on this wall? Never mind counting, I'll tell you, thirteen, at least one time too many."

She tried to look him in the eye and he looked away, scrutinizing the ceiling.

"I have been told that originally it was considered quite the love match," he said tensely. "That changed when it was realized that their firstborn son had, tragically, been born unexceptional. A disappointment. My Uncle would not allow his family name to be sullied by a child who was no better than a commoner, you see. Your curmudgeonly cleaning man Mr. Virgil is Stephen's older brother. Virgil Magesteri." He pointed out a spot beside his cousin's name where two names had clearly once been.

She thought she had made more expert erasures on disappointing embroideries.

"That explains quite a bit," she answered him, her mind filling in the blanks; Mr. Virgil's presence in the wedding party, the near adoring way the caretaker went to the Inventions Director whenever he had the slightest complaint, more than that, years of observation suddenly coalesced into a picture. In his own stilted way, Stephen showed a certain fondness for his brother. It warmed her, oddly enough.

"Which easily I could have told you tucked comfortably away in my study. One disappointment would have been an embarrassment to any parents but, in the eighteen years between Virgil and Stephen, my aunt Euphemia gave birth to six little corpses and another disappointment. He was named after my Uncle, Aurelius, before they realized he was no better than Virgil," he continued addressing the ceiling steadily. "I believe they held out hope for some time he would follow after Sidhe's strain and start turning invisible."

"How awful, where is he now?" she asked, touching his arm.

He shifted away without looking at her. "Oh, but it gets much worse, my dear. I'm sure it began harmlessly enough, a fertility charm here, a draught for health there, half the shops on Queen's Row sell amulets for the protection of expectant mothers, but Euphemia and Aurelius were a bit beyond their help, nothing worked for them until..."

"Until... yes? Until what?" she asked.

"They turned to Sorcery, not just any sort of sorcery but some rather questionable practices," he said looking her in the eye for the first time since they had started examining the wall.

"What do you mean?" she asked. Her knowledge of Dark Arts began and ended with an ankh and a handful of seeds on the floor for protection against blood drinkers. She had no idea what he was trying to imply.

"You don't have a clue, do you?" he asked.

She shook her head. "Sorry, it's not something there is much reference to in father's library. The study of Sorcery is a forbidden science to commoners."

"And it's not the kind of thing that exactly captures your bottomless curiosity, is it?" he said flatly. "I cannot say that I am surprised."

The silence stretched for several minutes before he leaned against the wall and stared into her face as if trying to see something located on the opposite side of her skull.

"There are a handful of dark rites guaranteed to spawn an exceptional offspring of great power, all of them... unsavoury, to say the least," he said, without a trace of emotion. "The night my cousin, Stephen was conceived, his parents slit his brother Aurelius' throat and bathed in his blood, his body went stiff whilst my uncle impregnated his mother not ten feet away. I believe Aurelius was six."

Looking up into his closed face, Polly felt decidedly ill.

"After Stephen was born, the recriminations began; he was clearly marked by his beginnings. As much as we may love him, Stephen Propertius Magesteri is an abomination," he said, the faintest hint of bitter humour in his voice.

"But it doesn't matter how he was made, Stephen is good," she said indignantly.

He laughed a short sharp laugh of disbelief. "Look at me, Pretty Polly. Look me in the eye and tell me you can stand within ten feet of him and not feel it.

The same way it is possible to look upon a beautiful child and feel the love with which it was engendered, people see Stephen and feel uneasy, he is a dark creation. It is an unescapable reality."

"I'm made out of dead babies, too, what does that make me?" Polly asked.

"That's hardly the same thing at all," Titus said testily.

Polly's brain was whirling rapidly. So that was why, as much respect as she had for him and fond as she had always been of Stephen, his approach still made her belly ache and the hairs on the back of her neck prickle. It explained so many things. She was nearly consumed with indignation on Stephen's behalf. What was done was wicked, but he was not the guilty party.

"I don't care, plenty of people seem perfectly pleasant until you get to know them, Stephen just happens to be the other way round," she said angrily. "Sort of the anti-Mr. Albinus."

"Mr. Albin…" He looked at her as if he were slightly confused. "What are you saying? Polly?"

"Look who's asking stupid questions," she huffed. "You have everything, money, family, fortune, you're so sodding charming, and yet everything you do is calculated to benefit one person, yourself. Now finish the story, what happened after Stephen was born?"

Titus looked disconcerted but he plowed on. "Aurelius Magesteri took to drink and eventually the whole sordid story came out. He assumed full responsibility, shielding my Aunt Euphemia, Stephen's mother, from any repercussions, legal repercussions, at least, and as a result ended his own life like an honorable Roman around my fifth birthday. Stephen's mother tried to love him, but she didn't not find herself up to the task, as you can well imagine." He looked away again. "She found her courage and took her own life soon after. In any event, there were many who said Stephen should not have been allowed to live. Full of fear and ignorance he was unable to control his abilities. Those with the power to decide such things sent one Uncommon trainer after another, each as ignorant as the boy himself, to teach my cousin to control his powers."

"They all failed?" Polly asked wide-eyed.

"They all died," Titus said. "Until a commoner with an interest in the how and why of things was sent. He was a climber, that one. He'd made quite a stir at the museum pestering all the departments with his suggestions; mind you he was right most of the time even though he technically nothing but a messenger. I believe Old Edney was trying was trying to get rid of him when he assigned him as Stephen's teacher. That commoner was Henry Plumber."

"My Papa?" Polly asked. Somehow this was the most shocking thing, to learn how her Papa had gained access to the halls of power.

"Of course as soon as Stephen was proven to be in control of his abilities he was sent to war in Her Majesty's service, as was I. In General Khufu's regiment and your father along with us," Titus said his eyes focused on something far away. "Though Khufu soon decided Stephen was a bit old for a wet nurse and reassigned your maker to the reclamation unit."

"But he was sickened by what he was asked to do, his heart wasn't in it," she said uncertain whether she was referring to Stephen killing people or her father sewing together pieces of dead commoners together in order to reanimate them and throw them at the enemy again. The wrecks were stupid lumbering things, barely aware enough to follow orders, nothing like her, even though she'd long known that was where her papa got the idea of making her. She wondered for a moment if Titus would prefer she be more like them, and in that moment she despised him.

He blanched, looking surprised.

"He might have been made by dark arts, but he's a good man," she said with her patented indignation. "I'm not so sure about you."

"You aren't so sure about me?" he asked, disgust clear in his voice. "After all I've told you, you call Stephen Magesteri good but you're not certain about me?"

"My Papa trusts you not to harm me, but I'm beginning to think he may be somewhat fallible," she said, then wondered if she had said the wrong thing. She decided she didn't care. "Everyone trusts you. And by the same token my papa trusts Stephen with his clerks and apprentices and they're all UnCommon.

He could kill any one at any time if he likes and yet he doesn't. He cares for people. In fact he cares for everyone far more than he's willing to let on. As far as I can see you make great show of being nice but only truly care for yourself." From her own experience, her own knowledge, she knew of a dozen instances of dangerous experiments in the laboratory where Mr. Magesteri had saved Will or Guy, and even Charlie, for whom Stephen Magesteri had roughly as much fondness as he had for a pile of rat droppings.

It was one thing to risk your life for someone you cared for, but something far greater to endanger your self on behalf of someone you despised. She knew Stephen Magesteri was driven to do the right thing, just as he was driven to say the most ugly thing he could imagine. Who could imagine fighting the darkness so hard as Professor Magesteri did? She felt quite certain she loved him, now.

"I most certainly do not," Titus said aghast. "What about you?"

"What about me?" Polly asked, angry and confused.

"I love you," Titus said through gritted teeth.

"You do not!" Polly shouted. "You take that back this instant."

"I most certainly will not," Titus insisted. "I love all my wives."

Polly couldn't help herself, she screamed.

"You are, without a doubt, the most selfish, willfully stupid, untrustworthy… you do realize, your line is practically identical to Stephen's father's? In fact it's technically slightly more incestuous thanks to your father's additions. Have you been telling yourself it's simply bad luck that you've lost four wives in child-birth?" Polly said

"What else could it possibly be?" Titus asked.

"You, stupid, you're a menace to womankind. Whatever it is you put in them, sooner or later it's deadly. Not so different than Stephen except you take longer, so there's more suffering. You think he's defective, but you're no better than he is. At least he bloody cares if he hurts people," Polly said grabbing Titus by his collar.

"I never," Titus said his eyes wide and his skin beginning to shimmer and fade but Polly kept her grip tight on the cloth. "I never forced…anyone. I have never forced myself on you."

"You couldn't force me if you tried, Titus Albinus," Polly said her brain speeding like a train. "But as for the others, you do realize, they had no choice, don't you? Or do you think the women of the Empire have nothing better to do than die to make sure Titus Albinus has a baby? What'll you do if you get one and it doesn't go with the décor? Women, babies, wallpaper, other people; what's the difference? We're all just things to you. The only reason you want a baby of your own is because you haven't got one and it's hard to go out and buy one that'll look good beside you in a portrait. It might as well be a diamond stick pin."

"Childbirth," Titus said narrowing his eyes, "is every woman's duty. She owes it to the Empire just as every man owes military service. Soldiers die in defense of Empire just as women die in childbed. I had no more choice than your precious Stephen when I was conscripted."

"That's what conscription means, isn't it?" Polly said. That's what had happened to her, hadn't it? She'd been conscripted into marriage and like a fool she'd followed the orders of her elders and betters because they were wiser and more powerful. She was beginning to question that wisdom of late. She despised Titus Albinus in that moment, even as she meditated on the taste of his semen in the back of her throat.

"But I serve happily and with honor, because I love my Empress as I love her Empire and if I were to die in her service, I die having done my duty, as my wives did theirs, and I will take my place beside them among the honored dead," Titus said, becoming solid to the eye again. "Duty and sacrifice are the lynchpins of the machine of state. If the individual shirks the entire edifice crumbles."

"You do know you're a bloody fool, don't you?" Polly said. "A selfish fool. Honored dead. Dishonored Dead. It means nothing. They're not any less dead simply because they got an extra line or two on their grave marker. "

Titus glared. "What precisely is that supposed to mean?"

124

"I think I explained that rather thoroughly," Polly told him. "Also I'll be sleeping in the spare room tonight."

"Which one?" Titus asked.

"I don't know, one that hasn't got you in it," Polly said then paused, remembering how all this stupidity had started. "And by the way, it wasn't your cousin I learned that from, it was Ovid."

"Ovid the writer?" Titus asked his head cocked to one side.

"And I got my practice on Charlie Edney," Polly smiled a wicked smile at her husband.

"Stephen's apprentice, Edney? The one with the horns?" Titus asked shock apparent on his features. "That pathetic excuse for a minotaur?"

"The very one," Polly said and made her way upstairs.

In the morning there was no note from Titus. Not that Polly cared. She spent some concentrated time with her ladies maid and took a hansom cab to the Museum.

"I've come to see the Viscount," was the very first thing Stephen heard when he turned off his blowtorch, in a familiar high pitched voice.

A whisper of "Polly" "Polly" "Is that really Polly?" "Our Polly?" rippled through the department.

Stephen removed his goggles and stuck his head out the door just in time to see a creature that was as much the work of some ambitious ladies maid as Henry Plumber.

"Your Ladyship," Stephen said, wiping the sweat from his brow on his leather apron.

Polly, being Polly, snorted and marched right past him into his private laboratory.

"To what do I owe the unexpected pleasure?" Stephen said raising his eyes to the clock on the wall. "I'm not due for tea for another hour and a half. You're usually still half-asleep in your jim jams at this hour."

"I can change my habits if I like," Polly sniffed at him.

Stephen shrugged. "Suit yourself, it doesn't make a whit of difference to me when you get up."

"Titus told me, he told me everything," Polly blurted.

Stephen turned on his heel and shut the door behind him with a click.

"I believe this is the third time you've told me that, forgive me if I find the statement less than illuminating; the other two times, he told you fuck all," Stephen said, his hands on his goggles ready to slide them back into place so he could go back to his blow torch.

"He told me about Aurelius," Polly said. "About my papa, and General Khufu."

Stephen could have asked which Aurelius she meant: his dear departed, never-known brother, or his shit-smear of a father; it hardly mattered. It seemed he'd left nothing out of this round of airing the stained sheets.

"What do you want, a biccy? Because if that's what you're waiting for. I get all my biccies from your house these days," Stephen said.

"I don't care. It's not your fault. You aren't at fault. Why didn't you tell me? I'd've still rather married you than Titus, he's hateful, positively hateful," Polly said, slapping the work table.

"No, he's not, he's a respectable member of the aristocracy, Polly," Stephen forced himself to say. "A decorated officer...."

"But you're the one I love," Polly said, with deadly focus.

"And Titus's your husband," Stephen reminded her.

"So bloody what?" Polly said. "He didn't give a fig how I felt when he asked me to marry him. Why should I care how he feels now?"

Stephen wanted to find a good counter argument, but he couldn't when the half-arsed Duchess Londinium Austri reached across him.

He thought perhaps Polly was attempting the secure the door latch, which was a stupendously bad idea. The two of them had far too much privacy already.

Stephen reached to stop Polly's hand and in a moment of utter chaos her foot tangled with his feet and they fell with a resounding crash, both of them on the floor.

"Did you hear what I said? I love you, Mr. Magesteri. Did you get that bit?" Polly asked, her right elbow planted firmly in the middle of his chest and her chin in her hand.

"Stephen, Polly, my name is Stephen," he said, and felt idiotic as soon as the words were out of his mouth.

Polly nodded, putting one gloved finger on his chin, then carefully, slowly used three finger tips to caress his cheek. Oh, but she was a horrid, clever, girl and drew her fingers up to his temples and through his hair, relieving him of his goggles in the process.

"I love you, Stephen and I'm fairly certain you love me back," Polly said, sitting astride him. He could feel the furnace like heat coming off her. That, and the fact that she still hadn't adopted the new fashion of wearing knickers. Polycorpus as always, was equal parts torment and delight.

"You belong to Titus," Stephen said stupidly. He was so hard he could barely think.

"Oh codswallop, you tried to give me to your cousin, Titus. You and my father, but I'm not yours to give. Do you know who I belong to, Stephen? I only just worked it out," Polly said opening his trousers and, oh, Set, Isis, Apophis, Apollo, pulling out his todger.

"You belong to me. You're mine, you were made for me," Stephen groaned.

"Umm no, try again," Polly said leaning forward to press her mouth to his mouth. Polly broke contact just long enough to speak again. "I don't belong to a person, because I'm not born, I'm made. I'm no one's child. I belong to this place. I belong to the Museum. And so do you."

"You're mad and this is the most pig-buggering shite mountain of an idea I have ever witnessed," Stephen said.

"Want me to stop?" Polly asked. She ground her hips for emphasis.

"Don't. You. Dare," Stephen muttered.

"And would you like to know something else?" Polly said lifting her hips and taking him inside her.

Stephen gasped. Polly was different than other women, this much had been proven, she wouldn't die from making love to him, but instead she might well kill him.

"What?" he asked his voice unrecognizable to his own ears.

"I've also worked out that you're good. You try to hide it but you work quite hard at being good," Polly said driving him mad.

Stephen reached up and with all his strength took a fistful of her hair and pulled her to him. Luckily for him Polly didn't decide to put up any resistance when he pulled her face to his. "Take it back," he whispered.

"I won't. You can't make me, because it's true," Polly answered him.

"I doubt Titus would agree with you," Stephen grunted, guilt and terror all that held his climax at bay.

"Titus is an arse," Polly said angrily.

"Titus is a good man," Stephen insisted between kisses, because he knew it was true.

"Titus is a nice man, there's a difference," Polly said, almost to herself, as Stephen spent himself inside her. She seemed to have been motivated by anger rather than pleasure. There didn't appear to have been anything in the ordeal for her.

After some moments Polly felt little drops of wetness roll down her cheeks but the tears were not hers.

Chapter 10 : A Surprising Conversation

Titus Posthumous Albinus did not sleep well after the row with his wife and as a result was out of sorts all morning.

He attempted to leave her the usual affectionate morning note but it was futile; the words obstinate and infuriating kept worming their way into the text, despite his wish to be charming and conciliatory. He had no idea what had got into him. He was charming and even tempered. It was an agreed upon fact. More than that, he was fairly certain that most people, if pressed, would agree these were his defining characteristics.

Titus never lost his temper. It was the rule he bloody lived by! In any difference of opinion, the best argument was no argument at all. Titus had perfected the art of agreeing with his opponent until he was able to slowly carefully turn their head round to his way of thinking. If forced into a direct confrontation, which he disliked intensely and inevitably saw as a sort of admission of weakness, the first man to lose his temper invariably, and without question, also lost the argument.

And Titus never lost his temper.

Until now.

Until Polly.

Which was problematic on a number of levels, not the least of which was the simple truth that he had no idea what they had quarreled over. Oh, he recalled the discussion from beginning to end and every single word between. It was one of Titus's unique gifts to recall every word uttered in his presence, though his memory for the visual was far less exacting. No, he knew precisely what had been said by both parties, what he was less than certain about was where the conflict lay.

All Titus had done was make perfectly sure that Polly understood about Stephen, and why he would never make a husband. Not for any woman. Not even for an extraordinary example like Polly herself.

Particularly not an extraordinary example like Polly herself.

Somehow it had all gone horridly…horrid and Titus had no idea how or why.

All he knew for certain was that it was not his fault.

He wondered, based on the anxious look Llewelyn gave him as he rose from the cold water, leaving the frigidarium behind him, waiting for his towel, if his usual masseur would be available. It was that sort of a day, where every thing that could conceivably go wrong appeared to be heading that way. An inadequate massage would only serve to compound his bad mood, and Titus was never in a bad mood.

He felt a bit presentient upon entering the Unctorium and seeing the Provincial Governor stretched out on the table of his favorite masseuse, Polonius. In fact the only empty table was manned by a short little commoner with a face like a turnip and the hands of a thirteen year old girl.

Titus cast a forced smile at Llewelyn and then at the masseur before lying on the table. If nothing else he needed to at least attempt a rub down before he straightened out all this business with Polly.

He wanted it all set to rights by tea. The trouble was the female was so unfathomable he hardly knew where to begin. He knew only that he was blameless, so the trouble must, by a process of elimination, lie with her. Then it hit him, the answer was so startlingly obvious he nearly leapt off the table midmassage; he'd go to Stephen, surely his cousin would come to his aid.

Stephen Propertius Drusus Magesteri had all his life been unwavering in his faith in the gods, now more so than ever.

It was the only reasonable explanation for his wretched life. The gods hated him.

Mere bad luck couldn't even begin explain it. The odds of one man being as put upon as Stephen Magesteri were astronomical.

The one, as in one and only, female he could touch without harm, had fucked him, without care, without concern, without so much as a single thought for his feelings, solely on account of her husband, his cousin and closest, perhaps only, friend. Polly had made a betrayer of him, slowly hardening his heart to the man he had once thought of as his other, better, self. Like a worm the very fact of her existence was eating away at what heart he had.

Of course she had only married Titus at his insistence. Never mind that it was for her own good and unquestionably best for all concerned. That was probably Aphrodite's idea of a joke; his reward for noble self-sacrifice. There were syphilitic goats with better fortune than Stephen Magesteri.

Choking back tears he did up his trousers and, wiping his eyes and nose on the back of his sleeve, put back on his goggles, starting up his blow torch once more.

Twenty minutes later - he could have set his pocket watch by it - Stephen was interrupted by the sound of shouting over the general din of the department of invention.

"What ho? What ho? What ho?" Titus called over the roar of machines, cheerful as ever, the stupid git.

"G'way, I'm busy," Stephen called back not bothering to dampen the flame on his torch.

"Oh, don't be that way, oh cousin of mine. I've run into a bit of a sticky patch with the Duchess. Not so much a sticky patch as a slight misunderstanding, a little nothing, these things happen... and I thought who better than to give me a smattering of insight than Stephen. He's known her since she was just so many pieces in so many jars," Titus said brightly.

For the first time in his life Stephen didn't, for a moment, considered telling the truth.

"What part of 'busy' is confusing you, Tight-arse?" Stephen said not looking up from his work.

"I wouldn't try for truculent if I were you, Stephen. A man in your shape tends to come off as merely dyspeptic," Titus said, thinking himself witty, the shit.

Stephen left his goggles on but turned down his torch. "What did you bugger up this time, then?"

"That's just it. I'll be damned if I know why the creature has taken offense, only that she has," Titus looking uncharacteristically serious. If Stephen didn't know him better he'd say…worried? Could that be right? Was Titus Albinus worried? "Stephen, she said, she said, she didn't like me."

Stephen watched in fascination as Titus shook his head in consternation. It wasn't worried. It was hurt. Polly had hurt Titus's feelings. Stephen was not going to be the one to tell him, there was a wagonload more where that came from.

"Did she say why?" Stephen coughed out the words somehow. All he wanted was for Mr. and Mrs. Albinus both to sod off and stop trying to pull him into their marital discord. Couldn't a man die alone and unloved in peace, anymore?

Titus scratched the back of his neck. Then he sat down on the edge of a work table. Then he crossed and re-crossed his legs.

Even through Stephen's green glass goggles he looked uncomfortable. Good, they were even. Stephen turned away and fired up his torch again, sparks arcing through the air.

"She says I'm stupid and self-centered. She also," Titus started in a rush but the words ran out of steam quickly, "she also blames me for the… the deaths of Hathor and the others. She says, she says the most extraordinary things. She says females, females, haven't…."

It was bloody peculiar, Titus never faltered in repeating a conversation, it seemed almost as though what Polly had said was so unbelievable Titus could hardly bring himself to repeat it.

"She seems to think they haven't enough autonomy to render meaningful consent. And this is somehow my fault."

Stephen snorted. From where he stood Polycorpus was a fine one to quibble about autonomy and consent. "Sounds like a load of overblown shit to me. There's only one freedom for any of us, and that's in the family crypt. What your wife needs is a hobby. She sounds bored. I've only heard a minute or two of it and I'm bored already."

Titus swung his feet and tilted his head to one side like a bloody bird. "So you don't think I killed them?"

Stephen paused. He wished Titus hadn't asked that question. He felt something squirming in his gut, unable to keep still. His hair had fallen in his face but he let it be, preferring to squint through the greasy black strands. He shrugged. "I'll be fucked if I know."

"Is that what people say?" Titus said.

That poor bugger, thinking he knew every shitty little thing people whispered behind closed doors. That poor bugger. Titus had likely heard it a hundred times and never for all the world imagined it was him, Londinium Austri, they were talking about.

Stephen knew he ought to apply some smooth untruth, but he'd done all the deceiving he could manage for one day; his lying muscles were sore. Instead, he said nothing.

Titus looked oddly inward, sitting very still and straight on the edge of the work table. "So Polycorpus married me, and you encouraged her to marry me, believing I had brought about the deaths of my previous four wives."

"I never said it was intentional on your part and Polly is more or less indestructible." Stephen felt compelled to make sure Titus understood he hadn't meant harm to either of them. No, it was for the best. He'd thought he'd solved everyone's problems at once going along with Titus's idea of marrying Polly. "I told her you were still a better choice. You are the better choice."

Even as he said the words Stephen believed it with his whole heart. Titus was a better husband for Polly, if only the girl would open her fool eyes.

"Thank you, Stephen, this does shed a rather different light on the situation," Titus said. "Oh look," he said, drawing out his pocket watch and everything about him changing in a flash. "It's almost time for tea. Get your coat."

Stephen shook his head, he couldn't face Polly again today for all the chocolate biccies in Londinium.

"Busy, remember?" Stephen said waving his torch.

"Suit yourself," Titus said with a sigh, and hopped down from the work bench.

It was about bleeding time. This wasn't the Duke's private salon; there was work to be done.

And so it was that Polly came home and cleaned off every trace of Stephen and had the Ladies maid, Bridgid, touch up her hair and makeup before tea. It was hardly the first time she'd managed to make a mess of herself before her husband came home, though it was the first time she'd felt bad about it. Duchess or not, even under the best of circumstance Polly didn't seem to be able to keep herself presentable for long.

After she was primped Polly occupied herself by feeling terrible, though she wasn't sure exactly why.

It was a nagging feeling in the gut, mostly.

Was it Titus? Did she feel bad for being unfaithful to Titus? Polly didn't think so, particularly since she hadn't been the one to give her word that she would be faithful. No, other people had given her word for her, and he'd taken it. So she didn't feel bad for Titus. Or, if she did it was stupid. She was stupid. His attachment to her was all image and no substance.

Stephen, then? Did she feel bad for Stephen? As near as she had been able to put together she was the only woman Stephen could be intimate with without fatal results, so why should she feel bad for being with him? Why should she? Polly wondered.

On the surface there was no good reason for her to feel so wretched. It was a good thing Polly knew a surface examination of anything was useless.

A feeling not entirely unlike a pain crowding in her head, Polly plopped herself down on an over-stuffed ottoman in the second best parlor. She wasn't sure why they rarely even set foot in the nicest one, and thought she would busy herself thinking until Titus and Stephen arrived home for tea.

"Polly." It was Titus's voice as clear as a deep rich bell but she didn't see him anywhere.

"Titus?" Polly called, suddenly terrified. Was that why she felt bad? Fear of being caught? If so it was the lowest, meanest form of guilt, like a naughty child. Still, she imagined Titus could hurt her quite successfully if he put his mind to it, so it was also fairly reasonable. She had learned enough in six months of marriage to know he was not an atom as harmless as he seemed.

Polly stood and turned slowly in a circle. "You know I don't like it when you do this," she warned him.

"Please, Polly, allow me to do this in my own way," he said, his voice coming from right behind her.

Polly would have turned to face the sound but invisible arms reached round her hips from behind and held her fast, she couldn't move without physically fighting him and physically hurting Titus was not what she wanted to do today.

It took her a moment to understand what Titus was doing in his invisible state. He was on his knees, that much was clear; he towered over her, ordinarily. He had his arms wrapped round her belly and his face, it felt like his face, pressed up against the small of her back. What on earth was he doing that for? It was not the position of a man who had come to confront an adulterous wife.

"Titus?" she asked nervously.

No answer came.

"Please, please, don't," she said, she could feel him speaking into the cloth of her dress but she couldn't make out the words.

"Polly, are Stephen and I, are we truly equivalent? Am I…like him?" he stuttered.

"He's not my husband," was all Polly could think to say because she didn't quite understand what Titus was asking her.

"Am I tainted, Polly? Is that what people say?" Titus said in a voice that was almost a whisper, still his arms held her tight. "Is that why you disdain me so?"

"I get angry with you because you're priggish and arrogant. I don't give a toss about what people say," Polly said with a sigh, and it was mostly true, unless the rumor meant she was in jeopardy every time she climbed into bed with him.

"What do they say, Polly?" Titus asked her backbone. "People?"

"Bad blood," she said, simply, and felt him shudder against her.

Against her back she could feel him shaking, his chest rising and falling, oh Isis, her back was growing wet. Was he weeping? He must be but it staggered Polly's imagination. First Stephen and now Titus, was she to make all the boys cry today?

"And yet, you married me," Titus said, sniffling.

"I hadn't much choice," Polly said honestly. "I've never gone against my papa's wishes. Not that he's ever asked much of me, aside from marrying you."

"I am grateful," Titus told her back sounding for all the world like Charlie Edney when she'd pulled his bacon out of the fire with some project for Professor Magesteri. "I will remain grateful for the rest of my days."

Polly didn't say a word, simply held still whilst he clung to her.

"Stephen is like a brother to me. The greatest friend I've ever had. Truth be told the only friend worthy of the name but still I bless the day the gods decided to reveal you to the oracle so that I could know to take you from him," Titus said his breath beginning to slow.

The Oracle of Apollo.

Nefrit.

"Why?" Polly asked quietly, in spite of the fact she wanted to scream it.

"I love my cousin, Polly. I want him to have such happiness as he can, but now I understand, I understand why the gods have put you and I together. I understand why my feelings for you are not like those I had for…the others. You are my destiny. My true love. My salvation," Titus said. "The one woman in all the world the gods have meant for me."

Polly was glad he couldn't see her cringe.

The Oracle had put all this in his head.

It was then, at that precise moment, that Polly realized Titus and Stephen were both as much pawns as she was, whether they understood what was happening or not, and she had done them both wrong.

She had every reason in the world to feel bad.

Just as a pig returns predictably to his slops and a dog is wholly incapable of leaving his own vomit well enough alone, Stephen returned the next day to Titus and Polly's house for tea.

He reminded himself that Titus would be suspicious if he didn't show up two days in succession besides some of the finest chocolate in the Islands was singing a siren song. He blamed his cousin, Tight-Arse habitually took the best of everything as his birthright.

The most delicious food, the sweetest perfumes, the softest linens, and then there was Polly. But Polly was hardly Titus's fault now was she? If Stephen had stood up to Titus when he'd asked Stephen to act as go between and told the bloody duke he wanted her for his own Titus might well have stepped aside. Possibly. Or maybe not.

Stephen wasn't sure and he refused to think any more on the topic, it was giving him a headache.

He rapped his knuckles against the front door and was surprised when instead of one of Titus's army of interchangeable servants Polly herself opened the door.

"Stephen," she said biting her lip

Since when had she done that? Stephen didn't like it one little bit.

"Polly." Stephen gave her a short nod; he didn't know what else to do. Coming at all was a mistake, Titus's suspicions be damned.

"I'm sorry for my behaviour yesterday. It was thoughtless of me. I'm very sorry, very, very sorry," Polly said as though she'd lain in bed all night practicing it in her head.

"You ought to be," Stephen said, because it was the truth.

Stephen's stomach was saved any further mutual soul searching by Titus galloping down the corridor like an unbroken horse, grinning ear to ear. He was both relieved and ground down ever so slightly to see that Polly was bright enough to leave her husband out of their shared stupidity.

"What ho! What ho! Oh, Osiris of the steam engine? Good to see you could take time from your hectic schedule to eat my biscuits," Titus said his hands on Polly's shoulders.

Something had changed between the two of them, apparently for the better. How fucking complimentary. Another round with Stephen had worked to convince Polly of Titus's relative merit. Lovely. Never mind that it was what Stephen wanted, what he prayed for, what he knew was right and just, it was still a bleeding kick in the gut.

Stephen felt it full force to see Titus kiss Polly's knuckles not once but twice before the three of them sat down in the parlor. When he threw himself on the settee the three of them usually shared, he was taken aback to see Titus take the chair opposite and tug Polly into his lap.

"Nooo." Polly giggled, twisting away from him. "I'll squash you."

"Cut it out, if I wanted to have tea with addle-pated juveniles, I'd've gone to the apprentice's dining hall. You're ruining my digestion," Stephen snarled.

"How droll." Titus chuckled giving Polly a fond, there was no other word for it, a fond look, as she plopped herself down on the ottoman, like no duchess before or since.

"So," Polly said leaning forward. "How is your focused light generator coming along?"

Stephen was frankly relieved to be granted a topic that was not only safe but also somewhat interesting. "Sod all for days but then yesterday I cut a hole clean through the wall to Oullette's work station. Six inches to the right and there'd be an opening for a new apprentice in the Department of Invention."

"Tough luck, that," Tight-arse, the ignoramus, said jocularly.

"No no, Titus, that's very good news. It's meant to do that, more or less," Polly said.

"There was a slight fire, nothing too big, nothing Virgil's crew couldn't deal with, and the whole blasted contraption melted itself again, but I am getting close," Stephen said round the biscuit in his mouth.

"It's probably a question of truly understanding the principles of light," Polly said leaning too far forward and putting those tits of her on display "If you truly understood the nature of light, the laws that bind it, its composition...."

"What under Nuut's starry sky are you two talking about?" Titus said, clearing his throat for Polly to sit up straight, not that she noticed.

Stephen wondered if Polly knew how to explain the project to an unmechanical git like Titus. Stephen certainly didn't.

Polly frowned. "Professor Magesteri is attempting to build a tool that focuses, that creates a pure beam of light."

"To what end?" Titus asked.

"I've got to build it first, don't I," Stephen said, taking another biscuit, accidentally a plain one this time "before I work out all the applications."

"And why did you say what you said? 'If you truly understood the nature of light, the laws that bind it, it's composition....' what does that mean? Principles of light? What are you talking about? Light is light," Titus said.

Polly turned on the ottoman to face her husband, half slipping off one shoe and turning it in a circle with her foot. "But what is light made of, Titus? What gives it its different properties? Why does it pass through glass and not through steel? Or, or, or why does your peacock waistcoat look iridescent in sunlight and a touch drab by candlelight?"

Titus made a concentrating face, Stephen wasn't sure if it was ridiculous or worrisome. "When put that way it seems an eminently sensible line of inquiry. It's a wonder I have never asked myself before."

"In order to make proper use of a thing, like light, it's imperative we understand its basic composition and rules that govern its workings," Polly said.

"What a load of fetid dog-rot, we constantly exercise powers we've no notion of…" Stephen started before the bloody duchess rudely interrupted him.

"You mean grope blindly, because we're wedded to asinine Aristolean…" Polly said.

It was an old argument, one they'd had been refining since Polly was 12. Stephen replied as he always replied. "You only say that because you're a commoner, if you'd been born with an ability, one you exercised as easily as taking a biscuit from a tray," Stephen said illustrating his point not realizing Titus had risen to his feet. "You would know that some things are simply gifts from the gods, to use as best as we are able."

Titus stood over him in two strides.

"Take it back," Titus said quietly.

"He didn't mean anything by it," Polly said jumping off her ottoman to wrap her hand round Titus's wrist.

Stephen wasn't quite sure what "it" was, so he took another biscuit.

"I will not countenance insults to my wife in my own house, not even from you, Stephen," Titus warned quietly.

Stephen shrugged, the big idiot was wounded to hear Polly called common. Stephen reckoned those society matrons said far worse. Still it was a good sign that he cared.

"Sorry," Stephen said. "Since you married Titus you're not common any longer," he raised his face to his cousin. "Really, Titus, she never was properly ordinary in any sense of the word. An extraordinary creation from day one."

Then Stephen took two biscuits and put both in his mouth at once. Purely as a precautionary measure. It was a funny turn where Stephen Magesteri was expected to calm Titus Albinus. It made Stephen feel confused and ridiculous at the same time.

Titus nodded and sat back in his chair.

Chapter 11 : A New Day

ow is your mother, Dearest?" Titus's mother, The Dowager Lady Aurora, said, because that was the first thing she said to her daughter-in-law every Monday at 10:45 a.m.

"Fine, Mrs..." Polly started but Titus leapt in, he should have put an end to the deception some time ago.

"Mother, perhaps I ought to have told you sooner, but Livia Canavan is Polycorpus's adopted mother," Titus said. "She was in fact built by Henry Plumber at the British Museum."

Mother clapped her hands happily. "I was wondering why you didn't smell like the other Canavans; they positively reek of saltwater, in a nice way, of course. Making a daughter! I've never heard of that before, Gussie," Mother said grabbing at the edge of Aunt Augusta's sleeve. "Henry Plumber is your friend, isn't he? Why don't you have him make you a little daughter? It would be so lovely to have a little girl to play with and love. Or didn't you know he could make you one?"

Aunt Augusta took Mother's hand from her sleeve and patted it. "Now Aurora, you remember what happened with the monkey."

"That was so sad," Mother agreed. "Still a little girl, a very little girl...would be terribly sweet to have."

Titus cast his gaze out the window to the garden where the now stone monkey, tail raised high, was a favorite roosting spot for pigeons.

"Some little girls are sweeter than others," Aunt Augusta said. "You should be grateful for what you have, Aurora."

"I didn't mean..." Mother said biting her lip for an instant before reaching out to Titus who leaned close for her to stroke his face. "You know I adore you, don't you, Darling?"

"Never doubted it for an instant, Dear Heart," he said kissing her hand.

"But did you know, Augusta, that Henry Plumber could make extraordinary children?" Mother asked.

"Of course, I did, Silly, who do you imagine he consulted when it came to her upbringing? Although he left it a bit long if you ask me," Aunt Augusta said with her characteristic waspishness. Apparently there was a strain of that sort of thing in his family that showed itself in Titus's cousin and auntie.

"So you haven't any mother?" Titus's mother asked, turning her head to where she estimated Polycorpus was. "Never, any mother at all?"

Titus eyed Polly closely as she grimaced. "No, only my papa, Henry Plumber, and the Museum."

Then Titus's mother reached out her hands, grasping both Polly and Titus.

"It's so sad and so perfect, Darling, you lost your father before you were born and Dearest Polly never had a mother," Mother tended to be very emotional, but she was right, she pulled Titus's young wife to her bosom "It's like poetry. From now on I am going to call you my Dearest to go with my Darling."

Titus couldn't help but grin at Polly, who had never known either the comfort or the embarrassment of being held to a mother's breast.

"Thank you," Polly squeaked.

"Let the girl go, Aurora," Aunt Augusta said with a sigh.

"She's never had a mother's love, Gussie, Completely bereft of feminine warmth," Mother countered.

"And no doubt our Polly is currently wishing you were a bit more manly in your affection," Aunt Augusta insisted.

"No, I'm, I'm fine," Polly said, her head still crushed to his Mother's chest.

"You're mine now, and I shall be yours, Dearest Polycorpus," his Mother said, petting Polly's head.

"I'm certain a warm handshake would suffice," Aunt Augusta said with a cough.

It was strange but with the new found blossoming of Albinus's marriage to Polly, which was accompanied by such treats as watching Titus kiss Polly's wrists a dozen times during tea when he was feeling restrained, just for the hell of it, Stephen Magesteri was aware for the first time in his life of the sensation of loneliness. That was not to say that he had never been lonely before, rather he had never been anything but lonely and so scarcely noticed it. He was now peculiarly aware of the sensation of not having Polly with him in the laboratory. He could make a request at tea that she come to the Museum and join him, he supposed, but he couldn't come up with a plausible excuse for the appeal. Besides it was inarguably a terrible, the worst sort of notion, a filthy cockroach of an idea.

He'd be buggered if he gave anyone the impression he required hand holding in order to go about his vocation. People would think he'd gone soft in the head.

There was nothing for it but to tolerate her absence and get on with his work. Yet he found he did not have the ability to completely leave behind the vision he had in his mind of her warm body breathing deep and even in Colonel Titus Albinus's bed.

The pain felt almost like his old curse acting up again.

He began to start the day with a breath or two of hashish, and if he was easier on his apprentices for it, they weren't complaining.

He also bought a little figure of Venus on the Queen's road to set on his personal shrine beside Imhotep and Apophis. He had no idea what he wanted her to grant him, only that he bleeding wanted it, whatever it was.

Titus stepped into his coach that had so conveniently required repairs, completing his reconnaissance at Wallace's house and falling onto the seat beside Polly barely holding in his laughter.

"Get anything good?" Polly asked.

"Nothing noteworthy," Titus managed to say though his words were strangled with the effort. "No plotting or disloyalty on Wallace's part. Not even petty corruption."

Titus bit his lip.

"There is something amiss, what is it?" Polly asked, her black eyes bright.

"His dogs…they're trained," Titus said.

"You mean the horde? They're like vermin; the plague of Yorkshire Terriers," Polly said.

"They're trained to lick…on cue…all of them…all thirteen…at once," Titus said starting to shake with the effort of holding in.

"Lick…lick what?" Polly asked looking worried. Polly's eyes squinted and her nose wrinkled.

"George Wallace," Titus said. That was it. He couldn't help himself. He burst out laughing.

"Should I ask where?" Polly asked.

Titus shook his head.

"You mean?? Ewwww" Polly said collapsing in a fit of giggles.

Titus had never had anyone to share these small silly moments with before, it was sublime. It wasn't until he was doubled over with laughter, more or less rolling on the floor of his carriage with his wife, that he realized how much he enjoyed being married to Polly in a way he'd never enjoyed being married before.

Oh he had admired Hathor, excessively. What else did one do with a siren but admire her? Lobelia had been perfectly dutiful and domestic. A veritable personification of hearth and home and wifely art. Drusilla had been, although painfully slow, as kind and comforting as any creature to walk this earth. He had hardly known Chandi but she was inarguably exquisite.

None of them had been fun. None of them were his friend, the way Polly was.

"Oh, it hurts," Polly said holding her side. "It hurts. I ate too much and my corset is too tight to laugh so hard."

And in that moment, laughing, his hands on her waist, stroking the silk brocade as well as the wheezing woman underneath, it occurred to Titus that while he would regret not having a child, and could, perhaps, never let go of the hope for one, he would be perfectly happy to spend the rest of his life like this, with Polly as his companion. Truly, the gods had been kind.

Polly inhaled sharply trying to catch her breath, Titus Albinus laughing and wheezing against her shoulder.

She'd never had as much fun in her life, not doing anything in particular, as she did with Titus Albinus. Charlie could never quite keep up with her and Stephen…she wondered why she couldn't stop comparing Titus, for good or ill, with Stephen. Particularly when she considered the way Stephen always, inevitably, shut down once things between them once they became too pleasant, like an engine with a faulty safety valve.

Polly wondered why no one else had ever taken the trouble to have fun with her. Her father was too busy and Mrs. Brolly too formal and Charlie Edney too slow, much as she hated to admit it. She turned her face to kiss Titus's forehead just so. He smiled, twisting the corners of his mouth and she inhaled the smell of him. He didn't wear a scent, which had surprised her at first, until she realized it was a dead give away for an invisible spy.

The smell of his body had grown on her over the past few months and gone from something she noted to something she anticipated.

Polly planted a kiss on his high sharp cheek feeling the rasp of a face that had last been shaved that morning at the baths.

"This is nice," Titus murmured resting against her. "I quite like…this… you…being together this way."

"The feeling's mutual," Polly said not knowing it was true until she said it.

And it occurred to Polly that while she did like it very much herself, at the same time she felt a bit bad about something she couldn't quite put her finger on. Perhaps that wasn't it at all. It seemed…the real feeling was she wished she'd had more of this. Sooner. Had she been lonely before?

Polly wondered what it might have been like to have attention and friendship like this all her life. For that she'd have to have a different sort of papa. A less busy, less distracted, sort of papa.

A papa more like Titus. Polly wondered what it would be like to be Titus's child while Titus kissed her earnestly on the neckbolt the way he liked to do. His warm breath made her shiver.

She reached up and touched his hair.

"Titus, I do wish you would let your hair grow, a bit, just long enough to run my fingers through properly," she said humming in pleasure at his affectionate kisses.

"Would you like that?" Titus asked. "Then your wish is my command. You know, I was thinking."

Polly suppressed the urge to ask if it had tickled, there was no point in being snide. "Oh, were you?"

"You know how you pleasure me at times? After the manner described by Ovid? Some women find it a questionable practice, but do you think I might try my hand at a bit of reciprocity?" Titus said nuzzling her ear.

"I thought you'd never ask," Polly groaned. Oh Mighty Isis, she loved Titus Albinus.

For the first time since marriage had been mentioned in her presence she thought of a child with something other than terror. It might be even nice.

She could quite easily picture Titus Albinus with curly headed boy on his knee, the two of them laughing. It was when she tried to fit herself into the pic-ture that the whole thing fell apart. Not that it mattered. Children belonged to their fathers, after all. And there would be nurses and governesses and nannies which was good because Polly had no idea what to do with a child, much less a baby. She supposed she was like her own papa that way. She felt for him, having built a child with no notion what to do with it after it was made and working properly. The difference for Polly being, she had Titus and it occurred to her she might want to give him a baby. The more she thought on it the more she thought she did, she did want to give him a baby.

And the oracle herself had sworn Polly could give Titus a child. Surely Polly's papa had been wrong about this; oracles could see the future. They weren't all drugged or mad or liars. At least Polly hoped they weren't.

As soon as they were home Polly would throw away her asafetida, lest her resolve falter.

Chapter 12 : A Change in The Weather

ed Shoes. Titus had never imagined a simple pair of red shoes could be so much trouble. All Titus wanted was to buy his wife a pair of fur-lined shoes with staggered heels to compensate for the unequal length of her legs in a blood red leather to match the Red Cathay silk lining of the fur coat he intended to give her at the same time. How difficult was it to make the outside of the shoes the same color as the inside of the coat? Apparently every bit as difficult as it was to make the fur lining of the shoes match the fur of the coat without sacrificing the quality of either. Was perfection truly so much to ask?

And the day before the start of Saturnalia.

The weather was cooperating perfectly with Titus's plans, turning dark and cold. She'd have good cause to make use of her gifts right away.

If only the furrier and the cobbler would do likewise.

Titus removed his watch from his pocket and checked the time. He was going to be late to tea. He struggled not to grind his back teeth. Beyond the front window of the shoe shop snow began to drift down in great lazy sooty grey flakes.

Seven months. That, in Stephen's estimation, was what it had taken for Polly to fall completely under Titus's spell. It was something of a record. Normally a female's petticoats simply melted as he walked past. Polly made him work at it, though. Even now that Polly was, in Stephen's estimation, in the bag, Titus was more off balance than Stephen had ever seen him. Swanning along by all outward appearances but paddling for all he was worth beneath the surface. He could only assume it was love, not reasonable staid husbandly love, no, rather a slavish trying to keep hold of a sodding electric eel beneath the table while dining with your Aunt Augusta sort of love, same as him. That or a head injury, one of the two.

Stephen watched the clock tick. Polly ate a tomato tart then rearranged the platter to make it look as though she hadn't. Six months ago, she wouldn't have bothered.

Stephen glanced at the clock again. That was a new one as well. Titus was late. Titus hated to be anything other than half an hour early, soirées not withstanding, though even with those his precious cousin had calculated the exact "proper" time of arrival and adjusted his jeweled time piece accordingly. The military credo of "Hurry-up and Wait" was a fully engrained part of his character. When they were boys the stupid git used to run, actually physically run, so he could stand at attention and wait to be whipped.

Stephen ate one of the biscuits from the stack on his plate and looked to Polly, or her décolletage, at least. She was finally at ease in her fashionable clothes and elaborate hairstyle. That had taken at least five months in itself. He wasn't sure how he felt about it.

"Titus has never been late before," Polly said her hand hovering over the sandwich platter.

"If you take any more you'll not be able to cover it up, not convincingly," Stephen said. "Titus isn't late, as a rule, it means something is on fire some place or he's been forced to stab someone and is having trouble getting the blood off his shoes."

Polly laughed nervously, as though he'd been joking. "Still he would have sent a message, you don't think he's vexed with me?"

Polly never took his moods seriously, why should she give a toss about Titus's?

A peal of thunder rattled the window and Polly leaped to her feet and rushed to pull back the curtain as though she was spring loaded and pressed her nose against the frosty glass. Stephen gripped the arm of the divan swallowing hard. In his experience Polycorpus and lightning were an unstable combination at best.

He craned his neck to search the blackened sky, but stayed rooted to his seat. He watched as Polly shifted from foot to foot, her head raised to the clouds. Then the world went mad. The walls shook and there was a roar and a scream like a great deal of glass shattering at once. Polly, clearly mad as a fish, ran towards the roar.

Stephen didn't care. He wasn't going to bloody follow her. He was not chasing Polly through piles of quivering bricks toward his certain death. She couldn't make him. Damn her. The least she could do was wait up.

Stephen steeled himself and made his way through the suddenly still house. The central rooms were a bloody mess. There was smoke everywhere. It looked like they'd taken canon fire but he didn't see Polly anywhere, which had been the bleeding point of following her in the first dog buggering place.

He opened the door to the Salamanderium, funny that. Half the walls were knocked down the ceiling had been shattered but the door was still standing. Still he opened the door, rather than step over the toppled bricks.

"Polly, you idiot girl, come back inside this instant," he shouted the minute he set foot on the muddy glass strewn ground.

"Get stuffed," Polly sang out. "If I can get the pumps going again I can save the bendies."

The whole business seemed past repair from what Stephen could see. The sky was black at noon except for the lightning that raced across the clouds from time to time. Stephen could only assume a lightning strike had caused the damage. Snow was blowing down hard and already beginning to accumulate on the ground. The peristylium itself was a shambles, twisted metal and broken glass everywhere. The eel tanks were shattered and the crustacean tanks as well. The cherry tree it had amused Titus to keep had been torn out of the ground by its roots. Most of the Hellbenders were dead and those few left alive were rapidly freezing. Not sure what else to do he picked one up, who was still moving, albeit feebly, and held it inside his top coat. It was then that he saw Malcolm, the damn thing's minder, dead, under the trunk of the cherry tree.

Too bad that.

He took the dead animal he'd held to his heart for warmth, all his snuggling hadn't done it a bit of difference, and fought against his urge to hurl it at the wall. Instead he laid it at Malcolm's side.

"Dammit, Polly!" Stephen shouted against the wind.

"If I can get these pumps up again I might be able to save some of them. They can't breathe without flowing water and the water can't flow without the pumps," she called.

"Did you see Malcolm?" Stephen said in a much lower voice.

"Yes, horrid, isn't it," Polly said, distractedly.

It was freezing and the wind was blowing, and his skin where he had held the dying animal was burning. He'd forgot for a minute the bleeding things were poison to the touch. That's what he got for his sentimentality, he thought, wiping his fingers on his trousers before rubbing his hands in the snowy stream.

"It doesn't matter, if they can breathe or not, they're all frozen to the ground," Stephen shouted still trying to get the burning sensation off his hands.

He looked up to see Polly, thoroughly soggy and disheveled, squinting at him.

"Of course, Stephen, you're a genius. Go get me a soup tureen, the big one blue one, for parties!" she shrieked, for all Stephen could tell having gone totally mad she reached down and stuck her arms in the muddy bank.

"What in the name of Imho..." Stephen started but Polly cut him off screaming.

"Go, Stephen, run," She shouted.

At a loss for an alternative, Stephen Magesteri obeyed.

When he returned, as good as his word, as quickly as he had it in him, Polly was sunk down into the mud to one shoulder, a wild look in her eyes.

"Give it here! No, don't hand it to me you numbskull, I've only one arm going at the moment," she chided like he was an apprentice. "There, that's a good boy."

With that Polly scooped a great armload of muck, like fishy tapioca, into the tureen.

The eggs. She'd managed to save the eggs. She really was as clever as he'd warned Titus.

"I got the lid," he said feeling stupid.

The two of them were standing there, snow piling on their shoulders, when Stephen saw Polly slowly raise her arms to the sky.

NO. Not now, not like this. He ran for all he was worth to get the eggs inside and get clear of Polly.

"Take this damn thing, will you?" He handed the tureen to Mrs. Hodson. "It's full of salamander eggs."

The servants were crowding the hall, looking at the smoking rubble.

Then it happened. Polly, being Polly, called the lightning down.

It broke like a scream and a crack and for a moment everything, the hall, the peristylium, everything, turned white. Then Polly, her dress torn and muddy and half burnt away, laughed, ringed in electricity like a thousand hissing blue snakes. She laughed and the whole house seemed to echo with it.

The servants seemed to step back as a group.

"I take it back, sir, I was stupid and ignorant when I told Plumly the Mistress was Common. Don't let her hurt us," one of the scullions whimpered falling to her knees.

"Don't feel bad, it's a common mistake," Stephen muttered watching Polly dancing in the broken glass and howling snow.

"Again, again," Polly screamed raising her hands to the sky. Beloved of Jupiter, was that why she was like this? Was it a god's favor that made her half-mad half the time and all mad the rest?

Stephen whipped round to address Titus's servants, he faced Llewelyn and Plumly as the senior staff. "I strongly suggest you all go quickly and quietly to your quarters. The Duchess doesn't mean harm when she's like this but that doesn't mean it's beyond her."

Another bolt of lightning shot down and Stephen observed how the silence seemed to echo this time, and how the blinding whiteness seemed to linger. It was only afterwards that the deafening roar came and he could see that the last vestiges of Polly's clothing had been burned away.

"Oh Stevie!" she said, laughing throwing wide the door. "Don't look so frightened. I've no intention of hurting anyone, least of all you."

"What of Titus?" he asked, hoping to distract her.

"I've no intention of letting dear Titus go without, in fact I'm rather hoping he might join us," Polly said stretching luxuriously, as though having sodding electricity arching and twisting and jumping over your skin was the newest beauty treatment. "Wouldn't that be fun? The both of you, at once?"

Somehow Stephen doubted Titus would concur.

"You think he'd agree to that?" Stephen asked backing to the far corner of the room.

"He ought to," Polly said looking and sounding confused.

"Why's that, Polly?" Stephen asked swallowing hard.

"Because I want him to and I do all sorts of silly things to make him happy; party after party," Polly said waggling her head. "This will be much more fun."

"I don't think your husband would think it an equal exchange," Stephen said, untying his neck cloth and setting aside his frock coat. He knew what was coming and didn't fancy having it ripped off of him.

"We'll have to see to that when he gets here," Polly said advancing on him with that look, that mad, mad look. "Ooops, almost forgot," she rapped twice against the exposed brick wall to dissipate the electric charge. "That could have turned nasty."

Stephen couldn't help himself, he laughed. From what he could tell it was as wide as it was tall as far as nastiness was concerned. Was this what he had prayed to Venus for? To have his cousin's wife in his cousin's house with the servants locked in their quarters shaking for fear of their lives. If this was all Aphrodite was willing to afford him, the goddess of love could get stuffed. Too bad he was too much of a pathetic wretch to tell his cousin's wife the same. He held out his arms to Polly. She positively reeked of ozone.

Polly crushed his lips against her own while he fumbled to undo his trousers.

She pulled him down to the floor and climbed astride him and Stephen struggled not to spend himself right away when she threw her head back and laughed.

Somehow, that ceased to be a problem when he noticed the blood, drip, drip dripping, out of nowhere onto the oriental carpet.

Titus.

Titus was here, watching, listening, the way he did.

Stephen's cock went slack.

"Titus, I can explain," Stephen groaned keeping his eyes fixed on the spot where the blood seemed to be coming from.

"Titus?" Polly ground her hips as her eyes scanned the room. "Come out, Come out wherever you are!"

Stephen was shocked to see his cousin Titus, arm bleeding, a dead salamander clutched in one fist, the stiletto he habitually kept secreted about his person in the other, point pressed to his own throat, touching but not quite cutting his own jugular.

"For the sake of Apophis, man, put the knife down," Stephen said.

"For the sake of Apophis what else am I to do but end this like a Roman?" Titus said.

"The Roman way to end this," Polly said, rocking back on her haunches to leave Stephen's cold wet limp cock exposed. "Would be to kill me, no questions asked, Why not start there?"

"Are you mad?" Stephen asked, annoyed, bewildered, and frightened. He wondered, on consideration, if all three of them weren't stark raving. "Don't mind her, either, she's mad, as well, I'm starting to believe we're all mad here."

Titus dropped the salamander. "I can't bear to hurt you, I … I love you so I shall have to kill myself, instead."

Polly ran her hands over her breasts seductively, like this was a sodding brothel instead of his cousin's formal dining hall. "Or you could join us."

"Join you?" Titus asked befuddled.

"Don't mind her, she's been struck twice by lightning in one day, she's not right in the head," Stephen said.

"Three times, actually. What's your excuse, Stephen, fall asleep with the moon on your face?" Polly laughed. "Yes, Titus, join us, it's what the gods want."

"What do you mean?" Titus asked, his blade hand relaxing and moving a fraction away from his throat.

"I mean, it's what the gods want; for you and Stephen and I to be together. The oracle told me as much before we were married. In order to bear a child I would have lie with the both of you. That's why Stephen didn't manage to impregnate me before you and I were married, and why you haven't been able to do it afterwards," Polly said rising to stand in front of stunned Titus and taking the knife from his hand.

"This is insane," Stephen bit out doing up his trousers and scrambling for his discarded neck cloth.

"If you're lying, if you're lying, it's blasphemy," Titus said.

"Shall we go to the temple of Apollo and ask Nefrit? It's easily done," Polly said.

Stephen was bothered that he didn't know whether she was lying or telling the truth, but if it was a lie she ought to try her hand at cards.

"You can't go see the oracle naked like that," Stephen said, noticing for the first time a mark, in the pattern of a great red tree was etched in her torso where the lightning had hit her, its branches spread across her breasts its roots descending to her belly.

"Put these on," Titus said, shoving a great white box at her. "They were meant to be a gift for the holiday. And bring him. Bring your lover." Titus seemed unable to look in his direction, much less his eyes.

And so it was that Stephen found himself taking the most uncomfortable carriage ride of his entire life, possibly anyone's life; Titus seething with rage unable to either look at him or speak to him, Polly wearing nothing but red high heeled shoes and a fur coat, in a blinding snow storm, heading for the temple of Apollo.

Wasn't he a lucky boy?

Titus Posthumous Albinus had never in his life entered the temple of Apollo without a sense of awe. It mattered little that he was hereditary priest of Apollo, a position dating back to before the founding of Rome, on the feast days he officiated he never could stop himself focusing on the fact of being in the god's presence, of generations of worship, of the knowable and the unknowable. Here in this place, if Polycorpus defiled this place with her lies, there would be blood on the altar of Apollo, he could not say whose but there would be blood.

Even as he strode in, Stephen and Polly trailing behind him, the hairs on the back of his neck stood at attention.

A junior priest, clearly impressed by his newly vested power to stand beside the door to the oracle's private chamber moved to block the doorway.

"The Oracle is not to be disturbed," the little nobody said, his hooves clacking against the marble floor.

"Do you know who I am?" Titus asked.

The stupid little man-goat shrugged unimpressed compelling Titus to explain in exacting detail…but was he cut short when Polly, her fur hanging open unattended simply pushed Titus, Stephen, and the goat-boy out of her way and barreled into the oracle's chamber.

He was disturbed by the sound of the oracle's laughter.

"Tell them, old woman," Polly demanded pointing a chubby, dirt-caked finger at his great-great-great-great-grandmother the Oracle of Apollo. "Tell them now."

"No one's allowed to address the Oracle without a certified senior priest of Apollo to act as intermediary!" the junior priest, who was unqualified by his own order's regulations, cried squeezing past Titus and his cuckolding bastard of a cousin.

In a rage Titus held his balled fist, with the ring bearing the insignia of the priesthood of Apollo on the smallest finger, precisely the right distance for punching the insolent little puppy in the face if he didn't recognize his authority immediately.

"Present and accounted for. Now get out!" Titus shouted.

The puffed up fool retreated instantly.

Nefrit failed to even acknowledge him, turning, instead, a death's head grin at the woman who had broken his heart. "Have you done it, girl? Have you? Are their seed now mingled in your womb?"

His blood ran cold.

Polly answered her without shame, running her hands over her loosened hair "Stephen seemed up for it until Titus came home and Titus is so melodramatic. Did you know he threatened suicide? Would you set him straight? Set them both straight. They are both such girls."

"What's wrong with being a girl, Polly?" the old woman asked, as if it weren't obvious.

Titus knew better than to disrespect an oracle but it seemed a stupid question.

"Aside from the obvious physical shite?" Polly answered rubbing her hands from her waist to her hips as if taking pleasure in her own body. "Girls are silly, and pointless, and afraid of breaking the rules."

"You are a girl and yet none of that is true of you," Nefrit said slowly.

"Never thought of that," Polly laughed merrily. "Would you please enlighten these two ninnies?"

"Only this woman, who was two and has been made one by a Commoner's hand will bear fruit for the tree, the roots of which feed when the Nile floods its banks. There must be a husband for each wife and a wife for each husband, else the rags run red. The seeds of the dying tree will mix or the great house will become a tomb. The God Has Spoken," Nefrit said.

And Titus felt an urge to vomit. He fell to his knees as he had been taught from childhood and kissed the hem of the oracle's gown.

"Blessed is the instrument of Apollo…" Titus started through his tears only to be interrupted by Polly.

"TE-DI-OUS" Polly sang out "Now that's been sorted let us go home and let me have my merry way with the two of you, as the god commands."

Nefrit began to laugh, a harsh wheezing sort of laugh.

"Polycorpus!" Titus began; he understood that she was high spirited and somehow affected by the lightning but this impertinence bordered on sacrilege.

"No, you can count me out of this little farrago, No, no, no," Stephen said baring his teeth.

"I don't like this any more than you do, Stephen, but the god has spoken, it's not ours to question," Titus said surprised at the ragged sound of his own voice. It was true, Stephen had wronged him, but his will was not his own and if the god Apollo decreed he was to be cuckolded Titus would frankly rather it was by the greatest monster of his age.

"You don't like this any more than I do?" Stephen said raking his hands through his hair and grimacing. "You don't…well, Titus, that is so sodding understanding of you …I must have missed the bit where you're used, once again, like a fucking tool, a bloody instrument, and cast aside as soon they've got what they want from you, because that's what's bloody happening to me, again, and I refuse. I can do that, you know, say no, to you, Duke Londiniumium Austri."

"I'm expected to sit by, approving, no, taking part, in my own cuckolding," Titus said somehow feeling his usual cloak of calm slip over his shoulders like a well made topcoat, he'd only once lost temper for so long before, and Polly had caused that as well. "Forgive me if my sympathy is not what it might be."

"What do you think it was like for me, acting as go between for your proposal? You knowingly came to me and asked for my assistance in taking for your own the only woman I ever loved, the only woman I could love," Stephen growled.

"What choice did I have? I lost four wives before The Oracle led me to Polly. Besides I specifically came to you so you could be free to object if you liked, and you didn't!" Titus said, his control beginning to slip again.

Polly sat down beside Nefrit on the dais and ate a bite of hothouse fruit from the bowl. "It's not very flattering to be the girl of last resort," she said looking from one to the other.

"Seems they want you badly enough now they've had a taste," Nefrit said, her body shaking with the effort of sitting upright. Polly stuffed a pillow behind her back.

"Not really, Stephen drools like a dog in a butcher's shop every day at tea but once he got me he barely seemed to know what to do with me." Polly shrugged.

"The poor boy is practically a virgin, you must remember he's never had a live woman, before, not one who stayed that way," the Oracle croaked. "You will have to instruct him in the ways of love."

"Love?" Stephen laughed. "The way of adulterous whores you mean? Well, I want no part of it."

It was not a thing that Titus had planned, or even thought about, but when Stephen turned to go Titus took hold of his lapel and said a single word. "Please."

"What?" Stephen asked, his eyes narrowed and his jaw set.

"It is the will of Apollo, and it is what Polly wants, and without it The Great House will be as a tomb, our house, our great house will be as a tomb. We are the end of our line, going back to the golden age of the gods, and without this it will end with you and I. We will be the last and I, please, I want a child." Every word Titus said was true and he had not known he would say a one of them until they began tumbling out of his mouth.

"The answer's still no, I won't be a tool to be used up and thrown aside, not for a god, not even for you," Stephen said. "And if Apollo's wrath follows, I can hardly be worse off than I am at present."

"If you do this, for me, I will give you anything your heart desires. Whatever it takes to make you happy. Name it and it's yours," Titus said, he knew Stephen had habitual money troubles. He didn't care if it bankrupted him if he could get his agreement out of him. It seemed ridiculous that he should be begging Stephen to violate his marriage bed.

When Stephen went deathly still Titus knew he had him. His cousin was simply waiting to name his price.

"Polly, I want Polly," Stephen said.

Polly meanwhile leaned over to straighten Nefrit in her seat and popped another grape into her own mouth. "Oh, this is getting interesting."

"Polly is my wife," Titus said.

"I could have told you he'd say that," Polly commented, taking another grape, she was often shocking but even for her this attitude seemed brazen.

"What is wrong with you?" Titus asked.

Polly rolled her head in a wide circle and popped her neck, the fur hung seductively open "I could say being struck by lightning three times in one day is a touch intoxicating but the truth is much simpler; Stephen loves me, and he desires me with a lust like a thousand cupid's darts. You love me as well. You never meant to but it happened just the same. And you know how much fun I can be in bed, not to mention on the desk in your study, pity about the leg, I told you I was too heavy. At any rate, I love you both and want the both of you for my husbands. The both of you wish, individually, to be my husband, and the Oracle said it would come to pass that I would have you both. A husband for each wife and the God Apollo seems to believe there are two of me."

Titus's mouth hung open and he had to will himself to close it.

"What if I said I wanted Polly to myself?" Stephen said his teeth grinding.

Nefrit leaned back against her cushions taking hold of Polly's hand. "I'd say it is unfortunate for you since that's not what Polly wants."

160

"Would you have me leave Titus?" Polly asked, her forehead wrinkled.

"Yes, once you've produced a child. It seems a fair exchange," Stephen said.

Polly turned her head and squinted. "But that would be just as bad as wanting you and not having you, so I wouldn't be any better off than I am now. I do love Titus as well, you know."

Titus could not wrap his mind round what he was being told to consent to, he could barely, just barely tolerate the idea of allowing Stephen to access to Polly once, because it had been foretold, but to allow him to be something like a husband to her? "And if I agree to this…unorthodox arrangement?"

"Why do each of you feel you must deprive the other in order to have what you desire," Nefrit's hand trembled as she adjusted the blanket on her lap. "If you do as the god commands you will have everything, the child you long for, the wife you adore, and Stephen Magesteri as your brother."

"Doesn't that sound cozy?" Polly asked, bright-eyed.

The effects of the lightning began to fade on the carriage ride home, at the same time the storm gentled to slow grey snow drifts growing higher by the minute and Polly had never felt more embarrassed in her life.

Her husband, whom she loved, had caught her in flagrante delicto with his cousin, with whom she'd been at least infatuated since she was old enough to use a welding torch. And she'd gone to the temple of Apollo wearing nothing but a fur coat. She'd never been exactly devout but even she knew that was beyond the pale. And now that she'd come, more or less, to her senses, she had to sit between Titus and Stephen in the carriage, glowering at each other's shoes.

She leapt from the carriage almost before it had come to a full stop. This was all her fault, all she had to do was tell the old woman "No," and no one would have been the wiser. As it stood she was afraid none of them might ever be happy again. She would have liked to run to the house but she was afraid of her coat slipping open as she ran, and the shoes, which were quite smart by the way, were not built for running on a slick walkway in steady snow.

"Don't take another step," Titus said so low and dangerous it stopped her, literally and figuratively, cold.

Polly turned round slowly to see the two of them, Titus and Stephen, facing one another snow on their shoulders like epaulets.

"You agree?" Stephen said, though from the look of them it could well mean they were about to nod and draw pistols. It seemed entirely possible.

Polly's gut churned as Titus carefully removed the blue gloves he'd put back on in the carriage. He was wearing blue today, it suited his complexion.

"I did not wish for this, Stephen," Titus said grimly.

"I'll be buggered if it was any of my doing," Stephen replied.

Titus nodded. "How is it possible that I despise my closest friend so much, without losing my love for him?"

"Fuck if I know, but the feeling, as they say, is mutual," Stephen answered.

"Brothers, then?" Titus said, extending his hand.

Stephen grasped his hand, skin to skin, and shook it, slowly. "Brothers. Now let's get in the house. It's sodding freezing out here," he said, before running for the door.

"Warm dry clothes, Llewelyn," Titus bellowed the minute they were inside.

Chapter 13 : A Tense Arrangement

hree quarters of an hour later Stephen Magesteri was more physically comfortable at least, and was trying to decide whether this was the worst or the best day of his life. He was fairly sure it was one or the other. Though the way it was headed he was leaning towards the former.

The three of them, Titus, Polly, and himself, sat in the second best parlor in front of a sweat inducing fire, as far as was geometrically possible from another within the confines of the room.

"Whose brilliant notion was this, again?" Stephen said.

"Don't look at me," Titus drawled.

Polly blushed. "I didn't come up with it on my own, it was the Oracle," she said.

"Any suggestion about how we proceed?" Stephen asked. "I'll be buggered if I know how to get started."

"I was hoping to keep that off the agenda." Titus smirked. "I would say age before beauty but since I've both I'll concede my unfair advantage, you first." Titus gestured to Polly as though he was offering Stephen a biscuit.

"Polly?" Stephen asked.

Polly cringed the minute she met his eyes. How encouraging. How utterly fucking encouraging.

"By all means, proceed, don't mind me, I think I'll have a cigar while I wait. I ran into Henry Plumber this morning and he practically forced this one on me," Titus said, pulling a slightly crushed cigar from his breast pocket. "It is somewhat the worse for wear."

It occurred to Stephen that if he didn't bring himself to act soon he never would, so he rose to his feet and stripped off his topcoat and neck cloth.

Titus lit his crumpled cigar and watched as Stephen ran his thumb under the notch of Polly's jaw. It had never occurred to him before how well matched the two of them were. Like Polly, Stephen was a bit shorter than average and somewhat broadly built. Together this way, they looked to be in good proportion to one another. He refused to consider even in passing that he had done wrong by taking Polly from Stephen in the first place. Titus's need was greater, not to mention the fact that Stephen remained completely unsuitable as a husband, not to mention a father. Polly never belonged to Stephen therefore Titus could not possibly have stolen her. Never mind the uneasy feeling that had never truly left Titus that Polly never wholly belong to him either, not in the way his other wives had. Titus sucked hard on the cigar and blew out a series of perfect smoke rings his eyes shut tight.

He was not some mewling and puking recruit who shied away from what was required of him, that didn't mean he was eager to watch what was transpiring on the tiger skin in front of his fire.

Titus disliked smoking in general and cigars in particular, but he thought back to their wedding night and knew he couldn't bear to smell Stephen's arousal. He sucked at his cigar until he felt slightly sick at his stomach but it was merely the tobacco. Nothing more.

He was not a child, or, no matter what Polly might say, a girl. He did not fall apart at the first hint of disaster. Jalalabad had been merely the first of a lifetime. He'd been in tight situations through out his career. This was simply another circumstance to be dealt with no matter how overwhelming it might seem at first glance. Today his house had been half-destroyed. The animals he had cared for since he was a child had been wiped out, and he was being asked, no, required to negotiate his own cuckolding. But Apollo had offered him the continuation of his line in return. Titus Posthumous Albinus was not foolish enough to spurn a gift from the gods. He'd read enough history to know how that went.

When he couldn't keep his eyes closed any longer the first thing Titus saw was Stephen grunting like a pig on top of Polly, slobbering all over her face.

Polly never expected to feel so tender toward Stephen's body with his broad back and soft gut. She felt a terrible twinge when she realized she'd never seen him without his shirt when he wasn't shivering and covered with blood, despite having been intimate with him twice. The twinge grew worse when she saw the tattoo over his heart identical to the one Titus carried. She hadn't recognized it before because the rest of their regiment was dead.

She kissed him softly, like she'd learned from Titus. Despite her explorations with Charlie she'd hardly kissed at all until she married Titus Albinus.

Polly had never known intercourse could feel so sad.

Stephen - Professor Magesteri every place but Titus's house - dark and frightening to everyone but her and Titus, came to her as awkward and shy and open hearted as Charlie Edney ever did. All Polly had ever done was hurt him, and she did not know how to stop. The cold she felt when he touched her had nothing to do with fear and everything to do with guilt.

His calloused hands trembled when he touched her. His mouth was red and raw and sought hers blindly. She fought the urge to cry at the desperation of his love, she could not lie and call it something else. He had wanted her love but all she had given him was sex. That changed from this moment. She decided emphatically she would give him her love, even if she had no idea how such a thing was done.

It did not take long, a handful of awkward thrusts and he was spent. Polly had never felt so sad before in her life. She kissed his cheek as softly as she knew how and tucked the greasy black hair out of his face, the way Titus did with her sometimes.

Stephen deserved something better than this, yet she could not imagine how he could ever attain it.

She was fully prepared to make Titus the villain. She was prepared for what passed between them to be a small scale war. It was he who wanted a child. It was he who dragged them to the Temple of Apollo to see the Oracle. It was he who had taken her from her father when it should have been Stephen and tricked her into falling in love with him. It was he who caused all this. Selfish Titus. Hateful Titus. Prissy Titus. Bully Titus.

She was prepared for him to come to her cold and vengeful. She was not prepared for him to kiss her hands. She was not prepared for him to brush his lips against the pulse in her throat, her lips, the curve of her ear. She was not prepared for his fingertips to trip gently over her cheek when she was still flushed and warm from Stephen's body on top of hers.

"Polly," Titus murmured pressing a kiss to the palm of her left hand.

It made her feel even worse than before. She wanted to have a focus for her anger. She wanted him to be the unreasonable, oblivious, selfish arse she'd married so she could blame all this on him. As it stood she had no one to shine her rage on but herself when Titus Albinus buried his lips in the crook of her neck.

"Polly," he said in her ear, his cock hard against her thigh.

"Polly," he said again and it seemed to be a question.

"Go on then," Polly said, knowing full well Titus was no Professor Magesteri. He would not be finished after a few minutes of groping and sixty seconds of turgid thick penis in not quite prepared vagina.

She had never longed for a sex act to be over before. Even a day earlier it would have been unimaginable. Titus, who always wanted to put his gloss of niceness, and manners, and convention over everything, clearly knew she wasn't enjoying any of it.

"Polly," Titus murmured low resting his hand on her belly. "Forgive me."

166

Polly tried to convince herself to take pleasure from it, sucking at his earlobe that always tasted so delicious and could be counted on melt away her self-consciousness, but he smelled of her father's cigar.

Titus slipped himself inside her, starting for a moment, perhaps at the sensation of her vagina already full of semen, someone else's semen, his hand still between them, rubbing at her clitoris. She wondered if he thought it was his duty.

Unlike Stephen Titus didn't bang away at her. His movements were slow and even, and with each rock of his hips he buried himself as deep as he could go. Then the dictates of her body overcame the distractions of her mind, in retrospect she was not sure why she was surprised.

Stephen knew why Titus, bloody fucking Colonel Titus Posthumous Albinus, Order of Apophis had made him go first, his cousin knew he was a coward and wanted to make sodding certain he followed through, even if he had to sit in the room while Stephen fucked his wife to do it.

Well, two could play at that game. If Londinium Austri had the bottle to sit there like he was at the bloody sex show at Club Aphrodite then Londinium Oriens could do likewise.

So sodding what if it made his breath come fast and his blood run hot and cold to see Polly open her mouth to Titus's kisses. He could avoid the whip marks on Titus's back as long as Polly's face or breasts were in view.

That was until Titus raised his head to look him in the eye.

Within fifteen minutes of completion Titus was dressed and directing the servants cleaning up the wreckage that used to be the peristylium.

Polly lie on the settee dressed in her shift watching Stephen scrutinize his reflection in the mirror now that he was dressed, trying not to look like he'd just had intercourse with the lady of the house, she supposed.

Much as she wanted to be nice to Stephen she was having trouble meeting his eyes.

"I'm heading to the kitchens to pester Mrs. Hodson, if I don't get something to eat soon I'll be tempted to buggering cannibalism," Stephen said. "Want to come along? I'll wait for you to dress. I don't mind."

Honestly Polly was starving.

"I'm good," Polly said, shaking her head.

"No, you're a bleeding liar," Stephen said, slamming the parlor door behind him.

Titus's dining hall was finally, not an exquisite entertaining arena, not presentable, not acceptable, but something recognizable as having once been inhabited by creatures capable of grasping a soup spoon.

He wasn't sure if his cousin Stephen had hurt his back or if this was his version of stealth. Nonetheless he watched from the corner of his eye as Magesteri made his way down the corridor lifting his knees high whilst lurching backwards and swaying slightly to prevent himself toppling over.

Titus gave in to his urge and disappeared, catching up to Stephen in a few silent strides, placing his hand on his cousin's shoulder, and allowing himself to shimmer back into view.

"Shit!" Stephen growled, a grimace screwing his features into something comically ugly. "I should have known you'd see me, Tight Arse."

"And where, precisely, do you think you're going?" Titus asked though he suspected he knew the answer.

"Home? You do recall that I live at The British Museum? In the basement? Have since I was seven and the world found out exactly what sort of monster I was? Did you miss that? Were you too busy being loved and coddled and oh-look-at-the-ickle-Duke-let's-give-him-pressies to notice what happened to an unclean creature such as myself?" Stephen said not bothering to mask his resentment.

"I will not allow you to make my home into a brothel, Stephen," Titus informed him.

"What are you on about, Titus? You've got what you wanted, the way you always do, you're free to wash your hands of me," Stephen said gnashing and baring his uneven teeth.

"What, so you can play poor little Stevie, yet again? I gave you my word you could be a husband to Polly. Since when do husbands show up for a quick one at tea time and go sleep alone in the basement of a public building?" Titus asked. "If you are under the impression I am going to afford you the opportunity to say Londinium Austri went back on his promise, I urge you to think again."

Titus was fully expecting it when Stephen laughed that bitter laugh of his.

"Are you trying to rub my face in it? Make absolutely fucking certain I know what an absurd request it was," Stephen shook his head in disbelief. "Have you even spoken to Polly about this? Asked the woman if that's she wants? Of course you haven't, what was I thinking? You prick."

"I don't have to ask," Titus said, hating the small sound of his own voice in his ears. "She's informed me on more than one occasion that she prefers you to me, not that I can discern any reasonable explanation for this notion of hers. It's clearly not aesthetic in nature. Perhaps the Duchess is simply... whimsical."

Stephen shut his eyes slowly. "She lied, Titus, that's got to be it. Polly was angry and she lied to hurt your precious feelings."

"What have I done now?" the Duchess in question practically shouted from the far end of the corridor. At least she'd put on her dressing gown over her shift, even if she hadn't bothered to dress.

"You lied to your husband and told him you were in love with me in order to hurt him," Stephen said, only the faintest trace of bitterness in his words.

"I never said that," Polly insisted. "I said I'd rather have married you and that was true. Is true. I was pretty cheesed off when I said it but I bloody loathe being a Duchess. It's all clothes and parties and being nice to people I can't stand. The horrid part is I think I am in love with both of you. It's as wide as it is tall.

I may have been slightly out of my head when I said it but..." Here Polly nodded, staring at the carpet.

If it weren't such an utterly mad opinion Titus would have been offended, as it was Titus simply filed it away in Pandora's box with the rest of the outlandish things his wife was apt to say and put it out of his head.

"There you have it; confirmation," Titus explained. "The lady prefers you."

"I never said that, Titus, stop putting words in my mouth," Polly said. "I love you very much, I just happen to love Stephen as well. Is that wrong? It might be wrong. It's probably wrong, but it is true. There it is."

Titus closed his eyes and nodded. It was, if he squinted, and thought about it from exactly the correct angle, preferable. Better than coercing her into the arms of a frightening man she did not want so that he could have an heir, he supposed. Better it was Stephen than someone else, anyone else, truly. He did love Stephen like a brother, even if he wanted to throttle him like a brother at the moment.

"You're both mad. Do you know that?" Stephen asked running his hands through his hair.

"I'll send my driver and a footman to collect your things from the Museum. I would offer to wake you for work when I rise and make my way to the baths, but I know for a fact you sleep less than I do," Titus said.

"What about Lily and Rose?" Stephen asked.

"Who are Lily and Rose?" Polly asked jealousy plain as day on her face. It made Titus feel a bit warm inside to see the shoe on the other foot.

"Stephen's cats; he's always kept cats. That's how your father taught him to control his abilities - he brought him baskets full of kittens. His reward for controlling himself was not having a basket full of dead baby cats," Titus said. "You can bring them as soon as the peristylium is repaired."

Polly wrinkled her nose the way she did when she was disgusted.

"So that's it?" Stephen asked wild-eyed. "We're all sleeping together in one big bed from here on out?"

"Don't be ridiculous, Stephen," Titus said tiredly, the fire in his blood starting to flag and his energy along with it. "I bunked with you in the barracks; you snore like a warthog. You'll take the blue room across the corridor."

Polly would have liked to say that after that everything was resolved and pleasant and Titus and Stephen tried to out do one another in their slavish adoration. She'd have liked to say that, but it would've been a lie.

Instead, it went something like this:

They were both gone, Stephen to work and Titus to the baths, long before she woke up.

Titus, as always, left a flowery note.

Stephen didn't, although he sometimes made a rude drawing or sarcastic comment at the bottom or in the margins of Titus's perfumed love letter, after Titus had gone, she assumed.

She didn't see either one of them until tea, when they would sometimes be very amusing but more often than not compete for her attention, Stephen by drawing her into discussion of his latest work and frustrations, sometimes unfurling blueprints atop the tea tray, and Titus telling stories. Titus also tried to cheat by bringing her presents; shoes in every colour, every design, every variation imaginable, pocket handkerchiefs too, to match her shoes, with her initials embroidered in the corner, combs for her hair, opera glasses, gloves, the list went on and on.

Stephen countered by bringing Polly machines he'd built with his own hands. A tiny device that when wound was capable of giving a beautiful little jolt of electricity was her favorite but there were others; notably a small portable clock, hardly bigger than a pocket watch, that would ring, loudly, at a predetermined hour and take off, wheeling madly about the top of her chifferobe, until Polly got out of bed, found the damn thing, and shut it off. Polly frankly hated that one.

After tea Stephen would return to work and Titus would go to his study to write his reports. As for Polly she would get out her paper and her pens and sit watching the work on the peristylium and continue her organization of moral reasoning.

Titus decided, through whatever process it was Titus used to make decisions, that Stephen needed to accompany the two of them to all their social engagements. She sometimes wondered if it was a form of punishment. She also wondered why it was that once Titus decided a thing, Stephen behaved, complaining bitterly all the while, as though he had no choice but to go along. Honestly, she stood up to Titus far more often than Stephen did.

Still the addition of Professor Magesteri to their social engagements had several interesting results. One of which was that Polly felt manifestly more adept at parties.

At a particularly boring do at Afrincanus Snodbury's the Effingham girl, whose first name eluded Polly at the moment, sidled up to Stephen like she was on a dare, simpering sweetly.

"It's such a treat to see you, Professor Magesteri. You usually keep yourself all shut up in the Museum." Polly had been watching Titus across the room, by the look of things he was telling witty stories to a growing knot of listeners, but suddenly Effingham had her attention.

To which Stephen held the flask, the one he thought was very discreet, to his mouth and grunted, literally grunted in Effingham's general direction.

Miss Effingham smiled as though she'd expected nothing less. "I told Julia, you know Julia Snodbury-Suetonius, I was so tired of seeing the same old faces over and over."

Polly half expected Stephen to belch in Effingham's general direction next, so she took control of the situation. "You'll be used to seeing my husband's cousin at these things soon enough, Cornelia." That was her name, Cornelia. "Titus has got the idea in his head now that he and I are so happily married that Professor Magesteri should find himself a bride."

Cornelia Effingham paled visibly then laughed, nervously, behind her fan. "How very kind of him."

"My cousin is the very soul of sentimentality. You may find it runs in the family," Stephen said, taking another drink.

It took all Polly's power not to burst out laughing when Cornelia's eyes went wide.

"Is that Julia calling me over? Coming, Julia! If you'll excuse me, Professor Magesteri, Polly," Cornelia said in a rush.

"Bye, Cornelia, so lovely to chat with you," Polly said, grinning as Cornelia practically scurried away.

"You're picking up Titus's ways," Stephen said. "What you did there, that was straight from Titus's book of tricks. If I'd done it my way and growled at her a few more times she'd have gone away sure enough."

Polly shrugged. "It's swim or be eaten by the Kraken at these things. Either you learn to maneuver or you don't. If you'd stood there grunting she would have gone back to Snodbury-Suetonius and the two of them would have spent the rest of the evening making sport of you in their little corner with all their little friends, as it stands I've put her in fear of her life. I count that a victory for our side."

"These people have whispered about me behind my back since I was old enough to write my name," Stephen said. "Do you and my cousin actually think you can rehabilitate The Great Abomination with a few rounds through the society circuit?"

"I don't think that's it," Polly said feeling uncertain. Perhaps it truly was a punishment.

"What is the point, then?" Stephen said grimacing.

"Did it ever occur to you I might simply desire your company?" Titus said from behind them. Titus did that thing he did, reaching out his long arms and pulling Polly close on one side and Stephen on the other and kissing Polly soundly on the cheek.

"Not for a sodding minute," Stephen answered him.

For his part Stephen was waiting for the whole bloody thing to go tits up.

Coerced sociability notwithstanding it was like a sort of dangerously good dream. The kind of life he had not been prepared for and had no firm idea how to respond to.

Eating the objectively best biscuits in England while he was pining after his cousin's wife was one thing. Eating the best food he had ever tasted at each and every meal, sleeping on the softest sheets with hothouse flowers on his bedside table in the dead of winter, after putting it to his cousin's wife; the woman they both loved, who, as far as he could tell, liked them both well enough in return, was another kettle of eels entirely.

It was the kind of luck you paid dearly for in the end, especially if you were Stephen Magesteri.

If he'd had Polly to himself he simply would have ended it and sent her away, rather than wait for whatever it was that was going to go wrong to get on with it and bollix itself up. He'd never had much experience with "too good to be true" but he was knew enough to recognize when it landed in his lap. Literally.

As usual he was grateful to his cousin Titus, and wanted to see him banished to Wales. The lucky sod had always been good with women, even Polly had fallen under his spell eventually. Stephen doubted he, himself, would have known what to do with her on his own but sometimes he thought he ought to have given it a stab. They had come to an understanding, he and Tight-arse, that neither of them trusted the other not to attempt to press for some advantage over the other during intimacy with Polly, and so unions took place together in full view of one another, and so far Polly, being Polly, was too insatiable to object. Titus was more adept at the act, that was unarguable, but Stephen was more familiar with Polly's little ways. Each was able to learn by observing the other and something like balance was maintained.

At tea that particular morning Stephen was able to head Titus off when he was about to put his foot in it with Polly, not for Titus's sake, mind, but he'd rather nip that sort of thing in the bud than spend hours listening to Titus pout and whinge on about Polly's inexplicable tempers.

In return it would be bloody nice if Titus did Stephen a good turn or two.

Not that Stephen expected it. Titus probably thought he'd done Stephen all the favors that needed doing by feeding him, and paying off his debtors and dressing him like a sodding fop so he could drag him along every time there was free food or drink on offer anywhere in Londinium.

And the sharing his wife thing, he probably thought that counted, too, though in truth it was closer to a creeping form of torture. Polly was Titus's. Even if Stephen had married her instead of Titus he doubted he would have been able to shake the feeling Titus had more inherent right to her by simple virtue of what Stephen could only describe as his "Titus-ness". Stephen was an interloper, now and for all time.

That particular evening, after a dinner party with two dozen tedious twats so pompous they made Titus Albinus look like the girl who scrubbed the chamber pots at the Museum, Stephen was in an especially foul temper. Titus as a rule made Stephen have first go at Polly. He probably thought if he went first, in light of Stephen's "gift", Stephen's seed would kill his. Stephen couldn't tell him it was a weak hypothesis.

That night though, nearing midnight, Titus kissed Polly while Stephen was still locking the parlor door behind them. That was probably why Titus'd given Stephen keys to every bloody room in the place, so he could make him responsible for locking up. When he turned round his cousin was lavishing attention on Polly's bolts in that way of his. Personally, Stephen avoided the knobs of bright metal at the base of her neck, he'd seen too many arcs of electricity leap from them to put his lips there. But for a layman his cousin seemed awfully distracted by the minutiae of Polly's construction, his fingers habitually tracing the seams that marked her skin like the borders between farmer's fields. One huge hand slipped into the front of Polly's dress to grasp the freckled white breast that was barely concealed by her dress as it was.

Stephen had spent his entire adult life unable to touch a woman before Polly so the only experience he did have was with his own right hand. That, and his eyes. He'd parted with more of his salary than he could afford some months, paying to watch sights less arresting than the one in front of him. Lovers less skilled, and far less ardent than those two.

Polly was particularly pretty that night, at least Stephen thought so. Titus removed her combs and watched the waves fall down her back so he could bury his nose in them. Stephen could feel his cock growing harder and harder to see the two of them. Was this what they were like when he wasn't there to put a damper on the festivities? With her dark eyes and red painted lips Stephen thought Polly was the most exciting woman he had ever seen. It seemed Titus thought so as well because he held Polly round the waist and kissed the back of her neck while he rubbed himself unashamedly against her arse.

Polly, being Polly, arched her back shamelessly and groaned, pushing her broad bum back against Titus's crotch. He didn't even bother to remove her stockings, and usually Titus bleeding loved to put Polly's little foot in his lap and slip off her shoes, then reach up under her dress and roll down her stockings. He liked undressing her in general, from what Stephen had seen. The one time Stephen had given it a try he'd embarrassed himself and come all over the both of them, and Polly called him "Poor Stephen". Titus had looked away, bored. That was worse, far worse, he reckoned, than being laughed at.

But not tonight. Tonight Titus was kissing Polly and rubbing against her with no indication he intended to hand her off to Stephen once her engine was primed, so to speak. He squeezed her nipple between thumb and forefinger as he sucked the side of her neck. With his other hand Titus navigated the folds of her skirt trying to get at her cunt.

Her breath was coming in gasps and her eyes were shining. Her lips were open and glistening. Stephen shifted in his chair absently giving his prick a squeeze through the cloth of his trousers and watched as the bastard whisper something in her ear.

Polly laughed out loud. Lovely, he did so fucking love to be the object of sport for those two.

"You are brilliant, Titus," she said with her black eyes unfathomable. She twisted out of Titus's grasp and crawled on her hands and knees to Stephen's chair.

"Polly?" Stephen asked a bit uneasy. This was not how it usually went. Stephen didn't usually appreciate surprises.

"You know I don't like talking in the bedroom, it's distracting," Polly said, sternly.

"If your ladyship insists," Stephen said suddenly feeling grim.

"Oh do stand down, Magesteri," Titus smirked. "But not literally, though I doubt you'll have much choice in a moment."

"Would you two be quiet? Or I shall go up to the library and read a book!" Polly said irritably. Stephen wasn't stupid, he buttoned his lip.

It was Titus's turn to watch as Polly, pretty Polly, on her hands and knees, freed Stephen's prick from his trousers and laid it against her lower lip. He was so hard he ached. His blood was pounding in his head and in his prick. It was a bloody sodding hideous filthy wonderful thing when Polly slowly opened her mouth and flicked her tongue against his foreskin before taking the head in her mouth like the lowest form of whore. She was right, it was brilliant. Getting more brilliant the deeper she took him in that wet mouth of hers.

Then she stopped, halfway down, and Stephen looked up to see Titus, instead of retiring to wait his turn in the armchair at the far end of the tiger skin rug like a civilized person, had Polly's skirt and petticoats pushed backwards and had raised her by the hips to hold her sex…to his mouth. His cousin was a barbarian, an over-dressed, pompous, barbarian.

Then Polly swallowed Stephen's cock down to the root, and Stephen didn't know whether he was going to die of pleasure or terror.

Stephen had killed enough people by his 12th birthday to never want to kill anything ever again. He had absolutely no desire to bring his cousin to his end, no matter how he envied him Polly's love, as opposed to her pity. Stephen knew without a doubt he could not control his ability as his ecstasy mounted. While he knew Polly was immune he was not certain the effect wouldn't travel through her body like electricity through a conduit, or he might accidentally touch Titus, or, or, Oh Heavenly Nuut, Polycorpus's tongue was a divine instrument. He could feel Polly shaking from Titus's ministrations. One day he was going to make her shake like that.

Then whilst Polly was there bent over him sucking, arse in the air, Titus buried himself in her to the hilt. Titus who took special care and hardly ever laid so much as an ungloved finger on him, had seen fit to take Polly from behind while Stephen was sliding down her throat an iron-spine length away, during the one time Stephen was at his most dangerous and had no hope of controlling himself. He didn't know if it scared Titus but Stephen was fucking terrified. Just not terrified enough to stop. He was amazed he had lasted so long, it was probably the abject fear of killing his closest friend. Even if he hated him.

Stephen could feel Polly's entire body moving in time with Titus's thrusts and Stephen felt sick at his stomach, and horrified and the pleasure was building and Stephen started to worry if he was in danger of some form of death by apoplexy. All because Titus was a show off. A twisty bloody show off.

Then.

Then.

Everything seemed to turn upside-down and inside-out at once and Stephen's brain and guts and love and terror all seemed intent on forcing their way out of the head of his prick. So much so that he hardly noticed Polly and Titus seizing similarly. His vision went spotty for a moment.

"Oh mighty Zeus," Stephen said when his eyes could see properly again, stuck for anything more appropriate to the situation. What was appropriate to the situation? What was the situation? He'd be fucked if he knew. Perhaps he already had been.

"A simple 'thank you,' would suffice," Titus laughed, luxuriating against the leg of the tea table.

Polly laughed merrily, wiping a blob of seed off the corner of her mouth. "Don't be a knob, Titus."

Titus held a hand to his heart in mock offense. "Oh, Lady, I'm wounded," and dove laughing into her arms. "Clearly you need to be kissed into submission."

"Think that's the way to get me on the run, do you?" Polly giggled.

This was the way of it, the two of them together, Magesteri was going to be left out again.

"Do you doubt it?" Titus said.

Polly raised her head to address Stephen. "I think this is going to take the both of you. Or don't you think the 87th can manage one stroppy girl?"

And they did.

They very much did.

So Stephen supposed Titus had done him a good turn or two, if only because he was a stupid bloody git. A stupid bloody brave git. And because he was a twisty twisty bastard.

Chapter 14 : The Wolf's Feast

Lupercalia finally came.

Which was significant to Polly because Titus, who usually let her sleep in and didn't make a nuisance of himself in the mornings, had opened all the blinds and was standing stark naked staring at the foot of the bed with his forefinger to his mouth. As her eyes adjusted Polly saw waist coats and cravats draped over all the available furniture, apparently someone couldn't make up his bloody mind.

Polly shut her eyes against the streaming light, but to no avail. Why was he doing this to her? She was so sleepy. She was endlessly sleepy these days. Hungry. Tired. Aroused. That was all her brain seemed to have room for. Hungry and tired and so full of semen she was surprised she didn't squish when she walked. As far as complaints went it was fairly minor. Given enough time she was sure tensions between Stephen and Titus would sort themselves out. They were quite fond of one another despite everything.

"Is there tea?" she asked shielding her eyes with one hand.

"Bloody bedside table, my liege," Stephen said, startling her. Polly hadn't seen him there lounging in a chair with a book in his lap.

She took a sip of her tea, it was tepid. She wondered how long it had been sitting and how long Titus had been dithering over his wardrobe.

"What are you doing?" Polly asked Titus. "I thought you picked out every-

180

one's clothes weeks in advance."

Titus didn't answer her, only hummed vaguely holding a cravat against first one waistcoat then another.

"Polly, you disappoint me," Stephen said taking a bite of something in between gulps of tea. "Don't you know your husband better than that? Two weeks ago Tight-Arse laid out his ensemble for today's festivities; he is currently deciding what to wear to the Temple of State to kick off the Lupercalia celebration of the She-Wolf of Rome and the continued fertility of its women."

"But," Polly sat up, "it doesn't matter what you wear to the temple, does it? No one's going to see. I mean, the first thing you do when you get to the temple is strip naked."

"The other Luperci will certainly see," Titus said as if waking from a dream.

"And Mt. Olympus forfend those other pouncy gits look askance at the cut of your trousers," Stephen said.

"Why don't you ever take part like all the other swells, Stephen? Viscount's pretty high up there and so's being head of Department of Invention. You'd think you were common for all your public spirit. I mean my papa engages in more public festivities than you do," Polly said.

"Dousing naked boys with dog's blood then running starkers through the city in February is not my idea of a good time," Stephen said.

"As if they'd have you… Viscount simply means he's the second son of an Earl, though I can't imagine Virgil being allowed to inherit Aurelius's title…" Titus said, looking hard at two remarkably similar cravats. "Besides, it's not dog's blood; dog's blood would be a good deal less expensive. It's only symbolic of dog's blood, rather it's good red wine."

"Why wouldn't they have Stephen?" Polly asked.

"Abomination, remember? Not exactly a good omen for a fertility festival," Stephen said. "Not that I regret not freezing my bits off."

"It's quite bracing actually," Titus said. His hair hadn't been cut in some time and a cascade of carefully arranged copper curls covered his forehead.

"Bollocks," Stephen said, taking another taste of tea. "You say that every bleeding time, about every bleeding thing. 'Come to the gym, Cousin, it's quite bracing first thing in the morning. We're going to spend a few bracing days hunting at the country place, care to come along?' It sounds bloody exhausting to me, you can have it; the gymnasium, riding through hill and dale for the sheer hell of it, not to mention running naked through the streets in the dead of winter."

"Julius Caesar was a Luperci; he ran naked through the streets in February," Titus said, his chin raised.

"He also had coitus with Cleopatra," Polly felt compelled to point out. "I suspect he was no stranger to vigorous activity."

Stephen set down his cup. "Just because I'm not some mincing fashion plate who spends half my life at the gymnasium doesn't mean I'm not accustomed to work. If the Museum weren't on holiday I would be there this minute. Working. And I would also like to point out in my defense that Rome in February is hardly comparable to Londinium."

Titus smiled with one corner of his mouth. "I've decided on the sapphire, it sets off my eyes. Cheer up, Cousin, there will be plenty of reveling in the Glory that is Rome and the ripe wombs of her matrons here at home once I've finished my circuit through the city. It's going to be the triumph of the social season."

It was astounding how he said that without a trace of irony.

Polly considered leaving her bed, but it was so very warm and comfy.

"The preparations do need some looking after," Titus said as Polly snuggled deep in her blankets.

"After I've another cup of tea," Polly whinged, silently assured the servants had it all well under control and did even better without Titus badgering them incessantly.

"Stephen, you could lend Polly a hand with the servants if you were so inclined," Titus said laying sapphire blue cravat against a silver waistcoat and smiling to himself.

Polly sat up and looked at Titus, there was something odd.

"You're different somehow. Did you, did you style your pubic hair?" Polly asked.

Stephen meanwhile choked on his biscuit.

Titus was still a bit high spirited from the run and the wine and being dressed in his finest when, crowd at his back, he opened his front door wide.

"Welcome to my humble home," he shouted above the din of every monster in Londinium behind him.

The roared response was deafening. The crowd surged behind him and Titus Posthumous Albinus stood, stunned for a moment, by the sight of Polly in the entry way.

He was perfectly aware, as far as beauty was concerned, Polly couldn't hold a candle to any of his previous wives. No matter how he liked her personally he was not deluded into thinking her exquisite or delicate or willowy or anything but thick set with the build of a cart horse. Her sensuality was that of a milk-maid or a common farmer's wife; all big round buttocks and breasts, and belly to match underneath her corset, but standing in his foyer, in her flame coloured velvet gown she stopped him in his tracks. Clearly it was the drink talking but if it weren't for the crowd he'd have her right there in the vestibule.

Titus bowed low and brought Polly's hand to his lips as the musicians started on cue and the music swelled.

"May I have the first dance?" Titus asked, it was expected and he didn't mind her awkwardness one bit when she was pressed against him.

Polly gave him a forced smile. "If you must."

"Oh it is absolutely imperative," Titus said. grasping her waist as the guests poured in. This was shaping up to be brilliant.

Stephen Magesteri was having a shit day. Not that anything particularly annoying had happened but as he sat in the farthest corner of Titus's ballroom he found his mood inexplicably growing more and more foul. Well, the entire house was stuffed to the gills with idiots making merry, laughing, dancing, and drinking, so it wasn't wholly inexplicable.

He saw Titus coming and wondered if it was possible to blend into the draperies.

"Greetings oh-cousin-of-mine," Titus said, his cheeks flushed with drink. "I see you're your usual ebullient self. Why don't you give some lovely maiden the thrill of her life and take her for a spin across the floor?"

"You mean scare the piss out of some poor girl out trying to entrap a stupid clot in unholy matrimony? Thanks awfully but I'll let the female population stalk their prey in peace," Stephen said, raising his scotch in Titus's general direction.

"Oh, come off it, there's no harm in simply dancing with them," Titus teased. "Polly won't mind. I think she's rather relieved when I do it, to tell the truth."

"Sod off, Cousin," Stephen said and took another swallow. His eyes fell on Polly across the room, speaking to her father and Aunt Augusta. When he glanced back at Titus his eyes were focused on Polly as well.

"This isn't a request. I'm sick of seeing you wallowing in self-pity when you've all you could ever wish for. Cousin, I'm ordering you to enjoy yourself," Titus said his eyes gleaming dangerously; Stephen felt something rise in his gut.

"No," Stephen said, finishing his drink.

Titus cocked his head curiously, as though he didn't believe his ears. "What did you say?"

"I said, 'no' as in no, I do not have everything I could wish for. Rather you have everything I could wish for, and merely let me borrow it, never forgetting for a moment it's all at your sufferance. You could take it every bit of it away at a moment's notice. Thus, you remain in control, as ever," Stephen said handing Titus his empty glass "Speaking of which, could I trouble you for the use of another glass of scotch? I promise I'll return it to you as soon as I'm finished, though may be a bit changed when you see it next."

Titus peered at the empty glass through slitted eyes and smiled enigmatically in Stephen's general direction. "It's not as though you're granted ample opportunity to …oh kill me… a dozen times a day. I'm sure Polly would forgive you, eventually."

As if Stephen wasn't painfully aware of the fact. As if Titus weren't the only man he knew capable of somehow turning his own power against him in such a way.

"Tell me," Stephen said feeling the scotch flaring inside him. "How do you think it will be, raising my son as your own while everyone whispers behind your back?"

All pretense of joking ended in that moment. "You were as incapable as I of impregnating her on your own or she would have come to me already with child," Titus snarled.

"Keep telling yourself that." Stephen gave him the sweetest smile he had.

"Sod off, Stevie," Titus sneered at him.

Polly never had this much fun at parties, ever.

Today everyone, simply everyone, she knew was invited, even her Papa. She had hardly seen her papa since she'd been married and it was all she could do not to break half his ribs squeezing him when she saw him. She wished she could understand why Titus disliked him so.

The way her husband said "social climber" you'd think it was a crime against nature. What an arse.

"So, Polly, how did Professor Magesteri manage to move in and your poor papa doesn't even rate an invitation to tea?" Polly's Papa said, lighting a fresh cigar.

It seemed Polly had grown unused to the aroma, but they hadn't stunk so badly before she was a Duchess. What was wrong with her? When she was little she used to sniff through the Museum for the scent of him, growing more excited the stronger the smell.

"Well…ummm…you know Titus," Polly blurted. "He doesn't like you. I think it might be your cigars. He has a very sensitive nose."

"Polycorpus!" Mrs. Brolly scolded her "I don't care what your title, speaking to your father in such an impertinent…"

"Let the girl be, Augusta, I'm hardly wounded. I'm well aware of Colonel Albinus's opinion of me. More aware, I dare say, than our Polly." Papa chuckled, drawing on his cigar. "I'm more interested in how you're finding Professor Magesteri these days."

Polly felt her face grow hot. "Oh you know Stephen. Same as ever, I imagine."

"You don't say," Papa said clenching his cigar tightly through his smile. "He's seemed quite changed to all of us at the Museum. Nearly pacified, for Professor Magesteri, that is. The edge is off his blade, in any event."

"I'm sure Stephen would be mortally offended to hear it rumored he may have accidentally been pleasant for once in his life," Mrs. Brolly said from behind her veil. "I'm certain it was an accident."

"He's not that bad," Polly blurted, because that was what she did, she blurted.

Polly's Papa leaned in. "Absolutely, Little Polly, now would you indulge your former Papa in a dance? I believe I hear the orchestra laying into a mazurka."

Polly had always been less terrible at the faster dances than she was at the rest. Her papa knew that.

"I'm honored I'm sure," Polly said only lying a bit.

Her Papa took her hand in his with a laugh and they were off. Papa holding onto Mrs. Canavan's tentacle with one hand and Polly with the other. Guy Ouellette took her by her free hand and Sekmet took Guy's hand. Always late, Charlie hurried to take Sekmet's other side. The chain went on and on until a good half the celebrants had joined the dance.

It wasn't bad. Polly only made a few mis-steps as the great circle went round. She was throwing back her head and laughing at the thrill when she passed Titus and Stephen near a potted palm. They were smiling so everything was fine.

Then the dancers broke apart, and the gentlemen went down on one knee and Polly skipped, more or less, round her Papa before joining hands with Mrs. Canavan, Sekmet, and Drussilla Everidge, that cow, and circling round to where they started.

It was the one time Polly had trouble counting anything. She always came up short or long when she was supposed to be dancing. Lucky her Papa grabbed her by the wrist before she could go past him and began to spin her round.

"I suppose I ought to congratulate you," her Papa said low.

"On what?" Polly asked, trying to keep track of the dance.

"The two most dangerous men in these islands, and you've reduced them to a matching pair of altered lap dogs. I hear that sort of business is considered quite the sport among the young ladies," Papa said smoke billowing from his cigar as the two of them danced their circle. "Still I doubt I'd have the brass to engage in it myself."

Polly had some difficulty not losing her place in the dance. Damned if she ever knew what to do with her bloody feet.

"Papa, I've no idea what you're on about; I haven't done anything to Titus and Stephen." Polly forced herself to smile when she said it. It was difficult to remember to smile and dance at the same time.

"In much the same way that you didn't take my pocket watch apart when you were five," Papa said her hands in his. "The mainspring was never the same again. I would ask you how you managed it but I think I can hazard a guess. We men are simpler creatures than we're generally credited."

"I still don't know what you're on about," Polly said as they changed partners. She counted her steps until her Papa took her hands and spun her round again trying with all her might not to think about it.

"Does Mrs. Brolly know?" Polly asked in spite of herself.

Papa laughed. "She very nearly took a strip out of my hide at the very suggestion, which is to say she refuses to believe the rumors."

"Oh dear," Polly said as the music sped up and so did the dance. "The gossip is fierce, then?"

"As ever, my pet," Papa said as the group joined hands and the music took on a breakneck tempo, "but I wouldn't be too alarmed. You know these society sorts, incapable of focusing on anything for an extended period and there are half a dozen more scandalous arrangements in the offing."

"There are?" Polly asked, the room starting to shift before her eyes.

Then her Papa said something. Polly knew he said something but she couldn't make out what the words were or what they meant. Instead, she felt her legs go out from under her and heard the sound of layers of cloth ripping in unison and two screams, maybe three and the scattering of the crowd to and fro. Everything seemed liquid and strange as if all the party goers and the ballroom had turned to raindrops and were washing down the gutter. Then she was being crowded, it felt as though she was being crowded.

"Stand back, Plumber," a voice that could only be Titus's shouted and Titus fell to his knees in front of her and it was only then that she saw what had occurred.

Her belly stood out hard and round and three times the size it had been when Florence had put on her corset that morning. Polly had never heard of such a thing. Clearly she was pregnant but still it was mad. Her belly had broken through her velvet dress, and her cotton shift, and above all it had ripped apart her canvas and steel corset. How was such a thing even possible? The crowd had reassembled in the tight circle around her, staring openly. Not a one of them liked her. She supposed she ought to feel embarrassed to have her naked belly exposed this way but she frankly cared less for that than she did for having fallen so publicly. Where was Stephen?

"Dr. Ng!" Titus called at the top of his lungs. "Bring me Dr. Ng!"

Chapter 15 : Piety's Reward

It was not the first time Colonel Titus Posthumous Albinus had been told he was going to be a father. It was however, the first time the doctor's news was confirmation of a promise given him by the Oracle of Apollo.

He looked to the little white fur-covered doctor, stooped over Polly in their bed. He was disconcerted by the way the hair made her expression unreadable.

"I trust all is well," Titus said, not that he required reassurance. The Oracle had promised him an heir, but so many things could go wrong.

"I do have some experience with the construction of standard Military Reclamations, though we never had much cause for treating them in the war; it was easier to reuse the parts than repair a serious injury, the parts reject each other in the long run so why bother," the hairy little doctor said. "We never made any females."

"I told you those stitches would hold fifty years, Ng!" Henry Plumber called from the doorway.

Titus whirled round to face the noxious little commoner who didn't appear to be paying him any mind as he drew a chair up to Polly's bedside.

"Papa," Polly said pulling the old man to her and burying her face in his smoky clothes. "There's going to be a baby."

Titus supposed girls were designed to have some sentimental attachment to their fathers, but he'd prefer to wash his hands of Henry Plumber. There was something grubby about the man, something immune to a good scrubbing. It mitigated matters somewhat to remind himself Plumber was not a blood relation, but had merely served the use of tradesmen the world over.

"Be a good girl and get your kit off," Plumber said pulling back the bed clothes. "Papa needs to have a look at the engine to make certain all the cylinders are firing."

There were some things Titus could not tolerate. Polly blushed, even her darker skin flushing.

"Sir," Titus said forcing himself to be polite for Polly's sake. "The Duchess has already got a physician; therefore I regret to inform you your assistance will not be necessary."

"Oh does she?" Plumber said "One who knows the creation better than the maker himself?"

"Dr Ng has been decorated for her work on the Reclamation battalions by the Empress herself," Titus informed the upstart.

Plumber didn't even acknowledge that Titus had spoken. "Put an end to this foolishness, Polly, explain to The Duke that as your maker…"

"I've been impregnated, not mortally wounded. Common women have babies every day without seeing a physician even once," Polly said, seeming quite herself now, which was to say unrepentantly stroppy.

"Polly," Plumber said as if speaking to a difficult child. "Polly, listen to me…"

"Papa, if you want to do something for me you'll go get Professor Magesteri and bring him here, to me," Polly said.

Plumber turned to look him in the eye. "With the Duke's approval, I'd be delighted to fetch the boy for you."

Stephen? Titus hadn't given him a moment's thought since Polly had collapsed on the ballroom floor.

"Do as she says," Titus said with a wave of his hand.

"What does she want now? Herd of Elephants? Just a small one? You could keep them in the ballroom but you're going to need to hire an elephant minder. I wanted to see if Polly was..." Stephen shrugged uncomfortably in the doorway. "In the ...um land of the living but she's...um not exactly...well you're not exactly living, are you?"

"Dr. Ng's prognosis is that Polly is in fact brimming with life at the moment," Titus said, kissing Polly's hand.

"The rumors were right, then," Stephen said shoving his hands in his pockets.

"Would you excuse us, Mr. Plumber? This is a private moment," Titus said.

"Come along, Stephen," Plumber said.

"No, stay, Stephen," Polly said holding out her arms to his rival, and Titus felt his stomach turn.

No sooner had Plumber excused himself than Stephen was on the edge of the bed with his face against Polly's breast.

"You scared the piss out of me, you horrid girl," Stephen said.

"Polly is fine. Polly is going to remain fine, we've the sacred word of the Oracle," Titus said keeping firm hold of Polly's right hand.

"Is that so? I seem to recall a great deal of talk about your precious heir but I must have missed it when Nefrit swore Polly would survive the process," Stephen said, his jaw tight.

Titus shook his head, Stephen was wrong. He had to be wrong.

"Don't be absurd," Titus said. "You're overreacting, as usual."

"Was that a knife I just felt at my back, you sodding liar? Is that how it is? I've done my part, the Ancient House is rescued from ruin, all those flowery phrases about brotherhood notwithstanding time to piss off, Stevie?" Stephen said.

"Oh, Stephen," Polly said running her fingers through his greasy hair. Titus hadn't grown his long enough to suit her, apparently. "We love you, both of us, Titus and I, both, and besides, you know Titus always keeps his promises."

Titus smiled broadly, giving no cause to suspect he had been wondering just how he might keep the appearance of good faith while avoiding actual practice. Then he slid beside Polly in the bed, his arm under her disheveled head.

"Let us not be tiresome, Cousin, this is a joyous occasion," Titus said.

"Agreed, Polly is, for the time being, still well," Stephen said stretching out on Polly's left side.

"Haven't we still got a house full of guests?" Polly asked, concerned, for once since Titus had met her, with propriety.

"Hang the guests, I'm going to be a father," Titus laughed, wondering how he was going to manage to rid himself of Stephen Magesteri.

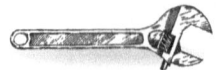

Professor Magesteri could not help but feel he had been brought low by the female. Not that he would admit it to anyone but he did not completely dislike the feeling.

The power of death had been his as long as he could remember but Polly, earnest, wild, patchwork-doll Polly could bring forth life without any particular effort. He could not shake the thought he ought to be kneeling at her little mismatched feet.

Stephen also had the distinct feeling that since that fateful day Polly had accepted Albinus's ring in her father's office, his life, his work, his very self had been taken apart and reassembled into something else entirely. A different machine with a function which was as yet unknown to him.

In self defense he renewed his habit of filing the ragged edges off the early mornings alone in the lab with a gentlemanly taste of hashish, just enough to prevent the clocks from clicking too loudly in her absence, just enough to keep abject panic at arms length.

It became his ritual. First thing upon rising he lit incense and made his obeisance to the goddess Taweret, much as he had worshiped at the altar of her husband Apophis as a young soldier. He even bought a small talisman for the protection of pregnant mothers on the Queen's Row and kept it in his pocket. Thus having done his duty to the gods he attended to the demands of his station and position and did as he must to keep hold of his manly stoicism. Were it not for duty and affection he feared he would run as far and as fast as will and money could take him.

But there was the rub; he felt a great deal of something for Titus's wife. Desire could not possibly be the right word because how was it possible to desire a thing already in one's possession? He did possess her, didn't he? Even if she had originally only been borrowed. He was inside her now. Even if he could now only watch as Titus made love to her for fear his seed would kill what grew in her. Polly loved him. It seemed to him most times he was the one securely tied in her little pocket. After all did the iron filings desire the rare earth magnets as they were dragged across the workbench? Desire couldn't possibly be correct. Still, whatever the word, he could not, would not, be parted from her no matter how Titus wished to be rid of him, and Stephen was perfectly well aware he did.

He would do all in his not inconsiderable power to protect and serve Polycorpus. Indeed, he had been her abject lackey from the moment the child began to swell within her, if not earlier, but he had no notion of how they would proceed once the childbearing was successful. The child would be Titus's regardless of piddling things like biology. Without a doubt the boy would have Titus's name and position and Titus would heap enough adoration on the boy to satisfy an army of offspring. There was no chance Titus would allow his heir's mother to leave and Stephen could no more leave Polly than he could leave his own right arm. Between Titus and Polly and himself, Stephen could not fathom a scenario which included happy family life. Strife and misery were fairly simple and straight forward, he could picture that. He could easily envision every foul accusation, every reproach he ever heard in his childhood coming from his own lips; it hardly required any effort at all. Death and despair were likewise accessible to him. He could imagine that. Polly dying in childbed. Killing himself. Killing Titus as well. All that was becoming surprisingly easy to picture.

It required a bit more time than was seemly at the hashish pipe but if pressed he could imagine Polly on the divan an infant sucking at her breast, after that it got rather fuzzy, and no amount of intoxicant would allow him to insert himself into the farrago. If he knew Titus, and he did, he was certain his cousin would no sooner allow his wife to nurse his child than he would allow her to clear the table so even that was buggering fantasy.

But even so where was Stephen going to fit in?

It was all he could do to put the future out of his head lest he run mad.

Within a week he noted white hair at Polly's temple when he kissed her cheek.

"Is she, or is she not, in good health?" Titus asked hairy little Dr. Ng.

All Polly wanted to do was sleep. She could hardly keep her eyes open and when she blinked she had tiny dreams like strange and vivid daguerreotypes.

Polly was having trouble focusing but the tiny Yeti gave the distinct impression that she'd been revising over night.

Dr. Ng adjusted her spectacles though you could barely see her eyes for all the fur. "As far as I can tell Polly's tiredness is to be expected during her current stage."

"She's not ill? What of relations?" Titus asked intently.

"Shouldn't be a problem," Dr. Ng said with a cough.

"You'll come back tomorrow. You must come every day," Titus said.

Polly wasn't sufficiently alert to remember Dr. Ng's reply but she couldn't imagine Dr. Ng disagreed. Not at the rate Titus was apt to pay.

It hardly mattered how much she slept because she was even more exhausted when she woke, as if she had been laboring in her sleep.

The next day at dawn Titus wrapped his fingers round hers and together they lit the flame in the Lares Familias. Then he guided her back to bed.

Other than that Titus woke her to eat, to bathe, and to kiss her face and hands a dozen times a day. Stephen sat on the bed and stroked her often tangled hair. At some point she believed he read to her. Or else she dreamed he read to her, she was hardly awake enough to be certain. When she found him missing she had him brought back to her.

She supposed Dr. Ng came and examined her over the next few days, sometimes she thought she vaguely recalled such a thing occurring.

Every evening, at bedtime, Polly supposed, Titus would slip her night gown over her head and slide his fingers, his tongue, his member inside of her. It was the only time she felt truly awake anymore.

Stephen watched from a chair in the corner of the room until she called to him to hold her hand as she writhed under Titus. If Titus blanched she hardly cared, she was much too fond of both of them to play favorites.

Her husband seemed younger since Lupercalia. Younger than her even. Young and hopeful and uncertain. He never seemed to see her without a look she could only describe as expectation.

Stephen was strange. Strange and silent, he kept one hand in his pocket at all times.

"The tiredness will pass," Dr. Ng said during a visit some weeks after it had all begun.

"You are certain Her Ladyship is not unwell?" Titus asked. It seemed Polly had heard her husband ask that before, whether it was once or a dozen times she was not sure and could not say.

"Despite the manner in which her exalted state came to light, there is no indication Her Ladyship's pregnancy is anything but perfectly healthy," Dr. Ng said wiping off the ear cone she used to listen to Polly's belly.

She was perfectly healthy.

Titus reminded her of this whenever she was awake enough to listen.

Stephen sat across the formal dining table from his cousin, in something that was little different than silence. Titus ate the way he always did, gracefully taking the meat and leaving the rest. Picky sod.

Stephen had been removed from polite society before it had the chance to make too much of a mark on him, so he had no problem taking Titus's plate so he could have his portion of honey carrots. He scraped the edges of the plate with his fork and used the crust of Titus's steak and kidney pie to mop up Titus's gravy.

"As soon as you finish those we'll pay Polly a visit," Titus said wiping his perfectly clean mouth with his perfectly clean serviette.

"No, we won't," Stephen said swallowing the food in his mouth.

"What did you say?" Titus asked turning his full attention at Stephen.

"I said 'No, we won't,'" Stephen said. He was sure he'd told his cousin 'no' before, even if couldn't remember doing it.

"Is that a threat?" Titus asked half-way between anger and curiosity.

"No, it's the way it sodding is, it's me looking after Polly, you self-absorbed git," Stephen said not really angry, not yet.

"And what if I were to disregard your directive, since I've the word of a medical expert that there's no harm in it?" Titus asked leaning back in his chair and crossing his legs. Stephen knew Titus was forcing himself to seem calm and relaxed, it still made him want to throttle him.

"No, bloody harm in it? She's half-asleep! You're not fucking disregarding me because you're not fucking doing it, you dog buggering git! You're not going to go climb on top of Polly and have at it like she's your fucking hobby horse. It's not as if it's going to change whose baby that is growing in her belly," Stephen growled rage boiling up inside him. Force of habit compelled him to rise, palms flat on the table. He wasn't laying a hand on Titus, despite the feeling racing through his arms.

Titus glanced carelessly at Stephen's hands out of the corner of his eye, and the muscle in his jaw jumped so slightly Stephen doubted anyone else would have been able to notice it.

"I've no idea what you're talking about, Cousin, everyone knows necromancers are congenitally infertile, besides which there is the Rule of the Pater Familias, a child belongs by law to the mother's husband," Titus pointed out casually, lightly.

Stephen wondered how many ways his cousin had worked out to kill him so far.

As for Stephen he only had need of one method, and despite everything, despite being the stupid mincing sod's heir, he had never considered killing his cousin, until that moment.

"Is that why you couldn't get Polly pregnant without me?" Stephen asked.

For a split second a look of rage crossed Titus's face and that was a thousand times better than killing; Stephen had busted his bloody façade.

"If memory serves, neither could you," Titus shot back. "The child is mine in body as well as name."

"You can have the brat for all I care, name it Titus, and buy it a pair of bloody lizards," Stephen spat. "Polly's my concern."

"Salamanders," Titus said through gritted teeth and quick as a wink he was on his feet. "Are you implying I don't care for my wife?"

"No, Cousin," Stephen said keeping his hands flat on the table, it was his turn to be calm "Not so much implying as stating it out right."

He could see his cousin's eyes darting round the room looking for potentially deadly weapons.

"I adore Polycorpus," Titus said, low and angry, like a roll of thunder.

Too bad for him Stephen Magesteri was the one man in England who wasn't afraid of the poncey bugger.

"You care for Polly as a brood mare. She's nothing but a receptacle for sperm to you, or I wouldn't be here. If you loved her, you'd have been satisfied to have her as your wife for the rest of your days and you wouldn't have bred her to an abomination, just so you could have your precious baby. You know what would serve you right? What would be just desserts? If Polly's baby were female. That's what you deserve, Titus, a daughter," Stephen sneered, "a swarm of daughters."

There was something strange about Titus all of a sudden. His eyes were open but unfocused his mouth likewise hung open as if searching for words, something Titus Albinus never did. Stephen had never seen him like this. Titus shook his head as if to clear it.

"I love her, I would love Polly even if she had a daughter, but I," Titus started no longer seeming angry at all and Stephen suddenly felt his stomach lurch as if he would vomit if he listened to the rest.

"No, you don't, you can't possibly love her or you never would have whored her out for the good of the family line," Stephen said bitterly.

"That's not what I did," Titus said his voice startlingly small.

"What did you do, then, Tight-Arse?" Stephen had to remind himself to keep the rage going.

"My duty, I did my duty and in the process I gave Polly what she wanted," Titus said, raggedly.

"Polly doesn't give a damn about babies," Stephen said.

"I wasn't talking about the baby, I was talking about you. Polly wants you, she's always wanted you. It doesn't matter to her that she's mine, that she's mine and I love her," Titus said very quietly.

Stephen shook his head. This was insanity. And his cousin thought he could fix it, remind him who had proper rights to Polly by making sure Stephen watched while he fucked her once a day.

"She doesn't love me, Titus, she pities me. You're the one she undresses with her eyes every time he walks across the room," Stephen said. "She never stares at my arse like that."

Titus shook his head again "That's not love, that's lust. She plays with your hair, all the bloody time."

"Is that why you stopped cutting yours?" Stephen asked. This was confusing; a moment ago they wanted to kill each other. Now they didn't, at least Stephen didn't. You could never tell about Titus.

"What's all the shouting about?" Polly asked from the doorway, still in her dressing gown her hair like a giant bramble.

"Oh, you know, mummy loves you best, that sort of thing," Stephen said sticking his hands in his pockets.

"Same old saw," Titus agreed, wrinkling his nose at her.

"Could you please row more quietly in future? Or not at all, I can't sleep properly when you row," she said, her eyes were black pits. "My room is on the other side of the house. I could use some assistance."

It was a preposterous claim, that their arguing affected her in some way. If Stephen were braver he would have told her so. Still she needed him, needed them both actually.

Titus took her right side and Stephen her left, and so, their arms braced behind her back, the two of them quite easily helped her back to her room.

"How long has this been going on?" Dr. Ng, the head of The British Museum's medical wing, said examining the cracked tips of Polly's fingers.

"You did examine her yesterday," Titus said looking down at both the tiny Yeti and Polly sitting up in the bed. "What of her hair?"

The number of white hairs at her temples was growing nightly.

"Still think she's perfectly well?" Stephen asked.

"The pregnancy is progressing nicely," Dr. Ng said peering closely at Polly's hands. "One of her kind has never bred before. This may be perfectly normal. Magesteri, get me the bandages from my bag."

"The baby is healthy? You're certain?" Titus asked, noting the dullness of Polly's skin and the dark circles round her eyes, not to mention the broken nails and bleeding fingers.

"Yes, the child is growing daily, the heartbeat is strong, the mouth of the womb is closed, the pregnancy itself is clearly stable," Dr. Ng said. "Professor, could you cut some finger sized strips? Open your mouth, Polly."

"All I needed was a few days rest," Polly said. "I'm more awake today." And then dutifully opened her mouth.

"It's been a month," Stephen said handing Ng the bandages.

"That's not funny," Polly said.

"Twenty-eight days," Titus corrected him as Ng wrapped the bandages round the ends of all ten of Polly's fingers.

"Truly?" Polly asked.

Titus nodded. "Truly and honestly."

"I've a theory," Dr. Ng said as she tied.

"Oh goody, a theory," Stephen said. "You're going to do medicine through trial and error."

"All doctors do medicine through trial and error," Dr. Ng said. "Anyone who tells you differently is a liar. My spectacles?" she said gesturing to have them pushed up.

Stephen looked at Titus and Titus obliged, pushing them back into place.

"As you were saying, you've a theory?" Titus urged her to continue.

"I believe the issue may be the extreme…health of the child. My theory," she said knotting the bandage round the nail split past the quick on Polly's smallest finger, "is that the child's vigor is draining the vitality of the mother. If I were able to fortify Polly's system with the necessary nourishments, her strength would return."

"What do you require?" Titus asked, wondering why she'd taken so bloody long to mention it. "I'll pay it."

"I've been acquiring ingredients and formulating optimum proportions the last several days," Ng said. "The Powders are in my bag, in the packet labeled 'Albinus'. She's to take a spoonful dissolved in her tea each morning upon rising."

"I will see to it, personally," Titus assured the doctor. Some things were too important to leave to the servants.

Between them Titus and Stephen saw to it that Polly took the powders dutifully each morning, whether she wanted to or not, and she didn't. It was three full weeks before Polly balked, declaring the whole business a foul tasting mess that served only to turn her urine funny colors.

Soon her nipples began to crack and bleed as well.

There was an unguent, of course. Dr Ng was very positive the unguent would help and Titus and Stephen were very enthusiastic and competitive about who would get to help her put it on her fingers and nipples.

The unguent did nothing but leave grease marks on the front of her night gown and frequently replaced bandages. Polly supposed they were a nice addition to the blood stains.

There were two solid white streaks in her hair as thick as her index finger.

That Titus and Stephen fussed over her like a pair of broody hens with one egg between them was not to say life came to a grinding halt. Stephen got up in the morning and went to abuse apprentices at the Museum despite the fact that Polly's womb was occupied. Stephen returned to the Museum after tea, as well, lest the brainless clots get too comfy.

As for Titus, he rose and went to the baths as he always had. The primary difference as far as Titus went was that he waited to leave until after he had forced a full cup of foul tasting tea down Polly's throat.

All of which was to say Polly had time to herself to think and time to write. Then when Titus and Stephen came home all she had to do was stow her work under her pillow.

In adherence to the new schedule after tea Polly slept deeply, took a stroll through the house to stretch her legs, suffered the bandages on her fingers to be changed and her hair to be dressed for the second time that day and laid in her bed, pen awkwardly in hand, struggling to work out her exact position on motherhood.

She had just shown to her own satisfaction that there was no meaningful difference between a commoner's and a monster's right to control her own conception, and she could feel her heart racing precisely the way it did when she managed to get an engine to fire properly, when she heard Stephen's tread in the corridor and shoved the pen and ink under the bed, her work under her pillow.

"Hullo, Professor," Polly said brightly, wiping the ink from her thumb on the dark coverlet.

"What a horrible word, and to think I could have gone into a noble profession like collecting barrels full of piss for the tanner," Stephen said throwing himself in the chair beside Polly's bed. "Skinning dead dogs…cleaning public lavatories."

"Bad day in the workshop?" Polly asked. "He doesn't do it intentionally… Charlie, Charlie Edney, I mean."

"Remarkably," Stephen said pulling his hair out of his eyes with both hands and gripping his skull in the process. "Just this once Charlie Edney is not the boil on my buttocks in desperate need of lancing."

"What's the trouble then?" Polly asked, shifting because she was uncomfortable. Polly was hardly ever less than ill at ease these days.

"Not what, who; Endymion Perkins," Stephen said pulling his hair. "I never imagined there could exist two catastrophes of such epic proportions in one empire let alone one Museum department. Natural Laws not withstanding young Perkins has achieved something of a feat in matching Edney's level of incompetence. Particularly at his tender age."

"I don't see how any act could be quite so tragic as that waistcoat," Titus said from the doorway.

"I don't see what your complaint is, aside from a few threadbare spots," Polly said sitting up on one elbow. "Stephen wears it all the time."

"Seeing as said article was just defended by a woman who thinks a French cuff has extra lace the evidence is conclusive. Throw it in the fire, Cousin," Titus said with a grin.

"I'd rather toss in Perkins, if it's all the same to you," Stephen said, not even bothering to turn his head to Titus.

"Since the boy's paternal grandmother is sister to the Provincial governor of Lettland that's not going to happen. The waistcoat on the other hand has no such family ties," Titus said sauntering in to sit by Polly's side. "How are you, my darling?"

"Oh, spiffing, sitting here, thinking of taking Stephen's velvet waistcoat as my adopted child," Polly teased, unable to stop herself toying with a copper curl that fell across Titus's forehead. Close cropped as it had been when she married him, Polly never imagined his hair was in truth so curly. It reminded her of a mass of copper springs.

Titus's eyes sparkled and a smile as wide as a pelican's split his narrow face. "Shall I call my solicitor? Tell him there's an unstylish and ill-kempt bit of haberdashery Mrs. Albinus is keen to bring into the family?"

"The baby will need a playmate, who better than Stephen's waistcoat?" Polly said feeling silly and happy until she looked to Stephen.

Stephen's face was strangely drawn and his fingers were digging deeply into the arms of the chair.

"If you two are quite finished playing silly buggers," Stephen rasped.

Polly could see the first of the letters begin to bleed red through the linen of his shirt sleeves.

"Budge up," Titus instructed Polly with a wave of his hand.

"Call Llewellyn, he and Cornelius can take me to my room, they can carry this chair if necessary," Stephen said his voice growing more and more forced.

"Don't be such a priss," Polly warned.

"I won't be gossiped over if I can help it," Stephen said sharply.

Titus rolled his eyes "You think they don't know? You honestly believe the servants have no idea? Let it go man, they're servants. It's like having the cats in the room while you move your bowels…"

"Titus!" Polly couldn't help herself sometimes her husband was as rude as his cousin.

"If you'll excuse me, I happen to be bleeding!" Stephen bellowed.

"And I will help you as soon as you can lower yourself to cooperate!" Titus shouted back before regaining his much vaunted self-control. "Besides which, if I've both of you in the same room I might be able to avoid running myself ragged keeping an eye on your conditions."

It was not until Stephen was lying beside her on a bank of pillows, swaddled in blankets and drugged to the gills that Polly remembered her book under his head.

Chapter 16 : Treason in the House

itus found the book, the thick sort of cloth bound blank book housekeepers used for household ledgers, when he shifted Stephen in a vain attempt to do something about his snoring, lest it wake Polly. It was not a book for reading; it was a book for writing.

Titus opened it up, well, because it was there and that was what one did with books, wasn't it, and because there was no good reason he could think of for Stephen to keep a book under his pillow. When he opened it he could see it was not in Stephen's hand, as neat and pedestrian as the sample in a child's primer, no, this book was in his wife's savage scrawl, and it was quite nearly full. Whatever it was. At the top of the first page were the words WHAT IS ACCEPTED TRUTH VS. WHAT EVIDENCE AND REASON SUGGEST.

Titus leaned back in his chair and crossed his ankles in front of him. It might be amusing to learn what Polly thought of the world.

Stephen drifted into consciousness to the smell of tea and cakes and the sight of his cousin looming over the bed.

"Wake up, will you," Titus said brusquely. "Are you well enough to answer questions sensibly?"

Stephen patted down his arms and legs. It had been almost two weeks since the curse had struck, the bleeding words had been reduced to red welts. Every bit of skin on his body ached dully but it was bearable.

"In as much as I ever answer questions sensibly, Colonel Tight-Arse," Stephen croaked, his throat rusty, wondering what the git was on about.

"This isn't a lark," Titus said between gritted teeth. "Time is of the essence."

"Where's Polly?" Stephen asked wincing as he shifted in the bed, too long on any bed, no matter how sodding comfortable, buggered up his back.

Titus waved his hand grandly, the way he was apt to. "Stretching her legs, having a private bath and getting her hair dressed, which is why I need you to come to your full senses as quickly as possible. Have you seen this book before?"

Stephen squinted, he needed his spectacles from his bedroom if Titus was going to expect him to read anything, then he recognized a stain on the cover. "Is that the book Polly likes to scribble in when she's at loose ends?"

"You've read it? You knew and didn't tell me?" Titus hissed.

Stephen shrugged rolling his eyes. "I happened upon it in December. One of the maids informed me it belonged to Her Ladyship."

"I allow you to share my wife's bed and you didn't feel it necessary to let me know that you'd found this!" Titus said waving the book in his face.

"I don't know what you're up in arms about. It's got fuck all to do with anything, just a load of philosophical twaddle. Made my eyes cross, what I could make out; your wife's handwriting is utter shit."

"This is not 'twaddle', Stephen, this is treason," Titus said laying the book on Stephen's lap. "I've seen men executed for less."

"Don't be fucking absurd," Stephen said picking up the book. "Polly's a girl. Girls can't commit treason. They haven't got the …they haven't got it in them. Can't do it. Not even Polly."

"What an erudite and well reasoned argument, though I doubt it would hold up in front of a tribunal, particularly since Polly's own reckoning is that a properly educated female is in every sense the equal of a male. Oh, but that's not the end of it; it's not merely females that are the equal of any citizen, but commoners as well," Titus bit out.

"She didn't say that, did she?" Stephen asked. Trust Polly to stick her foot in it up to the neck. "Even if she did, who cares what a pregnant girl says? I heard of a pregnant girl thought she was a manticore and took a bite out of her mother-in-law. No one much minded. Even the mother-in-law forgave her in the end."

Titus squinted. "Even you must recognize there is a difference between taking a harmless nip at the in-laws and denying the godhood of every Emperor who's ever lived."

Stephen's stomach churned "She didn't."

"I assure you; she did. What's more, that is the barest fingernail of Polycorpus's blasphemy." Titus grimaced. "I thought you read it."

"Well, skimmed, philosophy doesn't exactly make for scintillating reading," Stephen said.

"You do realize I am sworn to report all treason to my superiors? It's what I do," Titus said, his teeth gritted.

"You're going to turn Polly in?" Stephen asked. He was torn between resignation and grasping at a way to change Titus's mind.

"Don't be absurd," Titus said as if his allegiance to Polly was obvious and unshakeable.

Perhaps it was.

Stephen gave Titus a measuring look, trying sort it all out. There was something, something more Titus wasn't saying.

"Out with it," Stephen said. "Whatever you're holding back, don't make me wait all day, out with it!"

Titus frowned, deeply. "The duchess makes a very convincing argument."

"Is that bad?" Stephen asked.

Titus looked incredulous, as if the answer were obvious. "It is the worst thing in the world, for all of us."

The minute Polly set foot in her bedroom and saw Titus and Stephen staring at her, her book in Titus's hands, she very nearly turned around and walked out.

"What are you doing with that? That's my personal book, with my personal, private, thoughts. You can't help yourselves to my personal thoughts without asking, either of you," Polly said, feeling her face turn hot with anger.

She didn't know quite why it annoyed her so that Titus smiled blandly at her and Stephen scrunched his face worriedly. She quite forgot how weak and tired she felt for a moment.

"Polly, dearest, I know you are under the impression these are you're thoughts, but what I am interested in is where you initially heard this treason. Did Stephen teach you these things?" Titus asked placidly.

"Me?" Stephen all but shouted in surprise.

Polly couldn't help herself, she burst out laughing. It hurt her chest.

"I'm pleased you find it amusing," Titus said with false jocularity but his smile only went halfway up his face.

"First off those are my ideas; I came up with them on my own using my own powers of observation and ability to reason. I can only wish someone cared enough to tell me the truth rather than some storybook version of the way the world works. Secondly, Professor Stephen Magesteri is no more capable of thinking my thoughts than you are," Polly said counting off her points on her bandaged fingers.

"Quite right," Stephen agreed.

"He's every bit as stodgy and unimaginative as you are when it comes to the established social order," Polly went on.

"Hold off," Stephen said suddenly offended.

"No, I won't hold off. It's the truth. The only difference between the two of you, Stephen, is you believe a just society wouldn't suffer you to live and simultaneously thank and curse the gods for injustice. Oh, you whinge and whine about the way things are but given your druthers the only thing you'd change is your own predicament. You'd be just like him, given half a chance. Less than half. Your suffering hasn't improved your moral reasoning any more than Titus's advantages have improved his," Polly said, flushed at saying exactly what she thought but she could feel her strength beginning to falter.

"That's your statement on the matter?" Titus asked somberly. "These treasonous thoughts are yours and yours alone? No one led you to them? No one taught you to think such thoughts? You came to them purposefully and of your own accord?"

Polly sighed. "I came to them logically. Using the scientific method. Taking the facts into account they are the only logical conclusion I could come to. I had no choice."

"If your thoughts are so logical why doesn't anyone else think them?" Titus asked.

"You know as well as I do, the only ones who are taught logic and rhetoric, let alone granted the leisure time to use them, are well-born monsters with the luck to have come out with a penis, the very ones with the least incentive to put their brains to any uncomfortable uses," Polly said sitting down on the edge of her bed. She had no choice.

"You must also realize, then, that those who choose to think these thoughts despite their best interests are some of my primary targets of investigation?" Titus said and there was hardness to him Polly had never seen before.

"It's not treason, Titus. I swear I didn't intend them to be seen by anyone. These are private, my private thoughts," Polly said feeling her belly leap. Was it her child or was it fear?

"Then why, in the name of all that is holy, did you write this shit down!" Titus shouted.

"I wanted to get it all clear in my own mind, a sort of blue print, that's all," Polly tried to explain. "If it had been a machine I would have drawn a schematic."

Titus rocked back on his heels staring at the ceiling, his hands clenched behind his back. Polly guessed from his pose he was trying very hard to hold in.

"I could have lived the remainder of my life in peace, Polly, never having read your horrid book," Titus said and walked quietly out of the room.

Colonel Titus Posthumous Albinus, Duke Londinium Austri, Order of Apophis 1st class was a creature of duty. He knew where his obligations lay.

He knew without question his highest duty was to the Gods, of which the Empress was one. After that came his military superiors, his ancestors, his military inferiors, his living family, his fellow members of society, and finally his household to which his wife and servants belonged.

Yet Polly and her infernal book kept intruding on his thoughts. Her soft round brown buttocks. Her claim that the godhood of Emperors was mere political expediency. Her round white breasts with blue veins running through them, too large and exuberant for anything but a commoner. Her assertion that even the gods themselves were not divine at all but merely monsters of another age who used their natural differences to frighten commoners into worshiping them.

His wife was horrible. The very worst sort of atheist as well as intoxicating, earthy, and exotic. She was terrifying and dangerous. Exactly the sort of threat to the Empire he was supposed to eliminate.

Unsure what else to do Titus stalked down the corridor and up two flights of stairs to his study.

He lit the incense, splashed wine in the dish and fell to his knees in front of the altar. He felt nothing.

He raised his hand adoringly to the figure of Apollo Alexikakos but no feeling of peace washed over him. What if he had spent his entire life praying to beings who weren't there?

Titus took the figure of Apophis in his hand and pressed the worn smooth belly of the crocodile to his lips and felt no reassurance.

Finally he stood to take the framed likeness of the Empress herself from the top of the altar and settled back on his knees to bask in her Divinity, descendent of the Goddess Venus and the God Amun Ra.

He knew the features as well as he knew his own, but it occurred to him he'd never really looked at her before. What he saw was an ordinary looking woman with circles round her eyes, a hooked nose, and lines in the corner of her mouth, who could use a better dress maker. The materials were finest quality but the fit left something to be desired.

No, he worshiped Her Highness. He kissed the image's feet and for the first time in his life felt slightly foolish doing so.

He gazed upon her sacred countenance.

It must be his imagination that the smile that was wise and benevolent every day of the first 39 years of his life, could, in one day, turn ironic.

Titus lay the picture face down on the top of the altar and collapsed back on the rug.

What had Polly done?

Polly had ruined him.

Stephen would have said that Titus came home three days later, except that he had it on Llewelyn's sworn authority that his master never left the house.

Whether he'd left the house or not, when Titus returned he was changed.

For one thing he knocked on his own bedroom door.

"May I come in?" Titus asked opening the door a crack.

"Titus!" Polly cried hobbling out of bed, pressing her cracked lips to his face.

Stephen watched as Polly clung to her husband's arms. Stephen wasn't the least bit jealous, he'd known it was coming.

But something was strange about Titus, something Stephen couldn't put his finger on.

"Nice to see you again, Cousin," Stephen said, smiling.

"Likewise," Titus said with a shrug.

"Titus, are you growing a beard?" Polly asked stroking three days of patchy bright red stubble on her husband's jaw.

Perhaps that was it, but Stephen wasn't sure.

"I'm considering it, but, Stephen, Polly," Titus said taking hold of Polly's hands and holding them to his chest. "I want to bring this arrangement to an end."

Stephen sat down heavily on the bed unable to speak.

"Stephen, I love you, you are like a brother to me, we have been everything to one another, comrades in arms, boyhood companions, but I would like you to put aside all claim to my wife," Titus rambled on. "I went along with this travesty in the name of the gods, but seeing as I have come to the conclusion they don't exist I withdraw my agreement."

Polly opened her mouth as if trying to formulate a response but coming up short.

Stephen pulled his hair out of his eyes and looked up at his cousin an answer coming to him, without much pondering at all. "No."

"What?" Titus asked.

"You heard me, I said 'no' I know you haven't heard it much but consider this a new beginning. You say you want me to relinquish all claim on Polly and I say 'no' I don't want to give her up, because I love her at least as well as you do," Stephen said with a grin like one of Titus's old insincere ones.

"Stephen, Titus, how can you even measure love? It's not a contest," Polly said.

"Seeing as I'm the more powerful of the two of us I think that's the end of the discussion. Until Polly tells me to piss off I'm her lover. Since you've seen fit to drop your moral compass down the public sewer, you could always set Polly free, if you liked. I won't object," Stephen said.

"The day Polycorpus leaves my side is the day I die," Titus said his eyes gleaming.

"That can be very easily arranged," Stephen smiled back at him.

"Don't forget, Cousin, if you can be hurt you can also be killed," Titus matched his expression perfectly.

"Titus, Stephen, I want the two of you to stop it, this instant," Polly said holding her hand to her belly. The thought of Titus taking possession of the child, his child, inflamed Stephen.

"Look away, Polly, this will be over before you know it," Stephen said pulling the glove from his right hand.

Titus, being Titus, unsheathed the dagger and small pistol he kept who-the-fuck-knew-where on his person at all times then shimmered out of view.

"Stop it, you two idiots," Polly shouted, fairly flinging her body forward and collapsing there, in front of Stephen.

Titus's dagger clattered to the floor as Titus leapt in to keep her head from hitting the floor. At least it looked like that's what happened.

Polly had fainted at any rate and was hovering about the ground.

His own Polycorpus fainted like some society bint trying to impress everyone with her delicacy. It was by far the most girlish thing he'd ever known Polly to do.

He took her hands in his fully intending to shout obscenities in her face until she came to only there were trails of blood winding down her cheeks in the place of tears.

For a moment all Stephen could hear was his heart beating in his ears like thunder. Stephen wiped the blood away with his loose glove and succeeded only in smearing the blood across her cheeks.

He licked his finger tips and wiped harder, that helped a bit but he still felt a strange prickling behind his eyelids.

"We've got to get her to Plumber and Ng immediately. Call for Llewellyn and he can have the driver get the carriage," Titus said shimmering into view.

Stephen busied himself straightening Polly's clothes like a useless sod and blinking back tears trying not to think of the worst that could happen, trying with all his might to think clearly. "And what do you think they could do for her? Ng's already got every doctor, researcher, and engineer from Henry down to the lowest apprentice botanist working on Polly's case, the best they can come up with is a packet of powder that smells of rotten eggs and turns her urine pthalo blue."

"What do you propose? I'm not leaving her this way. I will not have it," Titus asked becoming quite solid. Stephen was taken aback to see Titus had cushioned Polly's fall by allowing her to land literally on top of him. Knowing how bleeding heavy she was he was surprised Titus had breath to argue.

"We need to go to the oracle," Stephen said told him, it was all he could come up with.

"What for?" Titus asked, indignant.

"Nefrit foresaw all this mess," Stephen said gesturing to the three of them. "If anyone has the answer it's her."

"Did she foresee this, or did she bring it about?" Titus said brushing a strand of hair from Polly's face.

"Yes, you and I have both been successfully out-witted by an old woman who is so feeble she has to be carried to the loo every 45 minutes so she doesn't mess herself. Does that sound likely to you?" Stephen shot back.

"Point taken." Titus inclined his head. "Ring for Llewellyn, will you? Polly shouldn't be left alone while we're gone. Besides, we could use a bit of help getting her to the bed."

Silence reigned for an instant, Titus's mouth drawn into a thin flat line.

"Did you truly intend to kill me a few minutes ago," Titus asked.

Stephen couldn't help grimacing. "Yes, but I would have felt terrible about it later."

Titus glared but Stephen supposed that was his right.

"I suppose I should be grateful. Would you mind terribly holding Polly steady whilst I pry myself out from under?" Titus said

"Proceed," Stephen said. The instant he touched her belly it began wriggling like a bag full of snakes. "Stop, Titus, before you do anything else reach those long arms of yours round the front and feel this."

Titus gave Stephen a hard look but he did as he asked. Then Polly's abdomen lurched violently and a visible shiver went through Titus.

"What have you put in her? We must go to the Oracle without delay," Titus said before turning his gaze over Stephen's shoulder. "Oh, there you are

Llewellyn, took you long enough. Could you help Professor Magesteri and myself to get the Duchess to bed? You are not to leave her side until my cousin and I return from the temple of Apollo."

Chapter 17 : A Grave Cure

he ride to the temple was tense but Titus managed to convey the appearance of nonchalance upon entering the Templum Apollonian.

"My cousin Stephen and I have come to see my Grandmother, Nefrit," he called loudly waving the back of the hand bearing the ring of the Priests of Apollo in the general direction of all and sundry as he strolled with practiced aplomb through the outer chamber.

The acolytes were duly impressed and stood back.

There in the inner sanctum, resting on a nest of soft cushions, was the Oracle, Nefrit.

Titus couldn't bear to play the willing instrument any longer, he went straight to where Nefrit laid and stood over her.

The Oracle's red eyes slammed open.

"Good, you're awake, time to keep your promises," Titus said.

"Good evening, Grandmother," Stephen muttered.

"What promises are those, boy?" The Oracle asked.

"You gave your word Polly would not die in her childbed," Titus said struggling not to shout.

"I said no such thing, I told you the girl would produce a living heir and fulfill your obligation to the ancestors," the old woman creaked.

"Told you," Stephen muttered behind him.

Titus felt himself turning round whip-like, without particularly wanting to.

"Would it be possible for you to be silent, Cousin?" Titus said, before addressing Nefrit again. "Not good enough, Grandmother, I will not lose her, no matter the cost."

The Oracle closed her terrible eyes once more, turning her face away. There was a chilling sound from her withered mouth; it took Titus an instant to recognize as laughter.

"Does my devotion amuse you?" Titus said through his clenched jaw.

"Please, Nefrit, I beg of you," Stephen said, behind him. "We cannot lose Polly."

Titus turned round to silence Stephen but thought better of it. Instead he turned back to Nefrit. "Tell me what you desire, and I will give it to you in return for my wife's survival. Simply tell me what is to be done."

The terrible laughing sound returned and the Oracle turned her terrible red eyes on Titus.

"Men are the same as they have been since the beginning of time. They never change. The world will always revolve around them and their pricks," Nefrit said. "It's not about your desires, either of you. It's about Polycorpus. It always has been."

"What are you saying? What is that supposed to mean?" Titus squinted. Perhaps Nefrit had gone the way all Oracles went in the end, stark raving mad.

"What it means, boy, is that the girl is not your wife, you are her husbands, both of you. She was not brought to you to give you an heir; you two idiots were drawn to her, inevitably, to get her with child. She is a stone round which the river of time swirls. The Duke and the Abomination are but grains of sand in comparison," Nefrit said.

Titus felt his knees weaken for the blink of an eye but he steeled himself.

"Then there must be a way to save her," Stephen said.

Titus swallowed hard. "Tell me and you shall be rewarded."

In an instant the air in the room seemed to turn too thick to breathe. The

Old Witch's back arched and her limbs twisted and the voice that came from the dark hole of her mouth was that of a beast.

"Midnight to midnight
In the fires of Cathay
Cut with a blade of sand
Stirred with a rope of sand
Boiled in a pot of sand
Served in a bowl of sand
A stone of heaven
An acorn for the New Year
Twisted branches of the Nile's tree
Flesh of Cypress and flesh of Chalybes
Soil of Conception
Waters of Humber
Wings of the World Maker
Tongues of the Suck Flower and the foreign wooly-headed hump back
Stirred night and day and served by the hand of he who brewed it." And with a rattle and a hiss the Oracle fell silent, her wizened body limp.

"What exactly does that mean?" Titus asked.

"Do you expect me to chew your food for you as well?" the old woman said in her usual raspy voice. "Some priest of Apollo you are, if you can't even interpret the words of the God."

"There are no gods," Titus said folding his arms across his chest. "That was nothing but gibberish."

Nefrit squinted at Titus as if waiting to see if she could make him blink. "I have given you the means to save your precious wife. If you don't make use of the gift it's none of my concern. When called to do my bidding, you must obey, regardless."

"That's it? No directions and I owe you now?" Titus felt his face grow hot.

"How exactly do I owe you?"

"You men are all alike, stupid. Yes, you owe me. Three times now I've gone out of my way to assist you. Boy, you tire me." Nefrit waved her hand to dismiss them. "You are free to go and take the Abomination with you."

Titus stood for a minute waiting for something more, but nothing came. He wondered how Nefrit's babbling could save anyone, let alone someone bleeding from the eyes. Polly was going to die. Like the others. Like the others it had been his fault. But unlike the others there was no replacing Polly. The thought of another after her was incomprehensible.

It was as though he forgot how to walk. He, Colonel Titus Posthumous Albinus, Duke Londinium Austri, Order of Apophis first class, had to remind himself how to first pick up one foot, swing forward, set down, lift next foot, swing forward, set down firmly. He had always been buffeted by the pronouncement of his name but tonight he felt strangely disconnected from the syllables. It seemed peculiar to realize he hadn't chosen any part of it himself, no, it had all been meted out by happenstance. Polycorpus, at least, had a name that reflected who she was. If he lost Polycorpus he had the feeling he might cease to exist, not just die, but vanish 'poof' as if he was never there at all.

"Titus, are you listening to a word I'm saying?" Stephen said, irritably.

"Hmmmm? Were you speaking?" Titus asked.

"I asked if you got everything she said in there. I believe I can parse it all out if you can recall it word for word," Stephen said, steering Titus through the foyer of the temple as though he were a ship.

"Yes, of course," Titus said swatting away Stephen's hand from his elbow, he was hardly infirm. "Though I fail to see the point, it's all nonsense. Honestly, Stephen, blade of sand?"

Stephen's brows drew together incredulously. "Do you know anything useful? Anything at all? Sand, My dear cousin, is the chief component in the making of glass. That wasn't nonsense, that was directions for an elixir to save Polly's life."

"Where are we going to find a blade of glass at 6 in the evening on a Saturday?" Titus asked hope, starting to glimmer.

"The Chinese make a superior tempered glassware for laboratory use, blades, stirrers, beakers. And Dr. Ng has the most extensive set I know," stepping out on the street Stephen called to the driver. "To the Museum, and don't spare the whip."

Professor Stephen Magesteri could not remember a time in his life when he hadn't known Titus Albinus. In most circumstances there was no one else he would rather have at his side. A military tribunal, for instance, there was no one he'd rather have at his side at a military tribunal. You could start out on trial for your life and end up covered head to toe in medals with Titus on your side. Titus was also unarguably an asset at any dinner party or trip to the haberdasher. It was simply that his cousin, Titus, knew fuck all about science and couldn't concoct a medicine if his life depended on it. Only it wasn't Titus's life was on the line, it was Polly's.

It would make so much more sense if it was the other way round. Polly would be an immense help in the laboratory and Titus, the smarmy bugger, would make an exceptionally apt invalid. He'd likely enjoy it.

"We'll go directly to Ng and make use of her facilities," Titus said peering expectantly out the coach window. "Perhaps you should compile your list now and you can present it to some underling when we arrive at the medical wing."

"I said I could parse the prophecy, not that I'd already done it, and if you think we can simply march into the director of medical research's office, hand a list of supplies to some grunt and have at it you're sadly mistaken about the functioning of Museum bureaucracy," Stephen said. "Not to mention the personalities involved."

"How it functions for you, you mean," Titus said. "I'm hardly a Museum employee. Surely my presence can only serve to expedite…"

"Your presence can only serve to cause the same sort of wankery as a fresh whore in an army barrack. The Museum runs on money, I know it isn't quite what you're used to but every department in the stinking pile is short funded and every employee lays awake at night scheming ways to get an increase," Stephen tried to explain.

"Then wouldn't my appearance motivate them to assist us," Titus asked.

"Your appearance would motivate them to attack each other like a pack of wild dogs trying to get at your purse strings. I can guarantee some would attempt to improve on the instructions given to us by the oracle. Someone else, at least one someone else, but likely more, would make an attempt at sabotage. I can also guarantee you at least three someone elses will, for reasons entirely their own, do everything in their power to obstruct us," Stephen said.

"Then how do we proceed?" Titus said.

Thirty-eight years Stephen had known Titus Albinus and he'd never asked him what to do before. Stephen coughed.

"You'll need to," Stephen waggled his fingers in the air. "Do your… thing; disappear. That also might prove more helpful than writing the usual requisition and waiting a week for ingredients."

"Right," Titus said still staring out the window. A moment later the carriage rounded the corner to the Museum and Titus began to shimmer before fading away entirely. In a flash the door flew open. If Titus made a sound as he leapt from his seat it was lost in the clatter of hooves on stone.

"You could've waited for the sodding coach to stop, dog buggering idiot," Stephen shouted. "You're no use to Polly if you break your fool neck."

Stephen at least, had the sense to wait for the driver to stop.

It was eerie walking up the service entrance of the Museum complex knowing Titus was close by matching his foot falls.

Stephen was barely inside when his brother, Virgil, turned onto the corridor.

"Don't often see you round here after dark these days," Virgil said with a look of undisguised scrutiny.

"Inspiration struck," Stephen answered without much expression, which was likely the best way to respond to Virgil.

"Couldn't sleep, then?" Virgil asked.

"Titus's place is shit for rattling round in after dark. Dull as ditchwater,"

Stephen said with a grimace, because it was partially true. If not for Polly he'd be bored shitless at Titus's place.

"Is that the way it is?" Virgil asked.

"That is the way it is," Stephen answered.

"If I didn't know better I might start to believe there was something to the rumors," Virgil said.

"What rumors are those?" Stephen asked, despite himself.

"Wouldn't know. I don't listen to rumors," Virgil said.

"Don't mock the afflicted, particularly when they can kill you with a touch," Stephen said.

Virgil didn't look particularly impressed, he never did.

"Well, see to yourself, I've rounds to do," Virgil said. "Night, Professor Magesteri."

"Night, Virgil," Stephen called heading toward the stairs.

"You too, Your Lordship," Virgil muttered under his breath.

If Stephen didn't know better he'd have sworn he heard Titus breathe for an instant.

Titus Posthumous Albinus, Colonel in her Majesty's, Duke Londinium Austri, Order of Apophis 1st class, had been to his cousin Stephen's private laboratory on countless occasions. He'd simply never paid any attention before. There was no need for it. It wasn't as though Stephen was committing treason or espionage or doing any thing interesting in there.

But now he saw beyond what a tip it was. Not a single device in the lab was self-explanatory and few of the individual objects were recognizable. Not to him, at least. He kept his hands to himself, because frankly, there seemed to be a great deal of soot and mechanical grease involved.

"Let's get started, shall we?" Stephen said putting his leather apron over his head.

Titus relaxed enough to allow himself to reappear, but not enough to touch any nearby surfaces. There was his frock coat to think of.

"Midnight to midnight," Titus began.

"Nonononono," Stephen interrupted. "I'm not having you repeat the bloody prophecy until I'm hearing it in my sleep. Write it down. That's more efficient in any event."

Titus patted his waistcoat. "I seem to have misplaced my writing set."

Stephen placed a strangely unfamiliar implement with a string hanging from one end in his hand.

"What am I supposed to do with this?" Titus said trying to hold it carefully, but to no avail. "It's left a mark on my glove."

"It's a grease pencil. It will do that. Best to take them off, and get writing," Stephen said.

"On what shall I write?" Titus asked.

Stephen rubbed his eyes. "The table ought to do."

Titus had never written on a table before. It wasn't the done thing. But for Polly he would make an exception.

Stephen leaned over the other side of the table, watching as he wrote. Upside down.

"Midnight to midnight, that's easy, it's the brewing time; 24 hours. I've a quarter past 8 by my watch, so we ought to be able to start on time, provided we don't take forever sorting this lot out," Stephen said.

"Indeed," Titus answered.

"Fire of Cathay is an antiquated name for coal. Burns around a thousand degrees; so the elixir requires an intense heat," Stephen said. "Which would also explain the need for tempered glass equipment."

Titus exhaled and continued writing. He went slowly to make certain it was quite legible despite the stained and pock-marked surface of the table.

"Stone of heaven and New Years acorn are obvious," Titus said.

"They are?" Stephen asked.

"Lapis Lazuli literally means stone of heaven. See what you get for killing all your tutors," Titus said trying unsuccessfully to rub the mark off his glove.

"Once upon a time acorns carved of amber and inscribed with good wishes for the Emperor were de rigueur for New Years gifts."

"If I gave you directions to the store room do you think you could get them for me without being found out while I sort out this next bit?" Stephen asked, staring intently at the words on the table.

"How do you propose to get the water, the Humber is some miles away?" Titus asked.

"Turn on the tap. Do you imagine we pipe this in from the Thames?" Stephen asked.

"How do you even know that?" Titus asked, puzzled.

"Killed all my tutors and had to pick up what I could from a gaggle of unkempt engineers," Stephen said, still scrutinizing the words on the table. "After you bring me the amber and the lapis, make your way to the menagerie. You've got to make quick use of that dagger of yours and you'll need your wits about you."

"For?" Titus asked.

"Tongue of the Suck-Flower as far as I can reckon refers to a bird of the family Trochilidae. In nature they are restricted to the Western Continents, north and south, but we've several species of the little buggers in aviaries 2, 3, and 6; all quick as a wink and no bigger than my thumb. You'll know them by their beak, like a long needley thing, a straw quite nearly. Wool of the Humpback has got to refer to Bison. There's a herd, well 6, in menagerie 1. Watch yourself, they're dangerous brutes. By all reports one of the most deadly creatures going on the Western continent, human inhabitants aside," Stephen said.

"And you'll have the rest deciphered by the time I return?" Titus asked, folding his frock coat neatly and setting it on the lower rungs of a ladder propped against the wall.

"If the gods smile, I will," Stephen said, not looking up from the table.

"Too bad for us there aren't any," Titus couldn't help but remind him, slipping off his waistcoat and laying it atop his coat.

"Don't worry, I'll pray for the both of us," Stephen told him.

Stephen Magesteri had ground the amber to dust and the lapis likewise. He chopped the hummingbird tongue fine. He was buggered if he knew how to deal with the Bison wool but he had taken the knife to the hair as thick and course as wire as well, cutting as small as he could manage.

Titus was watching him with his arms folded across his chest.

"Have you worked out what The Soil of Conception is?" Titus asked, Stephen could tell by his face that his cousin doubted him.

"I knew that one from the beginning," Stephen said giving the wool one more pass with the knife blade. "Remember the comet?"

"The one that hit outside Fayzabad a few months after our arrival in Afghanistan?" Titus asked squinting.

"No, the one that sucked your bloody cock, you knob! Of course, the one that hit outside Fayzabad, what other comet could I possibly be referring to? Well, Henry, took his footlocker and filled it with the debris from the impact site. You know how commoners are with their little superstitions. He put a pinch in the tank when he was making Polly. For 'luck' he said," Stephen said. "I went to Henry's private workshop and took a pocketful while you were giving the Bison a trim."

"Wings of the world maker is scarab, obviously," Titus said.

Even a school child would recognize the beetle that impressed the ancients by rolling balls of shit in mimicry of a god fashioning the Earth, and it chafed at Stephen a bit that Titus felt the need to point it out.

"Obviously," Stephen repeated.

"Well, don't forget it simply because it is so glaringly obvious. What of the others? Twisted branches of the Nile's tree ? Flesh of Cypress and flesh of Chalybes?" Titus said carefully placing a large handful of iridescent beetle wings on the work table.

"I've been considering that," Stephen said, uncertain of how his cousin would react.

"Yes?" Titus prodded him.

"And," Stephen inhaled.

"And?" Titus repeated as though he wanted to reach down Stephen's throat and fairly pull the words out of him.

"Ancient Cypress was the center of copper mining. In every language I know the metal takes its name from the place," Stephen said hoping Titus would take the gist of what he was saying.

"Go on," Titus said clearly not understanding.

"The Chalybes are universally credited with the invention of steel," Stephen said.

"Flesh of Copper and Flesh of Steel? Branches of the Nile's twisted Tree?" Titus said. Was he trying to be dense?

"That's not exactly it. A more precise reading would be Branches of the Nile's Twisted Tree; Man of Copper and Man of Steel. It means us, you and I, I suppose it's logical in a hair-of-the-dog sort of way," Stephen said feeling himself start to ramble but unable to stop.

"It doesn't say hair, it says flesh," Titus said. "We're committing sorcery, aren't we? It fits the definition; attempting to affect the conception of monsters."

The thought hadn't even crossed Stephen's mind until Titus said it, but the very suggestion was absurd and obscene. He shut his eyes tight.

"Of course not, we're doing our best to save Polly, that's all," Stephen insisted.

"You don't believe that any more than I do," Titus said. "I'm not losing my nerve; I want that perfectly clear. I simply wish to be decisive when committing a criminal act. Shilly-shallying is for cowards. I am perpetrating sorcery in an attempt to save the life of the woman I love." Titus tilted his head meaningfully. "And so are you."

"No, I'm not, I'm following orders," Stephen said. "The Oracle said..."

"The Oracle said the child would live but not the mother," Titus said unbuttoning his shirt. "What we do we do for Polly."

Stephen watched in horror as Titus methodically dipped the glass blade into the underside of his upper arm, not stopping until the knife hit bone. That done, Titus pressed a second cut less than an inch away from the first and followed its line until a piece of flesh the size of woman's palm laid across his knife.

All Stephen Magesteri's life he had made a conscious decision not to be his father. He might be a killer, by his very nature, but he was not a sorcerer. He would never do as his father did. He kept his distance from all magic no matter the cost. It was for the best an abomination like him was not welcome in the temples, because blood running red on altar stones caused his veins and arteries to sing inside him. It hardly mattered. Regardless of how he kept the supernatural at bay, it called to him and he knew it, knew it in his bones, the way a tear understands the deep salt sea.

He knew without question he would acquiesce. He understood what Nefrit meant the minute the words were out of her mouth and he knew immediately that he would do as she said. As if he could deny Polly the flesh of his body. As, bloody, if, he could deny her anything. Even if it meant the death of him. Even if it meant much worse.

"There's a blue paste in the jar behind you, for when there are accidents in the workshop," Stephen said taking up the knife and slipping off his apron. He supposed he ought to clean his cousin's blood from the blade first.

"That hurts worse than the knife," Titus hissed.

Stephen's cut was nowhere near as straight or efficient, but there it was just the same, in a matter of minutes, a hunk of meat roughly the same size and shape as the one Titus had laid on the table.

"See to yourself," Titus said thrusting the jar of paste at him and taking back the knife, ignoring the pools of blood running together on the wooden floor.

His cousin was right, it hurt like a bugger, but it worked, in two weeks time there would hardly be a mark on either of them.

Stephen wasn't sure what to say as he watched his cousin stack the two slices of flesh, one atop the other, and quickly cut the flesh into squares, one inch by two inches, more or less.

Bite sized morsels.

There on the table it was impossible to tell one flesh from another. He wondered vaguely if Polly would be able to taste the difference.

The tonic rose to the meat as Titus dropped it in and then began to boil, violently.

In twenty four hours, the elixir before him resembled nothing so much as the sort of clear broth one might feed an invalid.

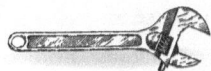

Polly was awakened by the sensation of a deft forefinger stroking the sole of her foot. As her mind rose to consciousness, the rest of her body quickly came to a pleasant anticipation of unfolding events.

The touch slipped to her ankle and she shifted her knees open slightly.

Next, Titus would say something snide about her choice of knickers. Stephen would comment on the fact that she was wearing knickers at all. She would not quite be amused. Then Titus would slip them off and there would be some sort of sex. She smiled sleepily in anticipation. She hadn't had sex with either of them in forever. Her mind was as agile as ever but sometimes she forgot her body gave every indication of falling apart around her.

In her mind she made love to both of them every day.

Actually as Polly began to float upwards towards consciousness she thought better of it. She tried to rub her eyes but her hands were bandaged and her muscles were so weak the best she could manage was to bat ineffectually at her face.

Polly tried a second time and succeeded in digging the back of her wrist into first her right eye and then her left. Crusted dried blood irritated her eyes and scattered across her face. It wasn't pleasant but she was finally able to work her lids open.

It was frustrating and she was already starting to feel knackered with the effort.

To make it worse Titus had stopped mid-stroke and was staring at her.

Only Titus wasn't Titus, he was Stephen.

She struggled to sit up and look at him then gave up and fell backwards against her pillows.

"Would you be willing to accept an offering, my dear?" he said, sitting against the foot of the bed, looking oddly stiff and formal for a man in his shirt sleeves.

Wait.

What was Stephen doing in his shirt sleeves?

Polly wanted to answer him but found she could not. She opened her mouth and all that came was a metallic sort of gasp and the feeling of something tearing in her throat.

"Don't force yourself to speak if it causes you discomfort," Titus said, across the room.

Polly closed her eyes, inhaled, and tried again.

"I beg your pardon?" she croaked, struggling to sit up, befuddled. It was hardly impressive but it was speech. A bit of blood trickled from the corner of her mouth, caused, she imagined, by the effort of speaking.

A look that was almost, but not quite, a sneer rose to Stephen's face, and his tone went instantly to offhanded sarcasm. "I've some soup for you, Mummy. You look hungry."

He held a clear glass bowl in front of him, like a talisman.

If this was his idea of a witticism she hated it. "Mummy." She more than hated it. It made her teeth grit and she wanted to slap him. He had an uncanny ability to make the word sound both ludicrous and obscene.

She might well love him, but that didn't stop him from getting straight up her nose sometimes.

"I'm not hungry," she said coughing out more blood, but remembering her manners, she blotted the blood on the back of her bandaged hands.

"Are you trying to make Cook weep? Mrs. Hodson is sufficiently repulsive without the added appeal of a runny nose," Titus said, off hand, the way he did.

She was instantly suspicious, although she couldn't say why.

Then Stephen produced a flat bottomed, glass spoon seemingly from nowhere and attempted to shovel something into her mouth.

She backed up until she was wedged between Stephen's spoon and the head of the bed.

"Cook did not make that," she said, her voice getting gurgly with blood and phlegm "What are you trying to feed me and why?"

Stephen set the spoon back in the bowl with a loud clank, clearly annoyed. Well, that made two of them.

"Very well." He frowned harder. "I made it. It's a restorative from a little known recipe I got from Madam Ng."

Polly looked at it speculatively and sniffed. It didn't look much like Dr. Ng's usual restoratives. It looked more like a thin broth that anything else. She peered down into the bowl and saw what looked like morsels of pork.

She looked to Titus leaning against the wall with his arms folded across his chest.

"You're not rushing in to rescue me from Stephen's concoction, are you?" she said with effort.

"All either of us wish is for you to be well," Titus said. "So, on the off chance it may do some good, no, I am not rescuing you from your medicine."

"Is that pork?" She wrinkled her nose. While not a strict vegetarian, she had disliked meat since she was a child and the prejudice had stuck with her.

"If you must know, it's bat. Of course, you would complain if it were nectar of the gods," Stephen snapped his spoon hovering inches from her mouth. "Now, be a good little mummy and open your fucking mouth, please."

"Isn't that contrary to some code, some brotherhood of creatures of the dark, serving up one of your brethren like that?" she said. He used the opportunity to cram a mouthful down her gullet.

"I would betray any number of winged rodentia for the health of the woman I love," he said, putting another spoon in her mouth as soon as she swallowed.

Whatever it was, the liquid seemed to be clearing out her throat, so it had some effect, which was more than she could say of most of the medicines they forced on her.

"There you go, dearest, you should be pleased, knowing you outrank the lesser mammals," Titus said pleasantly as Stephen jammed another bite into her mouth.

Polly fixed her lips shut, as she chewed the meat. Stephen loved her? He'd never said anything like that before. She was relieved and a bit surprised that Titus didn't object. And who knew bat was so like pork?

"Puts her ahead of my underlings at any rate." Stephen frowned over his shoulder at Titus before addressing Polly. "Does it taste too awful?"

That was funny: Stephen normally didn't give a fabled rat's arse about how a medicine tasted as long as she was able to choke it down. It was usually Titus who saw to it she had a spoonful of sugar or a cup of hot tea to take the bitter taste from her mouth. She gave him a measuring look. "If I didn't know better, I would think Cook did make this. Someone's cook at any rate. Though my father's cook never made anything this good."

He shoved another portion between her lips. She couldn't help savoring it. Titus was hanging back, scrutinizing her. It was almost, but not quite, as though Stephen and Titus had switched places; as if Titus was passively waiting to be invited in.

"It's clearly a potion. There is a complexity of flavour in spite of the way it looks like water. I'm betting you have over a hundred different ingredients in this. Isis, but it's delicious. You should make this for me again," she said, opening her mouth like a hungry baby bird.

"I think not," Stephen said. "It was pain enough in the arse to brew once."

Polly was beginning to feel strange. "What's in this? You actually made this, Stephen? On your own?"

"Tight-arse and I worked together …it was definitely a cooperative venture," Stephen said.

"My cousin is being generous. On this occasion mine was definitely a subordinate role," Titus said being careless in that way that revealed he was paying rapt attention.

Before Polly could say a word in comment a sharp pain cracked her chest like a blow to the heart.

She struggled for a moment to catch a breath that refused to come. Was this the end of her? Her body betraying her while her brain felt sharper than ever?

Her eyes went wide as the pain slowly subsided and the shattering feeling was followed by slow-burning warmth that went from her toes to the frizzy ends of her hair.

Stephen leapt back, careful not to spill any of the elixir, as tiny blue white threads of electricity jumped spontaneously from her hair and cascaded down her body.

Polly ripped the bandages from her hands to see her fingers, that had been bloody and cracked when the servants changed the cloth that morning, perfect and whole.

It felt like she was full of light, full of... she didn't have a word for it other than love. Not that she felt drugged - no, she felt sharp, more herself than she had since she was five years old, standing on the roof of the Museum with her father under the cloudy black hearing about the night the sky in Afghanistan blazed white from a falling star. She felt strong, like she could stride down the corridors and leave even Titus scurrying to catch up.

This recipe had not come from Dr. Ng. Whatever Titus and Stephen had done, they had done with magic.

"What is in this?" she asked him, flexing her shoulders as she tapped the night stand to dissipate the electric charge.

Stephen swallowed hard then feigned nonchalance, shrugged and tapped the spoon against the side of the bowl. "A tediously long list of exotic, costly, and yet essentially harmless ingredients requiring mind-numbing mincing, dicing, and several stages of boiling at rather precise temperatures. Finish up, Poly-corpus. I would rather not spend the entire evening feeding a grown woman as though she were an infant."

How perfectly like him. It was a fault of hers, she thought, that she managed to be annoyed with people she liked a good deal when they behaved the way they always did. To be honest, she was not annoyed so much as amused; Stephen didn't look half bad in shirtsleeves.

His hair was in his face and his lips were parted slightly. She felt wonderful and there was something so dear about him this way, looking so earnest and intent. Jupiter, she wanted him.

In between bites, she managed to ask. "Surely you've got something else you would rather put in my mouth?"

"Surely it can wait until after you finish, and don't be lewd," Titus said across the room, my but he looked as scrumptious as a tea cake himself, leaning casually against her chifferobe.

"I thought you lot appreciated a sexually aggressive female," she said.

"There is a difference between being sexually aggressive and sexually compulsive. One thing at a time. Let us finish with your restorative," Stephen said frowning in a way Polly associated with fondness.

Titus, still on the far side of the room nodded once, then again, then a third time slowly walking toward her.

"It's evening. You two are always gone so early in the morning. I was simply attempting to gather my rosebuds while the opportunity presented itself," she said in a very Stephenlike tone as he ladled the last delicious bite into her mouth. There was something about the weight of it in her belly that left her feeling supremely satisfied. It was mystifying. "Are you two going to tell me what I just ate?"

Titus shrugged, looking at her from head to toe, a grin creeping into one corner of his mouth. In the process of briskly feeding Polly the potion, Stephen had got a tiny drop on the bedclothes. Although it was a clear broth in the bowl, on the coverlet it was thick and dark red. Peculiar.

Polly was so shining with energy she forgot she had ever been tired, barely noticing the spot on the blanket. Polly felt brilliant in both body and mind; fairly humming with power. Oh she had an idea. She felt like such a clever girl as she reached over to smirking Stephen and took his hand.

She held the other out to Titus.

"I feel grand, don't you?" Polly asked.

"Absolutely," Stephen said giving Polly a hard look.

"Indeed," Titus agreed nodding vigorously.

Polly pulled them both to her.

Chapter 18 : A Complex Issue

imply because Titus Posthumous Albinus had thumbed his nose at duty, honor, and accepted practice it didn't mean Stephen Magesteri was going to join him in letting the side down.

Titus could keep his ingratitude towards the gods, thank you very much; Stephen wanted no part of it.

So it was that Stephen found himself for the first time in his life, in the temple of Apollo, on his own, making an offering, ostensibly on Titus's behalf, in honor of Polly's recovery.

"Pffft, useless! What would I want the girl's weight in incense for?" Nefrit asked. "If I was fifty years younger I'd throw my shoe at you."

"It is traditional," Stephen said in his own defense, in Titus's defense, though Titus had nothing to do with any of it, other than paying for it.

"What is that to me? Traditional? It's not my tradition. I didn't start it. It in no way benefits me. And you can tell Titus Albinus from me this in no way releases him from his debt," Nefrit wheezed.

"Would you rather have a statue?" Stephen asked. This was Titus's purview. He was a priest of Apollo; Stephen wasn't even properly welcome in a temple.

"Are you trying to be stupid?" Nefrit wheezed. "I didn't set all this in motion for a few baubles."

"Baubles?" Stephen repeated. The cost of that much high grade incense had been staggering. To him at least, Titus hadn't even batted an eye when he asked for the money.

"You are my servant now. You and your cousin, the red haired one, the young duke," Nefrit said, as though she couldn't remember their names. Perhaps she couldn't, though she clearly remembered Polly. She'd said it before. Perhaps she'd meant it. It wasn't about the two of them at all. Polly was the body around which they all orbited in Ptolemaic motion.

"You planned all this? You're behind this?" Stephen asked without thinking, he'd never learned to curb his tongue, he'd never needed to, and for once he regretted it.

A painful sound, like metal on metal rent the air. She was laughing. Nefrit the Oracle of Apollo was laughing at him.

"I have been working to bring forth what is coming for the last four decades," Nefrit screeched between the shrill cackles. "I made you all with an eye to the new life Polycorpus carries within her."

"You made me?" Stephen stuttered in horror.

"I did not hold the knife in my hand. I did not chant the words," Nefrit said. "But I know how to whisper a suggestion in a desperate man's ear."

Stephen did not remember what he said after that. He didn't even recall exiting the temple.

All Stephen knew was that by the time he stumbled home from the pub he was so drunk Llewellyn had to put him to bed.

"I can't believe you actually had a new cherry tree lowered in by airship," Polly said looking up and admiring the ripening fruit.

Titus never ceased to amaze her. It would never occur to her to do anything other than plant a sapling and wait for it to grow. But Titus had remade the peristylium into the loveliest little park Polly had ever seen. Perfect for a picnic.

"I can't believe you're sitting on the bleeding ground," Stephen said, shaking his head.

"It's not a proper picnic if you're sitting in a chair," Polly explained.

"And we're going to have to use a winch to get you up again," Stephen answered.

"Will not!" Polly said. "I'm perfectly healthy and as strong as ever, stronger even."

Titus bit into a peach and tried to let on he wasn't giving Stephen smug looks out of the corner of his eye. The peach was so perfectly ripe and fragrant Polly could practically taste it herself.

"It's not a question of strong, you nit-wit," Stephen said. "It's a question of logistics; you're the size of a baby elephant."

Not certain how she could materially argue with that statement Polly closed her fingers on the grass she had been idly toying with and threw a clump in Stephen's direction.

"To resort to violence is to admit defeat," Stephen said smugly.

"The least you could do is express your displeasure in a way that doesn't mar the landscaping, dearest, I've put a great deal of effort into that lawn," Titus said.

"You mean the workmen have," Polly said, feeling stroppy. Fond as she was of Titus he had trouble differentiating between paying for a thing and actually doing that thing himself.

"I have put a great deal of effort in, by proxy." Titus shrugged.

Polly rolled her eyes. "Did you draw up the designs?"

"I approved them, the garden architect dealt with the tedious little details, but I looked through an endless array of options. It was exhausting," Titus said reaching for a finger sandwich.

"So you didn't lift so much as a spade of earth. What you did ultimately amounts to shopping, as ever. Why am I not surprised? I'd throw grass at you except that it would mean more work for the gardeners." Polly laughed.

"And who better, really?" Titus said leaning close. "I have exquisite taste."

Then he kissed her. Polly's nose had been right; that peach was delicious. Titus's lips clung to hers longer than she expected. Still she was a bit disappointed when it ended.

"My turn," Stephen said leaning over the tea pot to take his kiss. Unlike Titus, Stephen used his tongue, but it was nice. He was definitely improving. If he were her apprentice she'd give him a glowing evaluation. Full marks to Mr. Magesteri.

"Stephen is right, though, you are huge," Titus agreed.

"Because I'm pregnant. That's how it's supposed to operate, reproduction," Polly asked. "Were your other wives not huge like this?"

"Are you going to talk like that when you're a mother?" Stephen chided her.

"You are no longer allowed to call your cousin Tight-Arse, because you have officially surpassed him in priggishness, Stephen, and stop trying to distract me on Titus's behalf," Polly said. "Why do you refuse to speak of them?"

Titus's chin dipped down and a slow shrug passed through him like a shudder, he started to speak, opening his mouth and then closed it again, shaking his head.

Stephen jumped to his feet and turned away from Polly, his hand on the trunk of the cherry tree.

"Titus courted Hathor Canavan for three years before they married. She was a siren. Literally. A bit fishy like all the family. There was a bit of greenish tinge to her, here and there. In spite of that she was, quite honestly, the most enchantingly beautiful woman I have seen, or ever hope to see, in my life," Stephen told the tree.

"She couldn't stand the sight of you," Titus said and for a moment Polly wondered who he was addressing, though he was looking at Stephen, now.

"You think I didn't know that?" Stephen sneered before he softened. "According to Titus she had a patch of perfectly opalescent scales at the small of her back exactly the size of his palm."

"What of the baby? What happened with the baby?" Polly asked.

"There was no baby," Titus said to the wall with an air of finality.

"What do you mean? What does he mean, Stephen?" Polly asked.

Stephen licked his lips and looked at the bricks above Polly's head. "When,

when Hathor was called to straw…"

"You mean when her pains began?" Polly asked.

Stephen nodded "When, that happened, things went to shit fairly quickly. The surgeons decided to attempt to save the life of the child, only it wasn't what you would call very childlike. Mostly a mass of jumbled internal organs, all inside, no outside, like my cousin said, there was no child to speak of."

Polly thought she was going to vomit. She wondered vaguely, if the surgeons killed her to save her baby, whether or not they could bring her back to life again. After all they'd done it once already. She tried very hard to wonder about that, rather than think about the thing Titus's first wife had grown inside her.

"And after that?" Polly knew she was pushing but it occurred to her she still might die and she wanted to know, she wanted to know about all the wives who'd come before her "What of the next wife?"

"Lobelia was a great comfort to me," Titus said stoically.

"She could pass straight through a flame, any flame, no matter how intense, without so much as a singed fingernail," Stephen said.

"She was loyal, steadfast, the very model of decorum and stability," Titus said.

"Did she hate Stephen, as well?" Polly asked.

"I got up her nose a bit," Stephen said warming to the topic. "Mostly I annoyed her, I think."

"Lobelia tolerated you," Titus said "She was very tolerant."

"Whether she meant it or not was another matter," Stephen interjected.

"What happened with Lobelia?" Polly asked before Titus and Stephen could derail the conversation with bickering.

"The Empty child," Titus said, still unable to look at her.

"Once again the surgeons acted heroically," Stephen sneered bitterly letting her know just what he thought of surgeons and their drastic measures, "and at first they had no idea why the child never lived or drew breath. He seemed quite perfect from the outside, but inside there was nothing, no heart, no brains, not so much as an appendix."

"I don't know which is worse, the first or the second," Polly said feeling gutted herself.

"It's a pointless distinction at any rate," Titus said softly. "It hardly matters."

"And the next one?" Polly asked, she dreaded hearing the rest but she could hardly turn back now that she'd started.

"I will not have you speak one word against Drusilla," Titus said pointing one long finger straight at Stephen.

"Did she hate you, too?" Polly asked "What is it with you and Titus's wives?"

"Polycorpus, darling, no one likes my cousin, save you and I, and even I have my moments of doubt," Titus patiently told the wall.

"Drusilla found me incomprehensibly terrifying. She once wet herself because I'd sneezed particularly loudly," Stephen said rubbing his eyes.

"Drusilla was the sweetest, kindest, gentlest creature to have ever graced the surface of the earth," Titus said fervently. It was silly of him not to look at her. "And pretty as a picture."

Polly wondered what he'd say about her when she was dead. Polly may not have possessed any of the womanly virtues but she was jolly good in bed? No, it might be true but it didn't sound like anything Titus would say.

"Drusilla was also a Cyclops," Stephen said plainly. It might not be the nicest thing to say but Cyclops were not, as a group, deep thinkers. Or thinkers at all, to tell the truth.

" 'Silla died in this house, in our marriage bed, soon after her pains commenced. The doctors said her heart gave up under the strain. When they cut her open in a vain attempt to rescue the infant in her womb all they found was a babe of stone," Titus said. "They were buried together in the family crypt."

"Oh," was all Polly could think to say.

Polly didn't know why she'd wished Titus would turn around a moment before, because when he did look at her it was utterly unbearable.

"That leaves Chandi," Titus said. "Her father, Sekar, was a military officer, like myself."

"We met him in Lashkar Gah during the war," Stephen said picking a leaf off the cherry tree. "She had eight arms, like her old man."

"Sekar and I respected one another, as soldiers, and as men of the world," Titus said, his focus on Polly unwavering. "Chandi conceived on our wedding night, or close to it. After four months of marriage I awoke in a pool of blood to find my wife already dead. I hardly knew her."

"She was perfectly pleasant to me," Stephen said ripping a leaf in half.

"I told her to treat Stephen as though he were my brother," Titus said tersely. "Unlike the others she has only a plaque in my personal vault. Her father requested I return her ashes to her family. I complied out of, oh, I suppose, friendship."

"It ended so badly for all of them," Polly said feeling frightened or sad or angry, one of those, but she couldn't make out which. "And all of them more lady-like, all better wives than me."

Titus simply stared.

"I've known artillery gunners more lady-like than you, Polly," Stephen said.

Polly had no idea why she started laughing, it wasn't funny at all. She was going to die. She knew it. Her gut was clenching so hard it burned. Still her shoulders shook up and down. If her eyes were leaking she'd have sworn she was crying, but her eyes weren't leaking. Besides, Polly didn't cry; it was axiomatic. The clenching wrapped all the way round to her back. It was awful.

"What are you going to say of me, when I'm dead?" Polly asked.

"Nothing," Titus said through clenched teeth. "Because you are not going to die."

"Then you'd better call for the coach and the driver and get me to the museum," Polly said as it occurred to her what was happening.

"What for?" Stephen asked, grabbing hold of one of the hanging limbs of the cherry tree distractedly.

"So Dr. Ng can bloody cut me open before whatever you gits have put inside me rips me in two on its way out," Polly shrieked without meaning to or wanting to. "Or have neither of you calculated the difference between the size of my belly and the size of my quim?"

It hurt so badly Polly wished she'd pass out from it, but of course she didn't.

Titus Posthumous Albinus had never expected it to go the way it did. He never expected it to go so quick. He had expected to take charge himself and see to it Polly was afforded the best care possible.

Rather Polly spent the entire time shouting orders at everyone, from the servants to the Museum staff, to him and Stephen.

She'd walked, well staggered, into the operating theatre on her own power.

"Don't touch me!" she'd shouted at either Titus or the theatre attendant. They both stepped back then she pointed at Titus. "Don't you leave my sight."

"I want ether and I want you to wash your hands, Dr. Ng, and don't you dare call my father 'til this is over with," Polly growled.

"I've sent Gillhooley for the ether and I've already washed my hands," Ng huffed.

"Wash them again," Polly insisted tears of pain rolling down her face. "Is someone going to help me out of this stupid dress?"

The attendant stepped forward to unfasten the back of her gown with naked terror in his eyes.

"You two," Polly sniffed wiping her eyes on the hem of her dress before gesturing at Titus and Stephen. "Up in the audience. Front row, center. I want you to get a good look at this."

"Polly, Your Ladyship, this is highly unusual," Ng said looking from Polly to Titus. "Speak to her!"

If the choice was between what the good doctor wanted and what Polly wanted Titus's path was clear.

"Is it wrong that I should wish to greet my much awaited heir upon his entry to the world?" Titus said as coolly and archly as possible. He did his sweating internally.

Stephen however, did not. Despite the cool of the theatre, his cousin's forehead was beaded with perspiration.

"Do I have to be here as well? Couldn't I just…duck out?" Stephen asked, swallowing.

Incredible.

Without thinking Titus struck him on the back of the head with the flat of his palm, then cringed. It wasn't the cleverest thing he'd ever done.

"Thank you, Titus!" Polly said. "I'd have slapped him myself if I could reach. If I have to be here, Stephen, so do you."

"Now that the hierarchy has been established, will the gentlemen please take their seats?" Dr. Ng said.

Titus straightened his waistcoat and took his seat, Stephen beside him.

Polly's knees buckled just in time for two attendants to help her onto the operating table.

Titus took out his pocket watch. He watched the minute hand move more slowly than it had since he'd purchased it in Vienna.

Another minute passed and someone, presumably, the much vaunted Gill-hooley, arrived with the ether.

There was some coming and going, both in the rear of the theatre and in the fore but Titus kept his attention divided between Polly and his pocket watch. It was an excruciating 13 minutes before little doctor cut open his wife's womb and fished, something, out.

"What is this? Hurt Magesteri Day?" Stephen asked.

Titus hadn't realized his fingers were digging into his cousin's leg. He let go and looked up to hear a cry.

It was wrapped in a towel in an attendant's arms but oddly shaped and moving vigorously as well as screaming its head off.

"Well? What is it?" Stephen shouted down to the operating floor. "Don't keep us in suspense!"

"Do be quiet, Magesteri! I'm not finished," Ng called out. "It appears our good director built your wife with two wombs and you've managed to fill both of them."

Titus glanced at his cousin beside him then back at the scene on the operating floor below them. A husband for each wife.

Titus watched in shock as the doctor pulled a dark shape from the slit in the top of Polly's second womb. The form wriggled and then somehow unfolded and expanded flinging blood and fluid everywhere, flapping. A child, brown skinned, with wings, before Gillhooley dropped the ether mask with a clatter to the floor to wrap the shivering cherub with a sheet.

"Show me the first! Show him to me! I want to see my first born!" Titus shouted rising to his feet.

The attendant loosened the cloth and got a face full of wing for his trouble. The first child was winged like the second but as fair skinned as Titus himself; the second no doubt had inherited Polly's complexion, or at least part of it.

"Your Lordship should be aware your first born son is, in fact, a daughter. The second, however, is male," Dr. Ng said as Titus raced down to the floor of the theatre.

"Give him to me," Titus said reaching for the boy "Perfect, you are perfect. I am your father, young man, and I am here to inform you, you are destined to be the greatest monster of your generation."

He'd like to hold them both at once but the logistics of it escaped him. Titus cupped the child's head in his palm. He could barely hear the doctor addressing him for the beating of his heart in his ears. The babe looked so like Polly. His face was broad and flat, his eyes jet black and slanted. Titus ran his thumb over the tip of a single feathered wing. Brilliant green, like his uncle Brolly. Titus didn't understand it. There hadn't been a putto born in The Roman Empire in over two hundred years.

He kissed the little forehead. It was worth the wait to hold this child in his arms. It was worth all of it. And he had not one but two. Two perfect little cherubs. Polly did nothing by half measures.

"Come along, Stephen, I haven't enough arms to hold them both at once," Titus called up to Stephen still glued to his seat.

"Perhaps your lordship is flush with fatherhood," Ng said her hands red with Polly's blood as she tied the thread holding her belly closed. "As I was attempting to tell your Lordship, the Duchess…"

He had quite forgotten Polly in the heat of the moment. Surely she'd forgive him. What if she hadn't survived, his stomach dropped.

"Polly," Titus rushed to her side. "Yes, Polly…"

"Hooray, Polly's still alive," Polly croaked, a strange and clearly drugged smile on her face. "Can I see my babies?"

"Polly … I … this is," Titus said holding the baby close to her. "Do you see how like you he is?"

"Where's the girl? I want to see my girl. The other one's a girl, isn't she?" Polly said weakly.

"There, there, darling, we'll get your girl for you." Titus jerked his head at the attendant. "Give your charge to the Viscount."

Stephen shook his head slowly. "I don't know, Titus."

"Don't be such a quivering coward, Magesteri, you're wearing your gloves," Titus warned him. "Take the child. Mind you support the head, the neck is weak at this age."

"What age? It's hardly been born," Stephen said, reluctantly doing as he was told.

"She," Polly said. "She's a girl and I want to see her."

Stephen came close, the babe in his arms. Where the boy's skin was a honey-eyed color and his wings were green. The fair skinned girl's wings were scarlet and the downy hair on her head appeared to be a pale reddish gold.

Titus lifted the boy towards Stephen, gesturing to exchange infants.

"Oh look at how she favors you, poor thing," Polly said sighing.

"And what's wrong with that?" Titus snapped. He shouldn't snap at Polly when she'd just given birth, but still, it was rude.

"Not looking like you, touchy," Polly said closing her eyes. "Poor thing being born a girl. It's horrid, being female."

"It won't be horrid for her. I swear it upon my military commission; behold the most fortunate girl child ever born," Titus said holding the child out that she could inspect the room. "You shall be the mistress of all you survey." He tucked a kiss on the side of her little neck. He thought for an instant she had a mole there, but on further inspection it was a bit of Polly's flesh.

"The Luckiest girl in the world is one born male," Polly said groggily.

"Says the woman who was never born at all," Stephen muttered.

Stephen looked from Titus and then to Polly in something dead center between awe and horror. "He's got me," Stephen said anxiously.

The boy had reached out and gripped the tip of Stephen's gloved finger.

"He has, hasn't he," Polly said, her eyes still closed. Titus had no doubt his wife might as well have gone to the moon.

"Gillhooley, come here, are you seeing this?" Ng said, from her position at Polly's belly.

Not only did the infamous Gillhooley sprint over to take a look but Titus and Stephen craned their necks as well.

Titus blinked.

The line where Polly's belly had been cut was disappearing before their very eyes, her belly shrinking back to its normal, plump-but-hardly-pregnant Polly state.

"Ooo that itches like buggery," Polly said scratching at the threads in her drugged haze.

"Fuck, that's um, um, you don't see that every day, or ever," Stephen said then pressed his free hand the baby boy's ear. "Sorry, you didn't hear that."

Stephen seemed to have got stuck in abject terror, somehow. Oh well, Titus was sure he'd get over it before too long.

"Mummy has an exceptional constitution, all due to Director Plumber's excellent work, no doubt," Titus told the child in his arms.

"And of course those remarkable draughts of yours, Ng," Stephen added.

"Yes, of course," Titus parroted. It was wise of Stephen to say it, even if they both knew it was far from the truth.

Gillhooley gave them both a sideways look that Titus chose to ignore.

"Mark my words, you will be handsomely rewarded," Titus added holding the child to his chest.

Ng made a little trilling noise, not unlike the sound of a contented cat.

Chapter 19 : Their Heart's Desire

Polly awoke in the Museum Medical wing, on the corridor where all the fine ladies went to have their babies, with a splitting headache, quite surprised to be among the living, or as among the living as she got. But here she was, alive, and a mother. She'd never pictured herself making it this far.

At least she thought she was a mother. She thought she remembered a red haired baby but then she also seemed to recall a different baby altogether, with bushy black hair and golden skin and both babies had wings so perhaps it was a dream. It was all very hazy.

Polly sat up, her head spinning, clutching her belly. It was as if she'd never been pregnant, her abdomen was its normal size and shape. Peculiar. Not that Polly was an expert but she'd always heard of ladies taking forever to go back to their proper form.

And here Polly was, back to herself already; or not quite, because her breasts were abominable.

They hurt like the torture of Prometheus and were easily twice their usual size.

Ow.

They were as hard as cement; hot, too. Something had to be done. Not whenever the attendants got round to it, but immediately. Right, sodding, away.

And every time she moved so much as an inch Polly's brain seemed to roll a league, bruised and bleeding, inside her skull.

She considered calling out. What if they brought her baby to her? What if they didn't? She was both eager and terrified to see what she had wrought. She wanted to live, but she hadn't been afraid of death. The thought of not existing didn't terrify her. Motherhood, now that scared her. Polly didn't realize it sooner because she'd never been properly afraid before.

What if something was wrong with the baby? What if the baby hadn't survived and Titus had left Polly on her own because she had disappointed him? What if the baby was perfect and Titus had no further use for her? But where was Stephen? What if she called out and they brought the baby to her? What if they didn't?

What if she called and no one came at all?

"Stephen!" Polly called out. "Titus! Dr. Ng! Gillhooley! Somebody!"

The effort of speaking and the sound of her own voice seared her brain. She didn't know how she felt about the sound of heavy footfalls running toward her, as familiar as the rolling of the Museum tea trolley.

"Professor Magesteri," Polly said with a sob, holding out her arms to him, no idea whatsoever why she was weeping.

Stephen took her in his arms and squeezed her tight. It was excruciating.

"Oww, you're hurting me!" Polly cried louder and Stephen jumped back, startled.

Stephen surveyed her misery and winced. "That looks…swollen."

"Because it is," Polly said grasping her head in her hands. "Where's Titus?"

"Oh umm, Titus? He's um, well you know…" Stephen fumbled.

Polly knew Stephen well enough to know he saved his hemming and hawing for when he was doing his best to lie.

"I'm right here," Titus said sticking his head in the doorway. "There's a bit of a hiccup with the twins. Nothing you need concern yourself with. Tawaret, herself, couldn't have done a better job, my dear."

Polly's head might feel as though it had been trampled by a coach and four but she knew Titus as well, he only put on the charm this thick with her when he was attempting to minimize his own anxiety.

"It wasn't a dream then. There are two of them? Tell me what's wrong. And don't sugar coat it my head is killing me. I think it's the ether. They did give me ether, didn't they?" Polly said, her hands over her eyes.

"It seems our offspring have inherited your difficult disposition," Titus said airily.

"They've rejected every wet nurse we've tried," Stephen said plainly.

"Bring them to me, bring them now," Polly said taking her hands from her eyes.

"Once they've suckled the nurse, yes," Titus said. "They can't hold out much longer."

"How long has it been?" Polly asked.

"Twenty six hours," Stephen said looking at his pocket watch.

"If you don't bring them to me, Titus, I am going to go fetch them myself," Polly said gritting her teeth from the pain. She was surprised by the fierceness of her own feelings.

She could feel her temper rising.

"I don't think that's a good idea," Stephen said slowly.

"Why not?" Titus asked.

"Are you going to tell him or shall I?" Stephen asked.

"Tell him what? That I'm unfit to nurse my own babies for some stupid reason..." Polly asked.

"I know it's a tad unbecoming but in a case where the children's health is at stake..." Titus started but was interrupted by Stephen.

"It's not a stupid reason, it's the children's safety that concerns me," Stephen spoke over both Titus and Polly. "When Polly was little Aunt Augusta brought her a puppy. Do you remember that?"

Not this. Mighty Isis, did Stephen think she was still four years old and not aware of her own strength?

Polly looked out the window and into the garden below.

"First day she had the poor thing she squeezed it and broke both its fore-legs," Stephen said. "Do you think she can nurse a child without accidentally breaking its tiny neck? What if she sneezes? Have you seen the way she goes through tea cups?"

At that moment Polly wanted to break Stephen's neck. She could do it. She could nurse her own babies. She would show him.

"I'm not an idiot. I haven't hurt a living soul since I was a child," Polly reminded him.

"What say we compromise," Titus said his expression thoughtful. "Do you think you might be able to …milk yourself?"

That had never occurred to her. Polly had to admit it, when Titus was clever he was very clever indeed and she would feel better about holding the babies herself once the effects of the ether had worn off.

"That's an idea," Polly commended him. "What have you named them?"

"I was planning on calling the child Arachnus after my late father, but there are two of them and it hardly seems suitable," Titus said then looked over his shoulder at the uniformed attendant who was creeping past the room with the tea trolley. "Just what we need, two clean tea cups!"

Polly filled nine cups before she felt empty.

Stephen stood over the twin babies, in their twin cradles, sleeping soundly. They were quieter in general since they'd been moved to Polly's room. Though how they could sleep with their mother snoring the way she did was beyond him.

Polly was calmer as well, with the babies close by. It was the strangest thing to realize all three of them were breathing in unison. All three of them had the same perfectly pointed M shaped upper lip. So did he and Titus for that matter. He wondered how common it was, that feature.

"Now that we're alone I would like to offer my sincerest congratulations," Henry Plumber said stepping inside the doorway.

Stephen suspected for some time that Henry suspected.

"It's a vicious rumor, nothing more," Stephen muttered turning back to the babies.

"Oh, that," Henry said waving his unlit cigar dismissively as he came to stand at Stephen's side. "I was talking about your successful foray into the work of a magus. You think one of these is yours? My money's on the boy."

Stephen nearly shit himself. "No, we didn't." Stephen whispered furiously "We did no such thing."

"So The Duke was involved as well, was he? I was wondering whether he'd participated or not. Thank you for clearing that up," Henry said keeping his voice soft.

"I did not fucking well say that!" Stephen struggling to keep his voice at a whisper.

"You didn't have to," Henry said cocking his head curiously. "Are you afraid I'm going to alert the authorities? Is that what this is about?"

"Sorcery outside the service of the Empress is a crime punishable by death," Stephen hissed. "Don't play fucking innocent with me, Henry Plumber…"

Henry kept his voice low. "I merely wanted to applaud you taking this final inevitable step. I saw it coming the first time they unlocked that basement door. This is your destiny, not mucking about with acetylene torches and metal grinders."

Stephen looked at the baby boy with his black hair sticking up like a hedgehog.

"Not that, dear boy. I am addressing the art of conjury. You can't fight your nature," Henry said. "I mean to say, it's possible but ultimately fruitless."

"Professor Plumber?" Stephen said keeping himself calm.

"Yes, Professor Magesteri?" Henry said lightly.

"Piss off," Stephen told him.

Plumber grinned. "As I said before, congratulations on your good work. All of it. As you watch the children grow, Polly at your side, I've no doubt you'll come round to my way of seeing things," Plumber waved his arm in the direction of the cradles as he made his way out the door.

The curtain beside Polly's bed waved, despite the tightly closed window, and Titus shimmered into view.

Titus looked unimpressed, but then Titus never did like Henry.

"Stop shamming," Titus said looking down at Polly.

"How is it you always know?" Polly whinged.

"If I tell you, my dear, you may learn to fool me, and why would I want that?" Titus said with a smirk.

"Then tell me," Polly said sitting up and throwing off her duvet. "What in Hades' realm was my father talking about?"

"Nothing," Stephen said shaking his head vigorously.

His cousin, Titus, of course, didn't know when to keep his mouth shut.

"You were ill and we made you well again," Titus asked.

"Ill?" Stephen said the understatement getting under his skin. "She was bleeding from her fucking eyes. You were bleeding from your fucking eyes. What were we to do? Let you die? We had no choice."

"It hardly matters," Titus said blithely. "Polly said herself," - then he appealed to Polly directly - "You said yourself, that magic is in all likelihood simply science we have yet to understand properly and thus terms like sorcery and maleficium are essentially meaningless."

"I'm sure a reading of Polly's little book of treason and heresy will do no end to end of good at our sodding trial," Stephen said feeling his stomach turn.

"What was that elixir the two of you gave me?" Polly said her expression uncharacteristically harsh. "Where did it come from?"

"The god Apollo," Stephen said. "Not that that's an excuse."

"He means Nefrit. We were given our directions by Nefrit," Titus said waspishly.

"And what was in it? What did you feed me?" Polly asked her black eyes as hard as flint.

Stephen exhaled slowly "Mostly water, a bit of amber, a bit of lapis, scarab wings, a few other things…nothing we couldn't get at the Museum."

"Don't forget a pound of my flesh and pound of yours," Titus said. "Would you like to see the scar? Stephen has one just like it."

Polly turned from one to the other with the sort of rage Stephen had never seen on her face before.

"Did you not for a moment think of the possible affects? Science or not? I know you are an arrogant twit, Titus, but you, Stephen, did you not for a moment consider the consequences for the children? Or have you learned nothing from your own conception?" Polly growled, she actually sodding growled at them.

"We love you, both of us, and we acted as we did because neither of us could bear to lose you," Titus said.

Even though every word of it was true Stephen couldn't help thinking Titus was an oily bastard for the way he said it.

Stephen wasn't sure how to stop her but he didn't like the way Polly had climbed from her bed and was lifting the babies from their cradles so she held one in each arm.

"If they've been tainted by what you've done," Polly let the threat hang in the air.

Titus, being Titus, practically skipped over to where Polly was standing and kissed the babies on the forehead, one after the other.

"Polly, darling, look at your children. Look at them," Titus said soothingly stroking first a baby's cheek and then Polly's. "Are they anything less than perfect? You've let Henry Plumber get you all worked up over nothing."

Stephen wouldn't exactly say it was nothing, but he was keeping his mouth closed.

"Henry won't turn us in, not really, I don't think," Stephen blurted when it occurred to him. "He's flexing his muscle, is all."

"He probably just wants you to be to be more considerate, Titus," Polly said.

Stephen was surprised when Titus grasped him by the back of the neck and drew him into an embrace beside Polly.

"We've everything we ever wanted, now is hardly the time to fall to pieces,"

Titus said holding both Polly and Stephen close.

"There you are," Titus said as the nursemaid laid his son before him on the library floor, as instructed. The sheepskin would keep him comfortable. Titus carefully unswaddled the boy. "Now you may stretch your wings without laying waste to the furnishings. Once I'm dead and all I have is yours you're perfectly free to smash it all to pieces but until that day, it's still mine and I would appreciate it if my exquisite possessions last long enough to be inherited."

Titus tickled the little belly and was gratified when he opened up his wings. Magnificent, his son was magnificent.

"Surely he hasn't broken so much, darling?" the Dowager Lady Aurora called from the seat she occupied beside his Aunt Augusta. Stephen's cat, Lily wound between her feet and those of the crimson tufted settee. "He's little yet."

"Not too little. I would say his wingspan is nearly as long as my arm," Titus said comparing the two carefully.

"Do you think I might, touch them, his wings? I've never, I don't know what they're like, the wings," The Lady Dowager said. "They're always swaddled."

"Come here, Mother Dearest," Titus called slowly allowing her to follow the sound of his voice.

He took her hand in his when she came close and helped her to kneel beside him, pulling off her glove. "Gently, Darling, feel here, here is the tip of the left wing. The furthest edge." Titus guided his mother's fingers along the tips of the stiff feathers.

The boy kicked and turned.

"Are they anything like Prince Brolly's? Wings that is? His wings?" Titus's Mummy asked.

"Very like, actually," Titus said, because it had been tickling at the edges of his thoughts since the children had been born. "It's most peculiar."

"Well," The Lady Aurora laughed lightly. "He was your uncle, silly boy."

Titus knew it was useless to explain that Brolly wasn't his uncle by blood and it didn't quite work that way as far as he knew.

Then Lady Aurora lifted her chin and tilted her head. A second later the sound of distant crying hit his ears. The other twin. The girl. His daughter. Titus knew he needed to name them but he didn't want anything short of perfect titles for either of them; something meaningful as well as dignified, something that couldn't be shortened to a common nickname or noxious sobriquet. Years of being referred to as "Tight-Arse Albino" had strengthened his resolve to give his children just the right names.

"Oh goody, she's awake!" Mummy said clapping her hands. "And Dearest Polycorpus is up as well. Don't you hear them?"

Titus smiled. "Of course I do, Mummy Darling." Although he didn't hear Polly, not at all. That meant nothing. It was part of his mother's charm that she was wholly incapable of not showing her emotions at any given moment. "Go play with your girls," he said kissing her cheek. "We don't mind. Do we, my boy?"

"Are you certain?" Mummy asked.

"Indubitably. Off with you, go enjoy your granddaughter," Titus smiled feeling benign and indulgent, immeasurably pleased with himself that he had been able to give his mother this.

Titus had always been grateful for the advantage his overlong reach granted him at fisticuffs and swordplay, now he would have to add turning his son on his belly without being struck in the face with a wing to the list. The boy flapped vigorously.

"You must not blame your mother," his Aunt Augusta said sternly from the settee.

"What on earth would I blame my mother for?" Titus said, sneaking up to tickle the sole of the boy's foot.

"I will not have you judge Mua'Ruhn too harshly either. Your uncle was a foreigner; their ways are not our ways. They are, in a word, uncivilized," Aunt Augusta said.

Titus turned almost completely round to stare at her. As always, her appearance revealed nothing. Her face was veiled and she was covered from head to toe. She sat still as a stone.

"What do you mean by that?" Titus asked, because honestly, he was baffled. His Aunt Augusta was many things but irrational had never been one of those things.

"I mean to say exactly what I said; do not blame Aurora. Your mother is perfectly innocent in this matter. Likewise Prince Brolly is not to be judged harshly for his actions. Certainly not by you," Aunt Augusta said stiffly.

"What actions would those be?" Titus asked, resting his hand on the boy's foot.

"Are you intentionally trying to be obtuse?" Aunt Augusta asked waspishly. "Or can you not recognize an elephant by daylight? Has it never occurred to you to question that an 86 year old man should father a child almost instantaneously on his second wife when his first never displayed so much as a swollen belly in 60 years of marriage? Have you looked at your son?"

"Aunt Augusta, surely you aren't suggesting..."Titus said making use of the broadest and most jolly grin in his arsenal.

"I don't believe it is necessary I suggest what is obvious to the most casual observer," Aunt Augusta said.

"My Uncle? You are saying..."Titus repeated letting his smile fall. "My Uncle? Your Husband? That he...?"

"He was perfectly clear with me regarding his intentions toward your mother," Aunt Augusta said. "I did attempt to dissuade him but as you're no doubt aware his people have a rather unorthodox interpretation of the institution of marriage."

"He used to tease my mother that when his people married one daughter they married them all and he claimed her as his second wife. But it was just a lark," Titus said. "It was only a lark."

"From your Uncle's perspective it was sheer generosity to grant your mother what her husband could not. He was aware that without an heir the Old Duke's considerable estate would have fallen prey to a viper's nest of litigation, from the first wife's relations as well as assorted cousins of Old Mr. Albinus, likely leaving your poor mother a pauper," Augusta said, petting Stephen's tabby affectionately. "As far as he was concerned it was a singularly selfless act."

Titus closed his eyes and sucked his lower lip into his mouth. Could it be? Could it possibly be true? He had never known his Aunt Augusta to lie or even be mistaken. The worst he could say of her was that she was occasionally unpleasant, though in light of recent revelations he could certainly see why she might be.

"He used to say, if ever I was in Serpentinia I was to tell them I was his boy," Titus said numbly.

"He would," Auntie Augusta said tersely.

"And my mother has no idea?" Titus said.

"Nor should she," Aunt Augusta said.

Titus tried to imagine his mother's reaction if he, or anyone really, were to tell her the truth. She could not bear to hear it. Furthermore he could not bear for her to know she was an adulteress, however unwitting.

"Agreed," Titus said licking his lips nervously.

All his life Titus strove for the gravitas and graciousness those old enough to remember ascribed to The Old Duke and inevitably he fell short of the mark.

Prince Brolly.

Known among his own people as Mua'Ruhn of the Quahadan family.

Titus supposed on some level he ought to despise The Prince for his use of Titus's poor simple mother, but he found it an empty notion. Titus knew what happened to childless widows. While he knew the act was immoral and wrong, he also knew that none of what the Prince wished to spare his mother was baseless.

And he had a father. He had a father whom he had known and cared for him. It was his Uncle Brolly who took him on his first real grown up trip to the haberdasher, who shared his own personal tailor. It was his Uncle Brolly who taught him that man is judged by his judgement. Brolly who, as a senior officer in his own unit, had taught him to make his way through the tangle of military protocol.

The Prince's behavior had been selfless and admirable, from beginning to end, regardless of what Aunt Augusta thought.

"In light of the birth of your children," Aunt Augusta said stiffly. "I thought you should have this. Your uncle would have wanted it to come to you."

Titus watched rapt as Augusta pulled something from her reticule.

Taking his boy, the boy who resembled The Prince so closely, only golden when the Prince was darkest brown in colour, up in his arms, Titus approached his aunt and took what she held out to him.

A ring.

He remembered it well. The Prince esteemed it; a gift from his own mother, the Empress of the Serpentine people. It never left his person while he lived. Finest gold, from the Southern edge of Serpentinia, cast with the literally meaning of the Prince's personal name.

Black Moon.

Mua'Ruhn.

The Prince had habitually worn it on the first finger of his left hand. Titus gave it a try. It was hopeless. Sometimes Titus thought there were cured hams smaller than his hands. Never let it be said Londinium Austri was defeated by a mere piece of jewelry. With some work he managed to force it on his smallest finger.

"Nigel? How does that suit you? Do you like that? Nigel?" Titus asked the boy whose wings tucked up naturally behind him as he buried his little face against Titus's chest.

"We could call that sister of yours 'Selene' after the Prince as well."

"Yet subtle enough to leave room for denial," Aunt Augusta said with a tilt of her head.

"I approve."

Titus gave her a nod of thanks.

Within a week the names were recorded in the official government registry.

HELIOS NIGELLUS ALBINUS.

Selene Eos Albinus.

In a few months, once fitting arrangements had been made, there would be a public ceremony marking the twin's naming to rival the splendor of the Lupercalia Ball when they had seen fit to first announce themselves.

~~

"Don't toss her into my arms that way! She's an infant, not a yard of salami," Polly said as the nurse handed Selene off for their ritual after-tea baby feeding. She'd never thought a servant could worry her half so much as the nursemaids worried her.

Titus waved both Selene's and Nigel's nurse away. "You may go do whatever it is you do. We'll ring if there's a nappy needs changing."

"I don't think she likes Selene," Polly said as Titus settled Nigel beside his sister in their mother's arms. "Perhaps we should get a new nurse."

Titus sighed. "This is the child's third nurse in two months, hire a fourth and you risk developing a reputation as a difficult employer."

Polly let Selene grab hold of her finger as she struggled with an explanation, although rationalization was closer to the mark. "None of them are quite... right."

"I don't fault you, Polly, truly, I don't," Titus said not minding the crease in his trousers. "It's laudable on your part to be so vigilant, but there it is, you've as much as admitted there is no nursemaid alive who will suit you."

"Am I that bad?" Polly sighed, feeling embarrassed for her feelings as he helped tug her breasts out of her dress so she could feed the babies.

"Only just," Titus said kissing Polly's bolts. "I think it's enchanting. You're like a she-bear watching over your young. I knew I'd find a pet name for you eventually, my she-bear. My Ursula."

Polly hmmphed at him as best she could, working not to smile.

She never quite understood what motherhood was before she was neck deep in it. She had imagined, before she got pregnant, she would give Titus his baby, and after that it would be in the hands of competent nursemaids and none of her concern.

She had never thought she would hold one babe, much less two, to her breast gripped by the sensation if need be she could fight off an entire pack of rabid wolves. Or worse, society ladies. Polly had only ever seen placid images of mothers and children, like everyone in the picture had been drugged. And she'd never seen mother and child interactions up close. Clumsy as she was, people didn't tend to expose their tender young to possible crushing by Plumber's monstrosity. She had never expected the feelings her children aroused in her to be so fierce. Never having had a mother herself she never expected to feel much of anything for Titus's child to tell the truth.

Or Stephen's, come to that.

As it was she'd never felt anything quite so passionate as her attachment to babies who, regardless of their paternity, belonged unquestioningly to her.

"I cannot wait for Stephen to unveil whatever is that's kept him working through tea all these weeks," Polly said looking at Stephen's empty chair. "He missed supper twice last week."

"Indeed," Titus said with a not quite amused smile. "I can predict with near perfect accuracy there will be gears, and a whirring noise, and you will make no less than three suggestions for improvement and at some point in his grand display my cousin will release a flurry of obscenity likely to loosen the wallpaper."

Polly would have offered her opinion on Titus's powers of prognostication but at that moment there was a knock at the door.

"Go away," Titus called. "What part of 'your master does not wish to be disturbed' do you find difficult to grasp?"

"Your lordship, Please," Llewellyn said through the heavy door. It was surprising, Llewellyn never contradicted Titus, ever. Polly had more than once thought Titus could tell Llewellyn to wait for him in the midst of the busiest crossroads in Londinium and the valet would be run down by a coach before he disobeyed his master's orders.

"Come in, and don't stare," Titus shouted.

Polly watched as Llewellyn made his way in, eyes trained steadfastly on the carpeting. Extended before him was the silver tray he habitually used to present

Titus with the afternoon post.

Only the afternoon post wasn't due for hours yet.

"What's this?" Titus asked.

Polly had several questions as well, only she didn't asked them. She never got a useful reply out of Llewellyn. No, all she got out of him was obfuscation and the certain knowledge that she made him terribly terribly nervous.

Of course, given what the servants understood of goings on between her and Titus, and likely Stephen as well, she couldn't much blame him. She had turned their unassailably orthodox and respectable master into one who participated in his own cuckolding and talked blasphemy at the dinner table.

"I'm sure I don't know, Your Lordship," Llewellyn said, keeping his eyes down.

"Then how do you know it's worth interrupting my private time with my wife and children?" Titus asked.

Llewellyn didn't raise his head so much as half an inch, he merely extended the silver tray to his master more insistently.

"Delivered by Imperial Messenger," Llewellyn said.

Polly's stomach turned and twisted and she sat very very still looking from her babies to her husband and back again. Was this it? Was this going to be the end of them all? They didn't execute the families of blasphemers anymore, did they? Titus hadn't said anything public or written anything down so he couldn't be prosecuted, could he?

Of course he could be prosecuted. Or summarily executed. The Empress wasn't above the law, she was the law. She could do whatever she liked.

Llewellyn slipped out so unobtrusively he could have been a ghost. Titus sat across from Polly still as death, holding the gilt edged envelope between two long fingers.

"Is this how they usually arrest you for blasphemy?" Polly asked.

"They don't usually arrest me for blasphemy, but no, this is not how they usually arrest anyone," Titus said carefully opening the envelope with one finger, allowing Polly to get an eyeful of the official Imperial crest emblazoned on the front. "Usually the Praetorian Guard comes in the night and you're never seen again."

"But that wouldn't be the way to get you, would it? I mean, if someone wanted to arrest an invisible man, they'd have to be clever, wouldn't they?" Polly said fear refusing to let go of her. Little Selene reached up and grasped her brother's hand.

Titus nodded. "I've an audience. With Her Majesty. It could be the making of me or it could be the end."

"Don't go. Why can't you stay as you are?" Polly said. "What if it's a trap?"

"I've no choice," Titus said calmly. "Refusing would only prolong the inevitable if the meaning is ill and risk exposing my family to harm."

"Couldn't we…" Polly started but Titus cut her off.

"I am going to pack my trunk and take the waiting airship to Alexandria," Titus said. "You, my dear, will carry on as though nothing were out of the ordinary."

"But…but…couldn't we…" Polly stammered flummoxed by the shrapnel of events unfolding like an exploding artillery round.

"There is nothing to be done," Titus said removing the lighter from his waistcoat and setting fire to the letter. This was new Titus. The old Titus would have slept with a letter from the Empress under his pillow.

"You know I love you, you wanker," Polly said unable to keep the sob out of her voice.

Titus grinned as though struggling not to laugh. "To hear those words from your lips, my children healthy and strong in your arms, means more than you could know."

He pressed a chaste kiss to her forehead and swept out of the room.

Jupiter, but that man loved a dramatic exit. Polly hoped Her Majesty would be impressed.

Chapter 20 : The Road to Destiny

tephen had been practicing what he would say to Titus for the better part of a fortnight.

He had composed it over tea-stained schematics and while keeping apprentices from killing themselves and one another. He committed it to memory to the sound of torches and metal on metal, the smell of acetylene in his nostrils. He had prepared himself.

Stephen trod through the corridor, hoping and dreading Titus was in his study. Knowing he had to say his piece before he went mad of it churning his guts to ribbons.

He threw open the heavy door and saw the familiar shock of curly red hair.

"Close your precious gob and let me have my say, Titus. You can spout off and protest however you like once I've finished but until then I want you to shut your bloody hole. I've thought long and hard about this and I won't have you working your magic and changing my mind in the sodding middle," Stephen said.

Titus raised his brows expectantly but said nothing.

"I know, I know I said I wanted Polly for my own. I know I said I wanted to be a husband to her but it's clear I'm like some sort vestigial tail or something, hanging about. Useless. I know that boy is mine," Stephen went only to pause when Titus made some sort of rumbling noise. "No, hear me out, but being that, being my son, is something I wouldn't wish on a dog much less an innocent babe. What I'm trying to say is, I'm going to collect my things and move back to my rooms at the Museum. It's for the best. The rumors will be put to rest and you'll have no more opportunity to drag my loathsome arse to every half-baked excuse for social masturbation in Londinium proper. The way you lot wank each other off with your forced admiration is beyond tiresome."

Titus looked more annoyed than anything. "Much as I would like to go on listening to you spout nonsense all day I can't so I won't. Instead I would ask you to close your trap and listen. I have been summoned, effective immediately, to court in Alexandria, to have audience with Her Majesty."

"Bloody Hell," Stephen said stunned.

"Indeed," Titus nodded. "It could mean a promotion or it could mean execution but I've no idea which. Even were it not for this turn of events, I would reject your withdrawal from our agreement. You are my closest friend, perhaps only friend, if by friend one means a man one trusts with his life. And Polly is inexplicably fond of you, in spite of your indulgent nature."

"Have you ever considered taking a day off from being a smug bastard?" Stephen asked.

"No, do you? Listen. I need you to give me your word you'll look after Polly and the children. You know how she is, she thinks she can run the world but she's less sense than a kitten when it comes to certain things. I will send word if it goes badly for me in the Capitol. Provided I have sufficient warning, of course. If I do not return in one month's time I am dead and you must marry Polly."

"Of all the addle-pated dung you've ever…are you mad?" Stephen stuttered. "I couldn't possibly debase Polly…"

Titus stared hard into his eyes. "You can and you will. If I am dead there will be those who insist a decent period of mourning be afforded my memory, ignore them. You are to wed Polly and adopt both children immediately. I want your solemn vow."

"Absolutely fucking not," Stephen said, his head swimming. How had he gone from resuming his bachelor life to being engaged in less than three minutes?

"I'm not joking, Stephen," Titus said.

"Neither am I," Stephen said.

Titus stopped and inhaled, it was only then that Stephen realized his cousin had been stuffing two separate valises with papers while they argued.

"Take this and keep it safe. It contains copies of all my legal papers including my will in case my attorney is not to be trusted. I've paid him enough but you know how these things go," Titus said grimly handing the larger case to Stephen. "There is always the possibility someone else is willing to pay more."

"More than you? Not bloody likely," Stephen said hoping to reassure him.

"Without a husband and father my wife and children will be utterly without legal protection. As bright as Polly is she is still female and as such is barred from even defending against civil suit from my creditors. And don't think a single one of them is above puffing up a bill when it suits. She'll be penniless in six months," Titus said.

Stephen hadn't thought of that.

"I hadn't thought of that," Stephen said.

"Well I have," Titus said leaning in close to stand nose to nose with Stephen. "Tell me, in all sincerity, there is another man you would trust to better protect Polly and the children."

Stephen shook his head, knowing he could not.

"Then you will marry her?" Titus asked.

Stephen tried to speak up but the sound that came from his lips was half strangled with emotion. "I will."

"Good man!" Titus laughed, pulling the glove from Stephen's fingers and clasping Stephen's hand between both of his. The show off.

"Oh, I nearly forgot," Stephen said pulling away to reach inside the pocket of his frock coat. "This came to you from the Temple of Apollo. It's Nefrit. She says your debt's come due."

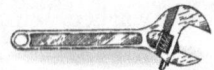

By the time Titus and his three trunks full of clothes made it within a city block of The Temple of Apollo evening traffic already choked Central Londinium.

His coach hadn't moved in, he looked at his pocket watch, 8 minutes.

"I've decided to head to the Temple on my own," Titus called out the window to the driver. "As soon as you can move forward, make your way to the Marc Anthony Aerodome, I'll catch up."

With his next breath Titus allowed the shining feeling of invisibility to cover him before he stepped out of the carriage and into the street. It was easier to walk the streets of Londinium unseen. No worries about squeezing too close to strangers. No worries about having your pocket picked. One could run without taking dignity into consideration, provided one had room.

He wove past the children and old women selling flowers, the chestnut vendors as well as those who peddled buns, women who pushed carts of eels and other things pulled straight from the Thames, in addition to a wagon full of urine barrels on their way to the tanner.

He avoided whores and stepped over crawlers. He narrowly dodged Marquises and Baronets as well as mothers, children, shop keepers, clerks, errand boys, managing to arrive, still invisible, in the main room of the Temple filled cheek to jowl with worshipers. He slipped by without notice into the inner chambers where the sibyl was housed, straightening his sleeves before he allowed himself to be seen.

"Good, you've come," Nefrit said, pillows keeping her propped up in her chair.

She was suspiciously alone.

"How could I refuse a summons from my delightful little grandmother?" Titus said suavely. The truth was he never felt completely at ease in her presence.

"Great great great great grandmother," Nefrit corrected.

"Of course," Titus bowed deeply, averting his eyes.

"You're wondering why I called you here. What price I require you pay," Nefrit's voice creaked.

"I have been summoned to Alexandria," Titus said, pulling his watch from his waistcoat pocket. He knew he was being impertinent, in fact, that was why he'd done it, to demonstrate his unworshipfulness. To Prove he no longer feared gods or their bent emissaries.

"Cleopatra Helene can wait until I have given you your task," Nefrit said sharply.

"I've already agreed to it, so give me my instructions that I may be on my way," Titus said.

Nefrit's body spasmed where she sat and her eyes gleamed red. Titus did not choose to look away.

"On the table beside me," Nefrit began as soon as whatever had wracked her passed.

"There is a chisel and there is a pen."

"Yes," Titus said glancing down at his watch.

"With the chisel you are to take the name of my father, Crassus Cato, wherever you find it, and you are to chisel it out. With the pen you are to blot out where it is written, until no trace of him remains," Nefrit said.

She had his attention now. Titus was no longer the believer he once had been, before he had been exposed to Polly and her wonderful terrible book, but the notion of defaming the name Crassus Cato, high priest of the Temple of Apollo in Alexandria and pride of the family line, was a transgression of the first order. Only a criminal would even ponder such an act, or a hero.

"Why?" he asked, levelly.

"Because I cursed him. I cursed him when I was a girl and he sold me off to a barely literate rural bumpkin in this forsaken backwater of the great Empire. I cursed him that dishonor and ill fortune would follow his descendents until his name was blacked out upon the Earth," Nefrit said, her voice growing stronger. "My brothers all died without heir."

"Why did you curse him? Not for sending you to England, that's motivation for tears not criminal sorcery," Titus said, seeing no reason to dissemble.

"You're beginning to sound like that wife of yours," Nefrit spat.

"Thank you," Titus said taking it in the spirit in which it was offered.

"Is it enough that the priesthood is drunk on its own power? Keeping the sybils drugged to control them? Holding the power to see the future for ransom to the highest bidder? Then interpreting the words of the oracle as they deem will benefit themselves and their cronies most? Is that not enough? Using the oracle for his own glory while treating the woman who gives him his power like a simple tool," Nefrit said, her voice as it must have been a hundred years ago.

Titus shook his head. "That's not all of it. I wasn't born yesterday. Tell me the rest."

"Compared to me you were," Nefrit sneered and her face was like a death's head. "What would you say if I were to tell you I came to my marriage carrying my father's child?"

Titus wanted to deny the depraved words she had said but he found his voice frozen in his throat. He shook his head.

"What if I were to tell you my child, William Tiresias Magesteri, the great hermaphrodite, who was both mother and father to your line, had no part of Waldo Magesteri in him?" Nefrit said.

"That cannot be," Titus muttered, not because he did not believe so much as because he did not wish it to be true. He knew such things occurred. He was an adult. But not in his line. Apollo, no, not in his line.

"William's son, Cornelius, did marry the child of his sister, Eulalia, so my poor husband did find his way back into the family line, still, not quite where he is usually placed." Nefrit shrugged. "It wasn't even classed a crime beyond a sort of breach of marriage contract, though I doubt Waldo could have afforded a wife of my status unless she was damaged goods. Still the right of the Pater Familias is absolute, and taking a little pleasure is negligible when you have the right to kill a girl every day of her life."

"Holding the lives of your family in your hands is a grave responsibility," Titus said by rote the line from his boyhood primer. "As Zeus is the father of gods, the Head of the house must be the god of his family." He could say it in Greek, Latin, and Egyptian as well, but he didn't.

"What a load of shit," Nefrit said. "Most men are no better than they should be, and some are a good deal worse. You will do as I bid you and free your children of Crassus's curse?"

"I will free us all," Titus said, a sort of hate he didn't know he was capable of welling up in him as he took up the chisel and the pen.

"Then kneel before me and receive my blessing," Nefrit ordered.

Titus obeyed.

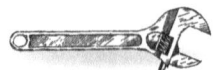

Polly sat nursing the twins until they were full and bored with milk and started playing silly buggers. She worked at not worrying over Titus. Meanwhile Nigel and Selene were drooling and grinning and pulling at her hair where it had escaped from its braid, and her dress, and each other.

She let them have their fun. It seemed so strange that it had only been three months, that was all, but she knew she would kill, outright, anyone who dared to lay a finger on either of them. It had been not quite two years since she'd married Titus and yet it seemed as though everything in her life had happened in those nineteen months. As if she'd been preserved in cold storage before, counting time, and waiting for her real life to begin without knowing it.

And yet.

And yet, it hadn't been Titus that made her life count. It had been herself, standing up to Titus, deciding things for herself. Before she was married, she more or less did what her papa and Mrs. Brolly said, because she trusted them to know more than she did and have her best interest at heart. But trusting other people to decide everything, knowing she had no power over anything, had left her, in retrospect, both frustrated and ignorant of the consequences of her actions. After all a difference that makes no difference is no difference.

Marriage to Titus had changed all that, simply because she wasn't about to let a goose like him have all the say, Duke or not.

And now, now that she cared for him, and what was more liked him, he might never return. It was unfair. And he was still more than half goose.

Who would dress the babies properly? Certainly not Polly. Who would love them the way Titus did if he never came back from Alexandria? Polly's love was fierce but nothing like the sheer delight Titus seemed to take from them. Stephen? Stephen seemed more frightened of the children than anything.

Which, in light of Selene's current nappy, made perfect sense.

Polly rang for the nursemaids to take them both, because invariably, when one baby's bowels went the other's were sure to follow.

"Is that all, Your Ladyship?" Mrs. Allison, Nigel's nurse asked.

Mrs. Duncan, Selene's nurse looked at her expectantly.

Polly fought the impulse to tell them the truth; that she was angry and worried and she didn't know what they could expect to do about it but stay out of her bloody way.

"New nappies all round should cover it. You can bring them to me in the peristylium after I've had my supper," Polly said feeling a twist in her gut when the nurses looked at one another when she made no mention of Titus. "Your master's been called to The Imperial Court."

Then it hit her. She didn't know why it had taken two hours of fretting over Titus before she realized the rest of them were in danger as well. Whatever crime Titus had committed, she and Stephen had committed as well. What if they came after them? What would happen to Nigel and Selene?

Her mind raced even as the nurses beamed at each other so hard they fairly glowed. Idiots. Oh it would be quite the coup to work for a family with Imperial honors. One where all the adults had been jailed for treason? Less so.

What a couple of ninnies.

Polly made herself smile back at them until they left.

She took her supper and Stephen was there. Neither of them said anything and when the dishes were cleared she couldn't recall what had been served.

She fed the babies in the peristylium but recalled almost nothing about it beyond the fact that it was done.

She lay in bed alone, expecting to fall instantly asleep the way she always did. Nothing happened.

She tried a book but reread the same line a dozen times without comprehending a word.

She moved to Titus's side of the bed. It made the back of her eyelids itch, and she wiped her face. She could feel the outline of his shape worn into the mattress. He habitually laid on his right side. She wiped her face again.

The room seemed so hateful all of a sudden; she could no longer bear it.

She jumped up, not even bothering to put on her dressing gown, and went to the Blue Room and threw open Stephen's door.

Stephen sat up midsnort.

Titus was right, he did sound exactly like a pig. His nightgown was graying and threadbare. How had she not known that? He needed a new night gown immediately.

"Polly?" Stephen asked rubbing his eyes. "Your Ladyship has sodding awful manners."

"Shove over," Polly told him. "And shut your gob."

"Yes, sir, your highness," Stephen said turning on his side.

Polly climbed in and curled up behind him, tucking her knees behind his and wrapping her arm around his belly, the way Titus did to her.

"Titus Albinus is an idiot," she told the back of Stephen's head.

"I was almost asleep," Stephen muttered, "and you woke me up again."

"You are as well," Polly said. "You're as big an idiot as Titus."

"And I love you too, Sweetheart, now, go to sleep," Stephen said tiredly.

He'd never said that to her before. She didn't question for a moment that he meant it. That night she did sleep. Eventually.

Colonel Titus Posthumous Albinus, Duke Londinium Austri sat down to break fast in the dining room of the Imperial airship wearing his second best uniform and his very best grin. There was nothing else for it.

Needless to say he was saving his best uniform for the Empress and he certainly wasn't going to drop the pretense of barely disguised self-satisfied delight, not in front of present company.

It might even be warranted.

But even if it wasn't.

"What extraordinary pain perdu," Titus said taking a drink of tea that he might choke it down. It was almost magically burnt to a char on the outside while still raw and wet in the middle. It was as bad as the mess in Afghanistan and the one in Burma, come to that.

"It's uncanny," Captain Smith said dissecting the bread, lengthwise.

"It's like every officer's mess in the Empire. I reckon they train them to do it. Intentionally. " Colonel DaSilva said.

"What for?" Titus couldn't help but ask. Polly was rubbing off on him.

"No idea, but at least they're consistent," DaSilva said. "We engineers usually consider that a virtue, consistency."

Titus eyed DaSilva's Engineering Corps insignia. He was probably one of those who measured his mistresses with calipers and wrote graduated charts in the place of love sonnets.

"Treason!" General Endymion Daar said brandishing his fork at them. Unlike the rest Daar had been gobbling the burnt gooey mess down as fast as the old man could shovel it in. Titus had imagined at his age and obvious state of disrepair the fat old general hadn't any ability to taste left.

The entire table paused and look to Daar, being the senior officer aboard, wondering if the general was potty. The eye in the center of Daar's forehead stared at them.

"Yes?" Titus smiled winningly at Daar.

"The reason the food in the mess is so bloody awful is to cut down on treason. Without the food to complain of talk turns to politics, war, women," Daar said waggling his fork at them. "And before you know it you've an unholy riot on your hands."

"Worked on us," Smith said.

"One does get inured over the course of a career," Daar said, shoveling more in. "Which is why the Imperial Airships employ army cooks, to make us feel at home."

"Don't look at me," DaSilva said "I go native whenever I can."

"I've my own cook," Titus said cheerfully. "Still this does bring back memories."

"Oh yes, the good old days, rum, buggery, and the lash," Daar said closing his eyes and wiping his lips. "She a good cook, DaSilva? This native of yours?"

DaSilva grinned. "French girls know their way around a stew pot."

Titus was purposefully not thinking about bad rum, buggery, or his time under the whip.

"What about you, Albinus?" Daar said. "Any scintillating cookery to regale us with?"

"Sorry to disappoint, no mistress here, only a wife, and as far I'm aware one who has never so much as boiled an egg," Titus said, sincerely amused at the idea.

"A lady, then," Daar said with a laugh.

"To fine ladies everywhere," Smith said raising his tea cup. "Without them there would be no need for mistresses, and what fun would that be?"

Titus raised his tea cup and let the General pour liberally from his flask like all the others. He couldn't fight the feeling if Polly were there she would give him an earful on the wrongness of the conversation. He knew there was something but he couldn't spell out precisely what it was. He smiled pleasantly at the General.

"To Ladies," Titus said, inwardly mulling it over as his teacup touched DaSilva's.

As soon as breakfast was finished he would write to Polly.

Stephen Magesteri woke up shit scared with arms wrapped tight round his chest. He tried to move but was held fast.

Polly.

Polly climbed into bed with him last night. He closed his eyes and willed himself to go back to sleep. It almost worked, until the snoring started.

And so was set a precedent of sorts. Polly would pretend to retire to her own room, her own bed, her marriage bed and then after a few hours creep in to sleep with him.

And when he said sleep, he meant just that, sleep. There were no dirty little games, as Polly was wont to play, no tossing him on his back and having her way with him, which was also part of her established repertoire. Only snuggling and dry kisses to the side of his neck and practically forcing him to start every morning with a good hard wank, before facing a department full of spotty faced little shits just waiting for something to snigger at.

Stephen came home for tea to Polly and the babies, who looked at him in a way that made him feel as though he'd done something wrong, which, knowing him, he bloody well knew he had. Spending the night with their mother, for instance.

But he didn't sit in Titus's chair and he went straight back to the Museum after he ate his tea. What he could get of it, that was. It seemed not even the grief of missing Titus could stop Polly stealing his biscuits.

At supper Stephen did his best to do as Titus asked. He sat in his usual spot and as usual kept Polly abreast of the goings on at the Museum. Let Titus's valet bully him about.

A week in, it got difficult.

Polly was ignoring him in favor of the babies, which was standard procedure these days.

Stephen was finishing the chicken livers on toast. There were only four left and Polly wasn't going to eat them. She hadn't let so much as a morsel of meat past her lips since she'd given birth. Which was a shame, because they were perfect little meaty buttery bites. Oh well, Polly playing picky-arse left more for him. Having eaten all the biscuits right away he was polishing off the last four savories before heading once more into the breach of negligence, ignorance, and gross incompetence that was his department.

"Surely Professor Magesteri is aware of his obligations," Llewellyn said when Stephen looked at his watch.

"What obligations? What are you talking about?" Stephen asked.

"The Crowleys," Llewellyn said meaningfully.

Polly's eyes wandered from the children, for once, and she shrugged. Clearly she hadn't a clue either.

"Don't know what you're sodding talking about," Stephen said swallowing the last mouthful of liver on toast.

"Master Phaeton Crowley's first birthday celebration. Master Nigel and Miss Selene's first social invitation? His Lordship left very explicit instructions," Llewellyn said as if they were all addled.

"Fuck, the bleeding baby party," Stephen said slapping his forehead. "There's no way to get out of this is there?"

"None, Sir," Llewellyn said. "I've laid out your better suit." He was no Titus Albinus. His entire wardrobe was worth less than one of Titus's outfits, but that was no reason to poke fun.

Polly looked like she was trying not to laugh.

Three hours later Polly had forgotten him again as he stood beside a potted palm hoping against wretched hope it would function as some sort of camouflage. Oh to be Titus Sodding Albinus and simply disappear, but no, he'd been spotted.

It was Thoth Phipps-Burnham, with the tusks. For the life of him Stephen could not work out why the poor sod habitually smelled of rotting fish.

"Ho, there, Magesteri," Phipps-Burnham said. "Good man, keeping an eye on your cousin's nest while he's away on official business."

He wondered if there was a subtext there but discarded the idea of insult as too subtle for dull Old Thoth.

"Mmm?" Stephen grunted noncommittally, watching the great ballroom full of babies, some on the huge rug that had been unfurled, some in cradles, others in cots, others proudly displayed in the arms of their nursemaids. Every

Uncommon babe in the British Isles under the age of three was there to be seen. Like pigs at a country fair.

"Titus has got insight, I must admit. When I first heard he was putting The Museum's Patchwork Doll in harness I reckoned it for sheer desperation on his part," Phipps-Burnham mumbled through his mustache. "But the old boy's cleverer than he lets on."

"I sincerely doubt it," Stephen said, his eyes, like Phipps-Burnham's, on the extra large cot where Polly hovered over her two babies, both powdered and perfumed within an inch of their tiny lives and dressed in the finest little silks to be had. Titus's two blue ribbon piglets, as it were. "That was nothing but dumb luck on his part."

The nursemaids stood, like sentries, stationed at attention at the north and south corners of the cot.

Livia Canavan bent over the cot, tickling both infants at once with her tentacles. Polly, who normally chafed under too much attention, was beaming at the smiles being thrown the twin's way.

"No, I'm in earnest. Not one, but two, extraordinary youngsters. That is an accomplishment," Phipps-Burnham said. "You don't happen to know if Albinus has looked into a match for them yet, the girl in particular? My Bert's going on eleven, come December, and as eldest he'll be coming into a reputable sum when he…"

"Not a clue," Stephen said, cutting Phipps-Burnham off before he could elaborate. Stephen'd never seen young Phipps-Burnham but if his father was anything to go by Titus wouldn't let the little ape near his daughter with a ten foot pole.

"No harm getting my bid in early," Phipps-Burnham laughed to himself. "Generally girls go begging, you know, they're weighed by the dowry more or less, but that girl of Albinus's…well… even at this age you can see the value of her. As sweet as a little tea cake, isn't she?"

Stephen couldn't disagree. There was no disputing the fact that Polly made beautiful babies. A whole cluster of ladies was grouped round the twin's cot, cooing. Who could blame them, really? Not that he was much of a judge but they were the prettiest babes he'd ever seen, far prettier than those other mewling brats.

Still Stephen was wise enough to keep out of the way. He hid behind his plant, straying only far enough to snatch food or drink off the tray when it came round.

By the time they came home Polly was practically glowing. She didn't wait as long as she usually did before coming to his room. Objectively, she had never looked so well in all the years Stephen had known her. Subjectively, she was stunning. She left him stunned.

Her hair was glossy and massive. Although the thick white streaks at her temples had not vanished, the hair there was as lovely as the rest. The effect was quite artistic, really.

Her skin was rosy in the paler portions and dusty rose in the darker parts, and all over tight pored and fairly glowing with health. Her lips and nails were smooth and perfect, like polished marble.

"How do you feel? You're not in your night clothes, yet. Are you not tired?" Stephen asked, not moving any closer.

Polly cocked her head wonderingly. "You know, I believe Titus can't help but come home. He's too...Titus, for things to go badly. He could talk anyone into anything. He's going to be fine. I'm sure of it."

That hadn't been Stephen's question and he had no idea how to respond. She did have a point, though. He'd never known anyone who was completely immune to Titus once he got going.

"You are perfectly free to sleep here if you like," he said.

"Don't be a tease," she said with a quirk of her lips. "It's unbecoming, besides, it's my house."

"Then by all means, allow me to make myself more comfortable," he said, sitting down so hard in his armchair it skittered back a bit. "And it's my room."

Polly rolled her eyes and folded her arms across her chest "Right then," she said only pretending to be annoyed "Will you please take off your trousers? Or do you want me to say pretty please?"

Stephen could see the grin creeping into the corner of her mouth.

It took almost no thought at all and out his cock sprang, with a force and motion that merited a clap of thunder. Not bad at all for thirty-nine. Still three more months until he was as old at Titus.

Titus.

"I'm certain Titus is going to come up smelling like a rose," Stephen assured the both of them.

Polly nodded.

She brushed one knuckle against her lower lip and he understood immediately. He'd never given her any pleasure, Stephen knew that. And here she was, so used thinking he couldn't please her, that she automatically decided to...Stephen must have gone mad because he shook his head.

"I want to...let me at least give it a try," Stephen said rising from his chair.

"Titus is going to be fine," she said.

"Titus is going to be bloody brilliant," Stephen agreed cupping her soft cheek in his hand.

Was it a lie? He didn't know, but he wanted it to be true. He wanted to want it to be true at least.

He wanted.

He wanted Polly. He wanted her entire body to hum at his touch the way she did at his cousin's.

He thought of the way his cousin had with theatrics, intentionally whispering so quietly everyone had to strain to hear. Always the tease. Never giving away too much. Always in control.

Stephen was an oaf who made a fool of himself practically blurting his love all over her thighs before he even started. But not this time. He refused.

Stephen wanted to devour Polly, crush her to him, but instead he brushed her lips with his thumb so softly he could almost sob with want. Titus wasn't the only one capable of pleasing Polly.

Polly stood still as stone, the gooseflesh rising on her shoulders, arms, the exposed portions of her breasts.

Stephen might not be as fit as Titus but that didn't stop him dropping to his knees before her, even as his cock throbbed, thinking of the offer she'd made as he pressed his face against the cool taffeta of her dress.

Her hands went to his hair.

Stephen was like a blind man rummaging through her underskirts for the hidden prize. He was surprised by the ferocious heat of her thighs, the smoothness of the skin there above her stockings, like a mouthful of sweetened cream, and then the thatch of hair so thick and coarse it felt almost dangerous.

Stephen inhaled. He'd always left this to Titus.

Not because he didn't want to. His mouth was already wet with anticipation.

But because it was filthy. Not literally. Filthy in the sense of not the sort of thing you did to a girl you loved.

The sort of thing only whores liked, as far as he'd ever heard. A decent woman would never allow it.

Trouble was Polly loved it. And Titus wasn't afraid or ashamed to give Polly what she liked. Was Polly indecent? He couldn't reason how she could be judged more indecent than him or Titus. Perhaps that blasted book of hers was rubbing off on him.

Closing his eyes, Stephen fastened his mouth against the top of her slit the way he had seen Titus do.

Polly made a little frustrated noise high in her throat. "It's difficult standing up," she said. "Let me help you," she said sitting in his armchair, her skirt raised, her legs wide, she opened herself. It was utterly debauched and it made him want to fucking cry with wonder at the beauty of it.

He was foul.

And at that moment he did not give a shit if the servants knew, or the society bitches suspected or any of the rest. He tasted her wet and slippery and musky as a fur coat, and he swore every single time he licked, she groaned and each groan resonated in his cock.

Her back arched and she grasped blindly behind her, nails scraping the wall for purchase.

He took the tiny lump of flesh, no bigger than a sugar cube, between his lips and sucked. Polly kicked her legs madly in the air her entire body stiffening. He didn't know why he expected her to keep her feet on the floor.

Stephen raised his head.

"Bed?" he asked her swallowing hard.

Polly nodded dumbly.

In his bed Polly's body was soft and warm everywhere it wasn't held in check by her corset. She didn't seem to mind the taste of her sex on his mouth when he kissed her. He in turn felt strangely excited by the taste of her lip rouge even though he knew it was made mostly of beetles.

The sensation of her legs in their silk stockings wrapping round him, while his cock unbearably hard and hot and heavy pressed against the mouth of her sex.

Silk spun by caterpillars, lip rouge made of beetles, in seemed their union was full of insects.

It was only fitting that he feel like a cockroach.

He was loathsome. The only reason she bore the burden of him was pity. Pure pity. It had to be pity.

"I have a, a , a request," he managed to force the words.

"Anything," Polly sighed breathily. "Anything you want."

"Polly, Sweetheart, would you smile at me?" he whispered. "For me?"

"Oh Stephen, always," Polly said sounding as though she might break into tears.

But she did smile, though it seemed a sad smile, to Stephen, even as he pushed his way into her. Even as her hips rose to meet his she smiled. The mouth of her cunt was as wet as ripe fruit and twice as sweet.

She smiled even as the sensation overcame him and he felt as though he might possibly swoon, which would be embarrassing, though he didn't in the end and was damn grateful for it.

And when it was all over and he'd wiped his prick on the sheet he laid his head on her breast and she kissed the top of his head.

"You know I love you. I love you just as much as, you know," Polly said toying with his open shirt, tracing his regimental tattoo with her finger.

Stephen didn't have it in him to either accept or reject her hypothesis under the circumstance, so he made his own query.

"I have made you happy? I've given you pleasure? Haven't I?" he asked, still breathing hard, staring at the ceiling.

He was nearly offended when she started laughing. "Mighty Isis, yes, you were wonderful."

It was good to have verbal confirmation.

"Now that's settled will you help me out of this dress? Unless you want me to call for my maid, that is," Polly whinged climbing out of the bed. "Corsets are murder."

"Do you make Tight-Arse do this? Help with your dressing and undressing? Or do you reserve the honor to the lesser members of the gentry?" Stephen asked lifting her hair to get at the buttons on her back.

"Oh, you know me, you know how horrid I am. I've forced him to help me since the first day we were married," Polly sighed.

Stephen couldn't help himself, he leaned forward and kissed the back of her bare neck.

"Thank you, Polly, thank you."

Too bad he had no bloody idea what he meant by it.

Chapter 21 : Between Duty and the Deep Blue Sea

olonel Titus P. Albinus was not some rustic provincial lord who had never ventured forth beyond the confines of his country estate. He was not the least bit intimidated by the sights and sounds and, most importantly, smells of the largest city in the Empire. He was not. He was unflappable despite the way the crowd, pressed cheek to jowl, flowed like a veritable river of flesh fairly sweeping one along so that it was more difficult to make one's way to a highly visible landmark like the Palace Complex than one might imagine.

Colonel Titus P. Albinus was a man of the world. Erudite, sophisticated, and above all self-possessed. He was not the least bit flustered by the time he arrived at the gate of the Imperial Compound; anyone would have needed a moment to straighten their topcoat and see to their hair after escaping the press of the crowd. It was only slightly warmer than Londinium at the height of summer.

Titus pulled his documents from the inside pocket of his best uniform coat. They were slightly damp but he handed them to the guards at the gate just the same.

They handed the papers back without a word. Of course they did. What did he expect, fanfare? The guards no doubt waved officers from across the Empire into the complex on a daily basis. To drive home the point Daar, the

Puntish General, queued up behind him in a shining blue uniga, pulled by a very haggard looking porter.

"Did you brave the foot traffic? Jupiter's hairy balls, Khufu was right about you, you are unstoppable. He told me once before Jalalabad, 'That young spy of mine, young Albinus, is utterly fearless. Tell the boy to do a thing and it gets done, no matter the difficulty. I swear the little cod could wade through solid rock up to his neck if given a direct order.' Didn't surprise me one bit to hear you made it out of Jalalabad," Daar said.

Titus shrugged graciously, folding his papers. "You flatter me."

"No, I don't. Khufu also said you were a smarmy prick, but a smarmy prick who can be counted on to do his duty. I'm surprised Her Imperial Majesty hasn't summoned you sooner," Daar said.

Titus smiled wider, the old man was past watching what he said in front of his inferiors, this in itself made him worth listening to. He was reasonably certain if Daar knew of any ill wind blowing Titus's way he would at least hint at it.

"That does sound like the late General Khufu," Titus said slipping his papers back into his jacket.

"Is it true what you said on the ship about not having a mistress? A man of your station should be able to afford at least one. Don't tell me you've run into money troubles," Daar said looking concerned.

So that was the rumor. Titus knew the old man had been trying to ferret out something since the ship.

Titus looked down at the old man sitting in his porter drawn cart.

"Have you by chance heard of the Commoner Plumber's rec? The female he built at The British Museum and raised himself from infancy?" Titus said as superciliously as he knew how, and that was supercilious indeed.

"Yes," Daar said vaguely. "I recall something about Plumber from the reclamation unit attempting something of the sort."

"I took her, less than two years ago, as my wife and I've already a son and a daughter, both strong and healthy and quite extraordinarily both are winged,"

Titus said unsure whether or not he should fight the genuine smile curling the corner of his mouth. "I've no need of a mistress. It's not a matter of finances. I simply haven't the energy for another female."

Titus knew it was unforgivably ungallant but he said it just the same. Polly wouldn't mind, though Stephen undoubtedly would.

The eye in the center of Daar's forehead blinked, but only for a moment.

"Is she …not…common, then?" Daar asked.

"Polycorpus Singularia maybe an artificial monster, but I assure you she is monstrous to her core," Titus said meaningfully.

"I would like to meet this creature," Daar said sincerely.

"It can be arranged. Next time you're in Londinium drop in for tea," Titus said, and he meant it. It was never too soon to position the children, socially. Daar would no doubt want to see the children as well and a general would be a fitting visitor to the nursery.

"If you don't hurry you'll wind up administrating latrine maintenance in Bulgaria," Daar said. "I'm afraid I've kept you here jawing so long you're going to be late."

"Shit!" Titus shouted in spite of himself, vanishing on the spot and breaking into a dead run.

It was no exaggeration to say he raced through miles of corridor, past bureaucrats and cleaners. Past serving girls and footmen. He narrowly avoided courtiers and their ladies by the score. He sprinted across mosaics and paved walkways. He ran through gardens and atriums and skidded, twice, on unexpected carpets.

By the time Titus reached the audience hall the clock was chiming 8 o'clock and he barely had time sort out his epaulets and arrange his curls before becoming visible directly in front of the dog-headed secretary's desk.

"State your name and business," the secretary said in surprisingly high pitched voice for such a decidedly masculine person. Perhaps it was the dog head that caused it.

"Colonel Titus Posthumous Albinus, Duke of Londinium Austri. I was summoned by Her Majesty," Titus said straightening his sleeve. There was the smallest loose thread on the gold braiding separating the sapphire blue worsted wool from the crimson red at the bottom third of his sleeve.

"You'll be called when Her Divine Majesty wants to see you," the dog-headed secretary said as though he said it all day.

Titus stood in the great marble hall, looking at row after row of hard backed chairs. For a period his mind was a void.

Stop blocking the bleeding egress and sit down, you useless tit. An inner voice that sounded disturbingly like his cousin, Stephen, rebuked him and so he did, allowing the queue that had formed behind him to, in the words of Canis Officialis, state their name and business and wait to be summoned into the Divine Imperial Presence.

By the thirty-seventh time he'd heard the secretary whine exactly those words he ceased to notice, because the poor bastard did, in fact, say them all day long.

He watched as the room filled up. The sea of chairs occupied, one and all, most of the available floor space was taken up by someone at some point. Supplicants leaned against columns, then walls and finally began spilling back down the corridor from which they came.

Periodically a name would be called, the room would shift to let them through, then surge to fill the void they left behind.

Titus sat and waited through tea time, then luncheon. By the time the hour for afternoon tea arrived the room had been winnowed down to a few dozen bereft souls and another dog-headed bureaucrat appeared, pen in one hand and book in the other, surveying the remains of the crowd.

"There will be no more audiences today, go home!" the crowd was told.

There was a disgruntled mutter from the populace. Titus stayed as he was, surely a mistake had been made. He had been summoned.

He watched as the rest of the supplicants funneled out of the hall.

Titus rose and addressed the secretary. "I believe a mistake has been made, my name is Colonel Titus P. Albinus, Londinium Austri and Her Divine Imperial Majesty summoned me, from my home, in The British Isles. She called for me."

"No mistake," The secretary said. "You're to stay in the upsilon wing, your baggage has been collected. A footman has in all probability already unpacked your things. Her Divine Majesty will call for you at her pleasure, not yours."

Titus stood still and digested that spoon full of medicine. "What am I to do?" he asked.

"Today? Whatever you like, so long at you're back in this room tomorrow at 8 o'clock sharp," the secretary said the hint of a growl in his voice. "But you must leave."

Titus, as he usually did when told to do whatever he liked, went shopping. He bought Polly a gold ring set about with rubies and fine enamel work, Selene, a dolly that said "Mummy" when it was turned over, Nigel, a stuffed crocodile, and for Stephen a new hat; the one he usually wore was a disgrace.

Between times he visited the Library, which was bigger than the Palace complex. It was late before he was sure he had a complete list of every book in which Nefrit's father was mentioned.

Out of sheer self indulgence he pulled out a few volumes on the Afghan campaign. In the center were a handful of color plates; photographs of the more noteworthy among the fallen; General Khufu and Prince Brolly in particular. Titus had never seen him like that before, in his barbarian get up. It was extremely gallant; Titus wondered where he could get something like that himself.

Before going to bed he took it on himself to write Polly a letter.

Titus laid out his pen and his heavy writing paper with his initials embossed up top. He unscrewed the lid on his inkwell.

He was more or less certain that any missive he sent would be well read before it ever reached Polly's hands. The question was…how long had they been reading his mail? It was entirely likely the Empress's spymaster had eyes in Titus's own house and had been reading his letters to his wife for some time. It followed therefore since any change in tone would only serve to worry his wife and make the Imperial Intelligence Office suspicious Titus was free write Polly the sort of letter he liked.

That night he dreamed of Jalalabad, of Prince Brolly, the skin completely stripped from his body when Titus arrived in camp. It had been a frequent occurrence in the weeks and months after the massacre but he hadn't dreamed of that day in years.

The second day in the audience hall was indistinguishable from the first, except that there was slightly less running to get there.

Afterwards Titus bought a velvet muff for his mother, for Selene a lace bonnet, for Nigel a pair of leather shoes, and for Polly a book of constellations. Although he knew she had one similar, the one he found in the shop was nicer with gilded edges and vividly colored plates. Then he slipped unseen into the library and spent six hours finding and obliterating the name of Crassus Cato in every book where it appeared. Afterwards he read three different accounts of the Jalalabad massacre.

That night he wrote Polly another letter secure in the knowledge if he had been free to share his mission with her she would no doubt whole-heartedly approve. Knowing Polly she might well ask to help.

After the third day of not being called, the dog-headed secretary suggested he pack a meal of some sort when he returned for his fourth day of waiting. Titus heeded his advice.

He also slipped into the Hall of Records, which instead of being anything like a hall, was a solid mile of clerks, floor to ceiling filing cabinets, and dusty tomes. He returned each evening, after the agents following him while he shopped were exhausted, but it was the better part of five nights before Titus was convinced all trace of Cato had been removed from the bureaucratic record. When that task was complete Titus decide to read what accounts he could find of the Afghan campaign.

Before he knew it eight days had passed. On the ninth day while he was doing his daily duty, sitting attentively, picking up all the gossip from the loose lipped crowd, his things were removed to another wing, one closer to the central Palace and Her Majesty. Still he sat and he waited. Still he was not called.

~~

The next morning at elevenses Polly got a letter in the post from Titus. She held it a moment, picturing his hand on the paper, holding the envelope to her lips like a distant kiss.

"Is that from Titus?" Stephen asked. "He must've sent it as soon as he arrived in Alexandria."

"Looks as if it were mailed from the aerodrome," Polly said gesturing to the red stamp on the front.

Polly opened the envelope. Like all his letters it was perfumed.

My Dearest Darling,

It seems as though I've hardly left but I find myself wishing I were home with you. There is nothing for it, I suppose, but to come home so heaped with honors and accolades as to make our separation worthwhile. My quarters aboard the Imperial airship are compact, but well appointed. Perhaps it is for the best that I travel alone as the sitting area hardly has room for two and if you were with me I would have no space to entertain. Speaking of which there is an officer with the Engineering Corps aboard. You would no doubt find him amusing. I had little success in explaining Stephen's experiments with light. I suspect my description was a bit muddled. I will close out my letter before it grows too long. Kiss Nigel and Selene on their noses for me and tell them their papa will be home as soon as he is able. Please check my cousin before he leaves the house. I know he will be a stained and rumpled wreck by the end of the day but that is no excuse for starting out in such a state. The least he can do is allow Llewellyn to press his suit before he puts it on. I trust you to take my part in this matter.

I promise to bring you home gifts, whether you wish me to or not.

Your Loving Husband,
Colonel Titus Posthumous Albinus
Duke Londinium Austri
Order of Apophis first class

Post Script- My Heart is, as ever, your domain, my Ursula, my she-bear.

Post Post Script- Enclosed please find enclosed twenty kisses, ten for each breast, as well as an additional five to be applied to your ruby mouth

Polly closed the letter and smelled the perfume once more. Rarely, had so many words been used to say so blasted little. There was almost no actual content. She had no idea what, if anything, was going on. It was almost like having him home. When would her husband learn to speak directly? Never seemed like a distinct possibility.

Polly sighed, wishing the kisses in the letter were real kisses.

On the evening of the tenth day Titus reached a fountain in a small public park, dedicated to the memory of Crassus Cato by his son, Aurelius. He found three such in the course of his search of the public records. By the end of the day all trace of the name had been removed.

He still had not been called, though he sat each day in the audience hall, waiting his turn.

He had six crisp new uniforms, still fresh from the tailor. He enjoyed showing them off to the brothers, Pollux and Aristarchus, who served as secretary and clerk for Her Divine Majesty.

He found a motherly old commoner who was easily induced to deliver the most delectable hot meals to order to himself and the two dog-headed brothers. They were young men, and quite dedicated. They often felt compelled to work through their luncheon hour to keep the wheels of Empire moving smoothly. It was the least Titus could do to share his repast with them. Besides, he disliked eating alone.

It was evening and the residents were gone to the theatre, when Titus removed his shoes and slipped, quite invisible, into the house where Nefrit was born. The house that had gone out of the family when her youngest brother, like the two elder, died childless. A stone in the corner of the peristyle bore her father's name. Titus gritted his teeth as he dropped hammer against chisel to obliterate the letters in a single blow. After this there was only one location remaining for him to visit; the Temple of Apollo where Crassus had been employed as priest.

Titus had come, at long last, to the conclusion he was probably not going to wind up shot or clapped in irons in some dark hole. For that they wouldn't have kept him waiting day in and day out.

Ten days turned to twenty and Titus was on his third room, in a third, entirely different, wing. He was also reasonably convinced that nowhere, in the record of the events at Jalalabad, were the extent of Prince Brolly's fatal injuries mentioned. It seemed strange, because Titus knew, without question, Brolly alone among the company, had had all the skin peeled from his body. It wasn't the sort of detail that was easily forgotten. The question was why? He also found it exceedingly peculiar that nowhere was in mentioned that his Aunt Augusta was heavy with child when her husband died, despite the fact that she later lost the child from grief.

Most of the aged photographs of Augusta Brolly on her sedan chair, carried before a cohort of recs, dated from before her pregnancy. But even pictures allegedly taken weeks before the massacre, a time when Titus had personally seen her and knew for a fact she was as big as a house, showed her slender and delicate and not even slightly pregnant.

It was canny but Titus could make no sense of it.

Stephen was thoroughly relishing the notion of spending the upcoming holiday with Polly. The bulk of apprentices had proved themselves utterly worthless with their woolgathering and general inattention and he had shouted them all out of the workrooms of the department. It wasn't entirely without precedent; most department heads released their thralls early this time of year time. The only thing that made it at all notable was that Professor Magesteri was the one granting the reprieve. The only reason Stephen noticed the approach of Saturnalia was it afforded him an excuse for a few hours alone with Polly, before

Titus's bloody social calendar demanded their presence.

The older apprentices, who watched her renewed presence among them with thinly veiled wariness, for the most part gave the Duchess the sort of unassailable deference and wide berth that belied polite mistrust. They had all gone to on some sort of outing, either to the brothel or the dog fights. There would be no intimacy interrupting juvenile delinquency this afternoon.

It was the little ones who required more work. They tended to cluster around Polly's skirts in the manner of nephews clinging to a pretty young aunt with loose purse strings and an overindulgent nature. She might be indelicate but Polly was decidedly soft hearted when it came to the little shits.

Stephen snorted to himself as he moved through the corridor.

He preferred to be the one to take advantage of Polycorpus's soft hearted, he occasionally thought it 'soft headed,' temperament.

He could frighten off any number of prepubescent Lotharios if need be. Not to mention enjoy himself thoroughly while he was at it.

All it took was forewarning of a fictional shipment of tools to be inventoried Monday morning to dislodge Mr. Cornelius and his little crew from her side. He was deeply gratified when they scattered like hunted animals.

"Do you have to do that?" she said irritably.

"It's my prerogative to defend my territory from incipient encroachment by rivals," he said honestly.

Her reply was a decided snort. Elegant.

"Dismiss it if you like; all the same, Mr. Cornelius fancies you." He frowned.

"I'm an awkward brute, no one fancies me," she groused.

"I believe it is Cuchulain Cornelius' opinion that your tits are the stuff dreams are made of, messy dreams," He scowled. "Otherwise, he would not adhere to you like a simpering barnacle."

"For your information, they were helping me." She sighed.

"I know I am no Titus Albinus," he said, "but perhaps I might be capable of rendering assistance."

They both paused at the mention of the name and looked at one another.

There had not been word from Titus in weeks. Some days Stephen prayed to Aphrodite his cousin was dead. On opposing days he prayed to Apollo he would return, and soon.

"It's Charlie Edney's birthday. Have you seen him?" she said, waving a package wrapped in the most amazingly garish colours. "I'd like to give him his present. Guy and Will don't know where he is, either."

Apparently Stephen took a second too long deciding whether or not to lie to her. "Why would I be privy to the whereabouts of Mr. Charles Edney?"

"That's not an answer and you know it," she said slowly, "but since you are bothering to dissemble I will assume you know something. Tell... Me... Now."

He gave her his best blank look.

"Stop staring at me like a codfish and tell me," she demanded.

"If you insist," he said disdainfully.

She crossed her arms threateningly. "I insist."

"Charlie Edney has eloped," he said with a soft smile.

"No, really," Polly laughed.

"With Sekmet Canavan," he went on.

"Come on, Stephen, did you give him an extra assignment on his birthday?" she asked.

"Whom he compromised with heavy petting in the cloak room during your rather eventful Lupercalia ball. Or maybe it was vice versa? I told you it was a terrible idea when you bought her that gown," he said "no good deed in the history of the world has gone unpunished." He watched her face as she slowly realized he was not joking.

"Why didn't he tell me?" she said, her voice rising with every word.

"Apparently, he was of the opinion that you would attempt to dissuade him," he said.

"Of course, I would; it's insane, irresponsible, muddleheaded. Is he out of his mind? Are you out of your mind?" she said at a level scream, leaving him to feel he was in the presence of a primitive form of alarm bell.

He stared. He was accustomed to screaming, not being screamed at, not even by Polly. It was shocking and slightly amusing. Ever so slightly stimulating as well.

"Is Guy part of this conspiracy, as well?" she asked, winded.

"Mr. Edney reckoned Ouellette would cave in under pressure from Livia Canavan and Will is the girl in question's brother," Stephen smirked. "Who else was he to turn to but his beloved master?"

"The world's gone mad." She sighed. "They're hiding out at Titus's country place, aren't they? What's more that's why you took my carriage this morning, to let those two have it?"

The corner of Stephen's mouth twitched at being found out so quickly. "Need I remind you that Mr Edney is of age? It is all perfectly legal."

"Why on Gaia's green Earth did you help him? How will they live?" she asked.

"Unless I am mistaken, Mr. Edney has recently passed his Engineer's exam." He shifted uncomfortably.

"You fudged it for him, didn't you? Where do you suppose they'll live? You do realize the Canavans are practically paupers and Charlie's granny will disown him. On Charlie's wages they won't be able to afford so much as a hovel," she said, exasperated.

"Not my problem." He shrugged. "I admit it, I gave Edney his articles for a wedding gift, despite the fact he doesn't deserve them. That should be of marginal assistance. I think I'll be giving every one of my older apprentices their articles this year until I weed the blighters down to a reasonable number."

It was a tempting notion, though he doubted he had the stomach to follow through with it.

"Stephen!" she said plaintively. "Why? Why did you do it?"

"You know me, my dear, always delighted to assist underlings in need," he said, the corner of his mouth twitching as he fought off a smile.

She glared, unmoved by his attempt at humor.

"If you must know, he put forth a convincing argument," he said, glowering.

"And that would be?" she asked, narrowing her eyes.

"None of your business," he snapped at her.

Stephen was not about to tell Polly that Edney had appealed to his own tender feelings as a man whose sweetheart had married someone else. What was more he would rather not shatter Edney's belief that he was simply trying to get rid of him and Polly never could keep her mouth closed. He wouldn't have it rumored Professor Magesteri had fallen prey to rank sentimentality.

Besides, he did want Charles Edney out of the way. That much was undeniable. It was even more true once he realized Edney wasn't quite as stupid as he had assumed.

She gave him a measuring look.

"You did it out of jealousy, didn't you?" she said, indignant.

That stung.

"And if I did?" he said softly.

He watched her gathering herself, her mind whirring before she spoke. "I need to make a visit to Livia Canavan and then she and I can take an airship to the Hall and get this mess sorted out. Would you arrange it with Noor for me?"

"I will do no such thing," he said, trying to control his anger "You will do no such thing."

"Excuse me?" She looked up as if she'd forgotten he was there "Simply because you're jealous of Charlie..."

"I believe it is the lady who is jealous," he hissed.

"What?" she said, aghast.

"Is your apoplexy affecting your hearing? I believe I said it is the lady who is jealous. Since you and I are the only ones present, I must have meant you, though it is a stretch, I admit," the words came bitter from his mouth.

"You are foul," she said angrily.

He put his hand to his breast in mock anguish. "You wound me, Polly. No one has ever said that before."

"You are ridiculous," she added.

"If your meaning is that I am subject to ridicule, that has been the case since I had the recklessness to fall in love with you. Now I only seek to limit the damage," he said. "For future reference perhaps you should keep me apprised of how many males you require."

"Pardon me? What did you say?" she spat.

He didn't stop himself from snarling. "Two? Or is it three, one for every hole? Or four, in case you misplace one? Since Titus is out of the picture are you looking for a replacement? It is a bit premature. At least give it a full month, darling."

"Charlie is my friend, he was my friend before he was my…you're a nasty jealous shit, do you know that?" Polly said her eyes shining but no tears falling. Stephen got the feeling she might sock him one, and he had no idea whether he'd earned it or not.

They were both horrid, without Titus to keep them in line.

"I require only you, bad as you are," she hissed then looked away. "And Titus… assuming he's…alive."

"Prove it," he challenged.

"How do you expect me to do that?" she asked, flushing, whether it was from anger or shame he couldn't say.

"Leave Edney be," he answered.

It was at that moment that Stephen Magesteri knew Titus Albinus was alive, simply because he knew for a fact he would never be so lucky as to have Polycorpus to himself. Besides he didn't think he could manage on his own indefinitely, they would tear one another to pieces.

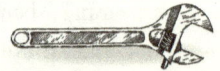

There were no audiences with the Empress the week of Saturnalia. The great machine of state came to a full stop and the normally conscientious clerical workers applied themselves just as conscientiously to drunken revelry.

Which was ideal for Titus's purposes.

The Apollon was near deserted, only an old priest nodding off in his chair with his jug of wine at his feet, in the outer chamber and in the oracle's inner chamber the sybils and their maid servants were trying out new hair styles.

Even if Titus hadn't been practiced in the art of silence it would have been impossible to hear his footsteps over the roar of traffic outside.

He carefully circled the Temple. The name of Crassus Cato appeared only once, carved deep in the wall of the atrium near the back of the temple, almost dead even with the one hundred seventy-seventh column.

Loud as the noise from the street was, there was no way he would be able to strike the name from the wall without rousing the few inhabitants of the temple. It didn't matter how invisible he was if it looked as though the name of Crassus Cato had magically been struck from the building. No, it was best to carefully stage an accident.

Titus had to do little more than peer out the front door of the temple to find what he needed.

He counted his way back to the correct spot, girded his loins, inhaled deeply, took the chisel in his right hand, grasped his hammer with the first three fingers of his left, a rather large but nearly empty jug of wine held uncomfortably between the last two.

Titus inhaled again.

Released his breath.

Then against everything he had ever believed in, ever been taught to believe in, he removed the last recorded vestige of the name of his great great great great great grandfather from the world smashing the glass jug against the wall in the same motion that defaced the name.

The old man nearly fell out of his chair, the sybils came running, maids trailing behind, and Titus Albinus ducked behind a column. Being invisible didn't mean people couldn't run into you.

"Filthy ruffians," either one of the maids or one of their mistresses said as Titus turned his back and did his best to hurry from the scene.

"It wasn't even empty," said the old priest clearly still drunk.

"Wasting wine and destroying public property, what is this city coming to?" asked someone else, indignant.

"Blasphemers!" one of the maids shouted into the street as Titus slipped through the wide door and out into the bustling crowd.

If the streets seemed rough and tumble when Titus arrived in Alexandria Saturnalia transformed them into pure pandemonium. It took him three hours to make his way from the temple to his rooms at the palace.

Titus collapsed on his bed picking a large shard of glass from his fore arm and examining the tears and stains on his former third best uniform, now a best used as a dust cloth. He wasn't even sure the glass had come from the Temple. He might've been hit with a bottle at any point in the melee that was his journey the four city blocks to the palace.

He would never consider Londinium crowded again. Provided he ever got home.

He had stripped off his shirt and almost drifted off to sleep without particularly wanting to when there was a knock at his door, the first since he'd arrived in Alexandria.

"Come in," Titus called, jerking awake.

"We've been looking for you," Aristarchus said, almost barking a bit at the sight of Titus in such dishabille.

"You shouldn't spend the feast day on your own," Pollux said.

Titus rubbed his eyes. "How gracious of you. Please forgive me, my undress."

Pollux shook his head, to wave off the apology. "It's you who are gracious to honor us with your company."

"Please, sir, don't tarry. We told our father we would bring you to dine and we've spent half the day searching you out," Aristarchus said sniffing the air.

Titus did his best to give them a winning smile. He didn't relish the thought of braving the crowd again but there was nothing else for it. He couldn't be so foolish as to decline.

Calling up all the vigor he could muster Titus leapt to his feet and threw open his wardrobe.

"I look forward to meeting the father of two such fine young gentlemen as yourselves," Titus said looking through his clothing options.

"But you know our father," Pollux said tilting his head first this way, then that.

"Our father is Endymion Daar, General Endymion Daar. Her Divine Majesty's Spymaster. You've been making reports to him for twenty years," Aristarchus said.

"He brought you from England," Pollux added helpfully.

Titus turned slowly to face them. "I only knew him by his nome de guerre. Well, I certainly feel a fair fool."

"You mean you didn't suspect? You had no idea?" Pollux asked.

"Father will be beside himself to have got the drop on you," Aristarchus said. "He has a very high opinion of your abilities."

"And best of all I won't have to brave the streets again. It's utter madness out there," Titus said and all three of them laughed.

It turned out to be a very jolly Saturnalia indeed.

The day after Saturnalia, proper, was not Polly's favorite.

She liked giving and receiving presents. She liked fine food and drink. She liked funny stories. She'd learned to tolerate the sort of social gatherings The Duchess Londinium Austri was expected to attend.

She did not care one whit for was being dressed up in her finest day gown, primped to within an inch of her life, and promenading down the Queen's Road with Stephen at her elbow and the babies at her back, prams pushed by their respective nurse maids.

Titus should have been home for this. This was precisely his element. And she hadn't had word from him in weeks.

Polly pulled her compress out of her reticule, using the mirror to look behind her.

"You're going to trip over your sodding feet if you don't start looking where you're going," Stephen said sounding prissy.

"All I'm doing is checking," Polly said. It worked better when Polly thought of the nursemaids as horses pulling little wagons rather than women, pushing her babies, in prams. Since the Charlie Edney business she had to admit she was a jealous cow and that was all there was to it, she was even jealous of her babies, even though plenty of other babies spent more time with the nurses.

All she really wanted the nurses for was the dirty nappies. That was very convenient.

"You're going to trip, and these bitches are going to laugh at you, and you'll get all belligerent..." Stephen said under his breath.

"I'm a jealous, stroppy cow what more can I say?" Polly answered him just as softly, nodding and smiling broadly at Mr. and Mrs. Everidge.

In her mirror she could see the passersby, who'd merely nodded at her, and curled their lip at Stephen, smile adoringly at Nigel and Selene. They had reached the point in the promenade at the apex of the hill where the circuit shifted and those who had been heading up the hill would suddenly find themselves on their way down. It was a perfect metaphor.

Except that it wasn't working the way it was supposed to. The crowd had thickened and a sort of living bottle-neck had occurred, pressing in, keeping the foot traffic at a stand still.

"Professor Magesteri," Mrs. Duncan, Selene's nurse called nervously.

Polly turned like a whip to see exactly what had brought the procession to a grinding halt.

It was her babies. Or rather a gaggle of people, commoners and Uncommon alike, crowding round, and the nursemaids trying to fend them off without cheesing off the nobles among them.

Polly took the offender closest to her, a bullheaded Minotaur making goggle eyes at Selene, and tossed him, by his shirt front, several yards back into the crowd.

"Come on. Don't hurt anyone, Polly, it's not necessary," Stephen pleaded.

Polly inserted herself between the twin prams and the crowd, managing only because she was very strong and very determined. They were growing more unruly by the moment.

Then a voice like she had never heard before; clearly Stephen but a Stephen Magesteri who was somehow a stranger to her, rang out.

"Step away from the children," The Voice said with what she could only describe as infinite menace. It was the creaking of a tomb and last rattle of a dying man and steel on bone and a dozen more terrible unnamable voices calling from the void. If the children were not stepped away from something very very bad would happen.

Longing still in their eyes the crowd fell back, some even scrambling over the fallen to get away.

"Go Home!" The Voice intoned and Polly looked at the source of the directive.

Polly had known Stephen Magesteri all her life, he was, in all likelihood, father of at least one of her children and yet he seemed a complete unknown to her. His sallow skin had gone grey as ash, his too thick lips as red as blood, his crooked teeth seemed capable of rending bones.

Much the way smoked glass is known to block the brightness of the sun, Stephen somehow concealed obscured the dark force that was…well himself.

Then, in an instant, Stephen seemed to shake, as though fighting off a random shiver, and he immediately came back to himself again. The self that Polly knew and had been known to throw olives at across the dining table.

"Shall we?" regular rumpled Stephen asked offering her his arm.

"No, I can't," Polly said.

"And why not?" Stephen asked indignantly.

"Because you've frightened the nurses away and we're going to have the push the prams ourselves," Polly said gesturing to the empty street, "You've scared everyone away by the looks of it."

"Oh," was all Stephen said, he seemed embarrassed.

And well he should have, Polly had never seen the city deserted like this. It was eerie.

"Is that the real you? How you were back there?" Polly asked trying make sense of what had just happened; the crowd, the babies, Stephen, all of it.

Stephen shrugged and kicked at the pavement like a boy "I dunno, could be. Is Titus more himself when you can't see 'im? Not my place to say."

"Whose is it, then? The postman's? One thing is for certain, you are the most stupid man alive," Polly said taking hold of Selene's pram and steering towards home.

"Hold up, what?" Stephen said, grabbing Nigel's pram and racing after Polly. "What?"

"You saw what happened; they're as uncanny as you are," Polly huffed. "You made them that way."

She could hear Nigel's pram rolling behind her so she kept on talking, saying all the things she couldn't let out while she was looking Stephen in the eye for fear she would sodding choke him, no matter how scary he was capable of being.

"It's stupid, just sodding stupid, you lot, particularly you. You know what it is to be tampered with…in the womb. You see how it affected the crowd back there. That was madness, sheer madness, and it's all due to your arrogant inability to leave bad enough alone," Polly said unafraid of being heard.

"It was love, they could see the love in what we did," Stephen said. "That's what every poor bugger wants to get his hands on."

"You say that as if it's a good thing, as if love were some magic sodding cure-all, some great panacea. Love is what drives sensible people mad. Love has caused me more headaches than anything else in my life. If I weren't in love with you, perhaps I wouldn't have felt so depressingly guilty for falling in love with Titus. And if I weren't in love with Titus I wouldn't have been so guilty about still being in love with your sorry sullen self," Polly said.

"Poor, Polly," Stephen sneered.

"The funny part is I don't even care anymore," Polly said in exasperation.

"Thank the gods for that," Stephen murmured.

"That's not what I mean, I mean, I love you both but I've these children to think of. I've other priorities besides who feels jealous of whom."

Stephen didn't say anything, just rolled along behind her.

"Have you thought of what it will be like for them? For the children? Can you imagine the hunted feeling of being wanted by everyone who sees you? Did you two geniuses think of that?" Polly glanced over her shoulder at Stephen.

"A damn sight better than being hated, I'd imagine," Stephen said.

Polly stopped walking, though they were nearly to the house. "You bloody moron! We won't be able to take them anywhere without a drape over the pram and once they're older, what then? The rest of their lives veiled like your aunt Augusta? Is that what you want for them? You think that's a damn sight better than a few looks of disgust when you walk down the street?"

Stephen stopped and came close to Polly, his mouth in a twist. "I'll tell you the truth. Neither of us had a thought for the children when we did it. And I could have stopped him, I could have, but I didn't. Instead I helped him. We brewed the elixir together, because neither one of us could bear to lose you, and mark my words, we would have. Without my flesh and his boiling together in that pot you'd be rotting in the ground. So I don't regret it, not for a minute. I don't care if it means these two have to wear veils for the rest of their lives and can't run the social circuit with the rest of the spoiled brats of Londinium. I don't care as long as it means you're here, with me, above ground. I'm an abomination anyway, it's not as though I can go downhill from here."

Polly didn't know what to say so she didn't say anything.

"Go ahead, tell me you despise me, wouldn't keep me as a lover if I were the last cousin your husband had left, which I am," Stephen said.

Polly exhaled slowly. "Why isn't anything simple? Why can't I have someone I dislike to blame for what's happened to my children?"

"So finally the truth rears its head; you do blame me. I'll return to my rooms at the museum. A necrophile is hardly a suitable role model for a child in any event," he said. "A separation would be advantageous for you as well, I imagine. I can watch out for you well enough from the Museum."

"You're afraid, you pathetic excuse for a man," she said, her face burning. "You're afraid of fatherhood. You're afraid of taking Titus's place. You're afraid to try to be happy instead of moldering away in the cellar feeling sorry for yourself."

His look was murderous, but she noticed he was not able to meet her gaze.

"You said you loved me," she went on, her tone accusatory.

"You said it yourself, Love is a pain in the arse," he said stonily. "I expect if we ignore it, eventually it will go away."

She looked into his perpetually sneering face for some hint of softening and found none. "I refuse to let you do this, Stephen."

"I am not giving you a choice, Sweetheart," he said, still not meeting her eyes.

This was clearly one of those times Stephen Magesteri desperately needed a good hard shake. Well, she was just the woman to give it to him.

She thought of a dozen ways to answer him, knowing in the end he could not stop her from following him back to the Museum, could not keep her from bringing the babies to the dungeon to plague him. But she could not force his heart. She did not let herself wonder how long he had it in him to play the arse if he set his mind to it.

She set Selene down in her pram and picked up Nigel instead.

"Take your son, sir," she said and thrust the baby at him.

Stephen Magesteri, with reflexes she never knew he had, all but flew backwards. She stepped toward him doggedly.

"What sort of game are you playing, woman?" he said, gritting his teeth.

"He's yours. You went through an awful lot of trouble to make certain I had him; the least you could do is hold him," she said steadily. "All this time and you haven't held him since the day he was born."

"I see him well enough from here," he said, though she realized he had thus far done everything he could not to so much as look in the baby's direction. "Besides I was under duress."

"Are you saying I forced you to impregnate me?" she said.

"You expected me to... take you every night," he said. She was surprised that her ears detected a hint of nervousness in his voice, "You and Titus."

"You could have refused. You weren't forced. You knew what would happen," she snapped. "What the oracle said would happen."

Stephen shrugged.

"Take him," she commanded. "Take him this instant; he's yours."

He gave her a mulish look, but extended his hands slowly, woodenly. He seemed intent on holding the baby as uneasily as possible, but he held him.

"Something is wrong with it," he said abruptly.

"Why do you say that?" she asked, peevishly taking up Selene in her arms.

"It's not crying." He looked into the baby's face hesitantly. "Shouldn't it be crying?"

"I imagine he's used to you. He's only heard your voice every day of gestation and every day since." she snapped angrily. "He's probably wondering why you've been avoiding him."

Stephen seemed to be slowly, almost imperceptibly, relaxing, settling the baby closer to his body, looking harder into the boy's face.

"You're a lucky little bugger to be so like that mother of yours," Stephen said, stroking the little cheek. "Just think, you could have inherited this ugly face."

Chapter 22 : In the Presence

olonel Titus P. Albinus, order of Apophis 1st Class, having drunk to the health and long life of Endymion L. V. Daar as well at that of their beloved Empress more times than he could precisely recall, woke to a pounding; both inside and outside of his skull.

From what he remembered, and that was precious little, he'd drunk to the health and long life of the table decorations as well.

"Colonel Albinus! Colonel Albinus!" came a voice beyond the door followed by a series of decidedly canine yaps. "You weren't in the audience hall and you've been summoned."

Titus's stomach lurched and he sat up, wide awake.

"Give me ten minutes!" Albinus shouted at the door.

"Her Divine Majesty called for you five minutes ago," Aristarchus whined through the door.

"I would rather apologize for my tardiness than for my stench. Ten minutes, Mr. Daar, and I will be ready to face my sovereign," Titus answered him.

After the quickest dressing and morning ablutions of his forty years Titus opened the door and followed Aristarchus Daar down the corridor.

Then another corridor.

Then two more.

His head throbbing and his gut rising and plummeting in turns, Titus Posthumous Albinus stepped through the door and bowed until his forehead was level with his knees. All the blood rushed to his head and he struggled not to vomit.

"Rise, Colonel Albinus before you fall over," a woman's voice said.

Titus righted himself.

"Please, Colonel Albinus, sit down and have some tea," The Empress instructed him in a voice that brooked no polite refusal.

Titus was no fool. He did as he was told.

"The generosity and magnanimity of your divine and august majesty outshines even the noonday sun," Titus said waiting for Her Majesty to drink first.

Her Majesty sighed then sipped her own tea. "Daar, make a note that Colonel Albinus is to be awarded full points for obsequious posturing."

It occurred to Titus despite the pain in his head that Her Divine Majesty, Empress Helene looked surprisingly human on her throne.

"On the contrary, I merely report your heavenly radiance as my lowly eyes perceive it," Titus said after his first swallow of tea. She needed to fire her seamstress and get a new ladies maid. Her make-up was too thickly applied and it aged her.

"Clever, Albinus," The Empress smirked in a way Titus would have considered cheeky from someone who was not worshipped as a living Goddess.

"You flatter me," Titus gazing up at her through his eyelashes. He questioned the wisdom of his actions, flirting with the Empress, still he knew his own strengths and it seemed a better course than not flirting with The Empress.

"I kept you cooling your heels in the audience hall for a month, some men would take that as an insult," The Empress said.

"A month? That long? Are you certain?" Titus said giving her his best smile. "The days simply flew by."

He felt droll. Very droll.

"Perhaps you would like to know why you were summoned," the Empress said.

"If it pleases your Divine Majesty. This tea is superb," Titus said. It was true.

It was very good tea and it was doing his headache no end of good.

The Empress gave him a hard look.

"How is your wife?" she asked.

"Quite well, thank you," Titus said conversationally, his stomach plummeting at the thought that it was more than mere pleasantry.

"She's very grateful, I imagine, but then it was your fault she was ill to begin with," Her Majesty said.

Titus closed his eyes and swallowed "Yes, well," he finished his tea in one painful gulp. "One does what one can."

"More tea?" Her Divine Majesty said gesturing toward General Daar with the pot.

"If I may," Titus said working not to wince.

"Which brings us to why you have been summoned to imperial court," Her Divine Majesty said.

"And why I spent a month waiting to be seen?" Titus said.

"That was a test," Her Majesty said.

"Of my backside?" Titus asked.

"And your character," Her Divine Majesty said archly. Though technically, he supposed, everything one did when one ruled a vast Empire, was, by definition, somewhat arch.

"I did tell you I was very interested in meeting Mrs. Albinus," Daar said, the eye in his forehead unblinking. "She must be an extraordinary female to inspire such devotion in the two of you."

Titus considered dissembling but abandoned it as a waste of effort.

Still, what passed between he and Polly was private and Stephen was part of their union only because they were both fond of him. They …loved him, he supposed. There was nothing sordid about it and it rankled to know that reports had been written on their intimacy. Missives had been read. What was the evidence? Eyes pressed to keyholes. Semen stains on tiger skin rugs. Love bites still visible at morning tea. Blood rushed in his ears at the thought.

Titus forced a smile and took a delicate sip of his second cup of tea.

"It would be pointless otherwise," Titus said.

"After all you did commit sorcery on her behalf," Her Divine Majesty, said, smile gone, eyes fixed on him like a dagger to the throat.

Titus looked to the door for the guards ready to clap him in irons though there were none there.

"That's one interpretation," Titus said. "Another is that my cousin and I utilized a decidedly innovative branch of medical science."

"I say this with all due admiration, you are as slick as shit through a goose, boy," Daar said. "And it's still a bald faced lie."

"You committed sorcery, the both of you," The Empress said stonily.

"It's a grey area, wouldn't you say?" Titus took another drink of tea, scrambling internally.

"I wouldn't say that, no," Daar said with a smirk. "But then I don't know a woman I would feed a pound of my flesh."

Titus refused to lose his smile; all he could do was shrug affably. It was hardly a pound but it seemed a pointless quibble.

"There's no question you committed sorcery, Colonel Albinus, and there's no question you committed it successfully. The only question is whether you committed it in service of the state," the Empress said, her face impassive.

"I don't get your meaning," Titus asked, flummoxed into responding without guard. He instantly felt a fool.

"Daar! Explain it to him," Her Majesty said gazing up at the ceiling.

"Put simply, boy, you have committed sorcery, you and that cousin of yours. We've seen it coming for years," Daar said.

Titus opened his mouth to protest but Daar cut him off, finger in the air.

"No point denying it, you are a pair of sorcerers, you and Magesteri. The only question is, will you be Her Divine Majesty's Sorcerers or will you be criminals?" Daar asked, the eye on his forehead blinking innocently.

Titus blinked. "Are, are, are you offering me a position as Imperial Court Sorceror?" Titus seemed to have developed a twitch in a matter of seconds.

"You and that cousin of yours; the abomination. You will go to Londinium, with all due haste, and you will fetch your family; Your wife, Polycorpus, the children Nigel and Selene, and above all your cousin Stephen Magesteri. Together the two of you will be invested as Imperial Court Sorcerers," Daar said. "The Imperial Court Sorcerers."

"Your wife will want for nothing. Your children will grow to adulthood in the heart of the Imperial Court. They will be denied nothing," Her Divine Majesty said, her voice level. "Or I'll call for the guards to kill you now. Yes, I know, you can disappear if you like but with Daar's sight that's not much deterrent."

Daar smiled placidly. "Her Majesty is, as ever, correct."

Titus found his tea had gone tepid but he swallowed just the same.

At one time he would have wanted nothing more than a position at the Imperial Court now the proposition terrified him.

"I gladly accept Your Majesty's magnanimous offer. I only hope not to disappoint, my foray into the art of conjury has been limited to healing my wife," Titus said, honestly, as lying would do him no good.

Daar actually rubbed his hands together. It was the most frightening thing Titus had ever seen.

"I wouldn't be too concerned with that if I were you," Daar said. "There's a certain predilection, it runs in the family."

Titus squinted. "Are you referring to my father, Prince Brolly?"

Daar moved back, his spine suddenly ramrod straight. "Who told you that, Old Boy?" for the first time looking honestly perplexed.

"My Aunt Augusta, Lady Augusta Magesteri-Brolly, she said, he did it in order to protect my mother from the poverty of childless widowhood." Titus felt faintly foolish, he knew he in no way resembled Prince Brolly. "When you see my son, my boy Nigel, you'll see it, he's as like to The Prince as a picture. It's as though my cousin restored him to life."

The Empress turned her painted face to The Old Spymaster, General Daar. All three of Daar's eyes trained on the Empress's face.

"If he is to be at Court, if he is to be Court Sorcerer, he would likely learn the truth on his own," the Empress said closing her eyes. "Tell him, Daar."

Daar slowly turned to Titus.

"Brolly sired that wife of yours, not you, you nitwit," Daar said squinting.

"Noooooo," Titus sputtered. "That can't be, Polly, Polly is, Polly is made of pieces. She hasn't got a father, a single father."

"That is true," Daar said letting out a long sigh. "It is also true that anyone who appears never to lie is merely more adept than average."

"May I have more tea, please?" Titus asked.

Daar looked to Her Divine Majesty and Her Divine Majesty nodded. Titus was allowed more tea.

Titus closed his eyes, allowing the facts as he knew them, to coalesce as he swallowed his tea.

Polly, then was Prince Brolly's child, at least in part.

All trace of his Aunt Augusta's pregnancy during the war had been erased.

All reference to the severity of Prince Brolly's fatal injuries at Jalalabad had been wiped away.

"Clearly there is a great deal I don't know," Titus said.

"Henry Plumber was her lover, of course," Daar said.

"Of course," Titus said, staring deep into his tea cup.

"When the barbarian Brolly threatened to shame Augusta with divorce, she and her lover, Plumber, plotted to remove the danger by making a widow of Mrs. Brolly," Daar said.

Titus's stomach lurched, but he forced it down, nodding, the story was falling into place.

"By the use of sorcery, of course, but it got out of hand. The Massacre at Jalalabad was no enemy attack; it was the work of an adulterous wife. That's why The Prince's injuries were so severe. It was he who opened the poisoned letter. Why remove all mention of her pregnancy?"

"Augusta Brolly did indeed give birth during the Afghan war, not to one child, but like her mother before her and her daughter after her, to two. One child from her husband, the Foreign Prince, the other from her lover, the commoner Henry Plumber," Daar said. "Plumber delivered her child, agreeing in advance to murder the child if it were common, but at the sight of his rival's offspring jealousy overcame him, and he smothered both babes."

"And from those children he made my wife, Polycorpus," Titus said, his head reeling "The question is why did you allow it? By your description Henry Plumber and Augusta Brolly have earned execution several times over."

"The Fayzabad incident," General Daar said.

"You mean the comet?" Titus asked.

"Yes, the comet," the Empress bit out.

"After the event the entire Cohort saw a rabbit with gilley flowers growing out of its back. They all saw the strangeness of the vegetation where the rock fell out of the sky. Only Plumber took the stone from the gods for what it was and used it in his reclamations, so that the creatures he made did not disintegrate after a few months, growing ever more putrid, but died, on the field of battle, like men," Daar said.

The unspoken part being that he had used the rock from Fayzabad in making Polly as well, so that like the rabbit that bloomed and the grasses with eyes on the tips of their stalks, Polly was two things truly made one. Child of the presumptuous commoner and Child of the Serpentine Prince.

"Did you imagine a nobody like Plumber became director of the British Museum because he was the right man for the job?" The Empress said scornfully. "Since the war Plumber has had special dispensation to uncover the secret behind the rock of Fayzabad. This is why he remains untouchable, despite his transgressions."

Titus sat back, careful of the tea remaining in his cup and crossed his legs at the ankle.

"I see," he said and he did. Polly was not a strange common creature he had once imagined, but rather his own cousin, nearly as close a blood relation as Stephen. And yet she was common. But also Uncommon. Just as she was foreign, in spite of the fact that the blood of Nefrit ran also through her veins.

Knowingly or not he and Stephen had used The Rock of Fayzabad along with their flesh in the restorative. In all likelihood his blood and Stephen's both ran through both children. Daar knew, without question. As did the Empress.

Polly was indeed the wheel round which all the world turned.

"I am to return here with my little family?" Titus said brightly.

"Within twenty-one days," Daar said just as brightly.

"Twenty-two, and you and your little family will be considered fugitives," the Empress said with a serene smile.

"I am by nature exceedingly punctual," Titus said finishing up his tea.

Chapter 23 : A Grand Departure

Stephen had come home on his tea break, and was sitting watching Polly playing on the floor with the babies, funny how they had recently picked up enough common sense to tuck their wings behind them when they were indoors.

He was tempted to get down on the floor with them. Either that or take one or the other of the little buggers in his arms for a quick cuddle. He knew it was a bad idea. Stephen knew the minute he was in arms reach of either child he would be late, well later, back to work than usual. Without him there, shouting, the industrious employees got busy doing stupid things, and the lazy sods got busy doing nothing. He was contemplating his escape when a vision appeared in the doorway.

Titus.

Only not Titus as he'd left them; clean shaven, if a little long-haired, in his pristine uniform. Standing the doorway of the every day parlor, Titus's hair was a mass of curls spilling down his forehead. He had a meticulously trimmed beard as bright as the fires of Hephaestus's forge. He wore a long-skirted slender cut suit of oriental silk in a color Stephen suspected his cousin would call midnight blue. Titus looked like a high priced astrologer, or decorator or something. Stephen supposed it was the latest fashion in the capitol.

Stephen wouldn't be arsed if Titus came home dressed as a juggler as long as he came home.

And now he was. Home that was.

Stephen jumped to his feet and threw his arms round his cousin. He didn't know when he'd been so pleased to see anyone in his life.

"I've so much to tell the both of you," Titus murmured in Stephen's ear.

Stephen felt his chest go hot and cold with simple happiness at his cousin's return

"Go kiss your wife, you gormless twat," Stephen said patting his back.

Titus grinned that happy open grin that made him look all of 12 years old and knelt down beside Polly on the floor.

The two of them sat there like a pair of imbeciles. Not touching. Not speaking. Nothing but soppy smiles and hungry eyes, fairly gobbling each other up.

It was a peculiar feeling when it occurred to Stephen he wasn't too bothered.

Stephen liked to think he would have grabbed hold of Polly and kissed the stuffing out of her, at least if he was Titus Albinus.

But no, Titus took Polly's hand and kissed her sodding thumb.

Of all the disappointing…

Her thumb?

Her Thumb.

Polly finally came to her senses, grabbed her great tit of a husband by the face and kissed him until they both came up gasping.

Polly took about six deep breaths and appeared to be gearing up for more kissing when Titus held her at arm's length.

"The Empress, Her Divine Majesty, Cleopatra Helene is fully aware of the means by which Professor Magesteri and myself restored your health," Titus said.

"Fuck," Stephen said, the words had passed his lips before the thought even finished its way through his brain.

"Hear me out," Titus said holding up his hand in Stephen's direction. "The Empress is willing to overlook the transgression."

"Provided?" Stephen said, knowing there was catch, there was always a catch.

"Provided we agree to take on the official position of Imperial Court Sorcer-ors," Titus said.

"We? As in you and I? That we?" Stephen asked, gobsmacked. "Did you tell her it was just the once? That all our great magicks amounts to a pot of can-nibal stew?"

Titus straightened his sleeve. "Her majesty is aware of the limited nature of our foray into the arcane arts."

"You silver tongued cunt!" Stephen groaned "Sure, you've saved our necks for now but what happens when we bugger it all to hell?"

"You'll have to see to it that you don't bugger it up, then," Polly said her jaw clenching.

"As our rise as spellmasters was foretold by Imperial Augurs some twenty years ago, Her Majesty is willing to assume we'll pick it up as we go along," Titus said, every bit the pompous shit he'd ever been. Stephen had missed him so much he'd nearly forgotten what a pretentious prick he could be.

"It's got to be better than going to prison for sorcery," Polly said picking up a baby in either arm.

"If only sorcery wasn't punishable by death," Stephen informed her.

Polly only scowled.

"Thank you, Stephen, for making my point," said Titus, the arse. "As it stands no one is going to be executed, you and I will rise to highest halls of power, and Polly and the children will want for nothing. What more would you like? A golden goose?"

"You're the sorcerer," Stephen said with a shrug.

"Oh, piss off," Titus answered him.

Stephen stood with his hands over his face for a minute and took the idea in. "Still, better than a plank upside the head, I suppose."

"As ever your gratitude is overwhelming," Titus said rolling his eyes.

By Hephaestus's Hairy Arse, it was true. Titus Albinus was the luckiest bas-tard alive and he could talk his way out of anything.

All that was left to do was live with the bargain he'd made.

Polly awoke the following morning between Titus and Stephen fairly zinging with the spirit of adventure. It was a minor miracle on several fronts.

First off Polly never woke up before either Titus or Stephen. They were absolutely unnatural. What made a person get up before dawn? Perhaps if she talked to Dr. Ng she could find a cure.

Secondly, Titus and Stephen had both fallen asleep in the bed after sex, exhausted. She might have been to blame for that, but it had never happened before either. She was counting that as a miracle, too, or at least anomalous, since neither seemed too concerned about the other.

Titus had insisted that the first order of business on his return would be to take the babies to see Nefrit. So instead of snuggling back down between her two favorite muddle-headed twits Polly experimented with her creeping, and slipped successfully out of bed without waking either of them and found her maid. And her treatise. There was no way she could take her treatise to Alexandria. It didn't bother Polly much; she still had the thoughts in her head. She could take the treatise in her handbag, from there she could find a way to slip it easily into the Thames and no one would be the wiser.

Which was how Polly found herself in the temple of Apollo Alexikakos with Titus, Stephen, Nigel and Selene at an hour when she was normally still asleep.

The nurses waited outside, in the main Temple chamber with the rest of the work-a-day, regular people, monsters and commoners alike. Polly would have preferred to stay with them.

The Oracle sat the oversized throne on her dais, surrounded by cushions to keep her upright.

"You have completed your task?" the Oracle asked.

Polly had no idea what Nefrit was talking about, but Titus rushed to kneel in front of the old lady.

"It has been done, all of it," Titus said, his head bowed, laying an abused looking chisel and fairly unremarkably looking ink pen at the foot of the dais.

"What did you do, Titus?" Polly asked jostling the babies in her arms to keep them happy, which was a mistake. Selene wanted jostling, or playing with, or better yet being set down to explore, all Nigel ever much wanted was a cuddle.

Titus whipped round and placed his finger to his lips.

"What did he do?" Polly whispered to Stephen.

Stephen shrugged.

"Here, take her, will you?" Polly whispered.

Stephen took Selene in his arms and turned to face away from him, the way she liked, with his arms crossed around her fat baby belly.

Nigel meanwhile clung to Polly's neck like a little monkey.

"He has freed the future generations from a curse, a curse that is almost as old as I am," Nefrit said with a terrible smile.

Titus seemed busy pressing his forehead to the ground.

Nefrit's red eyes went from one child to the other as if weighing something.

"Bring me the boy," the Old Woman ordered gazing directly into Polly's eyes.

It was strange because Polly felt an inkling of fear, though she knew there was no reason to be alarmed. Titus's however many great grandmother had no reason on Mt. Olympus to want to hurt a baby, and even if she did, what could she do? Nefrit Magesteri was as weak as a kitten.

"Get up, get out of the way," Nefrit said kicking feebly at Titus's head.

"Do you think you can hold him?" Polly asked skeptically.

"Put him here, beside me, move the cushions if need be," Nefrit ordered.

Polly, Nigel in one arm, carefully moved a cushion here, a cushion there, until she could safely slip her baby boy beside the ancient Oracle.

"Do you …um do you like him?" Titus asked anxiously.

"Very much," Nefrit said, her eyes blazing like Polly had never seen before. The withered hand stroked the fat cheek. She watched as the old woman lifted the hem of baby's lacy gown to tickle little round toes like a row of dun colored grapes "This is the child, the child I have worked so hard towards. This is the object of all my scheming."

The old hands fumbled to remove the ruby brooch Nefrit habitually wore at her throat. To pin it on the baby, Polly supposed, as a mark of something.

If it was humanly possible to burst with pride, Polly would be peeling bits of Titus Albinus off the walls any minute. He smiled so wide his narrow face looked to have reached its limit. Without speaking he took Polly's hand and kissed it.

Finally Nefrit freed the brooch, the pin dangling ominously.

The trembling fingers of her empty hand smoothed Nigel's unruly hair, as bad as Polly's ever was.

"This boy will be the instrument of my death," Nefrit said and in a flash jammed the sharpened pin of her brooch deep in the meaty flesh of Nigel's thigh. Almost instantaneously the boy changed and the soft baby-face became a masque of rage, but more than that, his skin turned grey and his mouth blood red, his tongue long and red and split as a snake's. Nefrit grasped his tiny hand and toppled down pulling them both to the floor.

Nigel screamed, his tongue flailing wildly and Nefrit lay on the floor, unmoving and unblinking.

Titus was on them pulling the pin from Nigel's leg before Polly could stop him.

"Titus, no!" Stephen screamed but too late and Titus toppled like a tree.

Selene screamed to match Nigel. Polly fell to her knees taking Nigel in her arms and kissing the blood from his leg. Nefrit was dead and Titus was…not breathing…his heart was not beating…but he wasn't…he couldn't be…

Selene struggled against Stephen with all her baby-might, reaching for Titus with both hands.

Stephen cowered, trying to hold Selene who wanted nothing more than to get Titus.

"Bring him back!" Polly ordered "Bring him back to me!"

Stephen shook his head. "It's no good, it doesn't last, he'll only live as long as I've got my hands on him, no, I can't. I won't. It's no good."

Nigel buried his face in Polly's breast, his sobs slowing. Polly put one arm round the poor little bugger. It wasn't his fault.

"Fix it," Polly said. "Fix him."

Stephen frowned, kneeling close by Polly and Titus but not touching either of them. He cast a little sideways glance at the back of Nigel's little head.

Then the strangest thing happened.

Selene arched her back and threw herself, literally threw herself out of Stephen's arms and onto Titus's chest. Once there, quick as a wink she grabbed hold of Titus's face and began gnawing on the side of that silly new beard of his.

Just like that Titus's chest convulsed. He took a deep breath and he sat up, barely catching the baby before she fell to the rug.

"Hullo!" Titus said. "What in the name of all the gods just happened?"

"I'll be fucked if I know," Stephen said.

"Oh, you know perfectly well what happened," Polly said, she'd seen too much to mince words. "Your great-great-great-great whatever great grandmother used Nigel to help her die, because he's like Stephen. Then you tried to help because he'd fallen to the floor and he killed you, too."

"But I'm not dead now," Titus said.

"You will be once you put Selene down," Stephen said, swallowing.

"She's got the other half of your powers, doesn't she?" Polly said, pondering.

"Looks like it," Stephen said.

"It certainly does," Titus agreed.

The three of them sat there on the floor of the sanctuary of Apollo in silence for a moment.

"When I pass Selene back to you I will be well and truly dead, there are some things I need to tell you," Titus said. "Both of you."

"Have at it," Polly said willing her brain to stop spinning, slow down, and think.

"The Rock of Fayzabad, Polly, we used a very small pinch of dust from the Rock of Fayzabad when we made our potion," Titus said.

"Your last words and you want to waste them jawing on about that old comet," Stephen said rolling his eyes.

"Dying declaration," Titus said holding up one hand. "Please show a modicum of respect. I do actually have a point, unlike some people."

Stephen looked like he was trying hard not to roll his eyes.

"In Alexandria, I learned that the Rock of Fayzabad has one very peculiar peculiarity. It seems to cause things that were previously separate and incompatible to come together harmoni…" Titus said.

"You mean the story about the bunny with the gillyflowers growing out of its back is true?" Stephen asked, as though he'd quite forgot Titus would be dead as soon as Selene was out of his arms.

"Precisely. Which means these children, whoever fathered them to begin with, when they ingested the potion in utero containing both our flesh and the dust from the Rock of Fayzabad, took on attributes from both of us," Titus said, then drew another breath, "Similarly Polly…"

"Similarly Polly what?" Stephen said. "What has this to do with Polly? Nothing, she's no abomination."

"The boy is not an abomination, he has a powerful gift, one that was badly used by an old woman desperate to die," Titus said.

"What were you going to say a minute ago, before Stephen interrupted?" Polly asked giving Stephen a stern look.

"Your father, he's a very dangerous man, don't cross him, but don't trust him either," Titus said.

"Henry Plumber is…" Stephen started indignantly. Stephen loved Polly's papa.

"Henry Plumber is utterly brilliant and utterly immoral," Titus said. "Do you know he's been given Directorship of the Museum because he's more or less holding hostage his understanding of just how the Rock of Fayzabad works its biological magic?"

"That's not…" Stephen started but Titus cut him off.

"I assure it is the truth. He used the rock's properties when he made his legions of reccs for the Imperial Army. He used it when he made Polly. Do you know how Polly came into being? Do you know even her name Polycorpus, many bodied, is a lie? It's only two; twins born out of our aunt, Augusta Brolly, and fathered by himself, Henry Plumber and our uncle, Prince Brolly. Henry Plumber smothered the babes and then hacked them to pieces," Titus said.

Polly knew she ought to have a something to say or at least a thought. "And she let him. Mrs. Brolly let him," was all that came from her lips.

"That can't be," Stephen said shaking his head.

"It can be and it is," Titus insisted. "Heed my words Stephen Magesteri; when I'm dead I want you to take Polly and the children to Alexandria immediately. There will be a place for you at court. You and Polly will marry, of course. You are to keep Polly and the children as far from Henry Plumber as you are physically able."

"My papa is my own physical father, the father of half this body, but he killed me. Mrs Brolly is my mother," Polly repeated, making certain she had all the details. "She's the mother of all of me. Prince Brolly, from Serpentinia, he's my other father."

Titus nodded.

"Not your hair though, Henry bought your hair off the back of an eel meat wagon. I told him curly blonde, you know, ringlets, were pretty on a little girl and as we were taking an evening stroll he saw this head on a pile of loose meat for the eels," Stephen said.

"How edifying," Titus said with a sniff.

"Titus don't go, we can find a way," Polly said with a catch in her throat.

"I can't very well spend the next 40 years carrying this child, my arms are bound to give out eventually," Titus said standing very very straight, straighter than Polly would have thought possible.

"Stephen, talk sense to him," Polly pleaded.

Stephen shook his head.

"The two of you will head immediately to Alexandria where you will marry. There may be rumors but disregard them, a certain amount of unconventional behavior is expected of an Imperial Sorceror," Titus leaned forward and kissed first Polly and then Nigel on the cheek. "Please see that Mr. Magesteri is clean and pressed. Left to his own devices he'll embarrass us all. You should keep Llewelyn on as his valet. He has a way with tailors. Do not allow the boy to blame himself for what has happened here, and remember always, no matter how many wives I have had, you are the love of my life, Polly."

"Titus, no, this is a stupid pointless death. It shouldn't be this way," Polly said, tears starting to flow. Dammit it was all so sodding stupid, she couldn't even bring herself to care that she'd turned into a blubbering mess. "It's wrong."

"Why look," Titus said smirking as he wiped her cheek with one finger. "You're a real girl after all."

"Oh shut your fat gob, you fool," Polly said crying harder.

Titus kissed her cheek, the babies, both of them, pressed between their bodies. Titus leaned down and kissed her lips, his kisses making a trail to her ear.

"Now take Selene and take two steps back," Titus warned.

Polly looked down, still on the floor Stephen was sobbing into his own arms, poor Stephen.

Polly took Selene on her free shoulder and stepped back. One step. Two steps.

She looked to Titus who was standing, very much alive, looking somewhat confounded.

"Not completely a chip off your block then Stephen," Titus said frowning thoughtfully.

"No," Polly said turning around. "I would say Selene is much more powerful."

"Where are you going?" Titus called to her back.

"I'll give you three guesses and all of them are wrong if they're not The Museum," Polly called behind her, setting a brisk pace, giving no thought to the dead oracle she'd left behind her on the sanctuary floor.

"Polly, wait up," Stephen called sniffling.

"She's not listening," Titus said somewhere behind her.

"She never does," Stephen agreed. "Don't know why you'd expect a little thing like death to change that."

Polly was too caught up in the seething in her brain to pay much mind to what else they said. A babe in either arm, unwieldly purse in the crook of her elbow, Polly strode down the pavements. She had a pressure in her head, like a storm cloud crammed into too tight a space, there was so much gathering. Polly had no idea what was about to happen, she only knew that it was fast approaching. The quicker she got to the Museum the quicker she would have an answer for the question she did not know how to voice.

She'd done as she was told. She'd trusted those who were wiser and more powerful, but it seemed to Polly all of a sudden they were neither.

It was seven city blocks from the Temple of Apollo Alexikakos to the British Museum. Seven blocks and she walked it so quickly she barely noticed except for Stephen and Titus trotting a few paces behind her.

"Polly," Stephen said.

"Polly?" Titus said.

But it made no difference. She could not think of anything, answer anything, was hardly aware of them as she turned up the back way. She'd only ever used the front entrance to the Museum when she came with Mrs. Brolly so she marched through a service door, where she almost ran smack, into Mable. Polly looked behind her. She must have lost Titus and Stephen when she ducked in the back.

"Polly! Begging your pardon, I mean, Your Ladyship, forgive me, Your Ladyship," Mable said all a dither.

"Oh Isis, don't say that, Mable, it makes it sound as though I'm to be launched at the docks with a bottle of champagne," Polly said.

Mable put her head down and only sniggered a bit.

"Mable, I wanted to say, I'm sorry I didn't realize before, what a friend you've been to me. You helped me when no one else cared. Thank you," Polly said.

"Don't mention it, Miss… I mean, your Ladyship. Don't mention it; I could find myself in a great deal of trouble," Mable said nervously.

Polly shook her head. "Not even a breath. But Mable, I want you to have… would you help me get this handbag off my arm?"

Mable curtsied and carefully lifted the bag off her arm without disturbing Selene, though it took a moment of wrangling.

"In there is a book, I wrote it, I'd like you to read it. I know you can read though no one's ever taught you. You picked it up working at the Museum, because you're clever. I know you're clever, clever as any apprentice. It hardly matters because you're a girl. If you're a poor girl it only matters how strong your back is, and if you're a rich girl it only matters how pretty you are," Polly said having her first coherent thought in some time.

"Your Ladyship?" Mable asked hefting the handbag.

"I'm giving you the purse and everything in it. After you've read the book you may do whatever you like, burn it for all I care. I just want one other woman, one other woman with good sense to read it and decide for herself what she thinks. There's some money in the bottom, I can't say how much, some pencils, I think there might be a pair of earrings as well. It's all yours, my gift to you," Polly said.

"Yes, your Ladyship," Mable said " I mean…Thank you."

"I'd put it out of sight immediately if I were you," Polly said.

"Yes, your Ladyship." Mable curtsied again.

"And Mable?" Polly asked.

"Yes, Your Ladyship?" Mable answered.

"Is my father in his office?" Polly asked.

"Yes, but he's taking his regular tea with Mrs. Brolly, he's not to be disturbed," Mable said.

"Thank you, Mable," Polly called racing up the stairs.

When she came to her papa's office Titus and Stephen side by side blocked the door. They must've come round the other way.

Titus had his arms folded across his chest. Stephen shifted his weight first to one foot then the other. They meant to stop her.

"Polly," Titus said.

"Do you know I rather like the new look? Stephen thinks it's silly I find it quite imposing," Polly said.

"Do you really? Because I saw a suit similar to this in Alexandria and I thought...that's not fair," Titus said when he realized Polly had played him.

"Life seldom is, take a baby," Polly said easing Selene into his arms before turning to Stephen with Nigel. "You too, Stephen. If you don't trust me you're welcome to come along."

"What are you doing?" Titus asked. "What have you got to say to him?"

"I want to know, I just want to know is all," Polly said because honestly she hadn't formulated any plan, she hadn't any idea; she simply knew she had to confront her father immediately or she was in danger of exploding.

"You already know, because I told you," Titus said slowly.

"I want to hear it from him, I want to hear it from his lips," Polly said.

Titus chewed the corner of his mouth but Stephen shrugged and stepped out of the way, kissing the top of Nigel's little head.

She threw open the door.

"Polly, I was just having my usual tea with Mrs. Brolly," Polly's Papa said.

"Hello, Mrs. Brolly," Polly said and took a breath. "Papa. I've come to ask, well, I've come to ask if you're my papa. I mean my natural father."

"Of course I'm your natural father, Polly dear. Could anything be more natural than the relationship between creature and creator?" her Papa said.

"You know what I mean. Are the two of you my ...my mother and father?" Polly asked, refusing to be dismissed so easily.

"Yes, my girl, you're very clever working that out, now toddle on home and get back to your babies or your whoring or however it is you occupy your time now that you're not spending your days seducing the Museum Staff," Polly's father said in a bored way that was meant to chastise her.

Polly started to object, two was statistically insignificant, hardly a dent in a staff of 300, but it was a merely distraction, exactly as her father meant it to be.

"It's true then?" Polly said. "And my other father was Prince Brolly?"

Mrs. Brolly rose silently from her chair across from Henry Plumber's desk. "You are poking into mysteries that are not yours to unveil. Your time would be better spent pretending to be an adequate wife and mother. No doubt that should prove sufficiently challenging."

Polly took a step forward without realizing it. "You are telling me I'm an inadequate mother? You?" she looked to her papa sucking on his cigar. "All either of you have ever done was to tell me I was an embarrassment and a bother and I should endeavor to disappear."

"What do you expect?" Mrs. Brolly spat. "You were 8 years old before you could be made to sit still long enough to have your hair combed through, you obstinate unnatural creature."

"I am, aren't I? One wonders why you made me," Polly said. "Particularly when you could have simply left me dead."

"Why does one make anything?" Polly's father said around his cigar. "Because one can."

"I don't think that's it," Polly said, the chain of events clear in her mind, one action precipitating another like interlocking gears. "I think Papa was only supposed to kill his own child, but when he saw your husband had given you a baby as well his pride couldn't stand for it."

"The Prince was dead," Mrs Brolly said. "I had only Henry and it is a man's right, the right of the Pater Familias to have authority over his household. How could I respect a man who was afraid to exercise the authority given to him by the gods?"

"You had to respect a man because he had the brass to snap your babies' necks? That's shit and you know it. You hated him and he tried to win his way back in your good graces by bringing your babies back to life," Polly said for the first time in her life unafraid of Mrs. Brolly and her unapproval.

"You think very highly of yourself, though I've no idea why," Mrs. Brolly began but Polly's Papa stilled her with a touch of his hand.

"How did you know that I snapped their necks?" her father asked, suddenly seeming interested.

"I worked that out from what I know of my anatomy. You made me an iron spine because you ruined both my other ones," Polly explained.

"Excellent reverse engineering, girl," her Papa nodded "Clever, very clever."

"But I think…" Polly paused, she normally would have been chuffed to bits over such praise from her father, but at the moment it seemed pathetic. At the moment it seemed she was seeing Henry Plummer unblinkered for the first time, and she didn't much like what she saw. "I think you miscalculated."

"How so?" her Papa asked.

"Henry, please," Mrs. Brolly said.

"No, Augusta, I want to hear this," Polly's father. "How did I miscalculate?"

"You miscalculated in forgetting I wouldn't be a baby you could shunt off on apprentices to have my nappy changed forever. I would want time and attention. I would become a pain in your backside," Polly said.

Polly's Papa inclined his head in acknowledgement of her point.

"You also forgot to take into account that every moment I continued to live was another moment your secret was on display for all and sundry. That's why you allowed me unhampered access to every dangerous experiment in the British Museum. That's why you sent Stephen Magesteri to me on the roof that day. You knew I'd fancied him since I was little. You knew what I'd do. You thought he would kill me like he did the whores in that Afghani brothel. More than that you hoped he would kill me,"

"I have heard enough," Mrs. Brolly said raising her hands to either side of her head.

"Is that because you know what's coming and you can't bear it? Something worse than how, when Stephen failed to kill me, you married me off to Titus, thinking I'd be like all his other wives. Dead? How you introduced subtle poisons into the medicines meant to heal me?" Polly said.

"You've no evidence of that poison nonsense," Polly's Father said coming round and taking Mrs. Brolly, Polly's mother's hand.

"I believe the part she's worried about is where I say you two killed my other father, Prince Brolly," Polly said.

"Dear girl, the Prince died in the Jalalabad Massacre," Polly's Papa said.

"I know he did. But the curse didn't come from the Russians. It was from the two of you, you sent it to him in his post, not realizing it would spread to the entire regiment," Polly said. "A fact I'm sure Stephen is very interested to know."

"You must trust that I am deeply sorry, Stephen," Polly's Father said. "It was an error in judgment on our part."

Behind her Stephen stood stock still.

"You're not sorry for killing my father?" Polly asked.

"I am your father, girl, and why should I be sorry for disposing of a foul foreigner? He was going to publicly humiliate your mother, divorce her, drag her name through the mud. As if it weren't bad enough marrying a barbarian, some insults are beyond bearing," Polly's father said, still holding Polly's mother by the hand.

"And you still love my father? Why? How is it even possible?" Polly asked Mrs. Brolly.

"Because, Polycorpus, Henry Plumber is more of a man than those two sorry sops of yours combined," Mrs. Brolly said. "A real woman loves the man who makes himself her master. She doesn't make her bitch of him the way you've done my nephews."

Polly turned round to Stephen and Titus, babies in their arms. Had she made them her bitches? She'd behaved badly a time or two, but so had both of them. As far as she could reckon all she did was treat the two of them as her equals. She didn't regret that.

Titus eyes grew wide and he raised his hand to cover Selene's face.

Polly spun round to see Augusta Brolly's gloved hand on the edge of her veil. Without conscious thought Polly leapt forward and grabbed her by the throat, holding the veil in place over her deadly face. Mrs. Brolly's voice came out a burbling gasp. She'd intended to kill them all; Polly, her babies, Stephen, and Titus.

Turn them all to stone. Nigel and Selene; the babies. She meant to kill Polly's babies. A thought like a buzzing insect in the back of her head warned Polly moving against Mrs Brolly could prove a deadly choice. It hardly mattered, Polly's decision had been made. A threat to Nigel and Selene was beyond her ability to address with half measures. It could only be torn out by the root, there was no other option.

Polly turned her wrist like twisting a key in a lock and her mother's neck snapped.

Polly would have expected someone to be screaming when a murder took place but all there was silence.

She turned to her father. "Aren't you going to threaten me, or call the security, or get the pistol from your desk, or something?"

"Why should I? There's nothing you can threaten me with. You could tell the Empress, I suppose. But then she already knows. I shall miss poor old Augusta but your lot are more useful to me as you are. I shall move on with my life. There's more than one woman in the world and poor Augusta was frigid in any event," Polly's papa said examining his crumbled cigar. "I shall tell them she fell down the stairs. It's simple enough to arrange."

"You should have got your pistol," Polly said laying her hand on his shoulder.

"Why is that?" Henry Plumber asked lighting a fresh cigar from the box atop his desk.

Without a word Polly placed her other hand on his head and broke his neck, like she'd broken Mrs. Brolly's, like Henry Plumber had broken hers all those years ago.

Polly looked down at her hands. There wasn't a spot on them. To think, she'd killed two people and there wasn't so much as a drop of blood on her hands. She could have laughed but inside her guts felt like lead. She didn't feel nearly as bad as she ought, it troubled her.

She faced Titus and Stephen who were, both of them, as silent as if Mrs. Brolly had succeeded in turning them to stone.

"We can't go to Alexandria," Titus said woodenly. "You father was under the protection of the Empress."

Stephen's shoulders were shaking with either dry sobs or mad laughter, Polly wasn't even sure if he knew which.

"I know what I'm going to do," Polly said holding out her arms. "Give me the babies."

Titus and Stephen traded a look.

"Don't be silly, I'm not going to hurt them, give me the babies," Polly repeated.

"Are you going to use Selene to resurrect your father?" Titus asked, wide eyed as Polly took the babes. Nigel as ever, was glad to hold his mother close. Selene, also true to form, wiggled like anything.

Polly boggled at the very suggestion. "No, not in this life. I'm not sure, given how we're all first cousins and the two of you jumbled up your genes with that potion of yours, which baby belongs to which of you but I am sure that they are both mine."

Polly strode down the corridors as quickly as her legs would take her.

"What are we doing?" Stephen asked to her right.

"Yes, you appear to have a plan of some sort," Titus said to her left.

"I don't know about we," Polly said climbing up the stairway to the roof. "I'm the one who committed both matricide and patricide in the space of three minutes."

"Yes, well." Titus cleared his throat.

"Would you open the hatch for me, Stephen," Polly said when she reached the door to the roof. "My hands are full."

Stephen squeezed past and pushed open the door. The sky was a brilliant cloudless blue.

It was cold on the roof. It would be colder in the air. It took some doing but Polly eased out of her fur coat, and wrapped it round her babies.

"Polly?" Titus asked.

"Polly?" Stephen repeated like an echo

Polly was busy finding the one airship gondola with the broken lock the apprentices used for their trysts and to hoard their caches of special foods, like potatoes and chocolate.

Polly placed her foot on the threshhold.

"The two of you are free, one or both of you, to go to Alexandria and be court sorcerers or you can come with me to Serpentinia. I hear my grandmother is Empress there. I'd like to find out for certain. It can't be any worse than here," Polly said.

Titus drew himself up to his full height and saluted. "Permission to come aboard, Captain."

Polly rolled her eyes handing him the babies. "Come along, you, I haven't got all day."

"Stephen?" Titus said.

Stephen stood, his hand resting against the wooden hull of the gondola.

"You killed Henry," Stephen said.

"I know, and he killed me, twice," Polly said swallowing. "From my count I still owe him one. You coming or not?"

"Not," Stephen said, "This is too...too...I can't."

Polly wanted to be calm and give him his choice, though no one had ever given her hers, she'd had to fight for every choice she'd made.

What she wanted was to grab him by his scruff and drag him along. But she would not be what Mrs. Brolly had accused her of. She would not treat Stephen and Titus as she had been treated all her life, like a mindless object to be moved about at whim.

"Right, then, you keep yourself safe, and get to Alexandria right away. We'll be fugitives or I'd tell you where to write," Polly said and gave Stephen a peck on the cheek and shut the door.

She went to the aft and began cranking up the anchor. The ship rose unsteadily, the way they always did at first. It was shaky at the start of any journey.

Titus laid the babies side by side in the Captain's chair, propping some poor apprentice's holiday hamper against the foot to stop it sliding in the turbulence.

There was a knock at the door.

Which was strange because they were roughly fifteen feet up in the air.

Titus opened the door. There was nothing but blue sky.

Looking down Polly could see ten broad fingers gripping the edge of the floor.

"I changed my mind!" Stephen shouted.

"Someday your dithering is going to be the end of you," Titus said reaching down to pull him aboard. "Good gracious, man, you are fat. Have you ever in your life walked past a pudding without taking a bite?"

"Have you ever walked past a girl without thinking you'd like to marry her? I know I'm fat but at least I haven't got a permanent callous on my fingers from untying so many Gordian knots," Stephen said.

Titus pumped Stephen playfully on the arm and it somehow devolved into... into...

They were both grinning like idiots.

Polly thought perhaps it was a hug.

"If you're quite finished I'd rather not have to listen to the two of you bicker your way across the Atlantic ocean," Polly said.

Polly looked out the window, Londinium shrinking below her. After her blood running like ice in her veins through the commission of two murders, it was only when she looked out at the water, with no shore visible on the other side, nothing but a vast expanse of sea and sky before her, that her heart began to beat like thunder.

She was the powerful one, she'd simply never known it before that day.

The End